A shuffling of startled him fully a he had slept, but someone was coming. He tilted his head and listened. Not an animal, nor a big man. Someone small, weary. Even with his wounds, he would have no trouble overpowering this one and slitting its throat. The musket lay in the dark corner, for he had not yet loaded it. He hoped this was a white man approaching, for he desperately desired to count coup, repay the slaughter of the day before. Ignoring the lancing of pain, he crept toward the door, waited out of sight until his prey entered. The only light filtered into the gloom through that opening, and he could be upon the enemy without ever being seen.

The fur-shrouded figure that stepped into sight radiated fire about its head, rays of sun brilliant in long strands of tangled red hair. Already in motion, his arm clamped about its throat, cut off a high scream.

A woman. A white woman.

The robe slipped from her shoulders when she clawed the air and kicked furiously with both feet, her full weight swinging on his forearm. One pointed boot toe struck his shin, another cracked his knee painfully. Gritting his teeth against passing out, he leaned against the wall and hung on, pressed the blade of his knife hard against her midsection.

Hissed in her ear, "Stop fighting or I'll gut you."

Praise for Velda Brotherton

STONE HEART'S WOMAN won a First Place for Historical Fiction from Oklahoma Writer's Federation, Inc. in 2010.

Stone Heart's Woman

by

Velda Brotherton

This is a work of fiction. Names, characters, places, and incidents are either the product of the author's imagination or are used fictitiously, and any resemblance to actual persons living or dead, business establishments, events, or locales, is entirely coincidental.

Stone Heart's Woman

COPYRIGHT © 2012 by Velda Brotherton

Cover Art by *Kim Mendoza*

The Wild Rose Press
PO Box 708
Adams Basin, NY 14410-0708
Visit us at www.thewildrosepress.com

Publishing History
First Cactus Rose Edition, 2012
Print ISBN 1-60154-997-0

Published in the United States of America

Dedication

To my husband Don and my daughter Jeri.
No matter what, they've always been in the wings
cheering me on.

Chapter One

Silence hammered in his ears like the rumble of gunfire that lingered in the haze of his memory. An arm, heavy with death, lay across the back of his neck, pinning his cheek against the frozen, blood-soaked earth. Stone Heart had no muscle or bone but sprawled limp, molded into the snowbank. Either he had perished under the white soldier's vicious attack or was frozen stiff. Perhaps this was only a vision of himself alive, his spirit determined to take one final look at what horrors had been visited on the Beautiful People before journeying to the afterlife. The only way he knew he lived was the fire that burned in his side and leg.

A stench of black powder hung in the frigid air that earlier had echoed with hideous shouts of bluecoats. To the west a huge silver moon poised on the horizon and slipped away, even as a wintry sun rose, nipping at ghastly thick shadows that lay across the battlefield. Everything glistened with a coat of new-fallen snow. Still afraid to move, he gazed into the grotesque face of his friend White Elk, who lay still in death, arms and legs splayed awkwardly. Eyes wide and unseeing, mouth open in a silent scream; blood matted the ebony braids, a rime of ice frosted his flesh.

In fear that a white soldier remained to guard the battleground, Stone Heart slanted his eyes to stare through the mist of his breath into the pearlescent sky. He would wait before learning if his spirit and body remained with the living. Had the soldiers butchered all his people? The women and children, the elderly, along with the exhausted, half-starved warriors who had rebelled one final time, with no hope for anything but death? They must have thought him dead too, or they would not have left him here. He felt a coward, submitting to his wounds while the massacre raged around him. Surely some must have gotten away. They couldn't all be dead, could they?

Lulled by the dangerous, creeping cold, he lay thus for what seemed like a full night embraced by nightmarish visions. Many who could not escape Fort Robinson had killed their wives and children to save them from the white soldiers, then taken their own lives. Boys armed with broken knives went up against the fiery blast of rifles. Yet still some survived and fled alongside him. When he stirred from the reverie and opened his eyes, the sky gleamed like the burnished blade of his knife. Only a few moments had passed, though it might have been an eternity. An eternity in which he punished himself for failing to save even one of them. The great elk-hide coat had protected him from the cold, yet its weight added to his dilemma. He must rise, for he would be dead if he lay here any longer. It was clear the soldiers had moved on.

He stirred. The slightest movement inflamed the agony of his wounds. Leather fringes on his leggings clung fast to the frozen, bloodied ground. Filled with sadness and a growing rage, he welcomed the lances of pain that alerted his senses. Pushing to both feet, jerking free of the chains of ice and shaking away the snow, he squatted there a moment to breathe raggedly of the carnage-tainted air.

And cursed his father's white blood with each beat of his heart. If slashing his wrists would rid him of every drop, he would yank his knife from its scabbard and do so. Let the hateful legacy of the Yellow Hair soak into the ground, mix with the blood of his mother's Beautiful People.

Fury drove him beyond the pain as he moved about among the dead, lifting a head here and there and recognizing one after the other of his dead brothers. His younger blood brother, Yellow Swallow, was not among them. Only nine summers in age, he too had been sired by the cruel Custer. A man who hated the Sioux and Cheyenne but loved to lie with their women. Neither son would ever call him father.

Little Wolf carried the precious Chief's bundle, and Stone Heart was filled with a need to find him and Dull Knife, the great elder leader. With frantic precision he passed from body to body, soon knew neither were among the dead, nor was Hog, the man who most recently had risen to lead the fight for the tribe's freedom.

From where he searched along the bluffs he could see the dead strewn in the snow all the way down to the bridge over the White River. Let them not all be dead. Let some have escaped onto the prairie. Others may have been taken back to the fort by the white soldiers. Hope diminished the sorrow that cut deep into his heart, but he refused to allow either of the emotions to blur a rage that swelled within his chest until his heart thundered like the drums of battle. His Cheyenne soul and spirit roared in defiance, the bellow cutting the cold air and hammering at the lightening sky. He would kill them all, every white man that walked this land.

If the soldiers had his people, they would be at Fort Robinson, but not for long. Soon they would be sent back down south to Indian Territory, a punishment worse than death. For six moons they had fled that place, only to be recaptured. They must be allowed to go north to their home where they could live and die in peace, yet he had so little strength left in his body. The wounds he'd sustained bled heavily, but no more. Still he felt weak, depleted. How could he make this happen when he could scarcely move? He must rest, recover, and then rescue all who had survived.

With the distasteful purpose in mind, he set about robbing the dead, for only in that way could he live. He would need weapons, medicines, clothing to ward off the bitter cold, and food, though he doubted he would find much to eat on these half-starved, escaped captives.

Hardening his heart and spirit, he searched the bodies of his friends, brave warriors he had lived and worked and played with. He amassed an assortment of items: an old musket engraved with a dragon denoting itself as a trade rifle, good enough only for Indians; a possible bag containing black powder, patches, and lead balls; a bundle of herbs and healing potions which he packed into a parfleche that already contained steel and a striking stone, candles, and writing tools. From the bodies of the dead he gathered up extra leggings, several blankets, and spare moccasins; from the lone soldier's remains he took jerky, hardtack, and a full canteen. The man's weapon was nowhere, probably retrieved by the victorious army. Constructing a backpack with a large four-point trade blanket, he shrugged into it and retreated from the haunted place of death. To leave his friends like this shattered his stone heart, but he could do nothing for them except save the living.

By full daylight he had traveled a painfully short way from the massacre, driven forward by something buried so deep within him he could not give it a name, moving beyond the pain and exhaustion into another plane where spirits guided the soul. Only temporarily, he left the White River and Fort Robinson behind. He would return, but for now he stumbled along the bluffs and over the endless prairie, looking for a place in which he could heal. Over and over he pitched face first into drifts swirled into mountains by the wind. Rose to move on only to fall again, until he could only crawl, leaving in the white powder a trail of blood. At last his strength gave out and he slept, in the bright winter sun on the open plains wrapped securely in brother elk's hide and the blankets he had taken, trusting his friends the animals to keep watch over him. Once recovered he would return to Fort Robinson, where he would live or die with what was left of the Cheyenne, whom even the whites referred to as the Beautiful People.

****

With a sigh, Aiden rose and went to the mirror to pin long blue feathers in her upswept hair.

"Stephan, if I could get my hands on your throat, I'd cheerfully squeeze the life out of you." She pinched her cheeks to redden them and adjusted the bodice of the filmy blue dress. The color made her green eyes shine like turquoise.

Though she wanted nothing more than to lie down and cover her head, she raised her chin and stepped through the door onto the boardwalk. A bitter wind tore at the filmy skirts, exposed her stockinged legs, and threatened to rip loose her hairdo. She fought to keep everything under control. Perhaps that's why she failed to see the preacher's wife until the lovely woman slammed her across the back of her shoulders with a broom.

"You're not welcome in this town, you godless creature," Amelia Durbridge screamed and connected with another swing.

Racing from the street, a mob of screeching followers descended upon Aiden, who threw her arms over her head in defense. Each attacker came armed with her favorite household weapon, beating her about the head and shoulders. The blows knocked her to her hands and knees, sent flashes of pain through her body. She tried crawling through the sea of swirling skirts, but the women quickly closed rank and trapped her. Some weren't so kind as Amelia Durbridge, calling her "whore" and "fallen woman" as they pounded on her. Embarrassment almost outweighed the pain. If her own dear sainted mother could see her now, she'd die of shame.

One of the women abandoned her weapon to rip Aiden's cloak from her shoulders, another tore the dress away to reveal her corset. A small bag filled with coins stuffed between her breasts popped out and dangled from the ribbon that secured it around her neck. Scrambling to all fours, she stuffed it back in place. Frantic to escape, she bumped into the solid legs of a man who dragged her upright into the shelter of his enormous bulk. She recognized one of her admirers, Wiley Lawson, and leaned gratefully into the whisky smell of him.

Lawson's voice all but drowned out by the uproar, he shouted, "Ladies, now ladies."

He managed to wrap her in a heavy fur coat that smelled of human and animal sweat, grain and tobacco smoke.

But the women had worked themselves into a frenzy and no mere man was about to slow them down.

"Out of the way," one shouted, and hit him across the shins with the handle of her weapon.

"Dang it, Miz Lucy," he yelled, hopping around on one foot and losing his hold on Aiden. "What's wrong with you? Does your husband know where you are?"

The rest of them turned on him in one huge roil of womanhood, and Aiden fled, dragging the heavy coat. She stumbled along the street, slipping and sliding through the churned, frozen ruts, past the theater where she would not be performing this night. The menfolk of town would have to find other recreation. Behind her the ranting mob finished with Lawson and turned once more on its original prey. She had to escape or they'd beat her half to death. Already her back and buttocks throbbed from the blows she'd sustained.

She rounded the corner into a bitter prairie wind that sucked her breath away. Gasping, stumbling, sobbing, turning her ankles in the absurd high-heeled boots, she jabbed her arms at the sleeves of the heavy coat. Gave up and hugged it around her half-bared chest. She dare not stop to put it on. Fury and outrage had turned the women from meek and obedient creatures to murderous predators. No doubt they'd had enough of their men worshiping at the feet of "that red-haired Irish hussy." If they caught her, they'd not only beat her senseless, they'd no doubt tar and feather her and run her out of town, as suggested by someone in the crowd.

At her back and closing on her quickly came the rattle of wagon wheels over the frozen ruts. Lungs on fire, she knew she was lost, for she'd never outrun a team of horses. They must have taken Lawson's wagon to run her down and finish the job they'd started.

Horror squeezed at her heart, boiled in her stomach, crawled up her back as she imagined them gaining on her. The wagon was right on top of her. If she was going down, she'd look her enemies in the eye. Out of breath and out of options, she turned to face the charging women, chin thrust high, the oversized coat wrapped tightly around her quaking body.

It wasn't the charge of the virtuous women she faced, but rather a lone driver standing, whip snapping in the brittle air.

He slowed the horses, hauled back on the brake,

and gestured frantically. "Climb on, quick. I'll get you out of town. Hurry, ma'am. Hurry."

She leaped onto the back of the skittering rig, diving over the tailgate to land with a painful thud on hands and knees, the buffalo coat clutched under one arm.

Lawson whipped the team into a full run, sending her tumbling around between bags of feed and wooden casks; an assortment of tools of some kind prodded at her skin. Finally she managed to grab the back of the seat and hang on. Kneeling on a fat gunny sack, every muscle throbbing, she twisted a quick look over her shoulder. The pursuing mob faded into the distance. Howling like a pack of wolves, they brandished their brooms at the glowering winter sky. A wedge of fear in her throat loosened. Sucking at the frigid air until her lungs nearly caught fire, she sank to her butt and held on tight while Lawson urged the team onward. Galloping hooves thudded across the wooden bridge that spanned the river at the edge of town. The cold afternoon air crackled with the noisy clatter of wagon wheels over ice. Hunkered behind her savior, out of the brutal wind, she wrapped up in the warm coat and tried to calm her racing heart. Patted the bulge between her breasts. If she lost the money she would be doomed. Or maybe she was anyway.

When they reached the rise above town, he braced against the reins, handled the brake once more and coaxed his team to a halt on the slithery surface. He glanced down at the small town of Benson, Nebraska, clustered in the snow-drifted valley below. She followed his gaze. The crowd of women had dispersed, leaving the street deceptively peaceful.

"Sorry, ma'am. I couldn't stop them. When a passel of females get the urge, a man just about has to stand back and let 'em have at it. You okay?" He fingered his swollen lower lip.

Nodding, she swallowed hard and shuddered. "What got their dander up, do you suppose?"

"Why don't you put that coat on?" He grinned wickedly. "Might of been that little bump and grind at the end of your finale last night, ma'am. 'A course, I'm purely guessing."

Dazed, she put her arms through the sleeves and felt instantly warmer. "I see nothing funny about this, Wiley." Her voice trailed off, lips trembling so she couldn't speak further. If she wasn't careful she'd start bawling and the tears would freeze on her cheeks.

"'A course not. I apologize." He angled heavy dark brows at her. "You got a place to go?"

"Home. Saint Louis," she murmured, "But I don't know how to get there."

"This weather, there won't be no stage to carry you to the depot for days, maybe weeks. I hear some of the trains ain't even running. You'd think in this day and age they'd have a way to clear the tracks."

The team danced nervously, and he hauled back on the reins, making gentling noises, then went on.

"Hell, the war's been over almost fifteen years, and still we live like we do out here. Did you ever see it so cold? And ever' dang time it warms up a tad, here comes another blizzard. Haven't seen the like in twenty year or more. Snow's piled higher'n an ox's ass." A sly grin twisted his gnarly features, a slitted gaze fastened on her bosoms.

With both fists she wadded the coat tight under her chin and moved backward. One heel came down on a short-handled cutting tool of some sort.

She ought to be more cautious than grateful. This could go from a bad situation to a worse one. Wiley could have his own reasons for rescuing her, nothing to do with sympathy for her plight.

Never once did he take his eagle eye off her as

he wound the reins around the brake handle and made to step over the back of the seat into the bed with her. She'd been right to be wary. She knelt and grabbed the adz, held it at her side hidden in folds of the coat.

In the time it took her to do that, he towered over her, no longer a rescuer but a menacing threat.

"Ain't nobody gonna come along here for a spell. Maybe we could get acquainted. I've seen the way you goggle down at us from off that stage. Looking to pick the one you want. Heard stories, too, 'bout how you like to have a little fun. I reckon you might owe me something for getting you out of your...little difugalty." He gestured crudely with stained fingers.

"I am not a whore, nor do I goggle, sir." She hoped not to be forced to hit him with the cruel weapon.

One look at the expression in his lustful eyes told her it would do no good to protest what he'd said. He believed it as surely as those women. But it appeared she could do nothing about their perceptions that a woman who sang and danced was also a whore.

His gloved hand shot out, and she jerked away, retreated till the tailgate pressed against her legs. Big and strong as he was, if he got hold of her, all would be lost.

"Leave me be. Go home to your wife."

"She ain't as purty as you. Besides, I got me four kids sleeping in the same room."

"Shame on you, you filthy man, for what you're thinking. And with a family to care for."

"Yeah, I know." Drooling, he advanced on her, eyes glazing in anticipation.

There was no place to go but over the side, and he'd catch up to her sure as the world. With a mighty heave she swung the adz upward, just like her brother Cormac had taught her. If Wiley hadn't managed to deflect the blow the thick blade would have buried itself deep in his throat. As it was, one side of the heavy iron head caught him across the jaw with a solid thunk. He made no sound as he fell backward into the seat.

"Oh, God, oh, Mother of God," she whispered, and dropped the evil thing.

She hadn't meant to kill him. What could she do now?

He moaned and stirred, driving both relief and panic through her. Thank God he was alive. She couldn't go back to Benson, but she could send him there. She didn't want him to freeze to death out here, just to go away and leave her be.

Carefully she crawled out of the wagon bed, her feet crunching in the churned ruts. The reins were stiff and difficult to unwind from the brake handle, but she finally loosened them, released the brake and went to the team's head. Leading them in a circle she turned the wagon back toward town, slipping and sliding in the button-up shoes. With a hard smack to the flank of the lead animal, she sent the rig off down the road, carrying its unconscious passenger. Without looking back, she started in the other direction, with no idea where she was going.

Many times during that day she wished she'd tossed the unconscious man out in the snow and taken the wagon. Inventing dreadful fates for him kept her staggering along the road while the cold whipped at her face. That subject exhausted, she kept going by damning Stephan for bringing her to this terrible place and leaving her like an unwanted piece of furniture. How could he have done such a thing when only weeks earlier he'd sworn his undying love? Vowed to marry and protect her, too. Back in Saint Louis, sitting in the swing on the front porch, arm around her, smiling so innocently when Mama brought them lemonade. What a terrible joke.

And what was even worse, she'd believed him. At her age, she should have known better. But that was precisely why she'd grabbed at the offer. Her thirtieth birthday bore down on her like a circling buzzard after carrion, dooming her to spinsterhood. No man to love her, no children to comfort her.

Occasionally she glanced over her shoulder, but there was nothing back there. Even the town of Benson had disappeared. Would someone come after her when the wagon arrived in town with its cargo? What if Lawson died? Would she be arrested and hanged? She probably ought to get off the road, but the idea of lighting out through piled drifts of snow held no appeal.

Overhead, the sky darkened, and spits of snow stung her exposed hands and face. Along the western horizon remnants of the dying sun purpled a gunmetal sky. Silhouetted against it perched a small house, nearly covered by a blanket of snow. Heart kicking at her ribs, she studied the soddie's black hulk. It wasn't quite dark enough for lamps to be lit, but it was quickly getting that way. No tracks in the snow to show someone had come or gone. And the wind blew so hard there was no way of telling if smoke came from the chimney.

No matter, this was shelter. For a while longer, she stared at the house, afraid it would disappear. But it was real, and good enough reason for leaving the road. Taking a deep breath and drawing the coat close, she started across the desolate, snow-covered plain. The longer she walked the farther away the house appeared against the darkening sky.

A bank of angry clouds swallowed the last of the light, and she staggered, almost fell. Drifts of deep snow were frozen and slippery, and she fought her way over or around each in turn. Ahead, the cabin held out its promise of shelter, but she was no longer sure she would make it. Legs numbed by the bitter cold, she dragged one foot after the other. Icy jags tore at her bare flesh like the fangs of wolves.

Damn the good women of Benson for tossing her out into the bitter January cold to freeze to death. She thought of dropping to the ground, letting the buffalo coat cover her, and waiting for the end to come. She'd be there come spring, all stiff and blue as the very sky above. And wouldn't that please those old biddies?

Before she'd halved the distance to the cabin, the howling wind thickened with icy pellets and fat flakes. If she didn't reach shelter soon she would certainly die out here. The shack remained just out of reach as if teasing her with salvation. The high button shoes with their cumbersome heels were nothing but trouble, worse in the snow, for they broke through the frozen crust with every step. She didn't dare take them off, but struggled on, falling, then rising only to fall again.

Climbing once more to her feet, she gazed around frantically. Only darkness. Where was the cabin? Gone. She turned, turned again. Dear God in heaven, she must have passed it by. Terror took her in its deathly grip. She was going to die. Head bent low, she forced one numb foot ahead of the other, unwilling to give up until she could no longer even crawl.

Off to her right a moon the color of ice rose above the desolate horizon and pointed across the treeless plain, lighting the cabin with its silvery fingers as if pointing out her refuge. Otherwise she would have continued to walk on into oblivion, for she had gone past the place and was headed away. Frozen on the plains of Nebraska, her body might never have been recovered. Her family would never have known what had become of her. Newfound energy sent her stumbling the last few feet, the brutal, incessant wind buffeting her up onto the porch and through the open doorway. She used the last of her strength to shove the door closed, leaned against it gasping at air that fired her lungs. The wind howled mournfully, battered and beat at the walls, as if furious to have lost her.

It was cold inside, but not like out there in that blasted gale. Dropping to her knees, she huddled in the total darkness and thanked God for bringing her this far. With each breath pain sliced through her lungs, but she was safe. At least for the moment. It was easy to see no one lived here, for the place was abandoned.

Exhausted, she curled up within the coat and slept, cozy in the shaggy fur that had once warmed the animal from which it came.

****

Stone Heart awoke shivering, cold to the marrow of his bones. Winter sunlight probed with tentative fingers at the elk-skin under which he huddled. He must move on. Though he struggled until a cold sweat covered his brow, he could not gain his feet. Scanning the unbroken prairie, he spotted an unnatural shape in the distance. It appeared to be a soddie or cabin, of the kind white settlers used. No smoke came from the chimney. For a long while he kept watch, saw neither man nor beast. He would seek shelter and if he found someone there, he would kill them.

Grinding his teeth, he wobbled to hands and knees and began the journey. Soon, he did not have the strength to crawl and drag the heavy bundle, but couldn't think of leaving it behind. His wounds ached, his palms wore raw, his thighs and upper arms trembled violently and would no longer hold him off the ground. He collapsed, lay in the snow, breathing heavily, smelling blood, his own and that of those he had robbed. He stared blearily at the cabin as if doing so could make it move closer. But it remained, taunted him as the sun slipped lower in the sky to darken its roof and reveal a door to one side. A door through which he must somehow manage to pass if he were to survive another night.

If he could not crawl then he would creep along on his belly like a snake. One knee dragged forward to shove, then the other, arms and hands numb and unfeeling, pulling him along, inch by inch, fighting to keep the heavy parfleche and supplies because to leave them meant sure death. The torturous trip would take a long time. Perhaps too long.

Memories of the battleground where the soldiers from Fort Robinson had slaughtered the pitiful small band of Cheyenne kept him moving forward. He would never forget this day nor what it had cost the Cheyenne. All his people wanted was to take their pitiful remnants home, home to the northern plains where the wind whispered of their heritage and the skies smiled with pleasure upon the land. This battle on a remote creek in Nebraska was not the first waged with the white man who would keep them on the reservation or murder them all. It must be the last.

After what seemed forever, he battered his way through the door, squatted in front of a mud-and-straw fireplace. Someone had piled dried buffalo chips in a corner, and he rested only moments before setting about building a fire. Fingers trembled weakly so he could hardly strike steel against stone or blow the smoking embers to life. Miraculously, he finally dozed in the blessed warmth of crackling flames.

A shuffling of feet, movement of some kind, startled him fully awake. He had no idea how long he had slept, but someone was coming. He tilted his head and listened. Not an animal, nor a big man. Someone small, weary. Even with his wounds, he would have no trouble overpowering this one and

slitting its throat. The musket lay in the dark
corner, for he had not yet loaded it. He hoped this
was a white man approaching, for he desperately
desired to count coup, repay the slaughter of the day
before. Ignoring the lance of pain, he crept toward
the door, waited out of sight until his prey entered.
The only light filtered into the gloom through that
opening, and he could be upon the enemy without
ever being seen.

The fur-shrouded figure that stepped into sight
radiated fire about its head, rays of sun brilliant in
long strands of tangled red hair. Already in motion,
his arm clamped about its throat, cut off a high
scream.

A woman. A white woman.

The robe slipped from her shoulders when she
clawed the air and kicked furiously with both feet,
her full weight swinging on his forearm. One pointed
boot toe struck his shin, another cracked his knee
painfully. Gritting his teeth against passing out, he
leaned against the wall and hung on, pressed the
blade of his knife hard against her midsection.

Hissed in her ear, "Stop fighting or I'll gut you."

Chapter Two

Gutting the intruder proved more difficult than Stone Heart expected. Weary as if he swam in thick mud, he could barely fight his own imminent collapse and hang on to the hissing wildcat encased in the enormous buffalo coat.

"Let me go, heathen."

No wonder she didn't understand him, he'd spoken in his native tongue and she was definitely white. What was a white woman doing out here?

The question scarcely registered before strong fingers clawed at his arm. Both legs swung free so he supported her full weight. She wiggled and kicked madly.

He could do nothing but release her in order to remain on his feet. Head reeling, he crouched as if to attack, knife circling about in front of him.

In the gloom, his prey emerged from the shaggy buffalo coat. Terrified green eyes reflected the stingy sun's rays; masses of red hair draped over pale shoulders and back. Full breasts swelled from a torn, fancy dress. His mind, slowed by the cold and exhaustion, at last grasped the situation fully. This was no bear nor man, no threat of any kind, as he had first thought, but simply a small, ill-dressed, creamy-skinned woman. By the look of her clothes, a white man's fancy woman.

How in thunder did she get out here?

He knew all about such women who sold their bodies to men for whom they cared nothing. This one had plenty of body to sell, but with his vision fading he had little strength to admire it. Her mouth

17

worked and she rubbed at her throat. He must be losing his hearing as well.

Finding her voice she screeched long and loud, soon clearing up that misconception. One arm thrust forward to ward him off, she stumbled backward, thunked into the dirt wall. Debris rained from the sod ceiling, dust motes floated in bars of thin winter light, clogged his nose and burned his eyes. Unable to move or make a sound, he widened his stance in an effort to remain on his feet. Smothering the wail, she hunched in the corner, facing him like a cornered rabbit, breathing heavily, making no other sound.

Cold air through the gaping door invaded the small, warm space and he quickly closed it, then turned back to the problem at hand. The white soul in him did not want to kill this poor terrified creature who had nothing to do with the slaughter of the Beautiful People. But he could not tell her so without breaking his vow to never let the words of his hated father's people cross his lips again. It didn't matter, though. From the look of her she wouldn't believe him, no matter what language he spoke. Overcome by pain and dizziness, his knees buckled under him and he fell to a sitting position.

For a terrified moment Aiden stared at the savage who had fallen on his butt when she fully expected him to scalp her. Warmth washed over her. He'd built a fire and she should be grateful, but was too frightened.

From his position on the floor, he circled the knife in a gesture that was plain. If he could rise from there he would cut her open.

Warily, she slid her gaze from him to the flames and back again, inched toward the coat, eyes aimed into his, pointing with a finger that trembled. "Don't touch me. Stay right where you are."

Foolish woman. She spoke as if he were her

prisoner, as if she held a weapon on him, rather than the other way around. He waved the knife, signaling that he would allow her to remain and share the heat. Never mind that he couldn't prevent it.

For a moment she didn't say anything, but concentrated on wrapping up in the coat, hugged it close to cover the exposed ivory flesh.

"Is this your place? When I arrived no one was here." She glanced at the flames again, as if to assure herself they continued to burn. "Who are you and where did you come from?"

She was either very brave or very stupid to face him in such a way and chatter on like a magpie. Glaring, he almost told her his white name, but in the end relented to her earlier perceptions that he was a savage. He had not been white since he had joined the Cheyenne in their battle to return home. Last fall, that was. The moon of the turning leaves.

It was annoying, listening to her speak and not answering. He wanted to tell her how close she was to dying. Threaten her. Pay her back for what the white man had done. Already, by allowing her to live, he'd broken his vow to kill every white man, woman, and child. He did not want to break another, so he clamped his lips over any reply he might have made.

Warily, she inched past him, dropped to the floor near the fire and wrapped up in the coat so he could see nothing but her face and that mass of hair that shimmered in the dancing light.

"Sit right there, just don't come near me." Her voice wavered and broke, but she lifted her chin and met his stern gaze. "I've never seen an Indian with golden hair."

Despite her attempt at calm, he could tell he had frightened her badly, even though he hadn't the energy to wrestle a rabbit. Pain from the wound in his thigh radiated down his leg and the muscles along his side bunched in agony. Still he was very good at covering up. He slipped the knife into the scabbard at his waist to show her he meant no harm and felt himself drifting off.

She touched a tangled lock of hair and glared at him. "I guess if you were going to kill me or...or scalp me you'd have already done it," she said, voice small and hopeful.

"Be quiet," he told her in Cheyenne, slapping three fingers over his lips to illustrate.

Warmth from the fire made him sleepy, and he wanted only to wrap up in the elk skin.

Leaning closer, she peered at him. "I guess you just told me to shut up."

Brave little thing, but too mouthy. He let out a sigh. If he had the strength he would gag her.

The wounds continued to throb. If he were to live, he had to clean them and not lie here sleeping while their poison invaded his body. In the light from the fire he surveyed the small, square room. Shelves on the far wall held an odd assortment that he couldn't make out. Perhaps there would be a vessel in which he could melt snow, for his first need was hot water.

Gathering his feet under him, he tried to rise, and she cried out, scrabbling backward. He stumbled to his knees, grunted angrily, and tried again. Getting to his feet was akin to trying to climb a mountain slippery with ice while someone stuck spears in his flesh.

"What...what is it? You're hurt." Though she sounded concerned, she did not approach, but merely watched him like an antelope watches a cougar.

Determined not to fail in this simple task, he shot her a dark look and heaved himself upright. Grunting against blacking out, waving like a flag in a brisk wind, he stumbled toward the shelves, hands grappling and knocking things all over the place. He went to his knees with a thud, and the last few items fell on him where he knelt, trembling with rage and helplessness. Despite struggling with all his might to hold on, he crumpled to the floor and passed into a world of darkness.

For a long while Aiden studied the savage whose fair, greasy hair had bright red ribbons intricately braided through it. He lay very still in a shadowy heap on the far side of the small room, no more than a few feet from her, his ragged breathing the only sign of life. After several minutes, when he hadn't moved or made a sound, she ventured close enough to reach out and poke him with one finger. No reaction. His feral smell assailed her nostrils, the scent of wild game and smoke and male sweat. Tentatively, she poked him again, harder. His body shifted, he grunted, and she dodged backward, almost falling into the fireplace.

"Hey, you. Hey," she yelled, but didn't touch him again.

He remained unmoving.

It was hard to know what to do. She'd only been gone a short while, awakening to find the night had passed, and trudging out into the snow to explore. How had he gotten here? Where did he come from?

His presence frightened her so she felt a fool for even thinking of helping him. But suppose she could get him to take her out of here? Not in his present condition, of course, but after he recovered from whatever was wrong with him. He'd probably as soon slit her throat as give her a helping hand, but there were few choices left to her.

In the hopes he would come to on his own, she studied him for a long time and decided to take his knife before he awoke. Probably not a great idea because he was so much bigger than her, but in his condition, she might be able to hold him off with it. Every nerve tingled, warned her to flee, run away from this dreadful hole and the wounded savage who looked white but certainly didn't act it. But where would she go? And come nightfall, should she not find shelter, she would probably freeze to death.

No, she would remain here. Take his knife, maybe even tie him up if she could find something with which to do it. When he came around she would show him that she was in charge. If he didn't agree, she would force him to leave, no matter his condition. The only way to survive in this harsh place was to look after yourself.

Silently, she crept close to the inert form. The way he had fallen, his body covered the knife, and she would have to turn him over to get it. The moment her fingers brushed his flesh, a shudder of misgiving swept through her. As if he had only become human with the touch. His braid tickled her knee and she touched it in wonder. Where had he come from, this fair-haired warrior dressed in beaded skins with features as stoic and chiseled as any Indian? She forced herself back to the task at hand. She tried to roll him over, but he didn't budge. He was heavy, his muscles iron hard beneath the hide coat he wore. Bracing herself, she heaved again, and he rolled over to sprawl face up. Moving him disturbed some pans that had tumbled off the shelf and they rattled over his groans, sending shivers up her spine.

She noticed the stains on his buckskins, at his waist and on one leg. Black like dried blood. He was hurt.

Suppose she awoke him? The knife's bone handle stuck out of the leather scabbard and she yanked it free. His hand slapped over hers, quick as a snake's strike, grip popping the bones in her fingers. Crying out, she tried to pull free, but despite his injuries, he had no trouble holding her fast.

Silver eyes glittered in anger. "You would kill

me?"

Amazed he spoke her tongue, she shook her head, pushed at him with her free hand. "No. I only wanted...I didn't want...to be sent away into the cold. If...if I had the knife...Turn me loose." She kicked both feet against him and tried to shove free. "You...you speak English."

He grunted from the blows, his features hardening, but he did not let go. "You wish to send me away into the cold. Is that the way of it, white man's whore?"

The words slammed into her, and she dodged as if they were chunks of rock. The heat of tears clogged her throat and burned her eyes. She brushed them away. What did it matter what this heathen savage thought? She knew who she was. He did not.

Nevertheless, the accusation brought back memories of the good women of Benson, and their dreadful treatment when all she was trying to do was earn enough money to go home. And she had never been a whore. Never.

Unbidden moisture trailed down her cheeks, causing him to stare at her. A tiny frown of puzzlement furrowed a crease above his finely chiseled nose.

Neither said anything for a long silent moment and, though his grip eased, he didn't let go her wrist. His palm felt hot and dry, little beads of moisture stood out above his lip and across his forehead, and he had an unnatural, flushed look.

"You are ill." She ventured into the sounds of their heavy breathing. "Why did you pretend you could not speak English?"

Abruptly he released her hand and curled one arm over his eyes. He could only ask her help by speaking with her, but he could hardly bear to look at her when he did. It was like betraying himself and his people.

"I need the wounds cleaned, the white man's lead dug out."

"Well, I've never taken out a bullet. I wouldn't know how."

"I can do it myself, but I need hot water. Melt some snow."

Without realizing it, she had begun to carry on a civilized conversation with this very uncivilized man. And he responded in kind.

He went on in a voice that rasped with weariness. "It is the only way either of us will survive."

That was all he seemed capable of saying, and she thought about his words for only the briefest instant before fetching two of the battered pots that had tumbled from the shelves.

He would help her, he as much as said so.

Even though her decision had been made she couldn't help thinking that once he grew strong he would probably kill her or worse. If they remained together until they escaped this dreadful situation, she could never dare turn her back on him. If she ever trusted another man again, it certainly wouldn't be this half-wild savage.

He didn't speak while she went about the tedious business of melting snow, but sat cross-legged and watched her every move.

"Put some of those chips in the fire before it goes out," he told her.

Puzzled, she glanced where he indicated. "I don't...is that how you built the fire? I thought they'd been keeping stock in here. Are you burning that cow dung?"

A ragged chuckle bubbled from his throat. "Buffalo chips. They dry out in the sun. Make a hot fire. Herds migrate through here." The staccato explanation appeared to exhaust him.

Delicately, she threw a few chips in the fire,

wiping her hands on the buffalo coat. What a disgusting thing.

His gaze followed her in studious silence while she shoved pans into the flames, and fetched mounds of snow to replace what had turned to liquid in the heat. It was eerie being in the small room with this frightening man and acting as if nothing out of the ordinary were happening. After a while the ponderous buffalo coat dragged at her until she could not do the work. If she shrugged it off it would mean parading back and forth in front of him in what was left of her dress. A rather tattered low-cut blue sequined affair designed to attract attention rather than serve as practical clothing, it hadn't worn well through her adventures in Benson and later with Wiley. The condition of the dress or its skimpiness probably didn't matter, for this man apparently had little interest in her body, for he continued to glare as if measuring her for a death shroud.

Yet the way he stared at her made her nervous. She readjusted the coat around her shoulders and knelt near the fire. When she stood, the cumbersome wrap fell to the floor. She glanced from Stone Heart to her own near-nakedness, to the shaggy coat, then back at him. His expression did not vary one bit. To heck with him. Not only was the thing uncomfortable in the heat from the fire, it didn't exactly smell too good. She left it lying in a heap on the floor, like some great dead animal.

Without warning he yanked the wicked knife out and brandished it. The long blade wavered back and forth in front of him like he might be trying to mesmerize a snake or something. Unable to take her next breath, she imagined her red tresses hanging from his belt, immediately felt a fool when he held the weapon out to her, butt first.

"Boil the blade. Do you wear an undergarment?"

His probing gaze sent shivers deep inside her, but she stiffened her spine and tossed the look right back at him. "I most certainly do."

"Take it off."

"I will not."

His glance cut off further protest. "Remove it and bring my bundle here. There in the corner. It has medicines for a poultice. We will have to clean the wounds."

"We?"

Ignoring her question, he removed layers of clothing, peeling the blood-stained shirt away where it had stuck to the wound at his waist. "The lead is there, I can feel it under the skin."

He palpated the flesh in his back. "The leg hurts like the devil, might have nicked the bone."

In silence she gazed at his hairless flesh gleaming in the firelight, the coppery skin of his thick forearms and flat belly a sharp contrast to the bruised and bloody hole just above his hip bone.

He repeated harshly, "My bundle, fetch it," and shook the knife. "Take it. What are you staring at?"

Flustered by the demeanor and blunt diction, as if each word were forced from some forbidden place, she did as he asked almost in a stupor. The blade dropped into the simmering water with a hollow thunk, and she glanced at him quickly.

"Are you sure you can do this?"

"No, but I must." He paused, flat gray eyes pinning her in an accusation. "Since you have said you could not."

"I didn't exactly say that. I said I've never done it before."

"Well, it does not matter. I do not trust you with a knife at my back." Unlacing the leggings, he tried to get a look at the leg wound, but the buckskin clung tight. "Bring me water to soak this. Then open the bundle of medicines. Move, woman. Are you daft?"

Daft? Quite possibly. The question fueled her anger. "If you're Cheyenne why do you talk like a white man? Well, almost, anyway."

"I'm working on that," he muttered and began to take off the shirt.

For a moment she thought he was going to remove the rest of his clothes right there in front of her. Not sure what to expect next, she kept a wary eye on him while shoving the pot of water within his reach. When she felt for the bundle of herbs her fingers touched a rifle lying in the dark shadow against the wall. Trembling violently, she picked it up, turned and braced herself, legs wide apart. Grunting, she leveled the long barrel at him. The gun was heavier than she'd expected and she could barely support it. The way it wavered she'd never hit him, even at close range. Him sitting there with a bullet in his flesh made her wonder if she wanted to shoot a man who had already been so badly wounded. A man who might be her only way out of this dreadful predicament. He might also kill her.

Lip curled and silver eyes flashing, he gazed, not at the gun but into her eyes. "It's not loaded, but shoot if it will make you feel better."

His features remained sternly set. Her worst vice had always been a quick temper. It had served her well with Wiley. Now it flared, almost blinding her with rage. She heaved back the thick hammer and pulled the trigger.

Oh, Mother of God, she hadn't meant to do that.

A loud, hollow click shattered her silent dismay. In disbelief she gaped at him. Sitting there, staring at her. Waiting so calmly for her to shoot him. It happened so quickly, so unexpectedly.

The rifle slid from her grasp. "My word, I could have blown your head off."

Without a reply, he let her think about what had

happened for a while, and she felt foolishly grateful and even more frightened. Not of him, but of her own willingness to kill this man. This land had truly done things to her. Terrible things.

"Now I know not to turn my back on you," he said. "Could we get to work? I will not scalp you just yet." He gestured at the knife. "I might pass out and you would need to finish this job. Maybe tomorrow when I am some improved. That hair would blaze like fire from my belt. Now, the bundle?"

Swallowing her indignation, she retrieved the musket and carefully propped it, butt down, against the wall. How stupid to have done such a thing. She knew nothing about guns or how they worked. She'd always thought all you had to do was point, force back the striking hammer, and pull the trigger. Obviously there was more to it than that. Not getting within arm's reach of him, she set down the heavy pack. He might yet think about what she'd done and take it out on her.

"Open it," he said, then calmly poured warm water over the blood-soaked leggings, grimaced and peeled them away from the wound. He made no sound, though it must have hurt something fierce. Blood spilled down his leg. He ignored it and inspected the area with his fingers.

Working to undo the bundle, she couldn't take her eyes off him until the knots in the blanket refused to budge and she was forced to concentrate on that.

"Well, that's good. There's an exit wound." With no hesitation he poured more water over the hole in his leg, held out a hand without looking up.

She would never have known the pain he was in had it not been for a fine sheen of sweat that broke out along the tight muscles along on his neck.

And his voice that grated with tension. "The parfleche, there. Open it and lay out those medicines where I can reach them. And give me your undergarment."

Leather pouch in hand, she glanced with confusion around the enclosed space.

"Well?" He raised his head.

She'd never seen a look like that on anyone's face. Pent up fury, a revelation of disguised pain flashing through the eyes, and despair so deep even his stern features would hardly contain it.

"I...I've no place to...to take them off." A need to cry caught her by surprise. This situation was so hopeless.

"I will close my eyes. Give me those herbs and do it, so I can take care of this."

She dropped the pouch beside him, and prepared to flee. Despite his wounds, this man exuded the power and intent of just what she'd called him: a wild man. It wouldn't surprise her if he lunged at her, cut her throat, and scalped her, all in the instant it would take to think of escaping.

"Don't order me about like that. I don't have to do any of this. You're a madman, uncivilized and wild." Even as the defiance escaped her lips, she wanted to take it back.

"Oh, I am worse than that, lady," he said softly. "Now would you please take off your britches, or whatever you wear under that...that..." He flung an arm in a wild gesture. "Because if I do not live it's odds on you will not either. Dammit, there is no talking to you without resorting to the white man's tongue. It comes back much too easily."

At times he sounded almost white, giving her hope. But he wasn't, and she had to face that. It had been clear from the outset she wouldn't live through this experience. She only hoped he made it quick.

"If you do live, I'm sure I won't," she said.

His laugh, anything but amused, sent shudders through her. "You're a tough one, I'll give you that."

His shimmering eyes raked her up and down, disdain warring with admiration. "You gonna run or take off your pants? Up to you."

Even though she could see he meant business, her legs refused to move. Only her mouth was capable of running, and now she'd angered him. Hugging herself, she could do nothing but wait for whatever he might decide to do. Movement to take off her undergarment simply wouldn't come. She might as well have been frozen out in that pitiless wind.

He glanced up from sorting through what looked like bundles of weeds, and stared at her with such evil intensity that she turned her back, lifted the dress and pulled down her drawers, fast so she didn't have to think. Fast, before he rose up from there and engulfed her in flames. Taking off her drawers was, after all, tamer than what he might have in mind for her later.

In her business she didn't wear layers of petticoats; men liked to see the flash of a thigh when she performed. But she did wear cotton drawers and they would have to suffice for his purposes. The corset that shoved her breasts up so they mounded out of the top of the dress, and shredded stockings were all that remained under the dress.

Without looking into his eyes, she held out the drawers. His warm fingers touched hers and she jerked back. He glanced at her with an unreadable expression that could have melted ice, then set to ripping the undergarment into pieces. Watching the strong fingers tear at her personal clothing sent a river of terror through her, and she gasped in surprise. He might as well have his hands on her, the way it made her feel. A disturbing tremor surged from the pit of her stomach into her breasts and she felt ashamed and vulnerable.

None of it mattered, though, for he was sure to

kill her as soon as he doctored himself and didn't need her anymore. She only hoped he made it quick.

He emptied some water out of the smaller pot, sprinkled the odd smelling herbs into it and worked them around with his fingers. Packing the mess into the leg wound, he used a scrap torn from her drawers to bind it before turning his attention to the hole in his side. This would be more difficult, for he clearly did not have a view of the area where he would have to cut out the lead.

Tightening her lips, she fetched the pot of water that held the knife and went to him, kneeling and placing the vessel on the floor. She reached to touch the wound, and he grabbed her hand. Almost choking with fear, she yelped and jerked against the vise of his grip. His murderous gaze held her as tightly as did his steel-like fingers. She might as well have stepped into a cage with a wolf. His hot breath washed over her, a scent of wildness that put her in mind of her worst fears. But he wasn't completely feral and, if she were to live, she must appeal to that hidden man she prayed dwelled deep beneath the animal.

Without struggling against his grip, she said, "You can't do this yourself."

Her flesh throbbed where he gripped it. In an attempt to soothe him, she laid her other hand over his. "Lie down and let me take care of it." How surprising that she could sound so confident when inside she was a mass of trembling jelly.

For several long moments they remained locked together. He tried to let her go, muscles loosening and tightening, could not. She felt so small under his grasp, the bones in her hands like those of birds. She could not hurt him, surely. The contact of their flesh promised otherwise. She could indeed hurt him, but in an entirely different way.

Though his expression didn't flicker, he finally

nodded, allowed her to help him lie on his side, baring his naked back. The back he feared she might plunge the knife in. For now she had tamed the wolf. Gently she fingered the hot, smooth skin that jerked under her touch.

He made no sound.

Taking a deep breath, she steadied the knife, tightened her lips and poked the point into the wound. After a bit of probing she felt an unnatural lump and he twitched, but again, uttered not a murmur.

"Is that it?"

"Yes." He hissed through gritted teeth.

With deep misgivings she shivered down to her toes, eyed the golden flesh which she would have to slit open.

"Dear God, help me," she whispered.

"Please do," he echoed. "Do it quick. Just cut me open and pop the thing out. Don't go poking around like some weak little girl."

"Shut up and let me do this. Or, you can try for yourself."

"Do it."

The knife handle felt smooth and deadly in her grip. She might kill him at this moment and be done with it. The shining blade trembled as she touched it to his vulnerable flesh.

Chapter Three

The swollen, bruised skin around the bullet hole twitched under the knife blade. Though Aiden briefly entertained plunging the knife deep into him before he could do her in, she knew at that moment that she couldn't kill this man. It simply wasn't in her. She tried thinking of all the scalps he'd probably taken, the many deaths he was probably responsible for, and still couldn't do it. The only thing she could do was cut out the chunk of lead and hope he would be grateful enough to let her out of here alive.

Staring at the weapon pressed into his flesh, she gritted her teeth and tried to cut deeper. But nothing happened. How hard could it be? Skin tore easily. Just slice it like a piece of fat back. Be quick. It was only meat, after all. She wiped her eyes, bit her lip, and pushed. A thin trickle of blood, like a delicate tear, ran from the wound.

"What are you waiting for? Go ahead, get it done," he gasped.

Her hand jerked and the blade went deeper.

He grunted, braced himself. "Can you do this or not?" His voice strained, the words spat through clenched teeth.

"I can, I can." *Okay, it's only a piece of meat, just cut out the bullet. Do it, now.*

And she did, shuddering at the feel of flesh parting under the blade and the sight of blood pouring. He stiffened and groaned. Gnawing her lower lip, she ignored him and continued to work until the tip of the knife touched the lead.

A low guttural noise rolled from deep in his

33

throat, tendons rippled along his neck, but he didn't budge or cry out.

With a bit of pressure it ought to pop right out. But it didn't, and so she pried the stubborn chunk of lead loose and slipped it out the opening, caught it in the palm of her hand. Blood from the fresh cut pooled on the dirt floor, then soaked away. For one relieved moment, she leaned back onto her heels and wiped her brow with the back of the clenched fist that held the gory thing.

She had done it. Now she had to stop the bleeding.

Taking deep breaths, he waited for his vision to clear. The woman's gentle touch eased the sharp pain that had threatened to drive him into a darker world, and he relaxed while she worked.

After cleaning the gash, she leaned forward to dress the entry wound. The tips of her fingers left tiny cold dots on his skin. A lock of coppery hair drifted onto his bare stomach. Her nearness caused a pleasant though strange sensation, one that he dare not enjoy too much. No woman had ever touched him in such a way. His mother's loving care had been taken from him when he was sent off to school. Snatched from the care of the Cheyenne to take advantage of his white heritage, he was told.

"If we understand the ways of the white man, we can learn to live in peace with them," his grandfather had said. What a rotten joke that had been.

The sound of her voice interrupted his musings.

"Tell me how to make the poultice so we can draw out the poison."

When he tried to reply, his voice rasped and he cleared his throat. He wasn't sure if his weakness was a reaction to her digging around in him with a knife, or his frustration at failing to overpower her. Whatever it was, it made him angry with both himself and her.

"There...in...the...water...do...what...I...did." His broken words came between deep breaths while he struggled to put away the burning pain.

While she worked, he drifted beyond the agony to concentrate on the gentleness of her small hand packing the medicines front and back into the wounds. Wisps of her warm breath flowed over his skin. Drifting off, he was surprised when he regained himself some time later to find the cabin empty.

He couldn't hear or see her, didn't know whether to be relieved or angry. It would be best if she had gone, yet for some inexplicable reason her abandonment angered him. From outside he heard the rattle and bang of pans. She hadn't gone after all. He let out a breath, amazed that it mattered what she did. After a moment, she returned, touched his forehead with the back of her hand, then covered him with her buffalo coat, tucking it snugly around his neck as if he were a child.

"Sleep is best now, you'll heal sooner. I'll keep the fire going." No longer afraid, she spoke gently in a soothing tone. "I wish I knew your name."

Warm and groggy, he whispered his name, then fell away from the lulling of her voice.

He awoke once in the dark of night, listened to the sharp silence of winter. The room was pitch black. The fire had died and the air was cold. Without being able to see outside, he could imagine that a storm was upon them, filling the night sky with snow-laden clouds. Listening intently, he finally made out the light whisper of her breathing close by. Wrapped in the animal skins they would survive another night on the unforgiving prairie.

When again he awoke, he sat up tentatively, inspected the wounds. They were not bleeding, and the pain was tolerable. She had left him alone again, this time, perhaps for good. If so it was for the best, though a strange, lonely feeling trickled through him. And oddly, he found himself wondering where she would go. Alone she would never survive.

But what did it matter to him?

He crawled from under the heavy buffalo coat and saw she had left water nearby, a strip of her torn underwear draped over the lip of the pot. He removed the poultices and used it to wash the wounds clean. How arousing to touch his flesh with what had once clothed hers. Where were these thoughts coming from? He had no time for them. Impatiently, he forced his head to clear itself of her, then stood up slowly, swaying for a moment on legs that trembled.

Eyeing the cold fireplace and the disappearing pile of buffalo chips, he decided to do without a fire during the day. As he pushed the door covering aside to step out, the woman, wrapped in the larger of his blankets, appeared carrying two pots filled to the brim. Her appearance startled him, as his did her. But she didn't flee nor spill the water, just let out a little "Oh!" and stared up and down his nearly naked body with those wide green eyes he found so delightful. In the white world...if he were still willing to be white...she would be much prized.

Choosing to ignore her, he nodded tersely and strode around back of the soddie, holding himself as tall and straight as he could and trying not to limp too much. Thinking about her and the way she'd regarded his bare body brought an unexpected twitch of a smile to his lips. Odd that a white woman who made a living satisfying the needs of strange men, should be embarrassed by a man's nudity.

He must indeed be quite a sight to her, wearing only his breech cloth. The cold morning air revived him quickly and he hurried with his morning ablutions. He would have to wash the bloodstained clothing and try to get the dark splashes out of his boots. Running around nearly bare-ass naked wasn't smart in this weather. Though the sky was a brittle blue, the sun shining, the air cut to the bone.

As he returned to the shelter, his earlier relief at finding her gone turned to misgiving that she remained. Alone, he could survive and recover, but having a woman around to feed and look out for would make it tough. And though he didn't like to admit it, she would also be quite distracting. Yet he couldn't toss her out to fend for herself, even if she was white and a whore. On the other hand, he wanted nothing to do with her. She was foolish, talked too much, and would soon freeze to death if she didn't put on some clothes.

He grunted. The two of them were quite a pair.

Maybe he could find something for her to wear in the bundle he'd carried from the battlefield. Certainly it would serve better than the tattered dress and silly looking shoes that must certainly hurt her feet.

He followed her inside where she set two more pots of water. She had lined up a row of battered old tin pots around the fireplace.

"What's this about?"

Eyes turned away so as not to look upon him, she said, "A bath."

"A what?"

"I want to take a bath, and melting snow takes too long so I'm carrying water up from the spring. Now, if you'd build me a fire so I can heat it."

For a moment he was speechless, then ventured, "If there is a spring, then why not bathe in it? Save yourself a lot of trouble."

"It's covered with ice...well, almost. Besides, it's too cold."

"The Cheyenne break the ice to bathe."

Now it was her turn to go mute, and she stared

at him, disbelief overriding her embarrassment at his lack of attire. "I...I didn't think Indians bathed. Are you truly Cheyenne?"

His eyes darkened. "One drop of blood would be enough. As it happens, I have a bit more than that. My mother was—" Breaking off, he turned and strode from the room that had suddenly grown too cramped. This was none of her business, and he didn't want her to know anything about him. Not anything. It would bind them together in ways he didn't desire. He did not know her name, had no interest in it.

Muttering in his mother's tongue, he followed her trail through the snow to the spring. There he squatted, found himself a large rock and chipped away the thin ice around the mouth of the spring. Off came the cloth tied about his waist, and with a howl he lowered himself in the water. The icy dunking cooled his temper, so that when he popped up and saw her standing there watching him with shocked disbelief, he actually laughed.

"Coming in?" he asked and reached out a hand.

She backed off, gaping at him as if he had lost his mind.

At least his action had served to shut her up. The woman talked far too much, so much he couldn't think. He took the ribbons from his braids and went under again, scrubbing at his scalp. His skin tingled pleasantly and his breath came in gasps. It was a matter of control.

Head tilted back, he stared through the crystalline water at her wavering figure. The red hair gleamed like copper in the sunlight, and in the rainbow colors reflected off the ice she resembled some spiritual being hovering above him. Blowing bubbles to ripple the vision, he surfaced and bounded out of the spring to stand before her. The shock to his wounds would have doubled him over if he had allowed such a thing. But he sucked in the pain, wondered why she stared at him so. Too late he realized she'd caught an eyeful of his naked condition and wasn't looking away. Stubbornly, he remained before her, hands folded over his manly parts as if it were a natural stance.

Her face flushed and she pinched back a cry, but this time those incredible green eyes didn't flicker, not even briefly as she closely examined the entire length of his bare body. Suddenly it was him who felt uneasy.

Before he could react, she said softly, "Would you like me to braid your hair?"

"I certainly would not," he said. "It is not your place."

She looked around, then back at him with an expression of deviltry. "Who would know? I'm good at it. My mother wears her lovely hair in a long braid wound around her head, and many's the time I've done it up for her."

He thought of this woman's gentle touch on his back, the way she'd applied the poultices, her own long tresses tickling his skin. Imagined her fingers in his long hair and gazed straight into her challenging eyes. "You have lovely hair yourself."

The quick shift in subject brought a look of flushed surprise to her features. Reddened cheeks heightened the beauty of her ivory complexion and for a moment he forgot he stood before her without any clothes on. Forgot that he did not want to get to know this woman who had interrupted his quest. They were alone together with no other living soul anywhere. Desire rippled through him, like a visitor long time absent. Shocked at the unexpected feelings, he took a step toward her, shivering in a light breeze that stirred her hair.

She reached out a hand that shook slightly, and he took it, oblivious to all else. Her fingers were soft against his. If she took another step, or he did, they'd be touching.

"You're cold," she said, and the words broke the spell between them.

Immediately, he regretted being so foolish. All he had wanted was to shock her so she would keep her distance. He hated her nearness, hated the way she made him feel, like some lusting white man. Hated that her very presence had made him go back on his vow to never speak the white man's tongue again. He knew all about the spell this kind of woman could cast on a man, for hadn't he been white before he came to his senses? All he wanted was to save his people and take revenge on the white soldiers. On all whites, and that had to include her. So he turned his back, gathered up his scant clothing, and walked past her as if she were invisible.

As he retreated through the trees, Aiden stared at the broad shoulders, the rippled wet hair that hung to his narrow waist, admired the muscled legs and taut backside. She had judged him a savage, was surprised to see desire for her written across his features. And then when she reacted, he looked as if he'd been caught peeking up her dress. She'd seen the expression before, and wondered at it, for surely he didn't embarrass that easily. And what of her own reaction? Earlier shame had quickly changed to admiration and wonder. Was she turning as savage as he?

On more than one occasion in her life lately, it had occurred to her that she was fast approaching an age when no man of any consequences would look upon her with desire. At any rate, not any man she could feel the same way about. Now here was this beautiful specimen of a man, no doubt her junior by a few years, sending signals she yearned to answer. In the overall scheme of things, who would it hurt?

By the time she returned to the cabin he had dressed in the layers of winter clothing common to Indians in the north, covering all his attributes quite well. He still refused to look at her or speak. And he had built a fire to heat the water.

"Thank you...for the fire."

He nodded. "We're almost out of fuel. Soon we'll have to be going."

He picked up a bundle of clothing. "I think you'll be more comfortable...after you bathe. I'll leave you to it." With the terse words, he whirled and left. Before closing the door, he added, "Shout when you are dressed, and don't be too long. It is getting cold outside."

"Oh, you don't want to play turn about and watch me?"

Face flushing, he snapped, "I most certainly do not."

"Uh-huh. Well, thank you."

When he aimed a puzzled gaze at her, she held up a shirt from the clothing. "For these."

"Yes, well, you're welcome. It is not good, you running around looking like..." He gestured and shut up. Stared at her with a look she couldn't read, and pushed the door firmly shut.

Arms crossed, she stared at the door. He'd said they'd be leaving soon. Not he but they. It appeared he was going to take her with him. But where? And to what purpose? Strangely, excitement and not fear built within her at the prospect.

In her temporary profession as a singer and dancer, her policy had been that the men in the audience could look but not touch, and those who came to see her perform honored that ruling, as if fearful she might disappear if they did not. And besides, they were either fat or bony old things, some filthy of body with tobacco-stained beards and dirty fingernails and the breath of a wild animal. She had no desire to look on them at all. But this man, Stone Heart, whose name quite aptly fit him, had some fine equipment in all the right places. And she'd seen it all. Thinking of it made her want to touch him, have him touch her. He was lean and muscular like a wild cat, and much cleaner than she expected a man like him to be. Especially delightful was that streaked blond hair hanging halfway down his back. Her fingers itched to get into it. No Indian had hair like that; no white man had a right to.

Still thinking of Stone Heart as he emerged from the cold spring, she removed remnants of the blue dress and began to wash, starting with her face and neck.

Mama always said wash the cleanest parts first, then work your way to the dirtiest, but she couldn't help thinking that she had no cleanest parts. All appeared equally soiled. The hot water felt good on her skin, and she wished she had some castile soap. How wonderful that would be. She could almost smell its light, sweet fragrance, see herself and Mama in the kitchen after her brothers had bathed and gone out on a Saturday night. Stripping down to bare skin, each taking a turn standing in the washtub near the stove. Soaping, each rinsing the other, then washing their identical hair. Dear God, how she ached to go home again. Ironic, wasn't it? That she had yearned so to get away, only to find that freedom was more of a trap than home had been.

Stone Heart had recovered remarkably well from the wounds, and she prayed he would help her escape this fix. Even if it meant she'd soon be on her way back to Saint Louis and civilization, never to see him again. Though she admired his masculinity, she wanted no more to do with this horrid country, its harsh winters and incessant winds. But it certainly didn't hurt to daydream a bit about being in his arms. His full, lush lips on her. She shivered, trailed fingertips over her taut nipples.

Shaking herself, she quickly finished her bath and investigated the bundle of clothing.

He'd given her a hand-laced buckskin vest with lovely blue and red beading in an intricate pattern on either side. A long-sleeved shirt made of blue chambray was obviously acquired at a trading post. Long buckskin leggings and a pair of fur-lined moccasins finished off the outfit. The clothing smelled of wood smoke and something wild and mysteriously akin to him. She shuddered to think they may have come off some dead Indian, but she slipped into them gratefully. Feeling warm and snug, she peered through the doorway, anxious to catch sight of him.

The setting sun painted lavenders and pinks across the metallic sky, sharpening minute shadows that cut the snow-drifted plains. For an instant her heart fluttered, for she saw him nowhere. But then he came from behind the cabin, limping toward her, a huge bundle over one shoulder. From the other hand hung a furry animal which he threw down in the snow.

With horrified eyes, she studied the offering. It was a dead rabbit. Revulsion washed over her and she stepped back inside where she didn't have to look at the poor little thing. Inside he deposited a blanket load of dried buffalo chips, and placed several in the fire. Without saying a thing, he went back outside, evidently to tend to the animal. There was only one reason for him to bring back such a thing, and that was so they could eat it. Her empty stomach roiled, growled, threatened to erupt. She couldn't make up her mind whether she was revolted at the thought of eating such a cute animal, or so hungry it didn't matter.

Perhaps if she remained inside until he had it

ready to cook, she wouldn't have to think about what she was really eating. To refuse would be foolish considering how hungry she was. The hardtack and jerky he'd shared earlier hadn't lasted very long.

He pulled back the blanket, stuck his head in. "What're you waiting for?"

"I don't know, what?"

"I can clean this animal without your help, but you must work if you are to eat. So come on out here."

She still wasn't sure she understood. "Me? I don't—"

"I know, and that's why you need to learn."

"But, I can't."

"Of course you can." He started to come inside, intending, she was sure, on dragging her outside.

"Okay, okay, but I've been working. I hauled up water—"

"For your bath." He reached for her arm.

Squealing, she dodged. "—and I...I took that bullet out of your back."

"And now you are going to help clean and cook our supper." He cocked an eyebrow. "Or you will not eat."

"You mean you'd sit in front of me and eat it all?"

"Indeed I would."

"I don't believe you."

He shrugged. "Watch me."

For an instant she thought about it, then decided it wasn't worth taking the chance. Her belly ached from hunger, and the idea of food of any kind made her mouth water.

Slowly, she peered out at him. The sun had set, left dancing colors that lit the sky, reflected on the surrounding snow.

"Close the door, you're letting in the cold." He stood over the poor dead bunny, knife in hand. At its throat blood matted the coat.

He didn't look up. She did as he said, then sidled toward him. He knew she was there though. Said without even glancing at her, "Pick it up by the hind feet."

She stared at the cute, furry little paws and swallowed harshly.

Without waiting for her to decide, he snatched it up and stuck the feet out. With one finger she stroked the fur.

He shook it. "Take hold."

Once again she gulped, did as he said and squinched her eyes shut. The remaining warmth of its life enclosed in her palms made her sick. A hard jerk and she let go. Looked to see him discarding the fluffy cotton tail.

The poor thing lay in the snow between them, one glazed eye pointing up at her.

"Pick it up," he said, impatience overridden by something she couldn't identify. But it sure looked like amusement.

She shot him a quick glance. Damn him, he was all but laughing out loud at her. Grabbing up the limp bundle, she held it by the hind legs. Steeled herself.

"Not that way. Belly toward me so I can skin it properly. We will want the fur."

She rolled the poor little thing over so its tummy was exposed for the knife, clenched her eyes shut.

"You had best watch. You might need to know this." He pushed her hands apart, the touch of his fingers warm against her clenched fingers.

Through slitted lids she watched him yank out tufts of fur on the inside of both the hind legs till he had bared a curved patch. She shut her eyes, opened them at the sound of his knife cutting flesh. He sliced around one foot about midway, inserted the knife point just under the skin and began to work it loose from the muscle beneath, two fingers following along under the flap the knife made. Fascination replaced revulsion. He was undressing the rabbit like it wore furry longjohns. When he'd done this to both legs, he unfastened the skin right down the center of the belly, like the longjohns had buttons and he was undoing them one by one.

She gnawed her lip, then thought of the feel of flesh to teeth and clamped her lips tightly.

When the knife point and the clever fingers reached the neck, he returned to work close to her grip again, cutting around each foot to loosen the skin.

"Okay, flip him over." He didn't wait for her to react, but tugged the feet from her steely grip, turned the rabbit with its back up and handed the dead little paws back to her.

Thank goodness he'd left the fur on the feet so she didn't have to hold on to that slimy flesh beneath. There was no blood except at the throat, and there a black blob that looked as if the rabbit had been wounded. It reminded her of the wound in his side and she swallowed hard to keep from heaving.

While she battled her thoughts, he took hold of the loosened skin and peeled it neatly away. She watched in amazement as he bared the hind legs, the back with its ridge of ribs and then the shoulders and front legs. Stared at the skin, a bluish-pink of tendon and flesh.

Before she realized what he was going to do next, he clasped the poor thing's head, inside all that skin, and broke its neck. The crack sent a shudder down her spine. Instantly, he cut through the sinew and left her holding the decapitated body.

Hot bile rolling up from the pit of her stomach, she bent forward, coughed and spat, but brought up nothing. Surely, this couldn't get much worse.

But she was deadly wrong. It did.

He didn't even give her a chance to recover, nor did he say anything in warning of what was yet to come. He simply slit the poor thing's stomach open with that deadly knife, spilling its steaming guts. An overpowering, hot, stench washed over her. Pale, steaming intestines hung in long dripping strands, attached to the rabbit in only one place, which she couldn't even think about. She turned away when he went to work to solve that problem, and so didn't have to see what he did.

"Okay, give him here," he said, touching her hands.

She couldn't let go, squinted through half-closed lids.

"Let go. You did fine. You are done." He laid both hands over hers, but all she could think of was what he had just done with those hands, and their easy touch did not soothe her one bit.

"I will clean him up. You go fix us a vessel to cook him in. One that has a lid."

Breathing raggedly, gulping over and over to control any upheaval from her stomach, she nodded and yanked her hands from his, shoved her way blindly through the door. There, with fists gripped at her sides, she regained a small amount of control over her lurching insides, steadied her dizzy head.

She had helped her mother clean plenty of fish, and occasionally a chicken, but none of that compared to what she had seen today.

It was entirely possible that she would starve to death before she let even a morsel of that meat pass her lips.

A while later, sitting across the fire from Stone Heart, she held the juicy hind leg of the rabbit in both hands as she ripped the sweet meat from the bone with her teeth. There was very little fat on the animal, but the broth from its cooking tasted rich, and they gulped it between bites. They took turns drinking from the smaller pan, for no eating utensils had been left behind by the former tenants.

He had cut the rabbit in four chunks and shared them equally with her, telling her, "You worked well, you eat well."

After his words, the only sounds were those of lips smacking and moans of delight. Neither spoke until every last morsel was gone and fingers were licked clean.

Wiping her mouth with the back of a hand, she glanced across the flickering flames. His lips gleamed with juices, and his metallic eyes shimmered as if about to shed tears. Of course, that wasn't possible. He was too tough to cry over anything.

"Thank you," she murmured.

Firelight danced across his features, giving him a frightening look.

"And you as well. We worked fine together."

Nodding, she wished she could think of something to say. Anything. This feeling of contentment washed away her earlier fears of dying out here on the prairie. He had brought it about. The clothing she wore, the food she ate, the warmth of the shelter.

"I guess I meant to thank you for more than...than the food. I would have died if it weren't for you."

His glance sharpened and he studied her intently. "How did you get here?" he asked, then looked away and waved a hand. "Forget I asked, it doesn't matter. I don't want to know. I only want to return to Fort Robinson and save my people...or what's left of them."

"The Cheyenne?"

A brisk nod.

"I thought...I thought they...you were sent back

to Fort Reno, to Indian Territory. I mean, that's what we heard over in Benson."

"That's not what happened. You can't believe what the whites tell. We will never journey to the south again."

He locked his arms around both knees and stared into the fire so long she thought he wouldn't speak again, but then he did, in a mysterious tone that sent shivers over her skin.

Chapter Four

Stone Heart gazed into the fire, as if to look at her would reveal his true self, a thing he kept well hidden. Then he began to speak. "They brought them up from Fort Reno down in Indian Territory last year, with Dull Knife objecting all the way."

"Were you with them?"

"Not until later. I had been away from my people...but I returned after..." He shrugged. "That doesn't matter, what does is that I rejoined them, and I shall remain, no matter what happens."

She despaired of him ever telling her everything. "It must be difficult, being of two minds and spirits, and pulled between the two."

He glanced at her, then back toward the flames. "Not any more."

"Because you have rejected the one?"

"Yes, I have."

She nodded, though she didn't think he spoke the absolute truth. Thus his sudden defensiveness. After all, he had reverted easily to speaking English soon after their first encounter. She decided not to pursue it, though, and instead urged him to continue the story.

"Because the leaders continued to tell the army they would not return, Captain Wessells stopped their rations...to convince them to be good and do as he wanted. They were hungry, but not ready to give in, so he cut off their water as well."

"Even for the children?"

"Oh, yes. The preening jackass sees us all as the enemy."

"And so they decided to..."

"Break out. Yes. Some of the women heard talk they were going to burn us out if we didn't give in."

"But they had you locked up, didn't they?"

"Yes, of course. But we all voted to die rather than return to Indian Territory. If they would not let us go home. And so we broke out."

"Where is home?"

"Montana, beyond the land of Greasy Grass. What you call the Little Big Horn." The sharp tone cut the silence like a sword.

"Isn't that where Custer was killed? The Little Big Horn."

He spat into the fire. "The son of a bitch. He will rot in hell."

She sent him a quick sideways look, reserved further comment when he stared with a murderous glint, appearing to see something far beyond the walls of the shelter.

He was silent for a long while, then went on in a voice tinged with grief.

"Braves were killing their own wives and children to keep from being taken. The soldiers were shooting at us, running us down like animals. I could not...I wanted to help, but there were so many. And we had so few weapons. Black Bear had his Custer rifle and Singing Wolf his Sharps. The rest—forty-four braves if you counted boys—between us we had five rifles and nine pistols, hardly any cartridges or lead or powder."

She lay a hand on his arm, found muscles clenched with rage. Imagined what it would be like to be so consumed with hatred. Yet how could she blame him?

Taking a deep breath, he went on, as if sorrow poured from a deep wound gouged in his heart and he could not stop its flow. "Knives, we had some, mostly broken. Little Wolf, who carries the chief's bundle, he escaped with some of the people. Even our women were strong and brave. And now so many are dead, I fear." The words at last halted, he returned to that faraway place where memories dwell.

It was an unbelievable tale and she studied him in horrified awe.

She wanted to put an arm around his broad shoulders, now hunched in defeat, and pull his head to her breast. No people should be made to suffer so. But she didn't, because when his eyes met hers, that half-wild expression carved a feral mask over his features, warned her off. He was in the mood to kill, not be hugged.

For a long while there was no sound in the silence of the cramped quarters. When he finally spoke again, the sharp tone startled her from a reverie that had carried her far from this place.

"Do not make the mistake of thinking we are defeated, though. Many were not among the dead, so I pray they lived. The soldiers dragged some of the bodies away, but they also must have taken prisoners back to the fort. I will go there, find out who survived. No one can stop me." He spoke as if to an enemy, refused to look at her. Perhaps in some twisted way he felt she had some part in all this. Once again the distant place captured him and he withdrew.

She let him be for a moment and rebuilt the fire. "But one man alone, how can you hope to free them?"

"I will or die with them. We will not return to Indian Territory. We only wish to go home." He glanced around, raised his broad shoulders. "And I cannot go without them."

In sorrowful silence, she nodded. She too wanted to go home, and the need to do so would not go away. It clung to her, squeezed at her heart and dug a great vacant hole in her belly. Made her feel incomplete. Perhaps if he knew he would trust her to understand his desire.

"I too wish to go home, to my family. I don't think I ever will, though."

"You can go where you please. There is no one to stop you. You are white."

"And so are you," she snapped. "You don't have to do this. You may think you're Indian, but take off that garb and you're almost as white as I am. No one would ever guess. So why do you torture yourself so?"

He grabbed her arm, twisted her around so they were nose to nose. She sensed his fury like a great palpable beast. Fear gnashed at her, stifled the cry that erupted from deep in her throat so that it came out like a croak. But she refused to look away, or show cowardice, instead stuck out her chin and held his burning gaze without flinching.

Lying her arm beside his, he clamped her jaw in an iron grip, forced her to gaze upon the contrast of ivory against copper.

"Look at my skin, look at yours. I may have the hair of my evil father, but my flesh is of the Cheyenne, and I will not live the lie of the white man anymore. You are white, I am not."

She tried to pull away from the vicious grasp of his strong fingers, but he held her fast. Teeth grating in an effort to speak, she found only silence and a dreadful sorrow. Hot tears slipped down her cheeks, and the spark of anger in his eyes flared and went out.

He pushed her off, turned away. "Go to bed. This is not a time to talk." Fiercely, he slammed through the door to disappear into the dark, cold night.

She had intended to clean his wounds, had put a pan of water near the fire to do so after they finished eating. Now he was gone, and she didn't even know when or if he would return.

Since she could do nothing about it, she made a bed using one of the blankets he'd brought and wrapping herself in Wiley Lawson's buffalo coat. This night she would again sleep in close quarters with a savage, knowing that he considered her part of an enemy that he would readily slaughter. Suppose he decided to take her first? Out by the spring she had sensed a definite attraction between them. While they performed their little mating dance, his desire had risen hot and fierce. The confrontation hadn't been that much different from the one that took place between her and Stephan before he lured her to this wilderness only to abandon her. There would only be one difference. Stone Heart would likely not bother to leave her alive after he had her. He would take her scalp, and she would not be able to stop him.

Despite her vow to remain awake and alert, her full belly and the warmth from the fire soon lulled her into a deep sleep.

Outside, Stone Heart dragged in a great breath that seared his lungs with the brutal cold, and waited for the passion of the last few moments to cool. For underlying the white-hot fury he felt against the white man had risen a renewed desire for the red-haired beauty whose courage so impressed him. Above him, stars blazed their cold fire and he gazed up into the heavens. The frigid cold caressed his cheeks, fell over his shoulders and enclosed him in its brutal embrace. He should have had the sense to pick up a blanket before storming out into the cold. Now he could stand out here and freeze, at least until she went to sleep so he didn't have to deal with what was happening between them. She knew nothing of his people, or of him, and it would be best left that way. Why had he spoken to her of what had happened at Fort Robinson?

What kind of woman was this that she could

affect him in this way? He had loved before, loved and lost, loved and discarded, even been discarded, but never had he felt quite like this about a woman. Like every time she looked at him she held his heart in the same hands that had bathed his wounds. If he closed his eyes, he imagined her sweet, soft lips covering his mouth. It was so hard to understand. She was such a tattered little thing, not only white but a whore as well. What was wrong with him? He had this one final duty to perform for his people that surpassed all else, and he would do it. What his father, the hated Long Hair Custer, had done to the Lakota and Cheyenne, he must atone for in some small way. What good it might do he had no idea. But he had to try, even if he died in the effort. Especially if he died. That would finally pay the debt, once and for all.

Gazing up into the blackness, he saw fast moving clouds swallowing the great bowl of sky. There would be no moon rise tonight, nor would the white man's drinking dipper show the way to travel in the dark. He thought of Little Wolf and his band, hoped they had made it over the bluffs and beyond. Headed home. They would at least die free.

But what of the others? The wounded and dead dragged back to the fort. The white man would have final say because he always did. But suppose Dull Knife and Bull Hump, Roman Nose and Little Finger Nail, Hog, and some of the others lived? He had to help them escape the prison that was Fort Robinson one last time. He could not leave without doing at least that much.

The white woman inside could not be allowed to deter him. She would have to be left behind. He could not help her and his people at the same time. It was not possible. All the same, he felt a great sorrow well up inside. Had he met her in that other world, the white man's world, they might have come together in joy, desire making them one. At least for the space of time it took to embrace the exquisite near-death of the mating dance.

Thinking of holding her, taking her in the wildness of passion, he shivered and hugged himself, sniffed the air that held the faint scent of snow to come; tonight, perhaps tomorrow. Very soon he would be fit to travel and fight, and he would leave her here because it was what he must do.

A gust of cold air and a slight rustling jarred her awake, and she listened to him moving about in the stillness. She had been afraid, but wasn't sure if it was because she feared he wouldn't return or that he would. Trembling, she waited, but he did not approach. Instead he made a small sound, and with great stealth, she turned to search him out. He sat beside the fire, leg propped awkwardly while he washed the wound, using water from the pan she had put on the coals earlier. What a man this was. Strong and filled with such purpose as she had never before seen. And despite what it might mean to her own survival, she admired him greatly for what he would soon attempt to do.

She let him finish, then sat up. "I'll do your back, if you want."

Though he appeared to hold fast to his anger, he nodded and grunted an assent, glaring at her defensively.

When she took the cloth away, he said, "Only because I cannot reach it."

"Yes," she replied softly, "Only because of that." But he could bathe the entry wound, and they both knew it. Yet he allowed her to clean it with the small square of cloth they had saved for the purpose.

"Does it need another poultice?" she asked, the tips of her fingers gently palpating the flesh around the hole in his belly.

The muscles under her fingers tightened. "I do

not know. Does it?"

"I never before even saw a bullet hole in anyone's flesh. It's not swollen anymore, and it's not red."

"Look at the back." He hunched up one shoulder and twisted so firelight played over the bunched muscles.

Dipping the cloth in hot water, she bent to examine the place where she had dug out the chunk of lead. Tenderly, she cleaned the flesh, felt goose bumps pop to the surface, experienced a violent desire she couldn't quite identify.

When finished, she dropped the cloth into the hot water and glanced up at him. His eyes, like twin mirrored lakes, studied her intently. Unable to look away from her double reflection captured there, she caught her breath. A fine bead of sweat lay across his upper lip, the only sign he was uncomfortable. But was it from pain or their nearness to each other? She wasn't sure.

At last she was able to speak. "I think they are healing." Never in her life had she been of such distinctly different minds. One feared what this savage might do to her, the other wished for his attention, his touch, his caring. She had been so foolish with a man once and ought to know better. But somehow she didn't.

"Good. I must go very soon. It will snow tonight, perhaps tomorrow. Too bad I don't have a horse. When we broke out we intended to make it to Bronson's ranch to steal some, but the soldiers prevented it. Attacked us before we could do so. Captain Wessells is a butcher with little sympathy. I will have none when I face him."

She thought of the slain women and children, remembered he'd said some of the Cheyenne killed their own families. What kind of courage did it take to do such a thing?

"I don't understand why they wouldn't just let you go home, if that's all you wanted."

"Because it was too late. The white man had dictated his terms, and to back down, even when he saw the Cheyenne would rather die than go, would not be possible. To let us return to our homeland would have made good sense, but the general called Crook would lose his honor. He and Long Hair were cut of the same cloth."

Sadly, she nodded. Men could be such fools. "Why do you hate Custer so?"

"He's a butcher of our people."

"And they killed him. Isn't that enough?" Tilting her head, she looked up into his eyes. "There's more, I'm thinking."

"No, nothing will ever be enough. While he murdered our people at every turn, he slept with our women."

Ah, so that was it. She nodded in understanding. Yes, that could explain such furious hate. "Others must have done the same."

"You will never understand. He sired me, turned me into a white man with no place to call his own."

"He's your father?" She could hardly believe it, but it would explain a lot.

"I will never call him that. Never."

"But...you're Cheyenne, you said—"

"And that is enough. None of the rest matters any longer. Now leave me be. You understand nothing."

"I understand being torn from those you love. I understand wanting to go home. It digs into your heart and the pain is almost too great to bear. I may not know the agony your people have endured, but I do know loneliness and despair and a desire to be with loved ones."

"It is time we slept," he said. Without acknowledging her pain, he moved a little away from her and made his bed. She watched in silence, then crept to her own blanket.

That night she dreamed of her mother and father, her brothers, Sean, Cormac, Blaine, Mulcahy, and the youngest, Ryan, born after her father was killed. She awoke with tears streaking her face. She would likely never see them again.

Fully awake, she cautiously dragged herself to her feet and started outside to tend to her toilet. The door had frozen shut and she yanked until it opened to face a solid wall of white. How could this happen overnight? They were trapped in a tomb and now would die here.

Yet she could hear nothing but her own breathing and the loud thumping of her frightened heart. Could it be he had gone, leaving her alone?

His voice came out of the darkness, filling her with relief. "I should have killed another rabbit."

"But, what...?"

"A blizzard."

"What are we going to do?"

"Dig our way out."

"I see." She gazed at her hands for a moment, turned on him in an explosion of despair. "I hate it here. How can you stand to live like this? How can any man expect a woman to live like this?"

He shrugged. "There are worse ways...there are better. You appear to be without a man. Yet you are here."

The intent of his statement wasn't lost on her. "Oh, I didn't come out here on my own. A man brought me. Lured me with sweet talk and promises he couldn't even keep long enough to marry me. And I still don't know why."

"You came. You must have wanted something from him...or this place."

"You think it's that easy? Stay or go? Women sometimes have to settle."

"Or they choose to?"

"You don't know anything about it."

He turned from her. "No, I do not, and I would rather not."

"I have to...have to...go."

He nodded in understanding. "I will fix you a place, just until we get out of here."

Later, they began to dig, using the battered pans and taking turns so they didn't get in one another's way. Close to the surface, the snow was frozen solid, and so they kept their digging low to the ground.

After a while, he tried to encourage her. "It is probably a drift and once we get out a ways, we should be able to break into the open."

"Should? What if we don't?"

He turned from his chore. "Then we will die. Either way the snow will one day melt."

"Is that your way of telling me what we do doesn't matter?"

"It matters very much, but it will not change what goes on out there. Just inside here." He pounded his chest with a clenched fist. "And what is in here remains with our spirit...forever." Eyes shooting sparks, he glanced at her. "Now, dig. It is your turn to make a difference."

He dropped his makeshift digger and spread a warm palm over her chest. "In here."

At his touch, heat soared through her, shot into the depths of her being. Immediately he drew back, but their eyes locked for a long moment before both broke away. Flustered, she scooped fiercely at the snow.

The tunnel opening advanced slowly, yet the pile of snow inside the small dugout grew to great proportions. The heat of the fire began to melt it, turning the floor to mud.

At last he moved completely out of sight in the

cave-like opening, and soon shouted, "We are out."

On hands and knees she squeezed through and emerged into a world of white. Sometime during the day the winds had calmed, the blizzard settled into a thick, wet snowfall. He gazed down at her through a thick curtain of huge flakes that clung to his eyelashes and covered his hair. Laughing with delight, she stumbled up against him. He was veiled in the white stuff, like a gigantic cake ornament covered with frosting.

"Isn't it beautiful?" Under her hands his heart thudded, and the heat from his body crept into her. A knot of incredible desire tightened deep inside her being. Without thinking, she reached up and brushed snow off his cheeks. "I wish...I wish we..."

Going deathly still, like he did so easily, he pushed a strand of hair away from her face, and cupped a hand over her ear. His gray eyes smoldered like embers coming to life. She licked away the melting flakes and waited for him to lower his mouth to hers.

His tongue traced his own lips, as if in anticipation, and she closed her eyes, inched closer. Leaned into the hardness of him and wished they wore less clothing. He did not make another move, so she snaked an arm around his neck, stood on the tips of her toes and pulled him downward. She could do no more, it was up to him. His warm breath caressed her tingling skin. Tiny rivulets of melted snow dripped onto her cheeks. All fear left her and she waited with anticipation.

But he pulled brusquely away, leaving her with arms outstretched into the falling snow.

"This is not the time." The harsh tone spoke much more than the few words.

Arms empty, body yearning, she stood deathly still, realized there never would be a time for them. He had but one purpose, and she was not a part of it.

She must go back to her world, leave him to his, and forget the way he made her feel by just glancing at her with those smoldering eyes, touching her with those fingers at once strong and gentle. They were strangers, and they would pass beyond each other all too soon. Forget each other even sooner. This storm would not last forever, and when it ended, he would be gone. She could only hope he would take her as far as Fort Robinson where she might get transportation back east where she belonged.

He could go on to his destiny. Which she feared was death at the hands of the white man.

She gazed at his stoic figure and knew he had already passed beyond that brief moment with her. All but forgotten her touch.

"I'm sorry, Stone Heart. Don't be angry with me."

"No, I am only angry with myself. I know of the attraction of women like you. For a long time I have not had a woman. I have been more concerned with staying alive and less with enjoying life. I am the one who is sorry."

Women like you.

How dare he say such a thing? He was still calling her a whore, and saying his attraction to her was only that brought about by an animal lust for her body.

"Don't you dare call me that. I am not a whore. You know nothing. You are as dense as this." She swung a hand around, cutting through the tumbling flakes, then ran mindlessly away from him, his voice echoing at her back.

"Come back. You will get lost. Do not be a fool. Come back."

The words faded, and she stopped, turned to throw his warning back at him. Fear twisted her insides. He had disappeared and in his place nothing but the solid white curtain. Whirling, she saw nothing in any direction but thick flakes. And in its center, herself, alone, lost. A husky dryness crept into her throat.

He was there, right there. She took a step, reached out. "Stone Heart?" Her voice sounded wispy as the falling flakes. Which way had she come? Where was the dugout? The tunnel they'd made? Only a little ways, she hadn't come far.

Behind her, the footprints she'd made filled. Soon they would be erased and she would be left here, in the middle of nothing, with more nothing all around her. She would die.

"Help. Help me," she cried as loud as she could, trying to retrace her way. "Please."

He would hear. Surely.

But no reply came. Over and over she called, flailing at the endless thick curtain, finally going to her knees. She could crawl, follow her prints back to where she had come from. And she did, for a few steps, then they were obliterated, filled as if they never existed. So she collapsed, sat where she was, afraid to move, afraid not to. Afraid mostly that she would die alone, so far from home.

When the heavy snowfall swallowed her up he yelled and kept yelling. She must stop, come back. Stupid, foolish girl. Now, he would have to go after her, take the chance they would both freeze to death, hopelessly lost within sight of the shelter. Even as he watched, her footprints disappeared. He ought to leave her be. After all, why should they both die for her stupidity? Men caught in such storms often died within shouting distance of camp.

The vague possibility that he could go back inside and forget about her crossed his mind, disappeared as quickly as a June frost. He was as much to blame as she, letting her taunt him with her body when he should never have touched her or allowed her to touch him. So he must find her somehow, someway and get them both back to safety. He only knew he could not be responsible for her death, even if he didn't understand why.

In the hope that she would see the folly of her ways and remain in one place, rather than running wildly over the trackless prairie, he took the time to go inside to find something with which to mark the trail back.

Pawing through his own supplies, the things taken from the dead in the battlefield, he came up with nothing. If he had a lariat, strands of rawhide, anything to secure at the tunnel's entrance, he could play it out behind as he moved in ever widening circles. If he didn't find her when he reached its end, then he would have done all he could. Sweeping a hand over the crude shelving along one wall, he found crammed back in the far corner a musty fat ball of wool yarn, the kind women made socks and sweaters from. It was damp to the touch and as ugly a color as the life these settlers had lived in this place. He feared the strands might be rotted, or perhaps chewed into pieces by rats, but it would have to do. Frantic to get back outside and begin his search, he only stopped long enough to feed the fire so he could bring her back to a warm shelter.

Aiden heard what sounded like a distant echo, and raised her head. Only silence. Crouched back down in the snow, she gathered her body into a ball to conserve what little warmth was left. Heard once more a faint sound. Someone shouting from very far away.

Cupping both hands around her mouth, she yelled as loud as she could, then waited for a reply. The monotonous distant cries continued, faded. He couldn't hear her above his own shouts. Still she kept calling for help.

She must have screamed a dozen times. Two dozen. Three. Her throat grew scratchy and she paused to wet her tongue with snow.

His reply came again. It seemed closer, but was it truly? Or was she imagining it?

"Hallow. Hallow. Hallow." Muffled, wavering, but surely nearer than before.

"Here. Here. Here," she cried into the silence that followed.

Then there was nothing, and when she tried again, her voice broke and she began to sob. Cold embraced her, her belly quivered and her teeth clacked. She lost the feel of feet and hands; felt sleepy and decided she didn't care if he found her or not, she had to have some sleep.Coiling into a tight ball, she buried her face into the curl of her body, took a deep breath and welcomed the darkness. Tingling in her toes and fingers faded, the quivering stopped and she felt at peace. Within the serenity of the dream she saw her mother's lovely, careworn face, heard the laughter of her rowdy brothers, felt her father's arms wrapped tightly around her. Rocking her, singing to the child that was her. She missed him so very, very much. How wonderful that he was here with her.

She'd inherited her Irish voice from him. His tenor sang the familiar words she knew so well.

Oh, Danny boy, the pipes, the pipes are calling. From glen to glen and o'er the mountainside...

In the depths of her mind she joined him, their voices blending like the singing of angels.

The summer's gone and all the...

Her father's arms enclosed her, taking her home.

Chapter Five

Caught in a frigid silence, Stone Heart stood very still and listened for any sound. A cry for help, moaning, shouting, a breath or heartbeat. From out of the thick curtain of falling snow floated a pure voice. A calling of the spirits. A song to break the heart. At first he thought he had imagined it, the sound was so ethereal. He swallowed, held his breath and listened. The delicate melody hovered all around him.

Perhaps he had wandered too far and himself frozen to death. This could well be a summoning from the next life, a vision. If it could be said that hearing music was a vision. He squinted into the thick blanket so intensely that his eyes hurt. And that was all he could see. Snow, snow, and more snow. Beyond it, out there somewhere, the beautiful music continued in the plaintive language of the white woman, burred by her vague accent of another land. It had to be her.

Playing out more yarn, he moved in the direction from which the soulful lament appeared to come. Slowly, slowly, he advanced, the music growing closer, more plaintive. Another step, then another, taken like a blind man, and he almost tripped over her, nothing more than a drifted-over lump huddled on the ground. Still. Unmoving. It couldn't have been her voice he heard, for she was nearly buried face down and so cold and limp he thought her dead.

On his knees, he brushed away the thick, wet cloak until he uncovered a tangle of frozen red hair, a head tucked between clamped knees. Fearfully, he lay a hand over the back of her neck. Stiff and as unyielding as a statue. Was she dead? Beneath his palm, a fluttering as fragile as moth's wings. Or was he imagining it, just as he'd imagined the song that had summoned him here? For surely she had not been capable of making so much as a sound. Curling his fingers, he felt for the pulse at her throat, found only frigid skin. His heartbeat quickened with dread. Had he come all this way only to find a corpse?

But no, there, under his touch, a faint pulse. Slow, barely discernible.

Leaning forward, he bent close to her ear. "Woman, woman, wake up. Hear me." What was her name? One of those strange names, foreign even to the white tongue. He had not called her by it, so he could not be sure. A'den, that was it.

"A'den, are you alive?" He shook her, searched once more for the movement of life's blood beneath the iciness of her skin. Found nothing. Odd how her death saddened him. She was the enemy, to be hated and destroyed. But seeing her lying there, features tranquil and lovely in a mantle of snow, tore at his stone heart as nothing else had save the suffering of his people.

She couldn't die. He wouldn't allow it. Already so many had perished in this place. This killing ground should be consecrated by the gods, forever left untouched, hallowed in honor of so many who had died here.

Removing his hand from the unresponsive flesh, he tenderly brushed snow from her hair, caressed her blue-tinged features, gathered her into his arms and cradled her. His heart beat against her, his warmth washed over her, his breath of life touched her face.

"I am sorry," he whispered, the words catching in his throat.

A harsh cough erupted from deep within her chest, sent a massive quaking from her body to his. She let out a broken moan, joined by his own startled cry.

She was alive! Nearly frozen, but alive.

Gratefully, he picked up the precious ball of yarn that would lead him back to the dugout, and rose, her fragile form in his arms. The pain in his side and leg slowed him down. Also, he must be careful not to dislodge the other end of the yarn, planted deep in frozen snow outside the tunnel they had carved. They would both die if he lost hold on that fragile line of life. Carrying her and following the length of yarn proved difficult. Every few steps he paused to draw in great drafts of air and fight off the stabbing pain in his side. Such a short distance, yet it seemed to take forever to reach its end and the welcome opening to the shelter. The hole they'd dug was already beginning to drift over, and he had to put her down to clear the way.

Taking her through the tunnel proved even more difficult. Finally he settled on backing in on hands and knees and dragging her along lying on her back, not so easy on either of them. He did not want to hurt her, nor could he ignore the pain of his own wounds. But they would heal, and keeping them both alive was more important than a bit of discomfort. Once inside, he lay her on a blanket, wrapped her snugly, and built up the dying fire. Dried buffalo chips burned hot but could not be banked like logs. One had to be vigilant or lose the coals. He could not afford to waste valuable time striking sparks and coaxing a new fire to life.

He must see to her quickly. Even if she lived she was in danger of losing her fingers and toes. He removed her fur-lined moccasins, lifted one small foot in his large hands, and rubbed snow over the blue flesh, wrapped it once again and massaged the other. Finishing that, he removed her coat and clothing and bundled her in warm, dry blankets. Even under the dire circumstances, he couldn't ignore the sweet beauty of her body. Pale as ivory, smooth and daintily curved, her breasts were delicate mounds with erect nipples the color of dark honey. A flat belly and tightly muscled thighs showed she was strong of limb and accustomed to walking.

Dragging his reluctant glance from the thatch of golden red hair at the vee below her belly, he massaged her hands. They were so small and still and cold that he tucked them beneath his arms and held them there while she cried and tossed about, trying to pull free. He knew she was in a great deal of pain as feeling returned, but she must endure this.

Several times she called out for her papa, her mama, but at last stopped fighting him and allowed him to cradle her in his lap and share his body warmth. He sat that way in front of the fire for a long while, staring into the flames and gently rocking the blanket-shrouded woman. His enemy.

Where her head lay against his chest her breath moistened his shirt. She lived and breathed, and holding her brought a flame into his own heart, so that he had to lie her down to quench a raging desire that grew in his gut. A desire beyond his comprehension. He had saved her, now he wanted to take her completely, make her his own. This he could not do. Strange how closely united were love and hate, that he could go from one to the other with no effort.

Wrapped in the cocoon, she lay as if already dead and did not respond.

Hope dwindled for her survival, and he kept a silent watch, as if by doing so he could bring her back from the brink where he was sure she tottered.

Once he would have killed her without compunction, only hours earlier he had planned to leave her behind, now he could scarcely bear the thought of her death.

From the diminishing supply near the fireplace he tossed more chips on the fire. He dare not use too many or they would both freeze to death before morning. Yet he must keep her warm.

Partially buried, the dugout held its heat well, and grew quite comfortable. Yet, if the storm continued, there would be another problem. He tried not to think of it, but if the outside opening to the mud and straw chimney became blocked by drifting snow the place would soon fill with deadly smoke.

Whatever happened now, he saw little chance they would live through the next few days. Had he survived the battle with the evil Wessells and his men only to die like an animal in this hole? And what of this beautiful young woman? Much as he hated the whites, he felt compassion for her plight. Besides, she had no control over her own heritage. How well he knew that.

He must lie with her, share his body heat and remain awake to keep the fire going all night. Tomorrow would be time enough to worry about fuel to keep that flame burning for another day and night.

Gently, he unwrapped the blankets from her bare body and snuggled in against her back. It took a few moments to fit his own long legs to the curl of hers, adjust his hard belly to the tantalizing curve of her hips and tiny waist, press his broad chest against the feminine softness of her back. How strange the feel of her body against his beneath blankets still redolent with the scent of his murdered people. Soon, a soothing warmth crawled through him to nudge at his stone-hard heart. How long it had been since someone had needed him.

Even his people looked upon him as having come from the other side, the evil white man. Wondered if they could trust him not to betray them.

To be all that stood between this young woman and certain death reawakened a tenderness long buried within his soul. Smothered the hate and rage and stirred a concern he felt ill-suited to accept. He had other obligations that would soon get in the way of such feelings.

He could only see to it that she lived, no matter what. And get her to Fort Robinson where she would be allowed to return home. How well he understood that need to go home. That all encompassing yearning to live with your own people. He must return with his people to the north land above the Platte River or die in the trying. Nothing could get in the way of that.

Aiden awoke in her sunlit bedroom, white lace curtains fluttering in a breeze off the river that smelled of summer. What a dreadful dream she'd had. In real life she would never have considered doing such a thing as going off to the wilderness with Stephan. They must marry and settle in St. Louis. How could she have thought for one moment about going west on such a dangerous adventure? What a relief to awaken from the nightmare of such a horrid experience. It had all seemed so real, the harrowing trip west by train and stage, Stephan's disappearance and her struggle to survive. And that gorgeous but fantasized savage who rescued her.

Thank God it had not been true. She must tell Stephan all about it when he came to court this evening.

Sitting up, she stretched and breathed deeply of the aroma from mama's kitchen downstairs: bacon frying, coffee perking; the laughter of her raucous brothers, who kept the small house in a constant uproar with their shouts and teasing and sheer enjoyment of life. Childishly eager to join them, she threw back the covers and poked her feet out.

They touched the floor and a pain she could not describe exploded up her legs. She moaned in agony.

"Mama, where are you, what's wrong? What happened?"

Strong arms enclosed her shoulders, steadied her. A man's voice, lyrical but gruff. "You're all right. You're safe. Lay down, cover up. It's not yet morning."

She opened her eyes, saw a fire blazing in the mean darkness. Smelled wet musty earth, a wildness she didn't recognize. Not her bright bedroom at all. Her heart plummeted. The arms tightened around her shoulders and she twisted from their grasp, felt herself swathed tightly in blankets. Struggled to escape and fought a rising rage.

"Let me go. Who are you? What happened? Where am I?" Her voice didn't sound like her own, raspy and broken. Her throat hurt, her feet throbbed, her hands ached. What was wrong?

He did as she asked, but before he could reply to her questions, memory washed over her and her eyes filled with tears. "Oh, dear, I thought this was a dream, and it isn't, is it? I'll never see Mama and the boys again."

"A'den, listen to me. You must stay under the blankets. You were so cold when I found you I thought you were dead. Please. Get back in the bed and let me cover you. Stop fighting me."

"You...it's you...the savage. Don't touch me."

"Yes, it is me...the savage." His sharp retort held a note of sadness.

It didn't matter. Stephan was gone and she was stranded in this terrible place. That's all that mattered. A burning anger rose within her, an anger that she awoke to find herself in this terrible soddy on the Nebraska plains, not home in her own bed. This was not supposed to be real, and finding it so made her want to lash out, punish him for what had happened.

Too weak and exhausted to struggle further, she sighed in surrender, curled up, and let him cover her. He lay down, arms and legs wrapped around her. Vaguely she wondered what he would do to her. If he would ravage her, then kill her, but she found no energy to object. She would go to sleep and not wake up. Maybe if she tried very hard, she could return to that place of her dreams, and if she died while she was there, then she wouldn't have to come back to this dreadful country. Ever again. Remembering at last, wandering off and getting lost, she wished he'd left her in the snow to die.

Blessed sleep encompassed, lulled, and soothed her.

****

"Stop, please stop," she murmured, tried to push away an insistent hand shaking her shoulder. The death she had wished for had not come while she slept, and now someone would not leave her be.

"Are you awake?" he asked.

"How could I be anything else with you taking on like that?" She popped her head from under the covers, shoved the mop of hair from her eyes, and peeked at him through slitted lids. Groaned out a muzzy reply. "It's true then, we are still in this place." Lowering her head, she fought back tears. "I dreamed...I thought it was a dream...a nightmare. What happened? I remember getting lost and the storm. How did you find me? And why?"

While offering a small pan of water, he told her about the ball of yarn and how he'd nearly fallen over her half-dead body. "Drink. We may have no food, but we must drink to stay alive."

Obediently, she sipped from the vessel he held

to her lips, making a face at the brackish taste of melted snow. "I asked why."

"I could not leave you to die. Now, take it all."

Shuddering down the remainder of water, she tried to move her legs about, but the pain was excruciating. "What happened to me?"

"You nearly froze. Here, let me have a look." Without waiting for her permission, he unwrapped her legs, took one foot in his hand and began to rub the skin briskly.

"Ow, that hurts." She tried to kick out with the other leg, but found she couldn't make it work right. "What's wrong? Why can't I move?"

"I told you, you almost froze. Can you feel my fingers on your toes?"

Eyes wide, she searched the concerned features and nodded. "But it stings."

"That is good. We will get you on your feet."

Without waiting for her consent, he hooked her under the arms and lifted her easily.

Frantically she clutched at his shirt to keep her balance. The blankets fell away and she cried out in dismay. "I'm naked. Where are my clothes?"

"There." He gestured where he'd spread them over the rickety shelves to dry.

She glared at him, fought, but he wouldn't let her go, just kept a tight hold. Muscles tightened beneath the deerskin shirt, building their own kind of fire against her bare flesh. Angry at her own body for betraying her, she tried to push him away. It was no use.

"Stop fighting me. They were wet. When they are dry you can put them back on. Let me wrap a blanket around you."

"Why didn't you let me die?" she wailed and punched out, catching him with a solid smack near the wound.

A grunt exploded from his throat and his grip

loosened. Before he got a good hold on her again she staggered and almost fell, but he caught her, breath rasping against her ear.

"Dammit, stop, now. I'm not trying to hurt you."

Because she couldn't remain on her feet without holding on to something, she bunched his shirt tightly in both fists and gazed up into his eyes that glinted like silver agates and remained stubbornly aimed at her face.

Defeated, and left with little choice, she said, "All right, but I'll dress first. Please get me my clothes."

None too happy, he raised his shoulders, gripped hers and sat her on the pile of blankets to do her bidding.

"You're about as mule-headed as any woman I've ever met," he said when he threw the shirt and leggings down beside her. "And don't bother trying to kick me out while you dress. I'm not going out there. You'll have to settle for me turning my back."

While she struggled awkwardly with the clothing, she could hear him muttering something about women acting foolish for no good reason he could think of. Something was different about him, his speech or manner, maybe both, but she couldn't put her finger on what it was.

Pulling on the leggings proved difficult because she couldn't stand without help. She absolutely would not ask him, either. Finally she lay on her back and wiggled into them, then turned over to fasten the waist.

"Okay, you can turn around."

He stopped his grumbling and lifted her from the floor as easily as if she were a bag of flour. When he set her upright, prickles of pain shot through her limbs, and she held on to him, even though she didn't want to. Helpless as a babe in arms, she had no choice but to allow him to help her. Speechless, she crossed her arms and glared at him. This savage warrior was nothing...no one, yet she had to accept his help. If she could raise her fist she'd punch him one right in the nose. How dare he show his civilized side? He'd reverted to the language and actions of his white heritage and made it harder to ignore a growing attraction toward him. Once she began to think of him as white, she might be lost.

He snaked an arm around her back to support her. "I won't let you fall. Can you move? Let's walk and get your circulation going. I'd hate to have to chop off those pretty toes."

"You'd pay hell doing that," she muttered. He pretended not to hear her, but she knew he did, for his eyes flared.

Around and around the small room they walked, if one could call it that. He limped and dragged her, yelling that she had to move her legs, to stand, to live, because he wasn't going to let her die.

"I'll die if I want to," she said, but all the same did as he ordered. Something deep inside told her it was not yet time for her to give up her life. Though, looking around the dreadful circumstances of their existence, she couldn't figure out why she should want to continue living.

If they didn't get out of here soon they would surely starve to death, or freeze when fuel for the fire ran out. But she walked and continued to walk until the feeling returned to her legs and feet, until she felt the pounded earth of the dugout floor beneath her soles. Until the pain receded a bit.

Firmly, she shoved his arms from around her shoulders. "I can do it myself now, let me go."

He did as she asked, stepped away, and she swayed, reached out to steady herself against the dirt wall, then began to totter around the room. After a few more turns, she glanced his way, caught him watching her, his silvery eyes still as a wood's pond, the usual hardness of his features gentled in an expression she found heartbreaking.

"What is it?" she asked.

As if someone had re-chiseled his countenance into marble, he glowered at her. "If you think you are going to live, I will go out and see if the snow has stopped. I will get us something to eat."

"Like a rabbit?"

"I suppose."

"I never asked, how did you...kill him? I mean, you didn't take the rifle."

"That worthless piece of trade goods is only fit for Indians. Cheap, probably misfire or the barrel explode in my hands. I prefer this." He rubbed the knife handle with a palm.

"You killed him with a knife? How?"

He yanked it from the scabbard, pointed at the rabbit skin he'd stretched on the opposite wall and with a move so quick she missed it leaving his hand, buried the blade hilt-deep at the edge of the downy fluff. "That was his neck," he said and retrieved the knife. "I will take some pots and bring in snow for drinking and cooking."

"Why don't I go with you? I can bring in the snow."

"And wander off and get lost again so I have to put myself in danger to come looking for you?"

Embarrassed, she gazed at the floor for a moment, then snapped her head up. "That won't happen again. I'm a quick learner."

"Okay, wrap a blanket around you. I will show you how to tie it. That buffalo coat gets in the way when you are working."

As he helped her wrap one of the smaller blankets around her shoulders, she sneaked quick glances at his glowering countenance. He had gone back to his Cheyenne self in speech as well as action. When he stepped close to tie a small, tight knot between her breasts, she held herself rigid. The brush of his fingers sent tingles through her. Head bent, he appeared not to notice the effect his closeness had on her. His loose hair tickled her cheeks and spilled across her bosom like melted gold. When he bent to tie yet another knot below her waist, she tried hard to concentrate on the intricate design on his shirt, analyze how each of the tiny blue and red beads had been woven together into the pattern. But he breathed on her and he smelled of smoke and the deep woods, and clean prairie air.

Dear God, what was wrong with her? Obviously, she was addled from being too long in this wilderness. Once back at the fort and then on her way home, she'd forget this man. Totally and completely.

He finished the second knot and stepped back. She let out a sigh of relief. What was wrong with her? This was no way for a reputable young woman to behave. Being shut up here with this savage obviously had brought out the worst in her. Mama would have a fit. Only trash gave in to lustful thoughts. But she hadn't given in. Not yet, anyway.

"Throw it back away from your arms when you work," he said in that musical chant he used when he wasn't yelling like a wild white man.

Though his words startled her from her reverie, she remained frozen to the spot for another instant.

Taking up one of the larger pots, he pulled the door open. "Well, come on; let's see what's out there."

He insisted on going through the tunnel first, and was forced to do some digging on the other end before they broke through to the outside world again. She waited patiently, for there wasn't room for them side by side. That she considered a very good thing indeed.

Fresh, clean air washed over her even before she squirmed from the hole and rose to her feet. She hadn't realized until that moment how stuffy the dugout had become. A crisp, bright day had replaced the earlier brutal cold. It was wonderful simply to breathe, and she took long, refreshing gulps, face turned toward the azure blue sky.

He stood before her, head thrown back, mouth open as he did the same. The brilliant sun reflecting off snow formed a halo of light around his head. For a long while she could only stare. A light wind lifted strands of his golden hair, tugging at something inside her. Forcing her gaze beyond him to the unbroken panorama of pristine white that stretched as far as she could see; nothing but snow all the way to the horizon. Even the dugout scarcely made a lump in the endless blanket. It was breathtakingly beautiful and horribly treacherous.

"Oh, dear God. We'll never get out of here," she said.

"We need to find something to burn for heat. We'll not find any dried chips out here. They're four or five feet under."

"What about wood? There's some trees around the spring, over..." She turned to gesture, found she couldn't locate either the spring or its surrounding trees. Even squinting, she had trouble seeing in the glare. Still, she knew she should be able to pick out the stand of trees from there.

"It can't have drifted over their tops."

"No, but it's drifted between us and them. They're in a low swale in that direction." He pointed. "We just can't see them from here. And if we get very far from the dugout we won't be able to see it either."

Studying the mound, she asked, "Could we make a flag?"

He regarded her for a moment. "That's a good idea. Wait right here and I'll fetch a blanket." He turned and fixed her with a hard gaze. "Don't move, you hear me? Don't take a step till I get back. If you hadn't sang for me the last time I'd never have found you, and you'd be frozen under all that snow, not even leaving a lump."

"Sang? I didn't..." But he was gone back into the tunnel, and so she didn't finish. For a long moment, she stared into the blue sky. But Papa had sung. In her mind, she'd heard his clear tenor voice singing "Danny Boy," so plain he might have stood beside her.

She began to hum the tune, and turned in time to see Stone Heart emerge from the tunnel, blanket in hand and a look of amazement on his face.

"That is what I heard. So plain I followed the sound to you. The pipes are calling, from something to something, o'er the mountainside. I heard them."

Excitedly, she nodded and sang the song for him. Neither moved until she had finished. Enthralled, she gazed up into his expressive face, tenderly touched his cheek with a fingertip. A muscle ticked there, his eyes blinked.

"I thought it was the singing of the spirits," he murmured.

"My father sang it to me. I mean, I heard him singing it while I huddled in the snow waiting to freeze to death. I believed I was joining him in death. How can that be? I mean, that you heard it too?"

He shook his head. "This is foolish. We must get to our tasks. Daylight will be short and the work hard."

She nodded, but could not turn away from him as their gaze locked. Something very strange had happened between them, and clearly neither understood it. He might want to ignore it, but she didn't and decided after they went back inside, she would ask him to tell her more of what had happened the day before while he searched for her.

Chapter Six

He carried two blankets from the dugout. Draping the smaller red one near the chimney, he piled snow around its edges so the wind wouldn't blow it away, and caught her hand. It felt cold, small and vulnerable enclosed within his.

"We'd better get started. I'll help you fill the pots with snow and we'll leave them inside to melt while we go down to the spring. It's not going to be easy making our way through this. Some places it will be piled higher than my head. We must stay together." He glanced quickly at her, saw indecision in the way she furrowed her brow and studied the situation. Being lost and almost frozen the day before had put a scare into her, and he was worried. Up till then she'd been ready to face any challenge.

"Why don't you stay here? You don't have to go," he told her.

Eyes flashing with bravado, she yanked her hand from his. "If I don't work I don't eat, and I'm starved. Let's get busy."

While she didn't refuse his help filling the pots, she insisted on doing her share, and once more he admired her fortitude. Soon the heaping pans were lined up around the fire, and they set out on the difficult trek to the spring where he hoped to find wood and game. He had brought along hide thongs to put together a travois on which they could drag their find back to the dugout.

"Stay behind me and keep up. If you fall behind shout, don't let me run off and leave you."

When she nodded, he said gruffly, "Answer me

when I talk to you so I know you are here."

Again she nodded, then said, "Yes, I will."

"Good." To keep her at bay he tried to sound gruff, and it wasn't difficult. Anger dwelled so near the surface lately. The presence of this enemy added to his problems, and even though she was not the source of them, he vowed to remain distant. Doing so was proving more and more difficult. Perhaps he hadn't shed his white skin quite so thoroughly as he'd thought. Her sweet vulnerability definitely presented a dilemma from which he must escape.

He led the way, keeping to cleared areas as much as possible and tramping through the deeper drifts to make a path for her to follow. It was tough going, and after a while the wound at his side began to pound with each beat of his heart.

They moved along for quite some time, the only sound that of their struggle, before they topped out on a rise that allowed him to spot the marshy, tree-covered area around the spring. He stopped and she bumped solidly into him with a grunt.

"Sorry, I was watching my feet."

Resting for a moment, he gazed into the sun, almost halfway along its low winter path across the southern sky. Despite the harsh, cold wind blowing over the prairie the exertion of ploughing through the snow had warmed him.

"What is it?" she asked when he continued to stand in one place, his thoughts drifting back to the fort and what might be happening there to the survivors of the breakout.

"Nothing. Just wondering if we might make it back to Fort Robinson if we lit out today."

She had leaned forward, hands on knees to catch her breath and snapped a quick look at him. "Why? We have a shelter and fire."

"True, but if another storm comes it could bury us till we could not get out. We would die, and it would not be quick. I think we might take a chance. Just wish I could bring down some big game so we would have food."

Cupping both hands around her mouth, she blew to warm them.

"Put them under your arms." His attention was drawn suddenly to a slight, dark movement against the white snow at the edge of the frozen marsh. "Hsst."

"What?" she whispered.

"Shh. Do not move, do not talk."

She didn't, but tried to see what he saw.

Dropping to his knees, he signaled her to do the same, held his hand out flat so she would know to stay there.

Without looking to see if she obeyed, he studied the landscape from his prone position, searching for sight of further movement.

"Slide down out of the wind and be quiet. I'll yell when the coast is clear. We can gather wood after I have found us some supper."

"*If* you find us some supper. There's nothing out here but us and all this snow. The smart animals left this place a long time ago."

Turning, he gazed long and hard at her. Huddled in the snow coated blanket, she hugged herself and looked completely miserable. Her beautiful red hair hung in tangled strands, her cheeks were reddened by the wind and sun and her eyes glistened with unshed tears. In all the white world, she was the most lovely woman he had ever seen. She had no business out here, but belonged in some ballroom dressed in satins and lace, swinging around the dance floor in the arms of some young white gentleman. He imagined her whirling round and round beneath glittering chandeliers, gazing up into the face of the man who held her, danced with her, adored her. The face became his.

Angrily, he flung away the image. His days of ballroom dancing were over. He would never hold a white woman in his arms again, and certainly not this one. He was Cheyenne. He was not Martin Stone, bastard son of George Armstrong Custer, but Stone Heart, the man who would free his people.

From the corner of his eye he again spotted movement within the copse near the spring. On his belly, he crept closer, wished for a bow and arrow, instead eased the knife from its scabbard while scarcely moving a muscle. After a long wait he made out a hawk poised on a limb watching something in the underbrush. A rabbit perhaps, or a rodent of some sort. Perhaps a ground squirrel or rat. Stupid to hope for a beaver. Even if it was, he probably could not bring it down with the knife. Why hadn't he brought the trade rifle, poor as it might be? Stubborn, that's what he was. So filled with a blinding hate for the white man he could not see what might be best for the both of them. No time to contemplate the consequences of his foolish action now. Whatever was down there, he would do his best to bring it down.

The hawk was about to lose his dinner to someone hungrier and more cunning than he.

Not budging an inch Aiden watched the Cheyenne creep toward the trees. He hunched forward low to the ground, every movement a study in grace as he all but disappeared from sight. Had she not been watching, she might never have been able to tell where he hid. Obviously the vigilant hawk couldn't either. Though in all fairness, the bird had its eye on prey and not the approaching predator. She thought the Cheyenne might be going to capture the bird for them to eat, was relieved when at last he let fly with the knife and sent it toward the thicket below the hawk's lookout.

The bird took wing with a loud *scree*, knocking

snow from the drooping branches. She thought the hunter might have missed for a moment, until he leaped from his hiding place and lunged forward. He clambered onto the ice, broke through with a splash and came up with a struggling animal. It looked like a rat only bigger. She stared with disgust, then turned away.

She had managed to eat a cute bunny, she wasn't going to eat a rat. Never, not even if she starved to death. With horror, she watched him remove the knife from the twitching body and wave her forward.

His tracks were easy to follow, even though the new fallen snow was nearly waist deep.

Disgust clear on his features, he held up the small, sandy brown animal by its hairless tail. He probably had no appetite for rats, either.

"Small pickings, won't fill much of a hole in our bellies, and me and that bird made enough noise to scare everything else off. I was hoping for a rabbit."

"What is that thing? It looks like a rat."

"It is not a rat, not really," he reassured her.

She swallowed with a loud gulp. "What do you mean, not really? Either it is or it isn't."

He swung the animal in front of her eyes. "This is a muskrat. A big, juicy rat would have been tastier."

"Musk-rat, rat. What's the difference?" Turning away from the dying, ugly creature, she swallowed hard to keep from gagging.

"This isn't a—"

"I know, I know. But I'll bet it tastes like one."

He laughed in that harsh way that made such a thing sound painful for him. "Well, now, how will we ever know? I have never had to eat a rat myself. How about you?"

"How can you joke? You're standing there dripping wet with all your clothes freezing solid, and you're holding a furry...furry dead animal that doesn't look like it would make a meal for me by myself. And you're making jokes."

"It is a *veho's* trait, one I am trying to break, along with my other white attributes. Now, let's gather some wood and get back. It will be getting cold soon." He eyed the sun that had moved much too fast toward the western horizon.

As far as she was concerned, it was already quite cold, with that brisk wind blowing across the prairie, occasionally picking up snow. Ice crystals hung from the long braid, clung to his stiffly frozen buckskins.

Together, they traipsed through the wooded area, gathering chunks of downed tree branches. He found two rather long sturdy limbs, lashed them together with some shorter ones and they stacked their salvaged wood lengthwise on the crude travois. When it was piled high he backed up to it as if he were a beast of burden and lifted the front end. Dragging it from the woods was difficult, but after that the makeshift sled seemed to move along over the snow pack rather well.

Following in his trail, she found the going easier. Once he stumbled and went to his knees. She started forward, but he motioned her back.

"I am all right."

Of course he wasn't, this she could tell by watching him struggle upright and take up the heavy burden once again.

"I can help."

"We're almost there."

He was right. The red blanket he'd plastered to the roof of the dugout stood out in the gathering dusk like a spot of blood.

At the end of their entrance tunnel, he dropped the travois and hunched forward to take in great gasps of air. She watched with some anxiety. If he died so would she, but there was more to her concern than that. She did not want him to suffer, moved forward and touched his heaving shoulder. The heat from his struggle had thawed the frozen cloth and it was clammy under her palm.

She could only imagine how much it had taken out of him to drag that heavy load of ice-laden wood so far. And then to realize that it would probably be burned up by morning, must be frustrating. He was right. They had to move on, and soon, or they would both die.

Leaning forward, she peered up into his face. "Are you all right?"

He took another deep breath and straightened, the expression in his eyes one she couldn't read. Not anger nor sadness, like she'd seen there before, but something else. Stubborn pride, perhaps.

As he stood, the disgusting dead animal hanging from a leather loop around his wrist caught her eye, and had something else to think about. They were going to have to clean the thing. The rabbit had been bad enough, but this would be a much nastier job, she just knew it. Maybe she'd tell him she didn't want her share and in that way get out of the job. Her growling stomach urged her otherwise, a grumbling she struggled to ignore.

"Well, we made it," she said, still eyeing the overgrown rat.

"We can't stop yet," he said. "Now we have to get all this wood inside. Why don't you crawl in and I'll pass it through to you? Stack it back in the corner as best you can."

"Can't we just leave it out here and get it as we need it? Surely no one will steal it." With an exaggerated stare, she looked all about.

The sun slipped beyond the horizon, shooting a brilliant orange blaze across the snow covered land. Above them the sky glowed like fire and, in what seemed to be a mere instant, a frigid cold embraced them. Stomping numb feet, she faced him with what little grit was left to her. His silver eyes dared her to complain.

"And let cold air in every time we come out to get more? Crawl out of a warm bed to fetch it? Inside it will begin to thaw, be easier to burn. Let's just get it done and it will be done."

Though her hands and feet felt like stubs, and her nose and cheeks were so numb she couldn't feel them, she stubbornly dropped to her knees and backed into the tunnel to do his bidding. He was a lot worse off than she, and still he remained like an pillar of stone. Did he never quit?

"Damn him," she muttered when he shoved the first bundle of limbs through the opening. "Damn, damn, damn him. And while I'm at it, damn you too, Stephan." She had never been angrier at him for leaving her than at this miserable moment.

Wiggling into the dugout dragging her awkward armload, she concentrated on her hatred of the man who had gotten her into this fix. It wasn't Stephan's fault, it was those damned savage Indians. With the help of that one out there, she'd live, if only to prove a strength no one thought she possessed, including herself.

By the time they had all the wood transferred, she was barely able to drag herself back to the entrance one last time. There was still that damned rat to deal with. Poking her head out into the darkness, she saw he was busy cleaning the ugly little critter, and to her surprise, realized she was hungry enough to eat it.

"Don't you need me to help you do that?" Be darned if she'd quit till he did.

"No, go in and build up the fire and put on a pot of water. I can handle this."

"Because it's smaller than a rabbit?" she

ventured.

"Any man can clean his own game."

If she hadn't been so exhausted, she'd have hit him with something. "So why did you...?" Even that didn't seem profitable, and she sighed and backed away. No sense in getting into that. Obviously he was having a fine time testing her, and she was too tired to play the game any longer.

While she put a pot of half-melted snow onto the briskly burning fire, she mimicked him. "Any man can clean his own game. Well, any woman can do some things herself, too." She wished she could think what they were, but in this situation, nothing came to her. Not out here in this godforsaken place.

When he scrambled in with the chunks of pink meat, the pot of water was boiling and she sat with her bare feet propped near the fire. She'd fed some of the wet wood into the hot fire made by the last of the buffalo chips and they sizzled noisily.

He dropped each piece of meat into the pot, washed his hands in some melted snow and removed his wet moccasins. To her surprise, he peeled out of the wet leggings as well. His long, muscular legs glowed in the dancing firelight. Though she tried to avert her gaze, her wandering eyes admired the supple limbs. He wore only a breech cloth, and the curve of his tight loins disappeared into umber shadows between his thighs. Blood poured from the wound above the garment. He'd opened it back up.

Raising onto her knees to inspect his back, she said, "Sit down, let me take care of that. Doesn't it hurt?"

He lowered himself to the blanket spread beside the fire, the expression on his face answering her question. It did hurt, but he'd kept going because he had no choice. She saw that and cupped a hand across his forehead.

"You're burning up. Lie down."

"It is fine. Do not fuss."

"I'll fuss if I want to. Lie down. It won't do for you to bleed to death, now will it?"

Casting a dark glower in her direction, he lay so that she could inspect the exit wound from which the blood came. She found remnants of her drawers, dipped the scrap into a pot of water, and cleaned his flesh.

"You've torn it open, but I think it'll be all right, if you'll just rest and let it heal." Fetching his parfleche she made another poultice and packed it over the wound.

He refused to make a sound, though she knew it must hurt.

When she had finished, he turned over, propped his head in one hand, and stared into the fire.

While the musk-rat boiled, she spread his wet britches to dry, then joined him, stretching her legs out to toast her toes. In the confines of the small room, she was extremely conscious of the attraction she felt for this savage. It left her limp and expectant, dismayed at her own weakness. Beneath the men's clothes she wore, her nipples tingled. If he were to touch her there, the ache would explode into a passion such as she'd never known. That secret knowledge settled down in her belly where another more urgent ache spread its claw-like fingers. She had never wanted a man in such a way, imagined his sensuous lips closing over her breasts. His tongue, warm and wet, tracing languid patterns across the right nipple, then the left, leaving a trail of sweet moisture that would lead finally to her very core. Then he would take her like the savage he was, with a great howling. And she would join him in like manner.

Stephan would never know her passions. Served him right.

Ashamed and embarrassed, she licked her lips

and remained silent. With the fantasy fresh in her mind she dare not look at him for fear he would read her mind. Wet wood crackled and hissed in the heat of the flames, and occasionally a sweet scent of its burning wafted through the room.

Suppose they died tomorrow. Then what would anything else matter? She wished he would take her in his arms, like he had the night she'd almost frozen.

Studying his profile in the firelight, she knew he wouldn't, and felt very sad.

Forcing her mind from the flight of romantic fancy, she murmured, "I'd kill for a bath."

"There is always the spring."

She shot him a withering glance. "No, thank you. I said I'd kill, not die."

He grunted, nodded, waited. Finally announced, "We will leave tomorrow."

The expected declaration brought fear to her heart, and she jerked around to stare at him. "Are you sure? I think you should rest another day. Let that heal."

"No time. We go in the morning. I am fine. Another storm could come at any time."

"What if we get lost, can't find our way?"

"We cannot stay here. We will have no more wood to burn, and if another blizzard hits we will sit here and die. It's better if we make a try for the fort. We are not that far away. We'll eat, sleep, and at first light bundle up and go."

"I thought you said the white men were killing all of...of...your people?" She couldn't bear the thought that he might walk into that fort only to die.

"They will let me come in, especially if I bring you unharmed. I will be another prisoner along with those who lived through the massacre."

"But you can't. I mean, I won't let you do that. You have to be free, you said so yourself. You have to go home."

His eyes held surprise when tears trickled down her cheeks.

"A'den, do not cry. It is not for you that I go back to the fort. It is for them, my people. I will help them escape and this time we will get away or all of us will die. I cannot leave them there. I must help them. You...well, you are just an added burden for me. So it is foolish for you to cry. I do this, not for you but for myself."

He turned from her, anger darkening his features.

Wiping the hot tears from her cheeks, she stared into the fire for a long time. The smell of the cooking meat permeated the close air around them and her mouth watered unexpectedly. It would appear she might be able to eat this rat after all.

Oddly, his words did not offend her, but she was curious. "And back there, when you risked your life to save mine. What was that? Why didn't you leave me out there to freeze? You came after me and so I'm still your burden. Because of you. I think you're lying to me. I think like all men, you cannot face the truth that a woman might mean something to you. Even Stephan was much the same way. Coming west meant more to him than our love did. I saw that, though I wouldn't admit it. I wanted so much to marry and have my own home. I won't make that mistake again."

With one trembling hand, she reached out, touched his arm. The muscles jerked beneath her fingers, but still he wouldn't take any notice of her existence. Earlier, something had happened between them, but he was deliberately putting it aside. She knew she should do the same, yet couldn't forget how he'd curled his body around hers to keep her warm, to save her life when he thought she was dying. And how safe she had felt when he held her in such a way.

If they made it back to the fort she would never see him again. She would go back to St. Louis and he would race toward his own destiny. And since he insisted on throwing in with the Cheyenne, that destiny could be nothing but dark and foreboding.

Angrily, she brushed a lock of hair from her face and stared at him, trying to force him to look at her. Shoulders hunched against the force of her words, he kept his back turned. She could not fathom what he might be thinking.

"Perhaps your wish to marry this Stephan and have a home meant more to you than his love."

The truth of the words tore at her reserve and she began to cry.

He paid no attention.

"Stone Heart?" she whispered, rubbed his arm again.

He stiffened, refused to answer.

"I know you care for me. You saved my life."

"It was nothing."

"It was everything. We'll never see each other again."

"No, we will not."

"Then...I wonder if...I mean, since we will soon part forever, could you hold me...love me...just a little?"

No reply, no movement.

She sucked in a deep breath.

"Don't," he said like a rifle shot.

"Why?"

"Do you have no pride that you would beg me?"

"Pride? You talk of pride? If I had any pride I wouldn't be out here. I would never have been so desperate as to follow Stephan around.

"A'den." His voice almost too soft to hear. "You tell me you are not a white man's whore. Would you become mine? I cannot be your husband, or give you

93

children."

"No, but you can teach me to love."

He took a deep breath, pulled her down beside him. "You know how to love, A'den. What you do not know is your value."

Lying so close to him, the very essence of his being washing over her like a soft caress, made her dizzy. "Then you don't want me?"

One hand spread through her hair, grasped the back of her head. "Oh, yes, I want you. I want the touch of you, I want to kiss you and have you kiss me. But this will not happen. It cannot. And it has nothing to do with how I feel about you."

Anger sparked in his eyes, but he gathered her into his arms and held her close. She felt a bereavement so harsh she could hardly contain it, but she knew there was nothing either of them could do.

A while later they ate the hot meat with their fingers. He divided the broth and they drank every drop. Not once while she chewed and swallowed did she think of that furry and disgusting little animal he'd killed. Could it be she would get used to living like this? God, she hoped not.

Stone Heart was up and down all night, keeping the wood stacked high on the hot fire so it could dry before burning. They would use it all and leave at dawn. He held out little hope for their safe arrival at Ft. Robinson, but at least they had a better chance than if they remained here with no food or fuel. If they made it, the trip would take two or three days, but only if the weather remained clear and nothing unexpected happened.

Most of the long, dark night he watched her sleep. More than once, when his hopes grew dim, he considered leaving her here and sending someone back for her, but then when he studied her face, so innocent in sleep, he knew he could not do such a thing. For if he did she would not live to be rescued. Once he tucked her hair off her face, made sure the buffalo coat covered her. Lingered to caress her soft cheek with the tips of his fingers. Perhaps he should have made love to her when she asked. For if they were both to die, it would be a good thing, a right thing. Though the passion raged within him like a caged beast, he couldn't bring himself to release it. She had placed her trust in him, and he would save her if he could, from both death in the wilderness and her misplaced desire. For surely she would regret allowing such a thing, once it was done. She called him a savage, and that is what he was.

He had killed white men in battle, yet he could not betray this white woman. She was so strong and bright and good-hearted, he wondered how a man such as the one she described could abandon her to such a terrible fate. He must have known what was in store for her out here on the frontier.

If things had been different, if he himself had chosen to remain white, he might consider taking her for his own. But the way things were, that wasn't possible. Never would be. He must turn from all things white, especially the heritage of his hated father whose cruel pursuit of the Cheyenne and Lakota was legendary. And all the time Custer committed his acts of murder, he continued to take to his tent the beautiful copper-skinned women of his enemy, siring children who would grow up hating him.

Stone Heart must have been the first, for Custer had been but a young man when he arrived in camp and wooed the lovely White Robe, daughter of Dull Knife's younger sister. Planted the seed that would produce Stone Heart, his first, but not last, child of the Cheyenne. How honored she must have felt, being singled out by the handsome, yellow-haired white boy. Lying in his arms on the river bank she could not have guessed that one day her lover would become the slayer of her people.

In the eyes of the Dull Knife band of Cheyenne, Custer was their relative because he had fathered children with their women. How could this white soldier, their kin, then turn on them with such ferocity? This they would never understand. Some continued to protect him with their silence until his death at Greasy Grass, what the white man called Little Big Horn.

Stone Heart yearned to dance on his father's grave, wished he had been at the battle and watched him die. Further, wished the death had been at his own hand. Now he could do nothing but try to save what remained of his people. Once he delivered this woman safely to Ft. Robinson, he would forever on be Cheyenne, until the grass grew no more, until the rivers ceased to flow, and the sun fell from the sky. He could sense the end coming for his people, and thus would he do penance for the deeds of Long Hair.

But first, there was this woman who lay beside him in sleep. He gently traced the curve of her determined chin, along the line of her jaw, brushed her full lips with the tip of his thumb. Drawing her in his mind so as never to forget her.

When he shook her awake, Aiden rose without a word and joined him in preparing the packs they would carry. She didn't want to leave the safe little haven, but knew she had no choice. He was adamant, and if she tarried he would go without her. The light had gone out of his eyes, and she sensed there would be no more kindnesses. He had become the terrifying Cheyenne warrior she had discovered in the dugout what seemed like a lifetime ago.

Once again fear filled her heart and her soul ached over the loss of something she'd never truly had.

Chapter Seven

Josiah awoke to wind rattling the makeshift shelter he'd built for himself up a ways from Hat Creek. His traps had been empty, owing to the soldiers chasing those blamed wild Cheyenne over half this countryside and scaring off the game. To get away from them he'd cut back cross country. It was cold enough to freeze the tail off a buffalo, and every time it warmed up a bit here'd come the snow. He'd never seen such a winter in ten years of trapping this country. The brutal cold cut to the bone, despite layers of clothing and fur wraps so thick around his feet he could hardly keep 'em under him.

Snugged beneath the buffalo robes he took stock of his surroundings. The lowering gloom of winter's dawn froze every breath into crystals in his chin whiskers. The snow had stopped, at least for now, but the wind continued to howl and rearrange what had fallen during the night.

This time any other year his pack animal would've been loaded down with pelts. Instead he'd trapped very little, and two days ago had been forced to shoot one of the horses. The other, barely on four feet and staked out back, was starved and half-froze. Probably couldn't go another mile. He'd have to remedy that situation and soon. Couldn't let the poor beast suffer.

What with the snow and cold it looked like he himself might not make it through this time. With a strange calm, he faced the imminence of his own death, discussed it aloud.

"Well, shoot, Josiah, you've had a good run. Trapping's 'bout petered out, nohow."

Who could ask for more out of life? Twenty years in the wilderness doing what a man was put on this earth to do. After all, he was nearing thirty-five. "Better'n being 'et by a bear like the most of us is."

Finally he sighed, ventured from beneath the pile of furs, and took up his Henry repeater. No sense letting that poor old horse suffer any longer. Should have put him away last night, but just didn't have the grit. Old Peg had been with him a lot of years, done her share and then some. How would he explain it to her?

Angrily, he fingered away a single tear, pulled on fur mittens and stepped from the shelter to greet another day in hell. Those who thought hell would be hot hadn't spent a winter in Ne-brasky. Stomping his fur-bound feet, he moved around back to where he'd tied poor old Peg.

Head hanging low, ears flattened against her head, she wobbled on weak legs. Didn't even bother to look at him with expectation of grain like she usually did.

"Aw, dang it, Peg," he muttered and rubbed a hand down along her neck. "I'm sorry as all get out, honey. It's time you rested."

Chocolate brown eyes rolled in his direction, but she didn't raise her head. Cupping one fur-covered hand over her nose, he bent his forehead to hers in farewell.

"I'm gonna miss you, old girl. Reckon I'll be along soon. Hell, may join you before this day is out."

He stepped back, slipped one hand free of its mitten, placed the barrel of the rifle behind her ear, squeezed his eyes tight, and pulled off one shot.

With a short chuffing sound, she crumpled. The sharp boom cracked apart the cold air. Without looking at the female he'd spent the last seven years with, Josiah cursed and shook the Henry at the gunmetal sky.

"Have ye took enough from me yet? Or is there more?" A bitter laugh echoed in the unearthly stillness. "Better not be, cause I ain't got much more to give ye but this tough old hide. Reckon you'll be seein' it soon enough."

Back in the shelter, he made a pack of what he could carry: frozen chunks of the elk he'd brought down a couple days ago, plus a bundle of jerky, hardtack, tattered blankets, the hide from the elk plus some other furs he carried for warmth, a leather water pouch, and his parfleche that contained cartridges, a striking stone, pencil and paper, a sliver of lye soap and his razor and strop. If he made it till spring, he'd surely take a fit to scrape his face.

Fitting the coonskin hat snugly over his head and ears, he shouldered the heavy pack, picked up the rifle, and moved out into the clearing. The rising sun stirred a brutal north wind laced with tiny pellets of ice, and he faced into it, staring in the direction of the Red Cloud Agency. Imagined a summer's day when he could easily walk it and be there for supper. Tried to remember how sunshine felt on his face. None of it made him the least bit warmer.

In weather like this his danged feet would likely freeze plumb off before he got to the agency, maybe his hands too. Could be he might talk some trapper friend into putting a bullet in his brain like he'd done for old Peg. Or better yet, maybe he'd just lay down on the trail a'fore that could happen and go to sleep. They said it was a peaceful death, curling up in a snow bank.

Oh, well. Time to get moving.

Sparing a last glance toward the shelter and the dark mound of Peg's still form, he headed out, carrying on a running conversation with himself now that he no longer had the mare to talk to.

****

They never truly got started on the long walk to Fort Robinson before Stone Heart realized he was going to have to teach A'den how to walk or she'd never make it. She minced along beside him like she wore a tight corset and a pair of those dreadful high-heeled shoes, the ones she'd had on when he met her.

Impatiently, he hooked her around the waist with one arm, lifted her out of the snow.

Kicking and flailing, she shouted at him. "Hey, let go." She pried at his arm, to no avail.

He shook her like a sack of feed. "Relax, stop fighting."

"I will if you'll put me down. You scared me. What're you doing?"

"Trying to stop you from wearing yourself out." He set her down. "You need to loosen up. Stop prissing along like something is about to break. I know it's hard to get along where the drifts are so deep. Take long, easy strides and stand straight. Stop leaning forward and wiggling your...uh, waving your arms about. I will clear the way for you, if you will stay behind me."

She swung and glared up at him, spoke through clenched teeth. "Well, you're the Indian, not me. Nobody ever told me I'd have to learn to walk in snow up to my...my..." Narrowing her eyes, she finished with a whispered, "ass."

He pretended not to hear, figured she was trying to annoy him, get back at him for pushing her around. She had a mouth on her and then some, but maybe he deserved it.

Still, he couldn't stop a sharp retort. "And that same nobody forgot to let me know I'd be dragging some wailing white city woman through Nebraska in the middle of the winter."

Hands on her hips, eyes shooting fire, she struggled but failed to get her mouth around a reply before he lit into her again.

"I should have left you behind and double-timed it to the fort. I could have sent somebody for you quicker than dragging you along." He met her stunned gaze with a harsh one of his own. "And I still might do it if we can find a suitable shelter for you. We don't have time to waste on you back-talking me."

She swung her arm in a wide arc. "Well, then, just go on. I'm a woman grown, and if I have an opinion I guess I can state it. You...you arrogant son of a—"

He wagged a finger under her nose. "That fire will get you in trouble. Now cool down and listen to me. Out here I know more than you, and it's time you admitted it. You either keep up or I leave you. And you are not keeping up."

Her chin began to quiver and the challenge went out of her eyes to be replaced by a wild terror. Her voice dropped so low he could scarcely hear her over the wind.

"Don't you dare leave me out here. I'll keep up. Just march on, and see if I don't."

A gust of wind whipped around and caught her hair. Her nose was red and tears she refused to shed stood in her green eyes.

Such a stubborn woman, and that only made her all the more attractive. He wanted to take her in his arms, break through that tough shell and explore her inner spirit. The urge ate at him and he fought it. Every time he rebuilt his own defenses, something like this would happen. He settled for reaching down and turning the thick collar of her coat up around her ears and adjusting the small blanket draped over her head. "Wish I'd had a hat for you."

She sniffed and nodded. "You won't leave me. I'd die, and then where would you be?"

"No, I won't let you die." A dire warning rose in his chest like the fluttering of buzzards' wings. Suppose he couldn't prevent it? They could both very well die out here, and him with nothing to say about it.

Snugging deeper into his own coat, he turned his back to her and the brutal wind. That kind of thinking had no place here if they were to make it.

It was better to put a growl in his voice and not be too gentle. Keep her riled and fighting back. "Don't fall behind. If we walk fast we will stay warm. The sun will not shine today."

Earlier he'd eyed the roiling clouds far off to the west and feared they would bring snow from the mountains before nightfall. If that happened, they had little chance of making it to Fort Robinson alive.

He could hear her moving along behind him, and the irate words she threw at his back. "I couldn't move fast enough to ever be warm again."

Keeping her angry could be the only thing that would save her life. He'd seen right quick that she hated being bested by a man. Had something to prove, he guessed, considering the actions of the last man in her life.

They trudged south across the flat lands, keeping to the windswept patches, leaving the Black Hills behind. Far ahead lay the high bluffs that looked down on the White River Valley and Fort Robinson. A day's walk on a sunny, clear day. That was not to be their fortune.

Dark clouds had cut their trail even as they got away from the soddie that morning, snuffing out the weak sunlight before it reached its apex. In the blustery wind, bits of sleet sniped at his skin. Filled the cold air with the taste and smell of the coming storm. He would have to find shelter and soon. They would not go much farther on this day. It was rougher going now that they'd left the flat lands. Downed wood littered the sloping ground and scraggly pines swayed against the gloomy sky. In the shadows under a stand of willow trees a slight movement caught his attention. A few antelope, trapped by winter's ferocity, milled about, peeling bark from the pale trunks.

Cautiously, he stopped in the lee of a huge drift and loaded the trade musket, tamping the powder down with a silent prayer that it had not gathered too much moisture to fire. Adding a patch and ball he prepared the rifle and signaled A'den to duck down out of the wind. She appeared only too glad to obey, disappeared into the oversized coat until he could see nothing of her but the red blanket above a drift.

Favoring a stitch in his wounded side, he tried to forget how their survival depended solely on him, crept downwind of the small herd. If he could get in a good shot and hit one of the delicate animals, they would have food to last them to the fort. If not, his failure could well mean her death as well as his own.

Raised in his mother's village until he reached puberty, he'd learned to hunt with bow and arrow long before he ever fired the white man's rifle. He considered himself only a fair shot with the black powder weapon, and the cheaply made trade musket would not be precise. He'd not fired it to know how it sighted in.

The area where the herd fed was free of drifts, and several dead trees lay around its perimeter, giving him the opportunity for some cover downwind of the game. The animals had nearly stripped the willows clean of bark and would soon move on. Unusual for them to be so far north this time of year. When he drew within range, he sank to one knee behind a fallen pine that had lodged at an angle among other debris. Only one of the animals showed a good target, and he steadied the long barrel against the rough bark to sight-in on its shoulder. Finger squeezing slowly, he held the heavy rifle steady, heard the hollow thunk of hammer hitting home and waited for the explosion of the powder that would send the lead ball on its way. Nothing happened. His heart sank. Dare he try again and have the damn thing blow up in his hands? Quickly, he thumbed back the hammer and fitted another percussion cap over the nipple.

The nearest antelope flicked its tail and turned to look toward him. He froze, held his breath and waited. Either they'd bolt or go back to eating. Now they all faced him, ears pricked, presenting no decent target. Gently, he let out his breath and waited some more. It paid to be patient.

Hunger must have overpowered their fear and curiosity, for one by one, they went back to peeling bark from the trees.

Slowly, carefully, he settled the stock against his shoulder, laid his cheek against it and aimed once more. On the verge of firing, his finger tightened over the trigger as a man staggered into the clearing, sending the small herd leaping into confused flight.

His first inclination was to shoot the fool. But much as he hated white men, he hadn't yet eaten one, didn't care that much for killing. Not like this. Damn rifle probably wouldn't fire anyway. Still, in this kind of weather, it was better not to leave it loaded. Shaking with rage, he aimed above the man's head and fired. An enormous boom shook the ground and knocked snow from the high pine branches.

The man shouted, sprawled to his belly, hands locked over his head.

Stone Heart trotted into the clearing under the pines, stared down at the man nearly covered in clumps of fallen snow. "I ought to've shot your blamed fool head off, scaring my game like that. What kind of man goes blundering around without paying attention to where he's at?"

The man slowly raised his head and peered from eyes dark as sloe berries. Ice and snow clung to his thick beard and fur cap. "What are ye?"

Clearly this man presented no threat. "Who I am is Stone Heart, of the Cheyenne. What I am is none of your business. What are you doing out here running off my supper?"

The man gathered himself to his feet, staggering under a huge pack. Peered at Stone Heart. "Ye don't look like no Cheyenne to me."

Impatient rage must have shown on his face, for the man backed off a few steps and held up a mittened hand. "Sorry, it ain't like me to be so careless, but I've been fighting this here weather and it's addled me some. Lost my animals and was hoping to make it to the agency." He arced a glance into the gloomy sky. "Don't look like I will."

He shifted his pack, stomped his feet and peered up into Stone Heart's face. "Maybe I can make up for you losing your supper by offering you a share of mine. Got plenty of elk meat. In this here pack. What say we throw us up a shelter, gather some wood and settle in until this storm clears?"

A spit of icy pellets blasted Stone Heart's cheeks, and he nervously eyed the threatening clouds. He didn't want to share a shelter with this fool of a white man, but it looked as if there was little choice. Besides, he hadn't tasted the sweet meat of elk in a long time.

"Hope you know more about building a lean-to than you do about getting along in the wilderness. I've got someone with me. I'll fetch her while you find us a likely spot out of the wind."

"A woman? You got a danged woman out here in this? What is she, a squaw?"

An inordinate rage roared through Stone Heart. He fisted the man's coat under his chin, lifted him so his feet swung off the ground. "Talk like that'll see you laying out here in the cold buck naked, mister. I could use those clothes you're wearing and what's in that pack as well, elk meat and all. Maybe I'll scalp you and take that fine fur hat and those mittens, seeing you won't need them anymore."

The trapper trembled and nearly fell when Stone Heart set him back on the ground. "I didn't mean nothing by it. You said you was Cheyenne. And I've always called Cheyenne women squaws. Meant no harm." Before Stone Heart could take further offense, he held up a hand. "You go get your woman, and I'll start cutting us some branches from these here pine trees for a shelter. I'll even gather up some wood and start us a fire. How'll that be? I apologize if I said anything wrong. I figure what we both want is to live through this. I'll be glad to fight you another day. When it ain't so blamed cold. How do you feel about that?"

Stone Heart actually felt sorry for the man, who was probably having as tough a time out here as he and A'den. Besides it was time to stop arguing and get under cover from the storm. Icy pellets thickened the air until it was hard to see. So he nodded curtly, and trotted off to fetch A'den.

His hand shook her from the burrow in which she daydreamed of another place far from there. Hunkered down under the blanket and buffalo coat her mind had been anywhere but in this remote and frigid land. She moved gracefully across a brightly lit dance floor, satin skirts billowing about her ankles as she waltzed in the arms of a handsome gentleman. Though her feet throbbed and shivers wracked her body, she imagined the heat from a mammoth fireplace, gazed with awe upon the glitter of candles in crystal chandeliers. Perhaps this hand touching her was only another partner begging for a dance.

The hand shook her again, and she moaned, returned to the wilderness from which there appeared to be no escape. If only he'd left her here a little longer she could have frozen to death and there'd be no more hunger and weariness to contend with.

"A'den, let's go. We have to den up for the night. A storm's brewing."

She tried very hard to move, but had no strength left.

"I know you're not dead," he said and gathered her into his arms.

Sighing, she snuggled close against his chest, rested her head in the hollow of his shoulder. Perhaps this too was a dream. Maybe she had frozen to death and this was heaven. But with the painful throbbing in her feet and the hole in her stomach where food belonged, she very much doubted it.

Even after he set her down, she clung to him so that he had to pry her fingers loose. There was little left of her reserves and she feared even that was quickly fading. If he turned her loose this one last time, she might give up. She did so want to sleep. But suppose she did and when she awoke he was gone? He'd threatened as much earlier.

He shook her a couple of times, repeated her name. "Don't go to sleep. You're too cold. We have to build a shelter and a fire. This man has food. We're going to make it. Don't go to sleep."

To reinforce the order, he pulled her to her feet. "Help me gather some branches so we can get a shelter built. The storm's moving in fast."

Though she groaned and pulled against him, he

wouldn't let her be. Finally she followed him into a thicket where he got busy cutting pine boughs which she gathered and dragged back to where the other man wove a sloped roof between two large pines.

By the time they had the shelter roofed and sided she could no longer feel her feet or hands. The storm had set in with a ferocity that stung the skin of her face and froze the blanket to her head. In the back of the shelter out of the wind and lashing sleet, the stranger built a fire and she hovered over it, hands held out to the warmth. If she ever got out of this place she was never, never coming back. Who could possibly live this way? Who could even think of it?

The two men continued to work gathering firewood, and when they had piled up a huge stack of limbs and branches, went to work lashing together the final wall of the shelter that would enclose them completely. She could no longer do anything but hug the fire, and neither of them paid her any mind.

Dropping to her knees she begged the Blessed Mother for a merciful death that would release her from this torture. A delicious, almost forgotten aroma tickled her nostrils. Her stomach rolled, her mouth watered and she opened her eyes to search for the source of this smell. It surely must be her imagination.

Stone Heart and the stranger sat cross legged before the fire, each roasting chunks of meat over the flames. Outside the wind howled, and while it wasn't exactly warm in the shelter, it was dry.

"Take off your moccasins and put your feet to the fire," Stone Heart said without even looking at her. "This is Josiah Meeker, trapper and fool, but we'll welcome him because he brings elk to the table."

He sounded almost human, his light manner

that of a nearly civilized man.

"It smells so good. I thought I'd died and gone to heaven."

The stranger laughed. "That well may be our fate before this night is out. Listen to that wind. Good thing we're in the shelter of these pines. And what might your name be, missus?"

"I'm Aiden Conner. Not missus, however." Unwrapping her feet, she removed the soaked moccasins and stuck her toes close to the flames. Soon the initial pain was replaced by a soothing warmth and she wiggled them.

Josiah stared at the pale feet. "Hell, she ain't no squaw. She's a white woman."

Stone Heart glared at the man, and Aiden glanced quickly from one to the other. Both were ready to do battle. If they fought in this tiny place it would be bad, but that's precisely what they appeared to be about to do.

"I wish I was," she said quickly. "Then at least I'd have me a tipi and a bed mate."

Josiah crowed and Stone Heart shot them each a dark look, but he didn't say anything. Maybe the battle had been forestalled, at least for the moment. Trapping this savage with two white people might be more than he could take. He could explode at any moment, skewer them with his knife, and take their scalps. The first chance she got she would warn Josiah not to bait Stone Heart. It wasn't the wisest thing anyone could do. Whoever this man was, she for one was glad he had come along. The meat smelled wonderful, and though she had never eaten elk it couldn't taste any worse than that ugly rat or that poor sweet little bunny. And besides, this meat came killed, skinned, gutted, and ready to cook.

She mimicked the two men, crossing her legs and sitting before the fire to enjoy the rich odor of cooking meat and soak up the heat.

Stone Heart threw her a scowling glare that she didn't quite understand, under the circumstances. Things looked a lot better than they had twenty-four hours ago, even with the storm raging outside. He was probably just mad at something this man had done or said. Or perhaps angry because he was there at all. It might have wounded his pride to accept help from the bearded trapper.

He said little while they ate, ripping a chunk of meat off his stick and handing it to her each time she finished off one. By the time they'd eaten their fill, her mouth burned from stuffing it full of steaming elk straight from the fire. Stomachs gorged on the sweet, juicy meat, Stone Heart attempted to settle the sleeping arrangements. She would lie nearest the fire with him next to her and the trapper next to him. Of necessity they would have to huddle together to share body warmth.

"Won't work too good," Josiah grumbled.

"Has to." Stone Heart frowned and began to lay out furs, as if his word was final.

"Then she can get up and put wood on the fire when it burns down, her being the nearest."

Drowsy and almost asleep, she listened to them argue one point after another. They could think what they wanted, she wasn't getting up once she fell asleep.

"I'll do that," Stone Heart. "And you as well."

"Then, put her in the middle."

The two men were quiet for a while, then Stone Heart shook her.

"What? Leave me be."

"Don't complain, just wrap up in this blanket." He proceeded to help her until he had her well bundled.

"What in thunder you doing that for?" Josiah asked.

"So you can't put your dirty hands on her."

"I'm damned," Josiah said, shaking his head. "I'm be-damned."

She peered at Stone Heart, who stood over her, arms crossed over his chest. He acted as if he was protecting her from this man. Sleepily, she wondered who would protect her from him, but fell asleep before she could come up with an answer.

Far into the night, Stone Heart rose, crawled out to gather an armload of wood, but decided to take a quick call of nature before doing so.

His moccasins creaked across the frozen land. There was no wind and it had stopped snowing. Stars lit the midnight sky. The air was so cold it burned his lungs with each breath. Turning his back to the shelter, he thought he heard something off in the distance. A cough, a laugh, a human or animal? He didn't know. Someone or something was nearby. He darted behind a thick pine and scanned the area closely. No one would be out on a night like this, surely. There it was again! It sounded like a horse...or more than one.

Hunched over, he crept toward the noise. Stepped deeper into the pines and spotted the dim flicker of a fire. Holding his breath, fearful his hammering heart would alert the camp, he slipped into a stand of willows.

From there he could see the hulking shadow of several tents like the Army used. What were soldiers doing out here?

Then it dawned on him precisely what they were there for. They were still hunting the Cheyenne that had broke out of Fort Robinson. And their orders could well be to shoot on sight rather than bring back the rebellious savages.

Slipping away, careful not to step on anything that might alert anyone, for surely they'd posted a guard, he hurried back to the shelter. There he put a quick pack together, making as little noise as possible. It was him they would kill, not these two asleep by the fire. Ride him down and butcher him in the snow so that his blood would flow with that of all the helpless women and children killed in the frantic breakout. And what of Dull Knife? He did not know if he lived or had been killed. And the others? Many lay strewn over the land, from the bluffs to the bridge at the White River and beyond to the fort. If he was to live to set those who had survived free he had to go, and quickly.

Quietly he fed the fire so it wouldn't go out. When the soldiers came A'den would be safe and so would the trapper. He had done all he could for her, and must now think of his people. He had to leave before the white men awoke and discovered the shelter.

For a moment he stood over her, curled in the nest of furs and blankets, locks of tangled red hair spread about. She dreamed of home, a look of serenity on her finely drawn features. This he knew, for he understood such a burning desire.

He would never see her again, but knew that he would not forget the touch of her hands, the gentleness of her lyrical voice, the way her eyes sparked defiantly.

"Farewell," he whispered, and could say no more.

His going made no sound nor shadow in the silent night. Behind him he imagined he heard her singing softly in a farewell of her own.

Chapter Eight

Horrific shouts ruptured the still winter's dawn, jerking Aiden awake. A uniformed soldier ripped away the side of the shelter and she screamed. Josiah Meeker vaulted upright, temporarily tangled in furs and blankets. While he struggled, his shouts muffled, he soldier prodded Aiden in the belly with the barrel of his rifle. Fear struck her mute and she could only bite her tongue, close her eyes, and wait to die, furs and blankets hugged around her.

Not so the trapper Meeker, who scrabbled about like a frantic trapped animal, shouting over and over, "Holy hell, holy hell."

From outside came a terse order. "Bring 'em out here."

The soldier grabbed her by one leg and dragged her from the shelter like a bundle of goods. Frozen in a grip of fear, she could only await her fate while her heart slammed against her chest. Behind her, the thunk of a solid blow cut off the trapper's cursing.

Fury released her from the frozen grip of fear and she kicked and struggled against the iron-hard grip. "Turn me loose, you demon from hell."

Dragging her a few more feet, he flung her into a snow bank where she landed face down. Finally able to dig her way free, she clawed snow from her mouth and eyes. Several soldiers circled around, their combined voices a rumble of indistinct threats. Other men poked about in the surrounding underbrush, obviously searching for someone or something. Stone Heart, no doubt, since he was nowhere to be seen.

She had no idea what had happened to him, but prayed he was long gone from this place. The way these men acted, they were ready to kill someone, anyone, and she feared it might very well be her. They might have already killed the trapper, for she saw no sign of him either.

Lying in the snow, surrounded by the excited young soldiers, fear filled her mouth like acrid sulphur water.

A couple of them dragged a limp Josiah Meeker from the shelter and tossed him down beside her. He appeared unconscious, but thank God, he was breathing. She had no desire to be left alone with these marauding soldiers.

"What do you want?" she managed to croak, throat dry as trail dust.

A young officer stepped into the ring, signaled the others to lower their weapons and addressed her. "Lieutenant Woods, ma'am. You this man's woman?" Face a snarl of disgust, he prodded Meeker with the toe of one boot.

"His...I don't..." Frantic terror crawled through her thoughts, still tangled in sleep. For a moment she couldn't clear them. All she knew was an unattached woman in these circumstances would be treated with less respect than a married one.

"He...we're together, yes."

"Ma'am. Begging your pardon, but we can see you're together. Is this man your husband?"

Shoving herself to a sitting position, she raked hair from her face and fixed the young Lieutenant with a contemptuous glare. "Do you think a woman like me would be with a man who was not her husband?"

He shrugged, grinned. "I have no idea what kind of woman you are, if you'll excuse my bluntness. Who might you be?"

She lifted her shoulders. "May I get up off the

ground? It's cold."

He nodded crisply, and the one who'd stuck the rifle into her belly helped her to her feet where she stood hugging herself and shivering, bare toes curled.

"May I have my coat and shoes?"

The lieutenant nodded again and one of the other men rummaged around in the shelter until he came up with the disreputable buffalo coat and the moccasins Stone Heart had given her.

"Looks too big for her, sir," he said, holding out the coat and glancing at the dazed trapper. "Him too, for that matter."

"Anybody with you? You seen anyone along the trail?"

"It's mine, I mean, a man gave it to me over in Benson. I didn't have one."

"Girl as pretty as you, looks like you could do better than this." Woods jostled Meeker again with his boot toe.

She grabbed the moccasins, slipped them on and huddled inside the coat without replying.

"Well?" he finally said sharply.

"What?"

"I asked for your names and if you'd seen anybody."

"No, no one."

An eyebrow arched toward the trapper. "And you'd be?"

The snappy question made her jump. Meeker was definitely in no shape to answer questions, and she didn't want him to have the chance.

"He's Josiah Meeker and I'm...I'm Mrs. Meeker."

The lieutenant sighed with exasperation. "And you're sure you've seen no one. Perhaps some renegade Indians. Cheyenne? We had a breakout down to the fort a few days ago and we've been following blood trails and rounding up savages ever since. Some are dangerous. You and your man ought not to be out here."

She glanced down at the bearded trapper.

"Mind if I ask why you are?"

The question pulled her attention away from her unconscious 'husband.'" "No, I don't mind."

After a long wait for her to go on, the lieutenant obviously lost patience with her. "I'm going to send the two of you on back to Fort Robinson. Private Cable here will escort you. Where are your animals?"

"We have none."

"You're out here afoot?" Renewed suspicion glittered in his brown eyes. "Sergeant, take a look around. Make sure this lady is telling us the truth."

Fearful they'd find Stone Heart hiding somewhere, she babbled, "We got caught up in the storm. Our horses died. We were trying to get back to the fort when last night's storm hit and we had to wait it out here. We were going to walk in today."

He scrutinized her thoughtfully, then made up his mind. "Cable, put her on your mount with you, take Ritter's horse for our friend here, and return as quickly as you get them delivered. We'll continue searching the area till you get back. If you follow Hat Creek Road you should be able to return before nightfall."

Meeker turned over and groaned, began to wave his arms and shout nonsense.

The lieutenant's lip curled. He obviously had little patience with civilians. "Stand him on his feet. If he can't sit a saddle, toss him over it. Gather their packs and get them out of here. Daylight's burning. And waste no time getting back. They can explain their plight to Captain Wessells. It's not our problem. We were sent to hunt down Indians not take care of greenhorns who haven't got any better sense than to wander around Nebraska in the middle of winter."

Cable saluted, reined his horse toward Aiden, kicked his left boot clear of the stirrup, and reached down to help her on. She was not an experienced rider and mounted awkwardly, finally settling herself behind the saddle and clutching the young soldier around the waist. As she watched two men help Meeker aboard the second horse, and another throw up his pack, she prayed he wouldn't get talkative and reveal not only Stone Heart's earlier presence but her lie about them being man and wife. Hopefully, she would get a chance to warn him somehow before they arrived at the fort. He appeared too addled to do much more than hang on.

Though she searched the surrounding area as they rode away, the Cheyenne was nowhere to be seen. She experienced a brief moment of disappointment, for she would probably never see him again. Still, she prayed for his escape. He had saved her life, and he had done it in a way she would never forget. No man had ever kindled her desires like he had.

Despite all her concerns, her heart sang with relief and joy when they reached the well traveled road. Once at the fort, she would soon be on her way home to Saint Louis where she could forget all about her dreadful experiences out here. It would be a long time, though before she forgot the touch of the golden-haired warrior.

By the time they reached Fort Robinson, it had become very clear to Aiden that she had talked herself into a complicated situation. All she wanted was to board the first stage headed east, but how to explain that to soldiers who would be told she was married to the trapper Meeker?

The fort was large, with many wood-framed buildings scattered over a huge area. It looked more like a good-sized town. Soldiers on horses and afoot moved about, wagons came and went, noise from all manner of pursuits added to the clamor. Along the perimeter, a cluster of tipis housed Indian men, women, and children who watched their passage dispassionately. She did not know their tribal affiliations, but surmised they weren't Cheyenne, for they didn't appear to be prisoners. She couldn't help peering at the dark openings as they rode past rows of buildings. In which one were the Cheyenne people being held? Was Stone Heart watching or had he already managed to get to them?

Private Cable reined up in front of a slab-sided building that sported both a window and a door on the front. A sign read "Captain's Headquarters."

"If you'd take my hand, miss, I'll assist you."

She did, but still made a poor job of dismounting from behind him. After helping her down, Cable threw a leg over the saddle horn and gracefully slipped to the ground. Meeker, who had said nothing to her on the way in, dismounted and staggered. During the entire ride in he'd spent his time grumbling about the cold and being forced to leave most of his supplies at the shelter. She had to get him alone long enough to explain her little white lie, though she had decided to come clean about her true situation to the commanding officer at the fort. Leaving out Stone Heart's part in it, of course. What could they do now anyway?

Meeker stepped close beside her and took her arm. "Well, looks like we're safe at Fort Robinson. Reckon what happened to our friend?"

Her heart dropped into her belly like a stone in a clear pool.

"Please, don't mention him to these men."

His gleaming dark eyes regarded her for a long moment, then he tightened his lips and nodded. "Nothin' to me, I don't reckon

She breathed a sigh of relief. The man had not registered her claim that she was his wife, and it looked like he was going to keep his mouth shut about Stone Heart. Now if she could just make things clear to this Captain Wessells, she'd soon be on her way home.

Private Cable rapped on the door of the captain's quarters, then went in, holding it for the two of them to enter. They faced a small, fair man, clean-shaven and immaculate in a crisp blue uniform, his nape-length hair parted and combed slick behind his ears. A black cheroot between his fingers trickled a thin cloud of smoke that filled the small room with a sweet, cloying odor. The large desk was strewn with all manner of papers.

"Captain Wessells, sir," Cable said with a stiff salute.

"Yes, what is it? I'm busy." The man's eyes scarcely spared a glance for Aiden and Meeker.

"We found these two, sir, in a shelter above Hat Creek. Say they haven't seen any Cheyenne, sir, but Lieutenant Woods wanted them brought in."

Wessells waved a small, almost delicate hand. "Yes, yes. Where's Woods and his men?"

"Still out hunting Indians, sir," Cable snapped.

A glitter of enjoyment filled Wessells' pale eyes before they strayed toward Aiden. "What manner of garb are you wearing? Looks like Indian getup to me. You been living with the Indians? You look white. Were you a captive, ma'am?"

Aiden shook her head vigorously. "Oh, no, sir. I...I was lost and...this man," she gestured vaguely toward Meeker, "helped me out with some...with these things. I don't know where he got them, sir."

Meeker snorted, opened his mouth to speak.

Wessells held up a hand just as both Cable and Meeker appeared ready to say something.

"Lost?" the captain asked, an edge to his voice. "What were you doing out there in the first place?"

Aiden swallowed over a knot forming in her

throat and tried to explain. "I...my name is Aiden Conner, sir. I'm from Saint Louis. It's a long story, but I would appreciate it if you could allow me to board a stage headed east. I have no money, sir, nothing. All I want is to go home. I have nothing to do with the Indians, sir, nothing at all. Nor this gentleman either." She gestured toward Meeker.

Cable again attempted to protest but was outshouted by the captain.

"Saint Louis?" Wessells barked. "How in the hell did you manage to get all the way out here to get lost?" Before she could reply, he waved vigorously in her direction. "No, never mind, I don't have time for this at the moment. Private Cable, show this woman to one of the vacant family quarters, and for God's sake have someone take her some hot water in which to bathe and wash that filthy hair. See if one of the officers' wives will lend her some clothes. Maybe then we can tell if she really is a white woman, like she claims."

Meeker raised a hand. "Sir."

Aiden stiffened, fearful of what he might say.

"And you are?" the Captain asked as if Meeker hadn't spoken.

"Meeker, sir. Josiah Meeker, trapper."

Wessells sniffed in derision. "You can bunk down in the infantry barracks. We're crowded here at present. You'll just have to make do. Cable here will show you."

"But, sir. She—" the private stammered.

"Not now, mister. Dismissed," the captain barked.

Cable shot a curious glance from Aiden to Meeker and back again, his eyes asking a question she hoped he wouldn't voice. He knew they were supposed to be married, and had tried to say so a couple of times. The short-tempered captain hadn't allowed it, but sooner or later he might. Considering his temperament, it was better if she waited till he brought it up, if he did. She met Meeker's gaze head on and hoped he could read her silent thanks.

They started out the door, and Wessells said sharply, "The two of you will join me tonight in officer's mess where I expect a much more thorough explanation of your presence. Be damned if I'll stand for anyone helping these savages, if that's what you've been up to. Now, get on out of here and let me work."

Standing outside on the boardwalk, Meeker studied her. "Well, I reckon there's more than one way to skin a cat. I'd a rather gone to the agency, but I suppose this place'll do till the snow melts. You reckon he got away?"

"I hope so. Thank you for...for not saying anything."

He grinned, revealing brown-stained, crooked teeth within the black beard. "Not my lookout. Got enough to take care of without getting involved in that breed's affairs."

Frowning, she glanced quickly in the direction of the young private who'd brought them in. He didn't seem to be interested in their conversation. He did appear somewhat puzzled as he hailed a passing soldier.

"Take this fellow to infantry quarters and see he gets a cot, if there's one available."

The young man took Meeker's arm. He stared back at Aiden as he was led away. She shuddered down to her toes. What would she do if he found out about her story and came to her to claim his rights? He was a dirty, smelly man who probably hadn't bathed in years. The idea of his hands on her drove a chill down her backbone.

Private Cable touched the brim of his cap, murmured "Ma'am," and led her across the compound to her temporary quarters in a row of small residences connected together and fronted by a boardwalk. At the door, he said, "It's none of my business, but if the gentleman is your husband, then why—"

"You're right, Private. It's none of your business."

He shrugged, touched his hat and left.

Stone Heart lay prone at the top of the bluff keeping a watchful eye on the movement of troops around and about the fort. He had seen A'den and Meeker escorted in and let out a sigh of relief. At least she was safe. Nothing going on down there at the moment hinted at how many of the Cheyenne were still alive, but he surmised they were being held in the same prison quarters as before. Though he stared until his eyes burned, he could make out no activity around the long barracks. Would Wessells continue to starve them and withhold water? He was a cruel man, punishing women and children in such a way, when his enemy should be the warriors. Stone Heart vowed to see that the brutal captain did not live to mistreat anyone else.

He would wait until dark and sneak into the fort. If he could find that coward, he'd put his knife in his heart before going to see what could be arranged for the surviving prisoners. The idea brought a bitter smile. Once he had wanted only to escape this dreadful place, and now he must put himself back in danger of capture by returning. He could see no other way in which to help those remaining in their struggle to return to their homeland. He knew any one of them would rather die than go south to Indian Territory, for he felt the same. He could not guess how many were left alive and what shape they were in. But even if there were only one or two, they must not be left to rot in that hell hole.

He had spent the afternoon scouting out a trail

that looked passable if he happened to be a mountain goat, memorized handholds along the perilous descent. A late-rising moon would be both a blessing and a hindrance. He had to decide whether to wait for it to light his way, or get down off the bluffs as best he could in the dark to minimize the chances of being spotted by a lookout. Once in the valley he would approach the fort using the sparse brush for cover. Shivering from the cold, he stomped his feet and rubbed his hands together. At last it was time to go, and he was filled with a mixture of dread and anticipation.

Because of the covering of snow and pale overhead clouds he could distinguish brush and outcroppings along the rim of the bluffs. On his stomach, he inched backward, felt around with his toes for his first footholds and slid into a precarious position that offered only one way out, and that was down. It was tough going. During the day the sun had melted some of the snow along the rock faces, but with darkness and the return of bitter cold, it had begun to freeze back. At times he was sure he would lose his grip and tumble to the bottom. Hands grappling for purchase, feet feeling for the next narrow ledge on which they could perch, he squirmed slowly down, hugging the precipice with his belly like a reptile.

A scrub brush to which he clung with one hand, suddenly uprooted and he was left flailing and kicking with the fingers of his other hand clinging to a jutting rock. His heart hammered so fast he thought he would black out before one of his feet, then the other found purchase. Resting there for a moment, he regained a somewhat normal breathing pattern. His stomach continued to churn, though, as he began his descent again.

At times his feet would reach out into space and find nothing. Frantically searching for handholds, he would lower himself from one to the next using only the sheer strength of his arms. The wound in his side sent jabs of pain that weakened his grasp and several times he almost lost his grip. He had no idea how much time had passed, and that mattered little anyway. All he knew was that the moon rose in the east and found him hanging precariously from one hand and waving a foot around for its next toehold.

Gasping, he found a ledge with both toes and clung to the sheer face to rest a while. Cheek locked against the sheer wall, he dare not shift around to get a look at the fort. What good would it do him anyway? He couldn't tell if they thought some crazy madman might be hanging from the bluffs and were keeping an eye out for him. Even if they did spot him, he'd probably never know it. One marksman with a buffalo gun could pick him off and he'd hear the shot a mere heartbeat before he fell dead onto the rocks below. Best to not even think about it. Just keep going until something happened.

The moon climbed slowly into the covering of overhead clouds and went out. A piece of luck for him, at least for a while. But then his luck gave out. Under one foot a rock shifted, pebbles rattled down the cliff face and the rock let go. The fingers of both hands slipped loose, clawed air as he fell. He swallowed a natural instinct to cry out and prepared in grim silence to meet a cruel death, dashed to pieces on the rocky bank of the river.

The thought no more than crossed his mind when he landed on both feet and tumbled forward. Surprise and shock washed over him, a sharp agonizing pain shot through the wound in his leg, his side cramped. The stars he saw were not in the sky above, and he thought for a moment he would pass out. He'd only been a little ways off the ground when he fell and the impact had rattled his teeth, but he was alive.

Lying flat on his face, one cheek jabbed by gravel, he heard the sweet song of the river and knew that he had come within an inch of landing on the ice and breaking through. Had he done so, even the short fall might have meant his death. To ease the pounding in his side, he turned over and pulled his knees up to his chest.

For a long while he lay like that, rolled into a ball like a damned porcupine, considering all the reasons he'd been spared and waiting for the throbbing of his wounds to subside. As soon as he could move about without setting off renewed torment, he sat up and checked himself thoroughly for any broken bones or ragged injuries that might cause him trouble later. It was a miracle that he found none.

Once sure he had actually come through the fall with only scrapes and bruises, he crawled to his feet and made his way toward the bridge. With the moon behind the clouds, he could cross the river there without getting wet and enduring still more discomfort. He had to make it into the fort before daylight. Where he would hide or how he would free his friends, he had no idea. As for Wessells, that would have to wait. Considering his chances of pulling off such a thing as killing an officer in the midst of a regiment of men and living to carry out his true mission, he decided against it.

****

Aiden reluctantly crawled from the cramped tub of cooling bath water, and stood warming herself beside a small, potbellied stove. Being there made her feel safe and she could hardly contain the euphoria. She was alive, bathed, and warm. A bed awaited her exhausted body. Private Cable had built the fire, sent to her a minuscule amount of bath water, a towel and soap, and told her he would return soon with clothing. He seemed little concerned that his captain had ordered his immediate return.

Obviously he thought better of his decision to return, though, for as she stood before the fire wrapped in a blanket off the bed, there came a tap on the door followed by a woman's voice. She bade her enter and was greeted with a blast of cold air that accompanied a dark-haired woman with sparkling blue eyes. She carried a folded dress of plain calico wrapped around unmentionables and a pair of soft slippers.

Studying Aiden closely, she lay them on the bed and joined her beside the small stove.

"It's cold in here," she said and hugged herself for a moment. "I'm Retha Woods. Private Cable said you needed clothing and decided mine would fit you best." Her glance swept over Aiden. "He has quite an eye for the ladies, I must say. I brought you a brush and pins as well. You have lovely hair. If you need anything else, please ask."

For the first time in days, laughter rose in Aiden's throat, and she studied the woman beside her. Same height, pretty much the same build if Aiden would eat a few good meals, and quite pretty with shiny black hair. Despite tiny crow's feet at the corners of her glittering eyes, she was probably not yet thirty. Married to a soldier and obviously content. Aiden wondered if she had children.

"Oh, thank you, Mrs. Woods. You don't know how I look forward to wearing civilized clothing again. It's been so long."

"Retha, please. And I will call you?"

"Oh, I'm sorry. Aiden Connor. Aiden is fine."

"You're not married?"

"Heavens no. Almost, but thank God it didn't happen."

"Then who is—"

"The trapper? I'm ashamed to say I lied to

Lieutenant Woods. Is he...are you...?"

Retha nodded, mischief lighting her face. "I do hope he was taken in by your lie. That would be delightful."

"Oh, yes, he was. I couldn't help it, really. I was frightened and didn't know how they'd treat me. They were pretty rowdy, well downright mean, if you want to know." She covered her mouth. "Oh, dear. I'm sorry. I didn't mean that your...I mean to say...he was decorum itself, but I was pretty ragged. Sometimes men get the wrong idea."

Retha chuckled. "Lieutenant Woods is always very proper, sometimes too much so. But I don't blame you one bit. They're pretty worked up over this Indian uprising when all we really wanted was to provide a safe home for those poor starving people. Several soldiers were killed for their trouble. It's made them angry and quick to shoot."

Heat flowed to Aiden's cheeks. "I understand many of the Cheyenne were also killed, including women and children."

Retha waved a hand. "War is that way. This Indian business has been a terrible situation all around."

Aiden's teeth clacked together.

"Let me leave so you can dress." The woman's gaze took in the ratty-looking buffalo coat draped over a chair in the corner. "I'm sorry, I should have brought you a cloak. I'll leave mine. I have another. I'm told you'll be joining us at officer's mess this evening?"

"Yes, but please don't worry about leaving your cloak. It's so nice. I don't need it."

"Nonsense, of course I'll leave it. I've only a hop, skip, and jump back to our quarters. Shall I call on you to take you to supper?"

"That would be wonderful," Aiden said, and watched as the friendly woman slipped through the door and was gone. All she wanted was to lie down and sleep, but she slipped into the underthings and calico dress. The clean fabric felt smooth against her bruised and aching body and, as she waited for Retha to return, she realized that she was starving.

****

Dark came early and found Stone Heart hiding in the shadows between the officers' housing and the mess hall. Mouth-watering aromas came from the place, but he tried to ignore them. Several large crates and empty barrels at the back of the building offered an excellent place from which he could watch the comings and goings and plan his next move.

When he heard the light tinkle of feminine laughter, he peered out to see two women walking arm in arm along the boardwalk from the quarters to the officer's mess. One had beautiful red hair coiled at the back of her head and she turned to say something to her companion. In the light issuing from the windows he recognized the familiar distinct features immediately. She was a different A'den from the raggedy woman he'd met in the dugout, to be sure, but he would have known her anywhere.

He'd been so right about her.

She was one of the loveliest creatures he'd ever seen.

His heart flip-flopped and he bit his lip to keep from crying out to her. He had no right to complicate her life any further, or his own either, for that matter. But still, he couldn't help remembering another time and place, when their bodies had entwined in sleep, her light breath fanning his cheek. He'd held her close then, to chase away her terrors, and she'd gotten a hold on his spirit that he couldn't shake.

But shake it he must.

For he had his own way to go, far from the white world, back into that of the Cheyenne, where he'd vowed to remain forever.

So he embraced in his soul the soft, gentle lilt of her voice and watched with deep sorrow as she passed out of sight.

Chapter Nine

On her way to take supper with Captain Wessells, Aiden walked arm in arm with her new friend, Retha Woods. Though dreading what the captain might have to say regarding her claim to be married to the trapper Meeker, she pushed it to the back of her mind. It was delightful to have another woman to talk to.

"It was so kind of you to lend me your lovely cape. I miss wearing civilized clothes. I can hardly wait to get back home to Saint Louis and my..." She broke off when they stepped from the shelter of the building into a brutal wind that sucked the very words from her mouth. But it wasn't the gale so much as a feeling that they were being watched that halted her.

"Pleased to do it," Retha said, and pulled up as well. "What is it?"

Aiden glanced into the dark passageway, frowned. "Nothing, I guess. I thought...no, never mind, I'm just being silly. Let's go, it's cold out here."

But she knew, absolutely, without seeing anything but blackness, that Stone Heart was nearby and watching her. She could almost see those silver eyes darken with distrust at the sight of her in the company of an officer's wife. Her heartbeat raced, her stomach quivered. Shivering, she snuggled the cloak around her bosom and followed Retha through the door into the bright warmth of the officers' mess.

The delicious odor of cooking meat greeted her and she sucked in a mouth full of flavors. Her stomach stopped quivering and let out a long, low grumble she was sure everyone in the place could hear.

From nearby the familiar figure of Captain Wessells rose, gestured toward them. "Mrs. Woods, bring our guest to the table, would you?" Uncommonly jovial, considering his early demand, he executed a half-bow in their direction and indicated two empty chairs on his right. Meeker was already seated near the foot of a long table adjacent to the captain's. A few officers and their wives glanced at the two women. Meeker half-rose and nodded in her direction, with an expression she couldn't read. What was he up to?

With a gleam in his eye, Wessells held out a hand to her and raked a long, deliberate glance down her full length.

"My, my, can this be the same ragamuffin our Private Cable dragged in here only this morning? Join us, Miss—or is it Mrs.—Connor?"

"Miss Connor, sir," she repeated and slipped her fingers from his damp grip.

"Well, *Miss* Conner, please be seated here, next to me." He pulled out the chair, then went to assist Retha Woods in a like manner.

Aiden studied Wessells, but then was drawn to the beaming Meeker who rose to his feet every bit as regally as Wessells and held out a hand.

"Well, my dear. I'm afraid they've found us out," he drawled. "The captain here is aware of our...uh, marriage, so I guess the cat's out of the bag. There's no keeping secrets, is there?"

"I'm sure I have no idea what you're talking about," she said stiffly and pulled her hand from his. At least he'd washed to his wrists, and the grimy face held some evidence of a quick scrub, though dirt remained in the lines around his eyes and mouth.

Beaming at the captain, she seated herself in

the chair he held. "I am not married, Captain, not to this gentleman nor any other. There has been a misunderstanding."

Wessells shot them both a quick, dark look as he seated himself. "I don't appreciate games, and since I see absolutely no reason for either of you to lie about this, why don't you explain what's going on."

Leaning back, he puffed on a long black cheroot and stared directly at Aiden.

She squirmed under the gaze. This was completely ridiculous, but she couldn't think how to get out of it now that the lie had taken hold.

"You'll have to forgive my wife, Captain," Meeker said and took her hand forcefully so that she couldn't pull away without making a fool of herself under Wessell's suspicious eye.

Several unaccompanied wives filed into the room, causing all the men to rise. During the distraction she jerked her hand from Meeker's grip and shot him an angry glare.

"Don't get any ideas."

"I'm not the one who said we were married. But it's not such a bad idea. I haven't had me a woman in a coon's age."

"And you don't have one now." She smiled tightly when Wessells took his seat and once again turned his attention to her.

"It was simply a foolish and harmless lie, Captain, and I admit that." She slid her gaze slowly upward to lock with his. She'd learned how to flirt with men from the girls her older brothers courted, and used the knowledge shamelessly to extricate herself.

Meeker snorted. "I should'a known you couldn't be true to me longer than a night or two. Shameless hussy."

"Here now, sir," Wessells said. "There's no need for such talk. Gentlemen watch their mouths around ladies, even if one is their wife."

Meeker puffed up and prepared for further comment, but she turned her attention elsewhere. Let them enjoy their egotistical male posturing.

Her eye caught reflections in the window that opened onto the dark alley. Stone Heart was out there, she knew it even though she couldn't see him. She had no intention of giving him away after what he had done for her. But why did he hang around? He should be with his people. His reason for being here was to rescue the remaining imprisoned Cheyenne. The way Wessells watched her, he could easily become suspicious, so, with a sweet smile, she turned once more to meet his gaze.

How did Stone Heart plan to set free the remaining Cheyenne, get them out of the fort without getting them all killed? And himself, too, for that matter. Many soldiers were out searching for the remainder of escapees, but plenty of them remained at the fort. They would surely capture him, and either kill him or throw him in the prison with the others. Once there he could do little to aid them in their escape.

Around her the dining room grew noisier as the food was served. The clatter of utensils against plates and cups, the tinkle of glasses, the buzz of conversation and laughter. Two young men with white aprons tied around their uniforms finished carrying in thick white plates loaded with food. They had served the captain, then other officers, and only now were serving the women. Unabashed, she stared at Wessells' plate, at the thick slab of beef swimming in gravy and brown beans in thick juice.

A bowl heaped with golden biscuits made its way around the table followed by small dishes filled with creamy butter, and she could not resist helping herself though her food had not yet arrived. Slathering butter over the hot biscuit, she took a huge bite and savored the flavor almost to the point of fainting in ecstasy. Opening her eyes she saw Wessells regarding her with amusement. Without shame, she took another bite, chewed in delight, and rolled her eyes. She couldn't help it, and didn't really care what he thought about her manners.

Her starving stomach reached up and grabbed the offering and pinched at her insides, begging for more.

Wessells snapped his fingers at the young man moving past with two plates. "Leave one of those with Miss Connor, Private."

He did so, sliding the steaming offering deftly onto the white tablecloth in front of her. She inhaled deeply of the combined aromas and nearly swooned. How would she keep from making a complete fool of herself?

Something touched her arm and she turned to see Wessels' wide grin when he offered the bowl of bread. "Please have some more, there's plenty. I apologize for the poor fare. These outposts seldom have much to choose from in the way of a balanced menu. But we never lack for meat. It comes in regularly on the hoof, if you know what I mean."

Eagerly she took two more biscuits, broke one and dipped it into the gravy pooled in her plate. The flavor was rich with beef drippings, and she finished it off before taking up her fork and knife to attack the slab of beef with renewed fervor.

Nearly halfway to demolishing everything on her plate, she noticed an unearthly stillness had fallen over the room. A room that earlier had been awash with the murmur of conversation and occasional laughter. She glanced up to find they were all watching her. A heated flush crept up her throat and flamed her cheeks. She lay down the eating utensils.

"I'm sorry, I apologize. You must think...I don't

know what you must think." Unsure exactly who she addressed, she stared down into her plate.

Mama had taught her good manners, but hunger had gotten the better of her. With the edge off that hunger, she had time to consider her actions and how they must have looked, even to these frontier dwellers.

As soon as she arrived in this country with Stephan, she'd noticed that women who came west did their best to carry with them the good manners from back east. They attempted to dress and conduct themselves as if they lived in splendor. It was part of their attempt to deny the harsh conditions under which they were forced to live.

Even in the midst of their kind exclamations that they understood, it was quite all right, she should enjoy the food, her thoughts suddenly turned to Stone Heart. How must he feel lurking out there in the darkness, while inside everyone ate and his people starved? How he must hate all of them, stuffing their bellies and not sharing with the Cheyenne.

Thinking of that she was unable to put the next bite of roast beef in her mouth, but stared at it for a long while. Finally she ate it, but some of the enjoyment was gone.

Somehow she must get him some food, try to help him in any way she could. It was only right, considering how he had taken care of her when she was lost and nearly frozen. A still, small voice accused her of another more personal motive, but she ignored it. Just because she was attracted to him didn't mean anything could come of it. Even if she did go to his aid. It was only to pay off the obligation she felt.

Covertly, she watched the waiters come into the dining area and carry out the plates, some still containing large pieces of meat. Part of that manners thing, she supposed. Ladies should eat delicately and leave a portion on their plate so they wouldn't be thought gluttonous. What would they do with the leftovers? There must be an outside door from the kitchen area, probably out back. Could she get in that door after everyone retired for the night? And if she could manage to procure some food, how would she find Stone Heart and his people? Obviously, this called for a midnight exploration.

"My, all this food," she exclaimed to Wessells. "Is it prepared right here?"

"In the kitchen there," he said and pointed toward the doors at the back of the room through which the plates were being carried. "Now, about this confusion concerning your marriage to Mr. Meeker there."

She widened her eyes, batted them. "I explained that. It was a spur of the moment little white lie. I didn't know what kind of men your soldiers might be, and a woman like me...well." She covered her bosom with spread fingers. "What about the rest of the soldiers? Where do they eat?"

Wessells gazed at her a long, silent moment, weighing her words, then replied to her question with a confused expression. "The cavalry barracks has its own mess hall, as does the infantry barracks." Lifting a fork, he said, "Now, if you don't mind, would you?"

Again, she didn't let him return to his earlier subject. Lifting her glass, she went on. "They certainly do feed you officers quite well. Do all the soldiers eat as well?" She forked up the last bite of beef.

He smiled, somewhat indulgently, she thought, but she lay down her fork to lean forward and look him straight in the eye, waiting for his answer. She needed information, not flattery.

"We receive canned goods by freight, comes in on

the train and is hauled up here. We keep a large supply, especially when winter's coming on. Of course the beans are a staple to fill the army's belly. The beef, as I said before, is purchased locally. I understand they have a contract with a nearby rancher." He lay down his fork and reached himself another biscuit and buttered it.

It was interesting that he avoided her question about the quality of the regular soldiers' food. She didn't insist, though, just let him continue.

"Of course, beef is easily kept during the cold months. It's butchered right here at the fort. We have a small house where it's hung, and there's a cold box where excess food is stored if they cook too much. The soldiers will have beans left from tonight's meal for their noon meal tomorrow, no doubt."

He shoved his plate away and lit another of the foul-smelling cigars. Wrinkling her nose, she tried not to show disgust. He went on without urging.

"In the summer, though, it's an entirely different matter. Meat grows hair quickly out here in the heat and cooked food sours fast." He took a puff and let out a trickle of smoke that joined the cloud filling the room. "Sometimes we get down to jerky and hardtack while we're out on patrol. Some local farmers grow vegetables and we can buy them."

"How nice." Glancing around, she leaned toward him as if to speak in confidence, and he tilted his head.

"How in the world do you keep...well, everyone...I saw Indians camped nearby...how do you keep them from stealing the food?

"We post a guard around the clock, storage units are locked, and I've got the only keys." Absentmindedly he rattled a ring of keys in his pocket.

Her spirits sank. They'd never get the keys and

get past a guard to the food. She curtailed the questions before Wessells grew suspicious, but she had found out what she needed to know.

By the time the young privates brought dishes of steaming and fragrant bread pudding and refills of coffee, she was more than ready to enjoy it, for she had developed a plan of sorts. It would take Stone Heart's help to carry it through, and some very dangerous role-playing of her own. Thank goodness, her questioning had put Wessells off further questions about her so-called marriage to the trapper.

****

In the dark alley Stone Heart hunched low and peered into the window across the way. Long shafts of yellow lamplight fell across dirty snow in the passageway. From his position he could see A'den Connor chatting amiably with that murderous Captain Wessells.

Despite her choice of a dinner companion, A'den drew his continued gaze. Lamplight glistened in her rich coppery hair. A long curl had escaped the twist at the crown of her head and hung beside her ear. Each time she smiled toward the captain, Stone Heart ground his teeth to control an animal-like instinct to burst through the window, plunge his knife deep in that mongrel's heart and drag her away.

Inside that room, warm from the potbelly stoves and reeking with the smell of rich food, they ate while his people starved. His desire shifted to taking a leap through the window to take the rotten bastard's throat in his hands and choke out his very life. Count coup on as many of the others as he could before they cut him down. Fists clenched at his sides, he controlled the urge and shifted his thoughts back to the woman.

Doing so only replaced his rage with another

equally passionate need, but one which might in the end cause him just as much trouble. She was a beautiful woman, and he knew something of how her mind worked, how kind she was and how her naïveté might eventually mean her downfall.

All kinds of men would be only too happy to take advantage of her. A few years ago, living his carefree white existence, he might have been one of them. But something had happened that changed his entire life, refocused his desire.

Had Custer not ridden against the People, the Sioux and Cheyenne, slaughtered them at the Washita and moved on toward the Little Big Horn, cutting a wide swath of death, Stone Heart probably would have been content to continue as the bastard half-white son of the great military genius. Living a lie, going under a false name, and building himself a white man's life. An easy existence indeed, when compared to the Indians' struggle to survive what was glibly referred to by the white conqueror as manifest destiny.

As a boy he'd been only too glad to pass as white, with the reluctant, secret assistance of his father's friends. Ironically, it was Custer's actions that had changed that forever.

Staring with eyes that for the moment beheld only the bloodletting of the man he would never call father again, he didn't at first notice A'den's quick glances toward the window. The sound of laughter brought him back to the present and he saw her looking in his direction, as if she could see him.

Heart beating like a drum, he hugged tight to the wall. Even though she couldn't possibly see him, she knew he was here, couldn't seem to keep her eyes turned away. How, he had no idea. If she didn't turn her attention elsewhere, they would all become suspicious. He started to leave before that happened, then saw her deliberately lift the napkin so it hid her lips and mouth something at him.

For a moment, he couldn't make it out, then realized she was saying, "Meet me. Meet me." The napkin was back in her lap so quickly he wondered if he'd imagined it. She took up her conversation with the captain as if nothing had happened.

How very strange that she knew he was there. Perhaps she did not, and he had only imagined her request. Even so, did he dare take a chance and go to her?

In the dining room, Aiden prepared to make a simple request of Captain Wessells. Whether or not Stone Heart had been watching and caught her appeal, she had no way of knowing. Yet she set in motion what must happen if he complied.

With wide eyes, she laid her hand on the captain's arm. "I find my appetite sorely dissatisfied. I was a long time without anything to eat. It would be wonderful to make a late snack of the delicious beef and beans." Raising a brow, she gazed at a slab of bread pudding drenched in rich cream that her companion hadn't touched. "And that pudding, too, if no one minds."

Wessells studied her closely, and she gazed at him with all the innocence she could muster, gently squeezing his forearm through the uniform jacket.

Taking a deep breath, he removed the napkin from his lap and wiped lips that appeared to tremble just the tiniest bit. She licked her own with the tip of her tongue and lowered her lashes.

It worked well. A look of abject pity came over his features, and he patted her hand, then gestured toward one of the privates removing plates from the tables.

"Please bring Miss Connor another plate of roast beef, gravy, and beans. And cover it with a towel so it won't cool off on the way back to her quarters." Turning to her, he said, "Please let me know if you need anything else. We'll speak further in the morning about your current situation. I really have no truck with Meeker's claim that you're man and wife. I see that as an attempt by a desperate man to secure your lovely presence. And I for one can certainly not blame him." He took her hand, held it to his lips much too long.

She smiled into his glittering eyes. "Why, sir. I can't imagine ever wedding a man such as him, but you're right. He threatened to do something like that. You are so kind. Thank you."

With reluctance, Wessells released his grip, rose when she did and helped her with her cloak before handing her the plate of food. "Oh, don't forget the dessert, either. It will be nice to see you put some flesh on those lovely bones."

Outside, she and Retha hurried through the brittle cold, each breath burning at her lungs. The young woman stopped at her quarters and gripped the doorknob.

"Can you find your way, or do you want me to accompany you?" Nose pinched and cold, Retha visibly yearned to go inside.

"It's only a few more doors down. Get inside before you freeze. I'll hurry along. Perhaps we'll talk tomorrow."

Retha had the door open, slipped through and shut it behind her in the blink of an eye.

Relieved, Aiden moved quickly toward her quarters where she paused to look around. Had Stone Heart understood her plea? Would he be watching? Behind her, laughter and conversations were cut off as each in turn entered their own door. She stood in the cold until all was quiet, then stepped out from under the shelter of the overhang. If Stone Heart had understood, he would be waiting for the opportunity to meet with her.

She was soon shuddering with the bitter cold,

and still no sign of him. If he didn't appear shortly, she would be forced to go inside. Turning, she stared in the opposite direction. Light streaked from windows to lie in a row of golden squares along the stretch of frozen snow cut by the many hooves of passing horses. Still, all remained quiet.

He wasn't coming.

Lifting her shoulders, she sighed, turned toward her door and realized she'd have to put down the dish of pudding to open it. When she bent over to do so, he approached, still as the fall of night over the land.

"Go inside but don't turn on a light," he said softly. "Leave the door ajar."

Though she'd been expecting him, he startled her so she almost dropped the small dish. Recovering, she nodded and slipped inside.

After a moment, he followed her into the dark room, the forgotten bowl of pudding in one hand, and softly closed the door. The room, vaguely lit by the outside watch fires, went totally dark

She gasped, stood very still, a sense of his presence like an old friend that embraced her. "I knew you'd come."

"I didn't." He touched her arm, then pulled away. "What is that I smell?"

"I brought you something to eat."

"Well, how in the...I mean, what did you say? I have a fugitive Indian I need to feed?"

"Hardly. Shouldn't I light the lamp? Won't it look funny if anyone's watching?"

"Maybe, but wait until I get out of sight."

"There's a table and chairs in the corner away from the door and window. Take this and eat it before it gets cold. It's absolutely the best food I've ever tasted."

Unerringly, he took the plate from her, though she couldn't see anything in the dark room except the small blaze dancing in the stove. After fumbling in the darkness to light the lamp she fetched a chunk of wood, opened the stove's door, and tossed it in. Turning, she saw he sat, not in one of the chairs, but on the floor, attacking the food with even more frenzy than she had earlier. He looked so pathetically beaten she turned away.

"I'm sorry," she murmured, tears burning her eyes.

He didn't look up, but finished off the food without words. The fork she'd carried along scraped noisily over the plate several times.

"The pudding, eat it too. It's sweet and covered in cream."

He snatched the offering, forked up a huge mouthful. Chewed and swallowed. With a terrible howl of anguish he rose and threw the dish and its contents against the wall.

The unexpected reaction so startled her that she let out a bewildered cry, and started to go to him. Stopped when he turned on her, loomed was a better word, arms raised and fists clenched, the most dreadful expression on his face. She didn't know him, would never have recognized him, he appeared so ferocious.

"What is it?" she asked, voice trembling so she could scarcely speak.

"How can I sit here eating like this when my people don't even have water to drink?" The ferocity faded, replaced by distress.

She went to him, placed an open hand over his heart and stood rock still, counting the hammering beats. "If you don't eat you can't help them."

Slowly, he calmed, some of the tenseness flowing from his taut muscles.

After a while he laid his own hand over hers. "I have to do something, A'den. I cannot allow this to go on."

"I know. I'd like to help you."

"But you mustn't. They'll kill you as soon as me."

"Not if they don't catch me. Us. If we're careful we can sneak them some food, then get them out of this dreadful place."

He squeezed her hand, then lifted it to kiss each fingertip, eyes sparking like struck flint. At the touch of his lips she shivered and her stomach convulsed with desire. Thighs gripped together, she tried to compose herself, had little luck. When she tilted her head to try to read his expression, he lowered his mouth and touched hers for the briefest of tastes.

She moaned, placed her arms over his shoulders. Touching him in that way, she sensed his exhaustion, held him as he had once held her, with tender care. As if he had no strength left, he leaned into her. For one brief moment of pleasure.

Sighing, he straightened. "How will we get them food?"

It took a moment or two to find her voice again, he had so affected her with his need. "From the storage shed. It's locked, but I can get the key. Then it'll just be a matter of taking care of the guard."

He nodded, heaved in a breath. "We must do it right away."

"No, I can't get the key until later, and you need some rest. I'll put out the light so no one can see."

She did so, then hooked an arm in his, and led him to the tub near the stove. Though it had cooled off, the bath water would be warmer than the icy streams he so proudly bathed in during the coldest winter days.

"Wait," she said, and left him to drag up a chair. "Sit," she added and he obeyed as if poleaxed.

Kneeling on the floor she removed his knee-high buckskin boots and leggings, still stained with the blood of the battlefield, then rose and stripped him of his jacket, vest and shirt. He appeared too weary to resist. When she took both his hands and pulled him to his feet, their bodies grazed, thigh to thigh, breast to chest. A shiver vibrated from her loins into her nipples. In the dancing firelight, she caught only glimpses of his bare skin. A shimmer of strong thighs and calves, a rippling of muscles across his stomach and broad hairless chest. The breech cloth left a skimpy, pale patch between his legs.

With trembling fingers, she untied the leather thongs at his hipbones and let the garment flutter to the floor. Trying to avoid allowing her gaze to wander below his waist, she took both his hands, guided him to the tub.

"Step in. I'm sorry it isn't perfectly clean. I bathed in it earlier, but it's the best I can do. You'll feel better after you soak a while."

He made a deep, humming noise in his throat and lowered himself into the tub, long legs folded so that his knees stuck up as high as his chin. She had fit much better. The cloth she'd used was draped over the rim and she rubbed soap into it.

"Lean forward and I'll do your back."

"It smells like you, A'den."

She swallowed hard.

Dear God, what was wrong with her that she wanted this man so desperately? Clearing her throat, she said, "Lean forward," and was surprised the words came out at all.

Hugging his knees, he obeyed and she touched the cloth to hard muscles, covered by warm, downy skin. Wood snapped in the stove, and she began to scrub in harsh, tight motions, carefully avoiding the wound which was well on its way to healing.

Anger caused a pain deep in her chest, and she didn't know where it came from or to whom to direct it.

All she knew for certain was that she must stop being such a fool over this man, who very well might carry scalps of white soldiers on his belt come morning.

Chapter Ten

Despite the circumstances under which he'd come to A'den's quarters, Stone Heart couldn't help grinning at her embarrassment. White women weren't used to dealing with a naked man and certainly not one scrunched into a bathtub with his knees under his chin. He wasn't sure how to set her mind at ease. He only knew that even in his exhaustion, it was indeed pleasant to feel her soft touch on his bare back. Though she denied it, she was what white men called a soiled dove, wasn't she? So what harm could his being here like this do? As a Cheyenne he could never lie with a woman who wore the rope of chastity. As a white man, he did not have that restriction. Was he being dishonest with himself? Trying to convince himself that it would be all right to give in to the passion he felt when he was near her.

It was hard not to, with her kneeling beside him, he who sat in water in which she had so recently bathed. And now washed him with a bar of soap that had touched her. He had smelled the fragrance on her earlier, shivered thinking of that slick, sweet bar so recently rubbed over her soft skin. Every inch of her soft skin.

Nervously, she cleared her throat and moved aside the thick, golden braid that hung down his back. Wood crackled in the stove, but the fire didn't explain the heat that washed over her as she knelt beside this virile and dangerous man. A soft moan of pleasure escaped him and he rested his head against his knees. Her heartbeat drummed a warning to

147

beware, she had not tamed him by washing his back.

She remembered how he'd burst out of that icy stream wearing absolutely nothing, every glorious inch of him on display while she stared without shame. To cloud the vision, she clamped her lips tightly and scrubbed his back with renewed vigor. Across his broad, muscular shoulders, down over his rib cage and along the outline of his backbone, careful to avoid the healing wound where she'd removed the lead. Water splashed up her arms and onto the floor, and she kept rubbing vigorously, as if she might erase the pictures cavorting through her mind.

"Whoa, don't take off my skin," he said.

She jerked her hand away as if caught at something sinful.

For a long while he remained hunched forward, and neither said anything. The fire popped and outside the wind plucked at the building. The roof creaked and moaned.

At last she wadded the cloth, ran it up over his shoulder and let it go at his chest.

He leaned back, grabbed her hand. "I will finish." His voice hoarse, his grip tighter than necessary.

"Yes, okay." But he didn't release her, and she wasn't sure what to do. The clean smell of the Castile soap hovered in the heat from the stove. A vague tang of prairie grasses came from his hair, and she saw herself running barefoot across a green meadow, him chasing her. Catching her.

Though he continued to hold her hand, the fingers of his other hand threaded through her hair, plucked out the combs and set the long tresses free. He pulled her close, buried his face in the long strands and sucked in a ragged breath.

Beneath their hands clenched together on his chest, she felt the hammering of his heart; his lips nibbled at her earlobe, sending shivers of delight straight to her core. Outside, the wind howled around the windows like a banshee trying to break in and join them in their passion. The mournful sound reminded her that she had slept with this man to keep from freezing. And what it had been like to have him curled around her under a thick pile of furs and blankets. His quiet assurances that had driven off her terror.

"I want you," he whispered, breath hot against her cheek.

She wanted him too, completely and forever, but that would never be possible for them. "Do we dare settle for just this night?" she asked.

"I must have you, even if for one night. We can set it apart from our life. Let it exist in another place that we can carry with us always. In our hearts."

"And when it's finished, then what?"

"I will do what I must do and you will do the same. It will have been the best thing that could happen for both of us."

For a long moment, she considered his argument. "Maybe for you. But I...I cannot do this with a man I do not love."

She might have struck him, the way he stiffened and jerked under her hands. "The white man knows nothing of love. You give yourself to any man who can pay. What has that to do with love?"

Her skin went cold and her head swam. "I've told you, I'm not that kind of woman. Why won't you believe me? I've never had a man, not in the way you're asking. Would you take a whore? If so, then you aren't much of a man."

In the darkness, he remained silent. She could hear him sponging the wash cloth over his skin as if that would help him with an answer.

"Stone Heart, will you never believe me?"

"If it matters that much to you, then, yes, I will

believe you."

But she didn't think he spoke the truth. Tears came to her eyes, angering her. "There is only one way I can prove to you I'm not a whore, but I don't wish to do it for that reason alone."

"No, no." He touched her cheeks, trailed fingertips down either side of her throat. "I believe you. I do."

"Are you sure?" He was only saying it to get her in bed. That, a warning from the place where she stored all her sorrows. The place that recalled the betrayal of another man and how much it had hurt.

He squeezed her hands. "I've told you. Now it is you who does not believe me. Say you do not want me. Say it."

Very softly, she said, "I can't."

He rose from the tub, skin slippery and sweet smelling. The towel lay over a chair and she picked it up, began to dry him slowly, starting with his shoulders and back, following the line of his buttocks and down his legs, then moving in front of him. The sensations that played through her mind tantalized her imagination. Performing such a ritual in the dark was indeed erotic. Her hands moved slowly across his chest, down each arm, then to his belly. There she stopped for a moment. He stood very still, made no move.

She was a fool. A complete, absolute fool. Yet she couldn't deny the attraction any longer. Must have something of this man to carry away with her. It would be different because she knew they could never be together. It would not be the same as with Stephan. Would it?

Along with a breathtaking desire to have A'den, Stone Heart felt a deep contentment, as if it would be all right if he rested here with her for a while. Let what would happen happen.

To have her rub him dry in the darkness of her

room was a strange and satisfying experience. The tentative movement of the rough towel over his chest, across his belly and down each leg produced an almost violent reaction in his gut. He waited with apprehension for her to touch him, felt a burning hunger rip at his sanity. Disappointment filled him when she avoided his private parts and handed him the towel so he could finish the job. He had wanted her hands there, touching him, caressing him in the way women were meant to touch and caress a man. Because she didn't, he only wanted her more.

Their fingers grazed, fire and ice. A small sound came up from her throat, almost a purr but laced with something more needful. He wished he could see her, look into the beautiful eyes, place his mouth at the pulse beat in her throat. He rubbed the towel briskly between his legs, hoping to settle down his rising manhood, but the action only made matters worse. It seemed a man was never too tired for passion.

Up until this moment, he had thought that to couple with her would be to satisfy an itch and nothing more. But if what she said was the truth, and she was a virgin, then he had no business satisfying his lust by lying with her. Still, she was not a Cheyenne and she wore no chastity rope. As a white woman, she intrigued him, and he knew that in another life, at another time he could love her. He'd best rid himself of any thoughts along that line. She belonged to a culture on which he had turned his back. A life awaited her elsewhere, and he had priorities that didn't include her. To take her now would be dishonest and damaging to them both.

She pulled the towel away and he could hear her breathing. Thought he heard the rustle of clothing. "A'den...?"

The tips of her fingers trailed over his chest. "Yes, what is it?"

The heat of her nearness, the feminine fragrance that enveloped him, awoke a rush of memories, and he couldn't remember what he'd been about to say. Could only recall the flicker of firelight on her lovely features, the blaze of winter sun flashing in her red hair, the gentleness of her touch when she tended his wounds. All he wanted was to take her in his arms, lay with her in the secret darkness. But he could not remain here alone with her. Had to dress and flee before he ruined everything.

Her arm crept upward, coiled around his neck. Her breath feathered over his throat, bare breasts and belly caressed his fevered skin, the silken flesh of her thighs pressed against his. She had removed her clothes, stood before him clothed only in the blackness of night, naked as he himself. He could not speak, dared not move. Desire blazed through him, burst into flames that licked at his loins until they shivered in anticipation. He dare not move, could do nothing but wait, paralyzed by a need such as he had never known.

"Stone Heart, I know it would make no difference to you...and I wish...uh, I want us to make love."

Throat filled with burning emotion, he enclosed her wrist to stop her, but could not reply. Make no difference? It would make every difference, but he would not tell her that. He could not do this.

With a small whimper, she said, "I'm sorry. Don't, you're scaring me." She tried to pull from his grasp. "I shouldn't have asked. I didn't mean..."

Curling her arm behind her back, he locked her against his chest. She grunted, began to pant and struggle, which only fueled his passion further. He should push her away, wanted to. Was helpless to do anything but hold her as if in anger. She couldn't know what was truly in his heart, and he would not tell her.

"Why do you want to do this foolish thing?" he asked against her ear. "Why?" He tightened his grip. "Because I am a savage?"

"No. Be...because...please, I'm afraid."

"I told you once you would be wise to be very afraid of me. I asked why you are doing this. Please answer."

"Because I'll never feel this way about a man again, and I can't bear to return home without knowing...knowing what it would be like to...to be with you. Truly be with you." She dragged in a breath, relaxed against him. "I'm sorry, let me go. Please. I feel like a fool."

"You are a fool if you're not frightened of what might happen. But I fear it is too late to let you go."

At last he truly spoke the truth, for he could no more release her than he could fly with the great eagle. Lowering his head, he kissed whatever part of her he touched in the darkness, an earlobe, the downy curve of her jaw, the satiny skin of her throat. Lifting her off the floor, he moved his mouth down to the rise of her breast and over a rigid nipple, took it between his lips. Helpless, hopeless, lost. He swayed, tasted deeply of her. Soft, sweet flesh nurtured him, filled him to overflowing and he drank in ecstasy.

She cried out, but did not pull away, and so he didn't stop. Could not have done so, even if he wanted to.

A great, glorious desire bloomed in his belly, spread through him like the warm light of summer. He took her to the floor, wrapped her in his arms and legs.

She curled within the curve of his body, opened herself to him while she moaned softly. Shifting until he covered her, he slipped into the moist warmth and felt his world tilt even before he broke the barrier of her maidenhood. What a powerful joy mixed with regret that produced in his heart. As a Cheyenne he felt shame, as a white man pride, for she had given her virginity to him. She had told him the truth.

For a long while he simply held her, letting her grow accustomed to the feel of him inside her, filling her. When his need grew beyond endurance, he growled down in his throat, took long deep breaths to tame the beast.

It was her first time and though he ached to continue, he knew to hurt her would ruin the experience. This would be their first and last act of love, and he wanted her always to remember that this was the most beautiful day of her life.

Smoothing tangled hair away from her temples, he covered her face with kisses. Tasted tears on her cheeks.

"Does it hurt?" he whispered.

"Yes, oh, yes, but it feels so wonderful."

He moved slightly inside her, drew away then pushed slowly, easily. Felt his world spinning.

She gasped, gripped his shoulders. "Do that again."

"Yes, yes," he said and did as she asked. Clung to her because nothing else existed beyond this animal hunger.

She locked both legs around him, rotated her hips until he felt himself ready to explode, then stopped and found his flesh with her tongue. Blazed fiery paths along his chest.

Spoke moist words against his flesh. "Stone Heart. It is not your heart that is made of stone, silken...hot...smooth...stone." With each word, she pulled him deeper within herself, soaring to the brink and taking him along.

Going with her, he held them on the precipice yet a moment longer to make sure she was ready, that what was about to happen would take her beyond the pain he caused and into the world of sweet rapture where only lovers could go. Her cries intensified and she moved to his rhythm. The pulse of his desire throbbed like the pounding of a thousand drums, and reality spun away. In the void of infinity, only the two of them existed. Both were plunged into a world of timeless ecstasy where all else was forgotten save this act of pure perfection.

Aiden rode the winds of his world, joined the howls of his gods, where their flesh came together felt the heat of the summer sun and the ice of an endless winter's night; offered herself to him with trust and desire and a love she could never have imagined. It had lain deep within her, waiting for this moment, and its release awed her. Frightened and delighted her.

He held her close, wrapped in a soothing pleasure that felt no discomfort, either from the hard floor or the chilly air. She clung to what she knew could not last. What she knew she would never find again. Not on this earth, perhaps not on the next. Being cherished in this way, by a man with whom she had shared such intimacy was like nothing she'd ever imagined. She felt sheltered, serene, and at the same time expectant. Lying there within the security of his embrace, overcome by the vague possibility that anything was possible. If only he would stay with her.

Somehow she had to make him see how wonderful that would be.

"Are you cold?" he finally asked.

"No." Sensing his withdrawal, she snuggled closer. *Don't go, please don't go.*

"But we should move to the bed. It will be cold before morning."

Nodding against him, she held on tighter, unwilling to be the first to break contact. *Stay with me, oh, stay with me.*

"Are you all right?" Concerned, perhaps impatient.

"Yes, oh, yes. So all right, you could never imagine."

His laughter enclosed her, soft as warm wool. "Oh, no? I could, I can. I went with you."

"Was it the same for you as for me?"

"How will we ever know?"

Both chuckled. Then she shivered from the cold creeping along the bare wood floor, and he unwound himself, dragged her to her feet. "In the bed with you, and under the covers."

She let him tuck her in. "Now you," she said, reaching for his hand but finding only emptiness. He would leave now, and she couldn't stop him. "Where are you?"

"Here, over here. I must dress."

"If you go they'll catch you, kill you."

"Maybe not. Even so, I have no choice."

Heart in her throat, she whispered, "You of all people have a choice. Please stay. You are more white than Cheyenne."

"You know I can't desert them."

"Stone Heart, this will happen whether you go or stay. Can't you see that? These soldiers, they won't let your people go free. They'll either starve them, take them back, or kill them outright. And you as well, if you are with them. Can't you see that? It's too late for them, but not for you...for us. I don't want to lose you."

He came to the bed, sat on its edge, found her hand in the dark. "A'den, you can't lose something you never had."

She cried out, but he silenced her. "No, listen. This is all there is for us. We stole a moment. There is no more, there can't be. You are to go home. I must as well. We will never forget."

She felt as if her heart had shattered into

thousands of tiny pieces.

"Wait, wait," she urged, holding onto his hand with both hers. "I have an idea. A better way for you to help your people than stealing food and breaking out. They'll kill you all, every one of you."

"Probably, but it will be better than this white man's prison."

"You've lived white long enough to fool them. You are only part Cheyenne."

Holding out his arm, he took her fingers and rubbed them there. "What part of me is Cheyenne, show me the part. Is it here?" He slapped his cheeks, "Or maybe this part only?" He doubled his fist and pounded his hard stomach. "Huh? You don't know? Well, tell me the part that is white and I will cut it off." Furiously, he dragged the knife from its scabbard and raked it across his chest, leaving a fine line of blood.

"No, don't. Stop." But she didn't touch him, couldn't.

In the flickering firelight his eyes glowed like coals, and she was sorry she had made him so angry. For even with the way she felt about him, deep down inside the pit of her secret self, she was afraid of what he might do. He was still, despite his white blood, a savage.

He reached out, touched her as if to calm her, but made no excuse for his actions. "I was doing pretty good as a Cheyenne till I met you. It rubs off, this white world, and I want no further part of it."

She was losing this battle, so took another tack, for she could not, would not let him go to his death.

"No, listen. Suppose they...the soldiers, thought you were a white man, an officer from some other fort. Perhaps here to inspect conditions. They do things like that, I'm sure. I mean, if you were white you could come and go as you pleased. You could set them free. Right under their noses."

"But I am not white." He rose, tried to pull away, but she held fast.

"But you could be, you don't understand. Please, give me a chance to explain." The idea so excited her that her tongue tangled so she feared she couldn't say the words.

Though he didn't speak, he also didn't move away. She could hear him breathing, standing there beside the bed, waiting. Hope crept into her heart. This would work and they could be together. And he might fit back into that white world so well that he wouldn't go away, wouldn't leave her.

"I can get you a uniform. We'll cut your hair, you can sneak out and ride in as an officer. Then you can have the time you need to save your people. You can move about freely. What do you think?"

"I think it is foolish. I swore never to live white again."

"But if you could save your people?" She waited, letting him think about what she'd suggested without interruption.

"I'm not sure. Where would you get a uniform that would fit?"

"Retha Woods. Her husband is gone, searching for...for your people. I could manage somehow to get one of his uniforms. I've seen him, he was with the soldiers who captured Meeker and I. He's as big as you. He's a lieutenant."

"I could never pull it off. Besides, how would you manage to get it?"

Exasperated at his reluctance, she sat up and stared at his shadowy form, wishing she could see the expression on his face. "You agree, and I'll get the uniform, one way or another. Now, come to bed and hold me. There's no need for you to go anywhere."

She didn't take a breath until she felt the bed jiggle when he crawled under the covers on the other side.

He snuggled against her, ran his hand across her bare belly and cupped a breast in a cold palm. There they slept off the exhaustion of the past few days, curled together in the warm darkness as they once had to survive the cold.

A knock on the door jerked Aiden awake. Her first thought was that Stone Heart would be discovered. But she needn't have worried, the space beside her was empty. He was gone. A great sadness crept into her heart. The knock repeated itself, but all she could do was stare at the indentation next to her where he had slept. She had lost him, despite everything.

"Aiden, it's Retha. Are you awake? They're serving breakfast and I thought you'd like to accompany me."

Shaking off the cobwebs of sleep and disappointment, she padded to the door, spoke against its panels. "I'm not dressed. You go on, I'll join you shortly." All she wanted was to throw herself down and weep. He had deserted her for a bunch of scraggly, hopeless people who were destined to die. After all they'd been to each other. She could only pray he would return.

"Yes, that will be fine," the woman said from the other side of the door.

"Retha?"

"Yes?"

"Has your husband, the other men, have they returned yet?"

After a slight hesitation, Retha answered. "No, why?"

"No reason, I just wondered. See you in a while."

"See you."

Without waiting a moment longer, Aiden rushed to the pile of clothes she'd discarded in the throes of passion the night before. Skin tingling with the

memory of all that had happened between her and
Stone Heart, she dressed as fast as she could.
Crossing her fingers that everyone would be at
breakfast, she opened the door and stepped out
boldly. Striding with purpose, she surveyed the
surrounding area. No one was about. Alert to any
change, she stopped at Retha's door and stood there
a moment with her back to it, fingering the latch.
When she sensed it was free, she shoved the door
open with the backs of her heels and stepped inside.
Closed it. Let out a shaky breath. Standing very
still, she waited for her heart to stop thudding. All
remained quiet. It surely couldn't be this easy, could
it? Any moment someone would burst in, drag her
away.

The quarters were larger than hers. On her
right an alcove with table and chairs, the parlor with
overstuffed furniture and a pot bellied stove, another
room inside of which was a bed, a chest and
wardrobe. No time to waste. She hurried to the
wardrobe in the corner, opened it and flipped
through several dresses before finding two uniforms.
Slipping one out, she quickly checked to see that it
was complete. Pale blue pants with a wide yellow
stripe down the outside of each leg, a boiled shirt, a
jacket. She had no idea what to do about a hat,
decided to worry about it later.

Heart beating so hard she could scarcely
breathe, she ran to the front door, opened it a crack
and peered out.

A soldier hurried along the boardwalk, almost
on top of her. He must have seen the slight
movement, for he paused in stride, as if expecting
someone to step out. Covering her mouth, she
backed away, slipped into the shadows and waited.

"Hello, anyone there?" he asked.

The door jiggled slightly, then swung open a
ways. "Mrs. Woods? You there?"

"Must've forgot to close it," he muttered, pulled the door shut and moved off along the boardwalk, boot heels thunking solidly.

Hand still clutching her mouth, she breathed a litany. "Oh, God. Oh, God."

She'd almost passed out when he opened the door. Thought he was going to step in and see her standing there holding Lieutenant Woods' uniform. And with no explanation whatsoever.

On quaking legs she went to peer out again, saw no one and ran as fast as she could back to her room. Plunging inside she leaned against the wall panting, the uniform hugged to her chest. Now all she had to do was find Stone Heart, let him know what she had done and convince him that her plan would work. Whether it would or not didn't matter. Getting him back into the white world did.

First she had to hurry to breakfast before Retha grew suspicious. Somehow she would manage to look absolutely innocent. Quickly winding her hair in a loose bun, she stuck in a few combs and headed for the mess hall.

Sitting beside Retha, Aiden had scarcely lifted her spoon over a plate of steaming cornmeal mush, when a commotion arose outside. A great volley of shouts followed by gunfire and the anguished cries of women and children. Everyone leaped to their feet and ran out to view the parade of a forlorn column of Cheyenne.

Past the mess hall they trailed, the pathetic wounded, starving men, women, and children. Soldiers of the cavalry rode on all sides, herding them like animals. A small girl stumbled along, her tiny face frozen in a mask of silent terror. Of all those she looked upon, this child's plight captured Aiden's heart. No one seemed to be caring for her. Leaves clung to her matted hair and torn dress. Her moccasins were worn through until her skin showed.

The poor baby. Aiden could hardly bear it.

Arms held out to the child, she moved forward, but Retha caught her arm, pulled her back. Shook her head and frowned when Aiden beseeched her in a silent plea.

"You can't help them. No one can. You can only cause yourself trouble," Retha whispered.

"But the babies, the poor little babies. How can this be happening? There must be something we can do."

A young woman marched past, even as Retha and Aiden struggled there on the sidelines. She clutched a baby to her bosom, its little head hanging over her arm limply, arms and legs blue with the cold. It did not move.

"My God, it's dead. Retha, that baby is dead." She couldn't stop the tears that came, nor swallow past the knot in her throat. "She's carrying a dead baby."

"Then you cannot help it." Harsh words from the genteel woman who continued to hold her back.

"But...oh, please, someone?" She glanced about at the stern faces of the onlookers. How could they all stand by while this happened? These were Stone Heart's people, the ones the white man once called the Beautiful People.

Tearing her arm from Retha's grasp, she shoved her way between two cavalry horses. Leather and animal sweat filling her nostrils, she caught up with the young mother and her dead child.

"Let me help you," she said softly, reached for the woman's burden.

The young mother shouted and jerked away, eyes filled with a cold hatred that cut through to Aiden's soul. From behind, a soldier grabbed Aiden. Strong fingers cut cruelly into her arm. He dragged her through the line of men. Deposited her on the boardwalk.

"Stay back, ma'am. Don't touch them."

Whirling, Aiden faced the crowd of onlookers. "How can you stand here and do nothing? Animals, you're all animals. Stop this, please." They only stared at her with flat, dispassionate eyes, and she felt as if her heart were cracking in two.

Captain Wessells appeared next to her and curled an iron-hard arm around her shoulders. "Calm down. I'll see you to your quarters."

"What will they do with them? The poor little babies...that one is dead."

"It's not your problem, ma'am. Come along."

She could not resist the force of his grip, and stumbled along beside him until he shoved her inside the door of her quarters.

"I will send someone to see you remain in your quarters. I'm taking fresh troops out to put down this uprising, once and for all." His anger spilled out to include her, as if she were somehow responsible. Without another word, he pulled the door closed between them.

She could only stand there and weep while the thud of his footfalls faded away.

Chapter Eleven

After he left Aiden's bed, Stone Heart spent the remainder of the night looking for his people. They were no longer imprisoned in the building from which they'd made their escape. Often, in his search, he would have to scurry into hiding when a guard approached. Several patrolled the grounds all night long. But they were awkward white men, not accustomed to going about silently, so he had little trouble avoiding them.

He slept not at all that night, but wandered throughout the fort, slipping in silence from shadow to shadow in what seemed an endless and hopeless quest. Hunkering in a protected corner when he grew too cold to move about. In the flickering light from the watch fires, tended by rotating guards who stood over the flames to warm themselves, he continued his search. If he didn't find the Cheyenne before dawn then it would mean another day and into the night they would have to endure the hardships of starvation. Some would die of it. He had to do something.

He did, however, find the dead, brought in and stacked behind the sawmill, looking like cords of wood. Frozen stiff by the bitter cold, the corpses lay one on top of the other. He saw some he knew, others whose features were no longer recognizable because of their wounds. He could not find Dull Knife or Roman Nose or Little Finger Nail, nor the warrior woman Buffalo Calf Road. But some bodies were frozen together, making it difficult to identify them in the pale, silvery dawn.

For long dreary moments he studied the grisly sight, hugging himself while his insides quivered. A brisk wind caught at his elk coat and beat relentlessly against the blanket he'd tied over his head. For fear his feet would freeze, he stomped back and forth alongside the stack of bodies. He spied an occasional army boot or uniform coat sleeve that told him some of the dead were soldiers. Thought it amazing that such poorly armed, nearly starved people could still manage to slay some of the enemy.

From the parade grounds came the morning cry of the trumpet summoning the soldiers to formation.

He had to move on or be discovered, but he knelt for a brief moment, back to the brutal wind, placed his hand on one of the departed ones and spoke to the spirits asking that they guide these poor souls to the afterlife.

Silently he slipped into the shadows of the mill to wait and watch his chance to move on without being seen. As the rising sun cast a glow through the low hanging clouds, he found himself within sight of the door to Aiden's quarters. There he remained hidden until she came out. In dismay, he watched her peculiar actions when she entered another door, shook his head grimly when she came out carrying a uniform. He had hoped that his absence this morning would put a stop to her crazy plan. He vowed not to return, therefore ending it for good and all. She could scarcely wear the uniform herself.

A while later, while he sneaked close to yet another building, he heard the uproar of approaching troops. Taking up a vantage point where he would not be seen, he watched with a great despair the straggling group of Cheyenne prisoners. Saw A'den try to help one of the women. Almost burst from hiding when the butcher Wessells literally dragged her back to her quarters. It was all he could do to stay put while that bastard put his hands on her. He must not give in and show himself, or all would be lost. Not only for him but for his people. Wessells wouldn't let this end here and would see that A'den was dealt with severely for her outburst in front of everyone. He might even lock her up. The man was relentless and pitiless, and would not brook any sympathy for the Cheyenne, who had disgraced him and the government by their latest escape. He would deal harshly with them and any who might stand in his way.

Torn between her safety and that of his people, he crept away. Following the parade of Cheyenne prisoners would at last lead him to the place they were being kept. Time enough to warn her of the consequences of her actions later.

Surely these would be the last of the lot. Any left out there after this length of time were surely dead. With no food and sparse clothing, they could not long survive this cold. Even so, he would not make his move until the last soldier had returned from the hunt and all escapees were confined in one place. When they escaped, they must all go together. He would see to that. And he must do it without involving A'den.

Hardening his heart against the pathetic string of prisoners, he kept them in view without showing himself until they filed into a long, low wooden structure near the hospital. Behind them a wagon loaded with those too injured to walk stopped at the door of the hospital. Several soldiers began to unload and carry the bloody Indians inside. To watch was enough to rip his heart from his chest. Rage overpowered him. It was all he could do to remain in hiding and not rush out to club as many white soldiers as possible before they took him down. Crouched low, he gazed through the open doors, saw the wounded lying side by side along the entire length of the building. Even as the new arrivals were taken in, the dead were moved out. Hauled to the mill and stacked with the others, he guessed.

Breath caught painfully in his chest, Stone Heart turned from the gory sight, hunkered deep into the shadows alongside the sutlers to wait. For what he was not yet sure.

****

After Wessells returned Aiden to her quarters, she sat on the bed trying to decide what to do. Seeing the young mother carrying her dead baby had made her understand why Stone Heart had to help these people. And she must help him. It would be impossible to live with the knowledge that she had done nothing while they suffered so severely. Nor would she try to stop Stone Heart. She had no idea how she would find him in this sprawling place, but after dark she would try.

Aiden had always pictured a fort as a place surrounded by high walls and lookout towers, but Fort Robinson appeared more like a large settlement sprawled across the plains. Row upon row of barracks were surrounded by many businesses, like any town. There was even a chapel and a hospital. All to see to the needs of the many soldiers stationed at this remote outpost, their families, and those civilians who passed through by stage. Finding him would not be easy if he was out in the open. That he was hiding would make it even more difficult.

In only a few moments she learned just how impossible the task might be when she answered a tap on the door to be faced by a young soldier.

He touched the brim of his hat. "Ma'am? I'm Private Hedges. The captain wishes me to see to your needs while he's gone. If you want anything, let me know."

"I want to take a walk."

"I'm afraid not, ma'am. The captain...I mean, you're to be confined to quarters until he returns."

167

"That's ridiculous. Why?"

Remaining at attention, the private never changed his solicitous tone. "I'm sure I don't know, ma'am. You'll have to speak to Captain Wessells about that."

"Well, get him then. I wish to speak to him."

"I'm sorry, ma'am. But the captain has already left."

"Left?" Stricken mute, she searched for something to say. Wanted to yell and scream but knew it would do no good, and so gritted her teeth. "I see, and when will he return?"

"I don't know, ma'am. Is there anything I can get you?"

Without answering, she slammed the door in the young soldier's face. If there'd been anything handy, she'd have thrown it. At the private or at the window through which she could see him leaned up against a post. Now what was she going to do? With no entrance or window at the back there was no escape save through the front door.

Then she lit upon a solution that might work. Fixing her hair and smoothing her skirt, she tapped on the window, motioned to the private.

He swung open the door, stood at attention. "Yes, ma'am?"

"I wonder if you could find out where my husband is and have him sent to me?"

The young man's features blanched, then turned a fiery red. "Your husband, ma'am?"

"Yes, that's what I said. I'm sure the captain didn't intend for me to remain here all alone. Did he?" She used one of the many gestures that had once garnered her hoots and whistles when she performed on the stage. Curled fingers stroking her throat and down between her breasts while her face conveyed sweet innocence.

"Well...uh...no. I mean, I...he did not mention a

husband."

"We were brought to the fort together. The trapper, Josiah Meeker? Surely you remember?"

"I was out on another patrol, ma'am. We only arrived back last night."

"Well, then," she said brightly. "I guess you'll have to ask someone else. I would really like to see him. It's very lonely shut up in here with no company."

She lay a hand over the cuff of his jacket and squeezed gently. "Unless you...?"

"Oh, no, ma'am. The captain would have my head." He backed off, pulling the thick fabric from her fingers. "I'll see what I can do."

"Thank you," she said and closed the door slowly, keeping her gaze pinned on him.

She'd begun to think her ploy hadn't worked when there came a loud knock. Eagerly, she opened the door to face a stunned Meeker, grabbed his arm, she hauled him inside.

"Jehosaphat, what in thunder's going on?"

The bang of the slamming door shook the walls. "I need your help. They need your help."

Confused, he glanced quickly around the room. "Who they? What's going on. I thought you said I wasn't to even come near you."

"Well, I've changed my mind."

Pulling the ratty fur hat from his head, Meeker grinned, showing stained teeth. "Oh, you don't say?"

"Don't be ridiculous," she snapped and faced him down. "Did you see them bring in the Cheyennes?"

"Yeah, I did. What of it?"

"And you remember our friend from earlier, Stone Heart?"

"Yeah. Again, what of it?"

"He wants to break them out so they can go home, and I want to help him, but they've put me under guard and I can't get out."

169

"Is that so?"

She pointed another sharp gaze at him, lifted her shoulders.

The black beard bounced, dark eyes gleamed. "Me? Oh, no, not me. I'm fixing to go over to the agency, replace my animals, and get back to my trapping. I ain't got no time to be fooling with no half-dead Indians." Gesticulating, he glanced toward the window.

She grabbed a waving arm. "Listen to me for a minute. It won't take long. I just want you to find Stone Heart and bring him to me tonight, after it gets dark. You don't have to do anything with the Cheyenne."

"And what about that'n?" Again Meeker waved a dirty hand, this time in the direction of the guard.

"Hush, he'll hear you. Hit him on the head."

"What?" he shouted, hunched his shoulders and repeated the word under his breath. "What?"

"Change clothes with him and pretend to be the guard while I go with Stone Heart. We'll be back before daybreak."

"If that ain't the wildest notion I've ever heard. And jest what am I supposed to do with the young man after I hit him over the head?"

She shrugged. "I don't know. Drag him off somewhere, tie him up, gag him. It's just till morning." She glanced in all directions. "I know, take him in the back of a building, the livery or the blacksmith, cover him up good. No one will find him before daylight."

"And suppose I get caught. What then?"

"You won't get caught. Are you afraid of a little ole captain and a bunch of green-behind-the-ears recruits? I thought you mountain men were braver and more foolhardy than that."

"Well, I reckon we are. But we ain't foolhardy enough to do something for nothing. Give me a good reason, I might do it." He leered at her bosom.

Mind racing she backed away. Maybe she had miscalculated. She could think of absolutely nothing to say.

He gestured with curled fingers. "Come here, give me a little kiss. I ain't had a purty woman like you in ages."

Probably never had a woman, "purty" or not, she thought, but struggled to smile. "Not now, he'll hear." Pointing at the door, she hurried on. "Later, after we do what has to be done."

"Well, now, missy. That ain't right. If I'm supposed to be your husband, then what would it matter if he heard? Why do you suppose he thought you sent for me, to pass the time of day?"

Crossing her arms under her breasts, she widened her eyes. "Oh, I just couldn't with him out there knowing what we're doing. Ladies don't do things like that. Once we're out of here..." She let the words trail off, not willing to voice a promise she had no intention of keeping. She'd deal with that when the time came.

He eyed her up and down, licked his lips. "What'll you do if I say no?"

"Have that young man come in and throw you out."

"Come between a man and his wife?"

Without hesitation she headed for the door.

"Never mind, never mind. I'll do it. But you'd better not try to cheat me out of what's mine after this is done and over."

"No, I won't. I promise you I won't cheat you out of what's yours."

After eying her for a moment longer, he nodded. "I'll have to wait till dark."

"Fine. Just find Stone Heart and bring him here."

"What'n if I can't ?"

Both jumped when a loud knock sounded. In a trembling voice, she called out. "Yes, what is it?"

"Dinner is ready. They've brought a tray. Sorry they didn't bring enough for...for your husband."

Quickly, before Meeker could utter a sound, she swung the door open. "Oh, that's all right, he has to leave now anyway. Just put the tray in there on the table."

Sticking her head outside, she spotted a few men running toward the mess hall. "Go on," she said to Meeker. "I'll be waiting."

With a frown that brought thick brows together above his scarred nose, he hurried away, turning once to stare back at her. He was none too happy, but she thought he would probably do as she wished, just on the chance he'd get his hands on her later. She shuddered to think of that and hoped she could handle the situation when it arose. In the back of her mind lurked the question she could not answer. Suppose he couldn't find Stone Heart?

****

Much as he wanted to hang around outside the back of the mess hall while they were serving the noon meal, maybe get his hands on some food, Stone Heart knew better. In broad daylight, he'd be caught, and he couldn't take the chance.

He had to wait till dark. Tonight after supper, he'd figure out a way, even if all he could find were the leftover scraps. The starving people would be glad for anything. So he hunkered down behind a stack of wooden boxes in a narrow alleyway between the sutlers and the freight office. From there he could see the main thoroughfare and all who came and went, and down the row a ways, the quarters where A'den was housed.

With a sinking heart, he had seen the guard talk to her, then take up watch outside her quarters. Saw Meeker come and go. Squashed an urge to wave at her when she leaned out the doorway after they brought her food. Obviously, the captain had ordered her confined to quarters, probably because of her action when the Cheyenne were brought in.

He'd never get to her now, even if he wanted to. On thinking about it, that was probably a good thing. In all probability, he wouldn't have been able to stop himself at least going in to tell her goodbye. One look at those green eyes and all their promises and he'd have been lost. Now he didn't have to worry.

A while later Meeker came out of the mess hall along with a lot of the other men and started slowly along the boardwalk, walking a ways into each alleyway as if searching for something or someone.

Blowing on cold fingers, Stone Heart stomped his feet and yearned to move into the pale wintry sunlight that slanted across the dark shadows around him. He dared not, for fear of being spotted. Curious, he continued to observe Meeker's strange actions until finally he figured out what he was doing.

The man was looking for him. She'd sent him out to look for him.

Couldn't let the trapper find him.

Sneaking around back of the sutlers he worked his way from building to building, until he was opposite the mess hall. Lingering odors of food cooking filled the cold air, making his stomach rumble. He could just imagine how his people felt after having been on the run out in the cold for several days. If Wessells remained true to form, he wouldn't bother feeding them. Not until they all agreed to go back south to the Indian Nation. And they would never do that.

All day the fort was a bustle of mounted troops, sometimes fifty and sixty at a time, leaving to hunt for more of the escapees, or returning with a few more half-dead captives. In all the excitement, he was able to make his way to the back of the main mess hall by late afternoon. A'den had said there was a locked shed where they kept the frozen meat, and that leftovers were discarded there as well. Leftovers would be by far the better choice, for they would be cooked, even though all mixed together in a hodgepodge of meats and vegetables, bread and desserts. Starving people would scarcely care.

Keeping careful watch, he could hardly contain himself as the aroma of cooking food wafted through the cold air. He could almost taste the beef and beans he knew to be common fare at the forts. Scrounging around, he found a barrel half filled with what looked like yesterdays discards from the kitchen. Already frozen around the outside. That's probably where they would put today's leavings, as well. A large tarpaulin was stretched over some wooden crates in front of the meat storage unit. Under it he found several small wooden kegs. Breaking one open, he saw it was filled with hard tack. Supplies for the soldiers when they left on patrol, he supposed. He broke open another, and dumped the contents so he could fill it with leftover food from the kitchen. He could carry both to his people. Then he slipped into a space beneath the tarpaulin to wait.

Wrapped in the elk robe, and sheltered from the wind, he squatted in the musty dark in relative comfort. Listened to the men as they arrived out front and went inside. Laughter and shouting crackled the air that turned bitterly cold as the sun disappeared behind the horizon. He scarcely breathed for fear someone would see the thick clouds of vapor coming from his mouth.

At last he heard the back door creak open, peered out and saw a man in a white apron carrying two large buckets. Scrunching deeper into the space between two crates and holding his breath, he watched him dump both in the barrel. Scrapings from the men's plates, no doubt. Men doing duty in this cold country tended to eat everything they could get their hands on. But cooks also prepared more than they could normally use, and that too would be stored in the shed.

After the door closed and all grew fairly quiet, he crept from his hideout with the empty keg. In the light of evening, he could scarcely make out the contents of the barrel. It didn't matter, it was food. With both hands he scooped out every morsel down to the frozen leavings and licked his fingers clean. He'd been right, potatoes and gravy, the flavor of beef. His empty stomach begged for more, but he didn't take the time. He had to get this food to the prison barracks, somehow get it inside to the people. Hefting a keg under each arm, he scurried through the darkness to the side of the prison barracks. There he set both kegs on the ground and leaned against the planking to catch his breath. From inside he could hear the feeble cries of children, women's voices strained by hopelessness, the low rumble of men arguing.

Cautiously he leaned out far enough to spy the barred double doors in front of the place. No guard in sight. Heart hammering, he turned to pick up the kegs, and knelt there, an arm around each one, he heard and saw the booted feet approach too late to do anything but wait and see what the guard would do.

The sentry did exactly as Stone Heart expected. He brought his rifle to bear and shouted, "How in thunder did you get out?" Then raised his voice. "Injun, Injun. Out back."

Another guard raced around the far end of the building. "Where'd he come from?"

"Danged if I know, I came around the corner and

there he was. See what he's got. No, wait, better sound the alarm and check the barracks. Savages must've made themselves a hole. Dang, keeping these animals penned up is nigh to impossible. Wessells'll kill us if we've got another outbreak."

All the while he spoke, he kept his rifle trained on Stone Heart. The other soldier ran between the buildings crying out in a loud voice. Men poured from the surrounding barracks, some hopping into their boots and snapping suspenders in place as they trotted across the yard.

Stone Heart's captor shoved him up against the barracks wall. "Whatch got here?" Keeping the rifle stuck in his stomach, the guard leaned over to inspect the keg. "Stealing food, huh?" He shoved him along roughly toward the front of the prison barracks. "Open up the door so I can get this one back in. The rest of you check along the back yonder, see where he got out. There may be more of 'em running around out here."

Before they could get the steel bar off the door, two soldiers approached carrying the kegs of food and hardtack.

"Look here. Looks like he was stealing food for 'em. Good God, this is garbage, this'n some of our rations. Danged heathens."

The one holding the kegs of food moved toward the door. "Poor buggers. What would it hurt to let 'em have this? They got women and kids in there."

"Not on your life. Wessells found out he'd have us up on charges. Probably court marshal the lot of us. Take it back where it come from. Besides, they're just a bunch of ignorant savages. Even animals deserve better. If you're smart you'll forget you even asked."

The corporal studied Stone Heart, then shrugged and walked off.

Stone Heart remained stoic and did not speak.

Fury blackened his vision. These brutal white men cared so little for his people they wouldn't even feed them discards from their table. He had failed, and now they would all die.

A soldier slid the heavy bar off and opened one of the heavy doors. Another one shoved him through into the smelly darkness where he fell to his knees. He wanted to cry out his fury, his frustrations, his anger, his disappointment.

****

Aiden heard a great uproar and assumed that another troop had brought in more prisoners. It had been going on all day. After a few minutes, someone banged on the door and she hurried to answer, wondering what had happened to the guard.

Eyes snapping, Meeker pushed inside and slammed the door behind him. "They got him. I couldn't do nothing. Caught him out back of the place where they're keeping the Cheyenne"

"Oh, no. What'd they do with him?"

"Put him in with the others. He was trying to take food to them. They found it out back in kegs, all the garbage from supper just dumped in there. I've a good mind to do me some housecleaning around here. I got me no truck with Injuns, but treating women and kids like that, well, I cain't stomach it."

Tears welled up in her eyes and she brushed them away. No time for such nonsense. She had to do something. Now, during all the hubbub.

"Where's the guard they put on my door?"

Meeker shrugged. "Didn't see no one. He must'a gone to see what the ruckus was about."

"Okay, good. Listen, did you mean what you said?"

He nodded, eyes wary as if reconsidering his earlier outburst. "But I don't aim to get myself killed."

"No one will get killed. We're just going to

177

perform a little rescue mission. We have to get Stone Heart out of there, but I'm afraid in order to do that I'll have to go inside the prison. I'll need you on the outside once I'm in there. Can you do that?"

"I reckon. But that's crazy. You go in there, even if the soldiers allow it, which I cain't see as how the will, them Injuns'll likely scalp you, or worse."

"No, I don't think so."

"Whatcha got in mind?"

"I'm going to turn Stone Heart into a white man right under their noses, and then he can walk out just like any other soldier, and no one will be the wiser. But we'll probably have to wait till things settle down a bit. Now, I want you on the outside so you can take care of my guard when the time comes. He's apt to come back any minute, and I have to be here so they won't come looking for me. Then when all is still for the night, you need to get me out of here and over to the prison barracks. Can you do that?"

He eyed her for a long moment, rubbed at his beard, then up under the fur hat. "I reckon I can. For a genteel white lady, you sure are addled, is all I can say."

"You may be right, but I refuse to sit here and do nothing."

Chapter Twelve

Meeker stared askance at Aiden who wore the uniform she'd stolen for Stone Heart. "You'll never get away with this. It's way too big, the legs are dragging the floor and...and, by God, I have to say this, you don't look like no man."

"We can roll up the legs and push up the sleeves. It's dark, they won't notice."

"They won't notice? A blind man would notice. You look like a kid wearing her daddy's clothes."

Her eyes burned with unshed tears. "Well, what do you suggest, then?"

"I don't know. Maybe we could just shoot the guards and break 'em all out, let 'em fend for themselves. At least they'd die free."

"They'd shoot them down before they got a hundred feet. Meeker, I have to do this. I won't just sit here and wait for something to happen."

"Well, hell's bells," Meeker hollered and began to shuck off his soiled buckskin shirt.

"What're you doing?"

"Oh, don't worry, I ain't gonna ravage you. I'm big enough to wear the blamed thing, and besides, I'm of the male persuasion. Tell me what you want me to do and I'll do it. Shoot me for a fool, but I'll do it."

Clutching the shirt over her breasts, she stared at him in disbelief. "Are you sure?"

"Better do it afore I change my mind," he said and went to work peeling off the pants.

Quickly she turned her back and removed the uniform shirt. If this worked it still wouldn't insure the escape of the prisoners, but it would set Stone Heart free to do what he needed to do. He'd probably get killed in the process, or go away and she'd never see him again. Either way would break her heart.

Without turning around she held out the pants and Meeker took them.

"Keep your back turned till I get my dress back on." She heard the slither of fabric against skin as he slipped into the stolen lieutenant's uniform.

"Go ahead, I ain't looking. But you just remember what you promised. I aim to collect."

If this worked and saved Stone Heart's life, she just might be willing to do what Meeker wanted, heaven help her.

"You got a plan or do we just play this by gosh and by golly?" Meeker asked and finished buttoning the uniform jacket. It was a bit loose, but looked better on him than on her.

She studied him, walked around and around. "I don't know about the beard."

He fisted up the wild growth. "Hold on a minute, you didn't say nothing about scraping off my face. I ain't a gonna do it, and that's all they is to that. Why, I'd freeze plum to death. This here don't come off till summer and the bugs come out."

Holding up a hand to hush him, she circled once more. "It'll be dark. It'll have to do. Yes, I have a plan. You've been sent to the prison by one of the officers to fetch the Cheyenne they just captured. They want to interrogate him. He may know where the others are hiding. Something like that. Then, you just go in, grab Stone Heart and drag him out. Only instead of taking him to the officer, you bring him here. Discreetly."

"You mean without anyone seeing?"

"That's exactly what I mean."

"What if they don't buy it? Ain't they gonna think it peculiar I don't have on a hat?"

"Yes, that's worried me all along. I don't know what to do about it, except I've noticed that the officers tend to choose a hat to their liking. Like maybe there isn't a set rule. You'll have to try and get something. Now, you'll need a name. There are so many men stationed here no one could possibly know them all, so we'll use a real simple name. Lieutenant Jones ought to do."

"What about the name of the officer?"

She had to think about that for a while. "Just say the major and say it real gruff like there'll be hell to pay if you don't get your prisoner."

Going to the window she peered out. "Hurry, get out of here before my guard comes back."

"How'm I supposed to get this Stone Heart fella past the guard?"

"Sneak up on him and bop him on the head or something. You'll think of a way."

"And what happens when he comes to and finds you got yourself a guest?"

"Stop asking questions. We'll deal with it when the time comes. The important thing is to get Stone Heart out of that prison. Now will you quit jawing and get on your way?"

He hadn't taken one step toward the door before a gentle rap sounded. "Aiden? Are you in there? It's Retha. Retha Woods."

"See? I told you," he hissed.

She waved a hand at him. "Keep your mouth shut."

"Yes, Retha, I'm here, but I'm afraid I don't feel too well."

"I'm sorry they put a guard on you, but I had a word with Major Klein and he agreed that was wrong of Wessells. Could I bring you some food? I'm sure they could heat up something at officers' mess."

Mouthing the major's name at Meeker, she replied. "Oh, no, that's okay. I'm just having my monthlies. Nothing to worry about." She wanted desperately to ask Retha to bring something. Stone Heart would be hungry when he arrived. But she feared having Retha present when and if the two men returned. "Thank you so much for your concern, I really do appreciate it."

After a long pause, Retha said, "Well, if you're sure. Perhaps we could get together tomorrow, since you're no longer confined to quarters. There's an ever so nice young man here from back east. He writes for one of those newspapers and came here to report on what's going on with the Cheyenne. I thought you might like to talk to him, considering...well, the way you feel."

"A newspaper reporter?" Aiden's heart leapt in her chest. If the world knew what was going on, would it help or hurt the Cheyenne people? Maybe President Hayes didn't know what these soldiers were up to. She couldn't believe he could condone such cruelty. "Yes, I would like that. Thank you."

"Yes, well, I'll be going then. See you tomorrow for breakfast?"

"Fine, yes, I'll see you in the morning."

Leaning an ear against the wooden panels, she waved Meeker to her side, listened a moment, then unlatched the door and shoved him out. "Don't come back till you bring me Stone Heart. And remember, it's Major Klein that sent you." She flicked at an imaginary speck on the shoulder of the uniform. "Get a hat."

"Yes'm." He gave her a mock salute and shuffled off, looking like anything but a lieutenant in the U. S. Army.

Hugging herself in the icy blast, she watched from the opening until the trapper disappeared into the darkness.

****

Stone Heart glanced around the smoky room.

The prisoners had built a few scrappy fires from what they could find to burn in the ramshackle building and the flickering light revealed a horrendous sight. He could not bear to look long upon the bloody and battered women and children huddled together for warmth. Several men, some with blood drying on wounds not serious enough to send them to the hospital, watched him warily from cross legged positions on the dirt floor. The stench of blood and human waste clogged his nostrils and his stomach heaved.

One of the men introduced himself, spoke in Cheyenne. "I am called The Sioux. The soldiers took me before I could make the river. What are you called and where do you come from?"

After he told his name, Stone Heart waited a long while before receiving a question in reply. "You are of the Northern Cheyenne, of Dull Knife's people?"

He hesitated a moment. "Yes, my mother was White Robe."

"And your father?"

"He is dead, killed at Greasy Creek."

"His name? Dull Knife's son Medicine Club was killed at Greasy Creek. And others of our people."

Stone Heart wanted to lie, to make up the name of a father, but he couldn't bring himself to do so. "He was a white man."

"Ahhh, but you are truly Cheyenne?"

"Yes, I am truly Cheyenne."

"I don't remember you."

"I was shot, they left me for dead along with many others at Hat Creek. I've only now been able to return. I was bringing you food when they captured me."

The Sioux did not speak for a very long time. Nearby a child whimpered and a mother's voice soothed.

"They could use food. Too bad they caught you. It seems I remember a Stone Heart. A son of the long-haired Custer."

While he searched for a suitable reply, raised voices from outside interrupted the conversation.

At his back, another of the men spoke to The Sioux.

"He is white. We do not need him here to spy on us. There is no escape, we must die with honor."

Another voice joined in. "Tangle Hair is right, The Sioux. We need no white men, especially not of the blood of the long hair."

With a sadness in his heart, Stone Heart strained to hear more. He was no longer welcome by these people, who had never before considered his white blood of any consequence. Outside the iron bar clanged to the ground and the doors creaked open.

The soldiers surely weren't bringing more prisoners this time of night.

The women and children in the dark prison wailed. The soldiers had come to kill them. Crying out, they sheltered their frightened children. Soon, they would die.

The Cheyenne words tore at Stone Heart's very soul.

A man in uniform stepped inside. "I come for the one called Stone Heart."

"He is here," The Sioux said before Stone Heart could stop him. No one should be asking for him, and he didn't trust what might be happening. It was clear The Sioux and some of the others wished him gone.

"The major wants to talk to you, now," the young soldier said. "Well, get up, breed, get a move on."

He did as he was bade, stumbled through the doorway where he was grabbed by a bearded man in a lieutenant's uniform and a hat too small for him. In the darkness he couldn't make out his features, but thought the smell familiar.

"Come along." The man grabbed his arm hard.

An inclination to fight back, to stand his ground, held him fast against the other's grip. "What does he want, the major?"

"Shut up and move," the man growled, shoved him hard through the door.

For the briefest of instants he wanted to charge the two soldiers, let one of them put a bullet in him now. Stop this hopeless quest once and for all. But hope continued to flare in his heart for the remainder of these brave people and he wished only to see them set free. So weary his bones ached, he stumbled along ahead of the bearded man. They walked along the perimeter of the road, away from the watch fires and a few sentries.

"Are you sure the major asked for Stone Heart?"

"Sure as rain."

"Where are we going?"

Glancing around in all directions, Stone Heart saw that they were headed away from officer's quarters. "Where are we going?"

A sentry approached and the bearded man dragged him into an alleyway. "Be quiet."

"What's going on here? If you're going to kill me, do it and be done."

"Be quiet, will ye? She sent me for you. It's me, Meeker."

A'den. She was the only one who could arrange something like this and figure she would get away with it.

When the sentry passed by, his captor signaled him to remain and peered out along the road in both directions. "Okay, all clear. Quit asking so many questions. She sent me to get you out and you're out. What she's gonna do with you I have no idea."

"By 'she' you mean A'den?"

"Reckon that's her name. She's Mrs. Meeker to

some." The man chortled under his breath.

"What has she got in mind?"

"Blamed if I know."

A'den's rescue both angered and pleased Stone Heart. He had wanted to learn more about Dull Knife and those who had escaped after the breakout, yet he looked forward to seeing the red-haired woman again. In his heart he knew that such a thing could only bring further disaster, but God help him, he yearned for her touch, the feel of her soft hands against his flesh.

It would seem he had not cast off his old life quite so completely as he'd thought. Making love to her had been a big mistake. Now he couldn't forget how it felt to be in her arms. He desperately longed to hold her, lie in the soft, sweet smelling bed. Put behind him the filth of the prison he'd just left, the strife and horrid conditions that would soon be his lot if he remained with the Cheyenne. And most surely, he would soon die.

He was no longer sure that was what he wanted. At the same time, he felt a traitor to his people to be thinking this way.

"Well, lookee there. She was right, there's no guard."

Stone Heart left his ruminations behind and saw that they were approaching A'den's quarters.

Meeker's arm shot out, blocking his way. "Hold up just a minute, here in the shadows while I take a better look around. She'll have my head if I get you caught."

Stone Heart leaned against the barracks in the darkness, his every breath ragged. Weariness seeped into his bones and he longed only to sleep where it was warm. Hunger squeezed at his gut. This was no way to have to live. He cursed the life with the white man that had made him soft.

When Meeker came back to fetch him, he

stumbled along in the man's wake. After a short tapping, she swung the door open and dragged him inside. Leaving Meeker to see to its closing, she threw her arms around him and he embraced her gratefully. Her smell, her touch, the warmth of the fire lulled him, and he felt his knees buckling despite a staunch effort to remain upright.

"Help me put him to bed, Meeker," she said.

He was only half conscious of sinking onto the soft mattress while she took off his clothes and moccasins. Heard Meeker adding wood to the stove while she pulled the covers up under his chin. Her soft, moist lips covered his and her fingers trailed through his hair. His mouth reached for the kiss, then fell away. He took A'den's caress with him into the sheltering darkness where peace and love greeted him.

Aiden regarded the sleeping man, glanced at Meeker, who had exchanged the uniform for his comfortable trapper's gear. "I need some shears."

"Well, don't look at me. I put my life on the line to bring him here."

She stared at him.

He looked down at his feet, shuffled. "Where would I get shears, anyway?"

"I don't know. Is there a barber? There must be. Or maybe at the livery. Or, maybe you could just walk into the mercantile and buy some."

"Now, there's an idee. What would I use for money?"

"I don't know that, either. What do you usually use for money? When you buy other things. Surely you do buy things."

"When I have pelts to trade, certainly I do."

"And you must have pelts. You'd been trapping a good part of the season when we came across you."

"And what pelts I had were left out there when we were dragged to this godforsaken place."

"Could you go get them?" Aiden rose, went to the bed and lay a palm on Stone Heart's forehead.

He stirred but didn't awaken, and she gazed at his face, so keenly sketched in repose. Though gaunt from his recent ordeal, he was beautiful. He would kill himself trying to save these people, and there was nothing she could do about that but help him. The lack of choices left her completely frustrated. And to think all she'd wanted was to go home to Saint Louis what seemed a lifetime ago. Now she loved this man and could see nothing beyond that love.

"Go get them, then," she whispered and moved away from the sleeping man.

"Do what?"

"Go get the damned pelts, Meeker."

"Now, lookee here, missy."

"And please stop calling me 'missy.' Go get the pelts, bring them back, take them to the mercantile and get some shears and some supplies for us to give to the Cheyenne."

He stared at her, dark eyes slitted. "You want me to walk all night, haul them pelts back here so you can have a pair of shears and them blamed savages can have some supplies?"

"Meeker."

"What good will supplies do without animals to haul them?"

"You get the supplies...sugar, flour, meal, whatever you can, and I'll see to getting us animals."

"Even if the pelts are still out there, and they well might not be if another trapper has come along, and say I do get the supplies, how on God's green earth do you expect to get the animals?"

She wanted to throw something at the man who continued to be as logical as she should be. He was perfectly right, but she didn't care.

"I'll steal them," she said curtly. "Now get going.

You can be back by morning if you hurry."

"And I reckon I'll have to steal me a horse to haul them pelts back here."

"You didn't have a horse when we ran across you."

Again he slitted that look at her. The one that told her she was winning the battle even though he didn't much like it. He wasn't half as tough as he liked to pretend.

"No, I reckon I didn't. I was prepared to tote it all to the Red Cloud Agency so I'd have something to dicker for me some fresh animals. Now you're asking me to give it all away so you and that'n can save a bunch of scruffy Injuns that'll be dead by spring no matter what you do. Does that seem right?" He rocked to his toes and crammed his fur hat down on his head. Went right on talking without giving her a chance to reply.

"No, sir, it don't seem right. But all the same, I reckon I'm gone, cause the onliest way I can put a stop to your haranguing is to go get them pelts. Then maybe you'll give me some peace. I know now why I never took me no woman on the trail with me. I surely do. And without a horse, by God, I cain't be back by morning, neither."

The door slammed behind him, cutting off further conversation.

She sighed, undressed and crawled in bed with her brave Cheyenne warrior, curled along the curve of his warm body and drifted off to sleep.

Sometime in the night Stone Heart roused enough to feel her lying there against him. Though exhausted, he turned over and wrapped her in his arms, tucking her head against his chest. Despite the hunger in his belly and the weariness in every muscle, holding her felt better than anything else he could even imagine. Guilt dwelt in his soul, yet visions of the Cheyenne locked in their dreadful prison could not change how being with this woman made him feel. Alive and hopeful of a future.

He didn't awaken again until dawn when the bugles sounded through the morning silence. Early sunlight slanted through panes of glass, crossed the floor and climbed over the foot of their bed. Fear shook him by the shoulders. Someone would see him. She lay between him and the small window, yet anybody could glance in and see them there together. How had this come to be? That he lay in the bed of this white woman when he had set out only to atone for his father's sins and nothing more.

Outside soldiers moved to and fro, headed for their various duties following formation.

Snatching the blankets over their heads, he whispered urgently in her ear, "A'den, wake up."

She squirmed against him, made a humming sound that sent moist, warm breath over his flesh. Her softness pressed so close, erupted waves of desire. He wanted to remain there with her forever, forget the cruel world that waited beyond this place. Yet he could not.

"What's wrong?" She blinked at him, sending back his reflection in the green pools of her eyes.

"Someone will see us, through the window."

"Uh huh. So stay under here with me." She playfully tugged at his braid. "No one goes around looking in windows in a place like this. They won't know who you are, under here like this with me."

Another moment stolen with her. He longed to obey his body's urge to explore all the secret places she had given to him alone. Looking deeply into her eyes, he cupped the side of her face.

"I missed you," he told her.

"Even so, you'll go away again. And I do understand. It has to be. But there's nothing you can do now, not until dark."

He sighed and pulled her close. "I don't think I

can do them any good at all. It's so hopeless. They have no food, no water. They're sick and exhausted, poorly dressed. There are children to think of. And they don't want my help because I'm white. Told me to go away and leave them be."

For one instant, hope filled her. They could go away together, forget all this and build themselves a life. Then she remembered the young Cheyenne mother carrying her dead child, and the tiny little girl with nowhere to go, the expression on her face one of numb acceptance. No child should have to feel like that. She should be running in the sunshine, playing, laughing, growing up, for God's sake.

Tears filled her eyes. "Oh, but you have to do something, we have to. I could never live with myself if I could have done something and didn't. We could never be happy. I want us to be together. Forever. We must do the one before we can search for our own happiness. We have to try to do what is right. We have to help them get free."

He held her so close that for a moment she feared something might crack. She could scarcely breathe. "*Ne mohotatse,*" he whispered. "I love you."

"Oh, I love you too. I didn't set out to, but I surely do."

For a long while they lay wrapped in the warmth of their love, oblivious to the outside world, as if, she thought, they savored this moment against a future that might well see them parting. This was a dangerous thing they planned, and it could mean his death, hers, or both. Even if the Cheyenne didn't want his help, he was bound by honor to give it, and she could no more back away now than he could. And the soldiers would do everything they could to stop them.

"I think my idea, to get you in uniform where you can move about without arousing suspicion, will work if you'll only give it a try."

He glanced once more at the window that exposed them to anyone who cared to look, snugged deeper under the blankets. "Go on."

"I sent Meeker after his pelts, you know, the ones he had in the shelter when the soldiers came. He can trade them for supplies for the Cheyenne. I have the uniform. When he returns we can cut your hair and get you outfitted. I'm afraid you're going to have to figure out the rest. You know, get the soldiers accustomed to your presence while we make a plan? I told Meeker I'd steal some horses to carry the supplies and—"

"Whoa," he said, horrified by her offer. "Stealing horses is a hanging offense. We'll think of something else. I won't have you put in that position."

She went on as if he hadn't spoken. "There's a reporter here, from a newspaper back east. I think we might be able to stir up some sympathy for the Cheyenne."

"A reporter? I wondered why they were taking the wounded to the hospital. Now I know. They can't let folks back home think they are barbarians out here. But I've an idea most people won't care. As a race the white man is entirely self-centered. It explains their acceptance of the idea of manifest destiny."

"That's not true. Throughout history conquerors have treated the losing faction like animals with no feelings. It's the same way in Europe. Winner take all. Most wars are fought for land and that translates to riches. The Indians did the same thing, I'm sure, before the white man ever came here."

Grimly, he nodded. "I'm not sure I agree with you. But it doesn't matter now. The Indians have to realize that the white man will never stop coming. All I want is to set these people free so they can go home. After living white, I know the end is near for their way of life. I fear that eventually Crook is going to send these people down south, just like was ordered in the first place. They can't let a poor little band of half-dead Cheyenne dictate terms of their imprisonment. But they'll fight back, to the last dying one. General Crook is a fool. He'd do better to let them go home and put an end to this, but it's gone too far and he's embarrassed by the breakout.

"Go ahead and speak to the reporter. Maybe some stories about what's really going on out here on the frontier could stir up some repercussions in Washington. But I still don't think so." He hugged her fiercely. "I would rather see you doing that than running around like some savage stealing horses."

"And you'll wear the uniform and let me cut your hair? You think that's a good idea?"

He pretended to think it over for a moment. "It's a very bad idea, but it could work. At least it's the only plan we have at the moment. What are you going to do, hack it off with a saber?"

"No, Meeker is bringing shears."

The remark silenced him. By God, she had this all figured out. He wanted to ask how she'd fallen back in with the truculent mountain man, but decided not to bother. It was bad enough that she was going to cut his hair and put him in a soldier's uniform. Send him back into the white world he so detested. He really didn't want to know too much about how she managed to convince Meeker to get him out of the prison.

A knock on the door interrupted their conversation.

Sitting up, Aiden called out. "Who is it?"

"Retha. Are you ready for breakfast?"

Though the woman was kind, she did manage to arrive at the most indelicate of moments.

Under the covers Stone Heart brushed fingers over her stomach, and she tried not to moan with pleasure. "I'll meet you there in a few minutes. I'm not quite dressed."

"Are you feeling better?"

"Oh, yes. I'm feeling fine."

He trailed his tongue along the laddering of her ribs and over her nipple.

She captured his hand, held it tightly, whispered, "Stop that."

"What?" Retha asked.

"Nothing."

He lay his cheek against her belly and cupped a hand over the mound of her sex. It was difficult to muffle her reaction. Going to breakfast became the very last thing in the world she wanted to do.

"You taste so good."

"I have to get dressed."

"Not yet," he said, "Not yet."

She gave herself to him wholly. She might have this man for only this day, or she might manage to keep him close a while longer. Whatever, she would accept it, for she knew that to have him for the brief moments they could steal was by far better than to never have known such an intensely beautiful love. She also knew that when she lost him, life would never be the same again.

It was a long time before she went to breakfast, leaving him there to wait for Meeker's return. He promised he would not leave again, and she believed him because she had no choice.

Chapter Thirteen

Outside the door to her quarters, Aiden balanced a plate of food and a cup of coffee and tapped at the panels with one toe.

"Let me in." She listened, tapped again. Her head throbbed with apprehension. Had he broken his promise to stay? Or worse, had they somehow found him and taken him back to the prison? She murmured his name against the door, and it swung open to reveal an empty room.

"Get in here," his voice urged.

She let out a surprised "Oh" and moved quickly through the opening. Turned at the sound of the door closing. He stood there in his buckskins, an apologetic expression on his gaunt features.

Lifting his shoulders, he grabbed the fork lying in the plate of food. "I didn't want anyone to see me. How did you manage this?" Without waiting for her explanations, he dug into a slab of fried corn meal mush slathered in molasses, picked up a chunk of beef steak with the other hand and bit off a huge bite.

The plate held out as bait, she led him away from the window. "Come, sit over here at the table where you can't be seen."

He followed, stuffing food in his mouth.

"Dear God, I'm sorry," she said when he lowered himself into the chair without missing a bite. "How long has it been since you ate?"

Mouth full, he stared at her, shrugged, grabbed up a fat biscuit and bit into it.

He devoured everything on the plate, and she

remained silent until he chewed and swallowed the last morsel and picked up the cup of coffee.

"It was all I could bring. I'm sorry."

Digging at something caught in his tooth, he said, "Stop saying you're sorry. There's more than enough sorrow to go around. How did you manage to bring me that?"

She grinned slyly. "Told them my husband was feeling under the weather. Asked them if I could bring him some food to keep up his strength."

"Your husband?" He gaped at her.

"Oh, I guess you don't know about that, do you?"

"Well, I don't know about any husband."

She told him about pretending she and Meeker were married when the soldiers came because of her fear they'd think her a loose woman and want her to service them.

"And what did he think of that?"

"At the time, nothing. Well, actually he was knocked out and didn't know about it till later. Then he got the idea that maybe he could collect on his husbandly rights, but I set him straight there, too. He's really an old softy."

Snorting, he finished the coffee and set down the cup. "So now how is it you've got him running around at your beck and call?"

She waited a moment, caught his gaze and said in all seriousness, "Hope, I guess."

He laughed, a joyous sound that reminded her of brighter days, the sweetest of times. "Hope? That's great. If only we all could exist on such a simple thing as that."

Cupping the side of his face, she said, "Yes, if only."

He covered her hand. "And what do you hope, A'den?"

"I think you know." She leaned down and kissed him, tasting the coffee on his lips.

For a long moment, he held on to the kiss, but didn't pursue it when she broke contact. "You need to go home," he said. "That's where you should be, not out here in this wilderness. It isn't kind to women."

"I know. But with all that's happened, going home has become a childish dream. I'm a grown woman and need to make my own home now. That's what I set out to do in the first place...with Stephan. I guess my initial reaction to being abandoned was to want to run home to my parents. But now...now...well, after this is all over, I'd like to make a home of my own somewhere. A comfortable house with a fireplace and a yard. A garden maybe. And children. I'd love children of my own. I'm not sure I can be my parents' child anymore, with all that's happened."

Her eyes burned and she moved away from him, went to the window and stared at the churned up, dirty snow and the monotonous buildings stretching across the bleak plains. "Not here, though. Not here."

If offered the chance to return to Saint Louis, she would go. Of that he was certain. It was just that she always tried to make the best of things. "Where would you like to be?" he asked softly, hope a broken thing.

"I don't know. Someplace not quite so brutal. Someplace safe."

"There is no such place." His voice took on an edge, and she was sorry she'd let the conversation drift.

"They don't want my help, you know? The Cheyenne. Their loathing for the white man is understandable. And they've decided I'm white. My being a son of Custer only adds to their dilemma. You can't blame them, after all that has happened at the hands of the white man. Though being a half-breed is only a problem in the white world, my connection to Custer has always been a problem for them. The Cheyenne believe that when a man fathers a child with one of their women he becomes family, one of them, and so it's been so hard for them to watch these children of Custer growing up in their villages while he runs around massacring the people. They never understood, and now most hate him in spite of the family thing. So it follows they'd hate me."

"How many children did he...I mean, with the Cheyenne women?" It wasn't only the chill in the room that caused her to shiver, but she went to add wood to the stove anyway. Perhaps a warm fire would help drive the dread from her heart.

"We can't know for sure. There is his son Yellow Swallow, who is nine, and we heard of a girl child named Yellow Tail, but have not seen her. I was born in 1857 from probably his earliest experience with a Cheyenne woman, when he was not much more than a boy himself, perhaps eighteen or nineteen, and traveling home for the summers from West Point." He rose, as if sitting in the chair did not suit him, stared beyond her with that vacant, savage look he sometimes had.

Mentally, she calculated the years. That made Stone Heart only twenty-two. My, and her getting ready to celebrate her thirtieth birthday. Perhaps she was too old for him. Gazing at his glorious physique, the golden tone of his skin that made him look like a white man who spent his days in the sun. The thick blond-streaked braid down his back. The nostalgic glimmer in his eyes. The age difference didn't matter at all, for he had an ancient soul. It was a shock, that's all, learning how young he was.

He continued the tale of his father. "One day, when I was perhaps thirteen summers, he returned to my mother's village. He had become a soldier, and he took me from her. Sent me east to live with some white people who could have no children."

"And they raised you?"

"Yes. They tried to bring me up in his image. Sent me to West Point as a white boy. Warned me many times that I must pretend to be white if I were to get along in their world." He grabbed a fistful of his hair. "Because of this I was believed. Many Cheyenne have mixed with the white, our skin is not so dark. Like adding cream to coffee. Our hair is often lighter. But this...the others have the same color hair, as if he left a brand to mock their heritage."

"Did you...like him? I mean before he did all those horrid things."

"I never saw him again, but I hated him for what he did to me and my mother. After a year at the academy I ran away. I went back to see her, but she had died of the smallpox. It is said, though I cannot prove it, that he delivered blankets to the Sioux and Cheyenne infected with that terrible disease, in an effort to wipe them out without firing a shot."

"How awful, if it's true. No wonder he is so hated." She paused, touched him like she once soothed her baby brother. "So you were white most of your adult life? Whatever made you return to...to such a hard life?"

His lips tightened and he looked away. "It was all a lie, that life. They were training us to go into battle against the Indians. I could not be, did not want to be like my father. When I learned of the horrible massacres he'd led, I knew I just couldn't live that lie any longer. Nothing matters now but that I help my people. The rest is gone, finished. That is why it is so difficult for me to put on this uniform and play white again. I vowed never to return to that life. I hate it."

"But you are going to do it. To help your people even though they do not wish it?"

"If I am not Cheyenne to them, then I must help them as a white man. Besides, I met you. Things are different."

Outside a horse whinnied, wood crackled in the stove, and she held her breath through the silence, finally was able to speak.

"And what does that mean?"

"I'm not sure, yet."

"Well, when you are, I wish you'd let me know." She tried to keep the anger from her voice, but it was there and he caught it. He had never spoken of their future together, never even said they might have one.

"A'den, please come here."

With the front window now in full shade the room was gloomy, and she couldn't make out his face. She rose from kneeling in front of the stove and reached for the hand he held out to her.

Starved for the affection he offered, she went to him. Even as she moved into the circle of his arms, she feared their love could never be. For despite what he said, he was and would always remain a Cheyenne warrior. Yet she couldn't stop the hope anymore than she could pull away.

He held her close, his arms like steel bands, and she leaned against the warmth of his chest, closed her eyes, and begged God for just a little mercy. Enough to see them through this terrible time. It wasn't a sin to want happiness, to yearn for some peace with the man you loved, and so that's what she prayed for. She knew, as she always had, that it was up to her to grab at her own happiness, up to Stone Heart to do the same. The only thing God could do was catch them if they fell, pick them up, and set them on their feet again. she could only pray He would allow them to walk the same path.

After Stephan left her, she had followed the path on which she was set, and now here she was, prepared to do the same thing yet again. Wiser of her if she simply caught the first stage that broke through the drifts of snow and went home to Saint Louis. But she had never been very wise.

She stirred in his arms.

"What?" he asked, lips in her hair.

"I have an idea."

"Yes." The flat of his hand spread over her back, still refusing to let her go.

"The reporter?"

"Yes?"

She struggled to lean away, looked up into his face. Wanted to see his expression when she said what she was about to say.

He loosened his grip a bit, lifted her chin and stared down into her eyes. "What is it?"

"If I could get him to come here, talk to you, I think that would make more of an impact than my talking to him."

Eyes slitted, he let her go. "I do not think so."

He reverted so easily to his Cheyenne way of speaking, moving, thinking.

"Why not?"

"I'm not sure why not, except that I'd feel like a freak of some kind. Him dissecting me, digging out all my feelings. I know how some of them are. When they get the truth they exaggerate or even change it. Besides, suppose he runs to Wessells with the story. They'd have me in chains before you could snap your fingers."

His refusal angered her. "All you want is to kill or be killed," she said sharply.

"And all you care about is keeping me here, with you." The realization of what the reporter's presence meant hit him, and without thinking what the outcome might be, he blurted it out to her. "His coming here. This means you could leave. The roads must be clear. You could return to Saint Louis any time."

She blinked, her mouth forming an O around the words she had been about to utter, that there was nothing wrong with her trying to keep Stone Heart there with her. Safe, away from harm.

"I...I no longer want to go home. You heard me say that."

"But I didn't believe you. Looking at you now, I still don't. Go home, A'den. Go back where you belong and leave this to me. I have to finish what I started."

"There's nothing wrong with my wanting to keep you safe."

"Not unless it gets my people killed." Her skirting the issue of going home convinced him that it was precisely what she wanted to do.

"What will get your people killed has little to do with what we might or might not do. Not now. Don't you see that? These soldiers are going to do what they set out to do. They'll never give in. You said so yourself. The most we can do is cause them some trouble."

He whirled from her. "Or kill as many of them as I can before they get me. I don't need a woman telling me what is right."

"No, I know you don't. Go on, getting killed will help your people, all right."

He slammed his way to the door, jerked it open without even looking to see who might be out there. "Go home, A'den before you get hurt."

"Please, stay." The door slammed, cutting her plea in half.

Fear knifed through her heart and she ran to the window to watch him stride away from the barracks, out in the open in broad daylight, like he hadn't a care in the world. At any moment she expected to see soldiers surround him, take him prisoner. But none did, and he disappeared around the corner of a long building across the way.

She had not gone after Stephan when he deserted her, but she would not do the same with Stone Heart.

Throwing on the cloak Retha had loaned her, she hurried out onto the street. She would find him, make him see reason. She couldn't help but believe that the story he could tell the reporter would sway many people. He was the half-breed son of George Armstrong Custer, and could speak as a white man with the understanding of a Cheyenne. They would listen and put pressure on the president to do something about this dreadful situation. But first she wanted to talk to the reporter, feel him out. Even though she wanted this desperately, she would not put Stone Heart in jeopardy.

The man in the mercantile told her she had just missed the reporter. "He writes for the *Evening Star* in Washington City. Came in on a stage from the depot down on the Platte." the man said. "Wonder why such an important newspaper is interested in a scraggly band of half-dead Indians?"

"It just might be that somebody cares what happens to them," she retorted. Came in on the stage, he'd said, and she managed to ignore it. For the moment.

Back out on the boardwalk, she glanced over the rows of buildings toward the distant horizon. The snow and mud, the drab surroundings. Such a remote, ugly place. Perhaps she should go home. She couldn't live like this, or like Stone Heart and his people. There was really nothing for her here but heartbreak and lost love. Her gaze drifted back toward her own mean quarters where Retha Woods and a citified young man stood outside her door.

Lifting her skirt, she crossed the road through

chunks of mud-colored ice. Reaching the easier footing of the boardwalk, she ran, waving her arms and yelling in a quite unladylike fashion.

Retha's hand, poised to knock on the door, fell away, and she watched Aiden approach with a somewhat astounded expression.

"My, but aren't you all a-twitter? We were looking for you. This young man is the reporter I told you about."

Aiden panted out a reply. "Yes, I know. I saw you." She grabbed the astounded man's extended hand and pumped it vigorously. "I was looking for you. We have to talk...I mean, could we talk?"

Retha eyed her strangely. "This gentleman is Marcus Young with the *Evening Star* in Washington City. Mr. Young, this is my newest friend, Aiden. I'm afraid I don't remember your last name, dear."

"Connor. My name is Aiden Connor. I'm from Saint Louis. Won't you come in? I mean, if you have the time, I'd like to speak to you." She glanced toward Retha. "In private, if you don't mind."

"Well," the young woman huffed. No doubt disappointed to be left out, she remained gracious nevertheless.

"I'm sorry," Aiden said. "I don't mean to hurt your feelings. It's just that...well, there are some things I need to tell Mr. Young here that are better not repeated. They could only cause you grief, Retha. You do understand, don't you?"

Though itching to get the reporter alone, Aiden took the time necessary to assuage Retha's injured feelings. She certainly didn't want to alienate the only friend she'd made here.

Obviously miffed, Retha finally gave in. "I'm sure he'll be interested in your thoughts on this unfortunate situation with those poor savages. I can't imagine what you might say that I shouldn't hear, but never mind. I'll leave you two alone."

Aiden took her hand, gazed into her troubled eyes. "Thank you so much. I'll never forget what you've done for me, it's just that this...well, if you don't know certain things, then you won't be in trouble later."

The gray eyes widened. "I can't imagine what you might be talking about. Oh, never mind. I'll just be on my way."

Aiden turned back to the reporter. The dapper young man, who looked like a greenhorn in pin-striped pants, wrinkled white shirt, and vest, tilted his black bowler and smiled. "You certainly have my curiosity stirred up. I'd be most interested in what you have to say. I seem to be running up against it trying to get any of the officers or men to talk much to me. They took me over to the hospital, let me see that they're caring for these poor souls, but wouldn't let me talk to anyone there.

"The president is concerned, and I believe a story or two out of this remote fort about what is really going on with these so-called savages, might make him sit up and take notice." He beamed as if he personally had the president's ear.

"But not concerned enough to send an emissary, it would appear," she said. "Oh, never mind. Let's go inside out of this cold. I'd be happy to tell you what I think about this abhorrent situation." Though sure his reports would be self-serving, Aiden supposed they might inform the rest of the world, including President Hayes. There was nothing like pressure from voters to sway a politician.

She spoke to the reporter at great length about what she had seen, then cleared her throat. Heart hammering until she could barely hear herself speak, she got around to what was important.

"I...uh, I have a friend...he...well, this is very difficult. I must have your word that you won't go to any of the officers here on the post with what I am

205

about to tell you. It's very important, a matter of life or death, you might say."

Young leaned forward in the straight chair, pad on his knee, pencil poised. "I never divulge where I get my information. However, I must also say that your telling me something someone else told you is not reliable enough to print."

"Oh, that's exactly why I wanted to speak to you in private. I think I can arrange for you to speak to him directly, if only I can convince him that you won't trick him or twist his words. If he is caught, he may well be killed. It's that serious."

Young gulped audibly and his eyes shimmered. She was right about one thing, he wanted this story bad. The desire was there in his eyes, the way his fingers gripped his silly little hat, the nervous licking of thin lips. Just how truthful he would be, she could only guess. But if he refused to take secondhand stories as fact, then he must be somewhat honorable.

"Just who is this...this gentleman?"

She gnawed at her lip, shifted in the chair. "He is a Cheyenne, but his father is General Custer."

"George Armstrong Custer?" Young's close-set eyes bulged.

She merely nodded.

"My God." Young breathed out the exclamation. "Can he prove it?"

"Oh, I seriously doubt that he can, but I think what he has to tell you will be enough proof in itself. You can check it out, though I'm sure the trail has been obliterated quite well."

"Do you know this for a fact?"

Twisting her hands in her lap, she finally had to admit that she didn't. "Only from the stories he's told me. You have to listen to him. You have to tell his story, these people's story to the world. They're going to kill what few of them remain. Dull Knife's

Beautiful People will be no more if someone doesn't do something."

"Morningstar," he murmured.

"Who?"

"Dull Knife is only a nickname. His true name is Morningstar. Tell me, does...ah, your friend...does he know if Dull Knife is still alive?"

"I'm not sure."

"I'd go anywhere, promise anything, do anything, to talk to Morningstar if he is alive. And I swear to almighty God I would never tell where he is."

"Will you make that same promise about my friend, Stone Heart?"

Young scribbled the name in his pad, stared at her intently. "I most certainly will. You find him, set it up. I'll be there, and I won't tell anything he does not wish me to, not to a living soul, ever."

For a long while she stared into his earnest face, could read no deceit written there. Only a burning desire to find out the truth. At last she made up her mind.

"Okay. I'll have to find him, that could take a while. You come back here tonight after dark. I'll do my best to have him here. Just please be careful. If you do anything to put him in danger or get him hurt, I'll kill you myself. That's my promise."

He blinked in surprise, then allowed a small, wry grin. "Why, I do believe you would."

Closing the door behind the reporter, she stood there with both hands gripping the latch. She could never find Stone Heart. All she could hope was that he came back after dark when he knew Meeker was due to return.

On the chance that he would return, Aiden answered the call to supper by hurrying to the mess hall to fetch two plates of food, again begging off for her imaginary husband, who remained under the weather.

Despite her protests, a young private accompanied her to help carry the food. She could only hope that if Stone Heart were hanging around, he would remain out of sight. It was entirely possible that he would be inside, and she could barely breathe as she reached for the latch, speaking loudly to the private as she did so. At least she could give him a chance to jump in bed and cover up. She imagined falling down in front of the young man to keep him from stepping inside and finding her Cheyenne savage. She couldn't help but smile at the vision, even as she slipped the latch.

Even with the door cracked open she could not see enough of the room to know if it was empty. Suppose he was in there, sitting at the table, big as you please? What would this young private do? She turned to him with a wide smile.

"It was so sweet of you to help me carry all this. I never would have made it by myself. I'm sure my husband will be appreciative too." Sticking her head inside, she saw only a pile of unmoving blankets.

"Sweetheart, dinner," she called gaily. "He's probably still sleeping. Just put those on the table there. Thank you again."

The private, a tall, gangly, red-haired youth, glanced at the bed then back at her, flushed and scuttled from the room without saying a word.

"Oh, my goodness," she said and fanned herself with an open hand, trying to steady her thumping heart.

When the lumps on the bed remained still, she went over to shake him awake. So sure that he had come back and was hiding under there. She found nothing but pillows and covers, all in a bunch. No Stone Heart.

Where was he, and why didn't Meeker return? Nothing could force either of them to come back to her, and she feared that neither would. All Meeker had to do was fetch his pelts and keep right on going. At the Red Cloud Agency he could trade his furs for a horse and supplies and be on his way. He owed her nothing. As for Stone Heart, his one driving desire was to rescue the Cheyenne, and he thought he knew better than anyone how to accomplish that. He might well have gone back to the place where they were being held, for he seemed to have a wish to die with them. Perhaps he thought he could atone for the evil his father had done only by such a death.

Sitting at the table without touching the food, she waited. An ashy dusk crept out of the corners to surround her, the windows grew dark, but she didn't bother to rise and light a lamp. She was alone again, waiting for a man to return and fill her life. And she hated the feeling. Once she put him in touch with this reporter, she would do as he asked and go home. Placing herself in this situation where she depended on the whims of a man again was foolish. Let him ride to his destiny. She had her own survival to worry about. She did not belong out here, that was obvious.

Activity on the roads and byways curving through the large fort grew less frantic after dark. Here and there soldiers walked in groups of twos and threes. Windows in most of the businesses were darkened, with only the places of entertainment showing light. The officers club and the recreational facility where enlisted men played cards, dominoes and various other games were open when Stone Heart returned from reconnoitering the fort. He had planned a route of escape from the prison, using various buildings as shields. Even as he did so, he was filled with a tremendous doubt that he could bring this off. What few of his people were left were weak from hunger and hiding out in sub zero weather could well mean their deaths. The most important thing was not to attract attention in the first place. To sneak away with no one being the wiser. He tried to imagine quieting crying babies and upset children, dragging them into the dark, frigid night. Maybe A'den's way was best. Go back there, speak to the reporter about all that had happened. Perhaps put on the white man's uniform so he could remain apprised of Wessell's plans. In that way he could save what remained of Dull Knife's Beautiful People. There had already been so many deaths.

Two hundred eighty-four men, women, and children left the south country six moons ago. How many were left he would have no idea until the last of them still hiding out in the hills were brought in. That afternoon, he heard sporadic gunfire from beyond the bluffs. The soldiers were still out there, still shooting his people. How many days had passed since the outbreak and the ensuing battle he did not know. Eight, ten, twelve?

He would ask A'den, if he saw her again. Thinking of her brought a dull sorrow to his heart. Why did he have to find a woman he could love when it was too late? And what a cruel joke it was a white woman who deserved all the things he could not give her.

As it grew dark, he made his way cautiously toward her quarters. Though he felt guilty lying in a warm bed and eating hot food while his people suffered, he was drawn back to her.

He told himself he returned to find a way to set them free, but he knew it was her beautiful eyes and warm, soft touch that called to him. And he was ashamed.

He waited in the alleyway until some soldiers passed, then crept out and headed for her door. A man crossed the common diagonally from the direction of the mercantile, and he ducked into the shadows to watch.

He appeared headed for A'den's place. And surely he was. When she opened the door, lamplight showed him that the man was the trapper Meeker, and he hurried along to get there before she closed the door.

He stepped inside on the heels of the bearded man but scarcely spoke before A'den was on him.

"I thought you'd left. Oh, come on in. Look, Meeker is back, too. Isn't this wonderful? There for a while I was afraid neither of you would return. And look, here you both are. I have food, food. Sit down, eat. You must both be starved."

She released him, steered them both to the table.

"I could eat a buffaler," Meeker said. "Never expected this kind of greeting." He picked up a fork and dived into the steaming plate of food.

"I wasn't sure you'd come back."

"Nearly didn't," he said past a mouthful of meat and beans.

"I meant Stone Heart, but that's okay."

Stone Heart hadn't spoken at all, but the food smelled good and he began to eat, watching A'den as she danced around and babbled. She'd been afraid he wasn't coming back, and he almost hadn't. Still wondered if he should have.

Why didn't she go home where she belonged, so he could stop feeling so responsible for her? So damned drawn to her? Why did he keep coming back?

Someone tapped on the door and all three froze.

Gaze darting between Meeker and Stone Heart, she rubbed the palms of her hands down the front of her dress. Moved to the door.

"Who is it?"

"Marcus Young."

"Are you alone?"

"Yes, ma'am."

With hands that trembled she slipped the latch and let the young reporter in.

Chapter Fourteen

For a moment Young stood just inside the door, huddled inside his coat. His cheeks glowed red from the cold. She smiled, invited him to remove his things. He took off his bowler and leather gloves and rubbed his hands together vigorously. Across the room, Meeker and Stone Heart paused in like positions, forks suspended above half-empty plates, astounded gazes pinned on the newcomer. The only difference between the two was Stone Heart appeared ready to fight or flee.

She tried to reassure him. "He's a friend. I invited him."

"I see you have a guest," Young said when no one spoke.

Turning from Stone Heart's accusatory glare, she managed to reply. "Oh, do take off your coat, Mr. Young. This is the man I spoke to you about, Stone Heart, and this is a friend, Josiah Meeker. I'd forgotten he was coming. I do apologize, and hope you don't mind. He's been...uh, helping us."

"Gentlemen," Young said. He shrugged out of his coat, allowed Aiden to take his things, which she laid on the end of the bed. "Please continue eating. I just finished myself. Good, wholesome food they serve out here. Puts meat on your bones." He slapped his slightly rounded stomach with both hands. When neither man replied, he removed a pad and pencil from his waistcoat pocket.

Caught between the challenging stares of the three men, Aiden felt like a referee in an Irish bare knuckle fight. A beat or two of silence was all she

213

could endure.

"Oh, for goodness sake," she finally said. "You two finish your supper and Mr. Young and I will visit. He's really come to speak to Stone Heart."

"Who did not plan to be here," Stone Heart grumbled. He went back to his food, scowling occasionally in her direction.

She offered Young the only other chair, a rocker near the bed, and perched on the edge of the mattress, hands folded primly on her knees.

"I apologize for the accommodations, Mr. Young. I did not expect to be traveling to this place, so brought no furnishings with me."

Obviously, the reporter had been in worse situations, for he took this one in stride, opening the pad on his knees and poising the pencil above the white paper. "No bother. At least it's warm. I'll just get a bit of information about you while these gentlemen finish their meal, and then perhaps Mr. Stone Heart and I will talk, if he's amenable."

"Not particularly," Stone Heart grumbled, took another bite and glowered some more. His demeanor reminded her of the first day they'd met when she found him in the shelter, wild, unkempt, and ready to slit her throat. Only now he looked so tired, almost as if one more disappointment might break him.

"I do believe I can assist with your cause, if you'll permit it," Young said. "But do finish your meal."

Aiden watched the two of them. Young showed just the right amount of deference, and she thought perhaps Stone Heart would come around. Meanwhile, she filled the reporter in on her reaction to seeing the badly treated Cheyenne herded into the fort like animals.

"And how do you come to be here?" Young asked after making a great deal of slashes and loops on the paper.

She leaned forward. How in the world could he read such scribbles?

"Miss Connor?"

"Oh, yes. Of course. Mr. Meeker and I were brought in by the soldiers after we got caught in a blizzard. They were out chasing the Cheyenne."

Young's eyebrows climbed his smooth forehead, forming furrows there. "Ah, yes. Could I ask, what were you doing with...uh, with Mr. Meeker?"

"Is this a part of your story?" she asked sharply.

He peered at her from the tops of his eyes, cleared his throat. "No, of course not. We'll skip that and go on."

"Very good." She sat straighter.

"What do you think should be done with these people?"

"They should be allowed to return home."

"To...?"

"Montana."

"Is it true that there are no facilities for them up there? That the United States government has made arrangements to house, clothe, and feed them down south in Indian Territory?"

"I don't know about any of that. I only know that the urge to go home is inherent in all of us. Would you like to be trapped here, even though the government fed you and housed you and clothed you? Only one thing, you couldn't go back home? Ever. I think not." Trapped here in much the same way she was, save for better accommodations. But that was another matter and one she didn't wish to address as yet.

"Fortunately, that isn't a possibility I must consider. These people are savages living on land that the government wants. What else did they expect?"

"I don't know what they expected, Mr. Young. To

live on the land of their ancestors, perhaps? To be left in peace, do you think? To be allowed to raise their children without seeing them butchered? Or worse, having to kill them to keep the brutal white man from getting his hands on them?"

"Oh, dear. Surely that can't be true. These soldiers are only carrying out orders. They wouldn't."

Stone Heart lurched to his feet, kicked away the chair in which he'd sat, and covered the distance between them in what appeared to be a gigantic leap, though she knew his feet must have touched the floor at least once. The reporter gazed up at him almost benignly. Didn't so much as flinch. A slight smile tilted the corners of his mouth. Not at all like a man expecting to be scalped. Aiden was amazed at the young man's affability in the face of such a frightening threat.

"Are you ready to talk to me now, Mr. Stone Heart?" he asked in a soft voice. "Or do you wish my hair?"

Stone Heart loomed over the seated man, hands fisted at his sides, eyes shooting fire. "Don't call me 'mister,'" he said. "That is a white man's title."

"And I understand you are only half white?" Young replied and turned the page to a fresh sheet. "Tell me about your true heritage."

Amazingly, Stone Heart sank to the floor, and there, seated cross-legged, began to speak to the man he'd earlier appeared ready to kill. They talked for what seemed like hours. Aiden listened as if she hadn't already heard the stories. Young filled page after page, and occasionally Stone Heart would jab a finger into the air to make a point. Young never wavered, his expression compassionate without being demeaning.

At last he asked, "And what is it your people wish to ask of the president?"

"They ask only to be released so they can join

216

the others up north. If they are to die, and they are
sure this is the case no matter where they go, they
wish to do it on the land of their ancestors. They vow
to die at their own hands, to the last man, woman,
and child, if Wessells tries to send them back to
Indian Territory. You can bet they will; many
already have."

"And you as well? You chose this life, probably
certain death, over the life of the son of a famous
white man? Can you tell me why?"

Stone Heart glanced at Aiden, then at Meeker,
who had long ago finished his meal, but remained at
the table, chair tilted back against the wall.

Young's gaze followed his, then settled on Stone
Heart. He waited patiently for a reply, pencil poised.

"When I was eleven, my father," he spat the two
words, then continued in a tight tone, "my father
massacred the very people who became a part of his
family when he lay with their women. He was young
himself, but learned quickly how to destroy the red
man."

"Sand Creek," Young said.

"No, that was another barbarian. Chivington.
Custer cut his teeth at the battle of the Washita
when he tried to do what Chivington couldn't at
Sand Creek. Destroy Black Kettle. Two years later
he sent soldiers to tear me from the arms of my
mother and her people.

"We were called the Beautiful People by those
same white men who cut us down. I was taken away
and molded into a white man. By the time I
returned, Little Wolf had taken all the Northern
Cheyenne from the land of our cousins, the Southern
Cheyenne, and began the trek north...to return to
the land of our ancestors. I caught up with them,
hoping to become a great warrior and thus make up
for what my father had done. Soldiers pursued us,
but we were determined. Some of us were captured

and taken to Fort Robinson. Little Wolf managed to escape with a few followers. I hope they are waiting up north.

"A few nights ago, I have lost track of how many, we broke out and tried once again to go home. We were pursued and attacked. General Crook sent many soldiers and Wessells has been like a rabid wolf in his pursuit. Morningstar, called Dull Knife, and a few others have thus far eluded capture since the breakout. If they haven't frozen to death out there, they will soon join Little Wolf.

"Somehow, someway, I intend to see that those they are dragging back here, for God knows what reason, are set free to join them."

Young nodded, finished scribbling, glanced up with eyes bright. "And you are willing to go with them, die if necessary, just to be free?"

"Yes, that is true." Stone Heart glanced at Aiden and she refused to look away. She wanted to plead with him, beg him not to go, but said nothing. It had all been said.

"So you rejoined the Cheyenne because you were ashamed of being the son of Custer and you thought to die to atone?"

"I have said it, I will say it again. If I must, I will die. But I could not help whose son I was. I was ashamed that he was such a coward, that he could not be trusted, that he slaughtered the very people he claimed to love."

"That he could not be your true father."

Eyes glimmering in the lamplight, Stone Heart studied the young man. "My true father is Morningstar. I will never call Long Hair father. He spilled his seed in my mother, but he thought nothing of the child he might sire. Because of the kind of man he is...was, I am glad he never called me son. I would rip out my own heart if he claimed me."

"If you could speak to our president about the

predicament of your people, what would you say?"

Stone Heart stared through the darkened window for some time. "I would ask only that he allow us to follow the path of Morningstar."

"Even though that probably means the death of your people?"

"My people died when the white man came. It has taken them many moons to pass from the earth. I ask only that they be allowed to do so in peace."

Tears filled Aiden's eyes and she gazed in wonder at the distantly serene countenance of Stone Heart.

"And if they are released, you will go with them?"

With that question, his eyes met hers again, held them for a long moment. Then he replied. "Yes. I must."

He might as well have struck her, she felt the blow of his words so solidly. After all they'd meant to each other, how could he so calmly speak of deserting her? Of fleeing to his own death without a second thought? He would abandon her just as Stephan had. Yet she had known it all along and shouldn't be surprised.

Young sat there a bit longer, but it was clear he had nothing more to ask. Finally he closed the pad, stuffed it and the pencil in his pocket and rose.

"I'll write this up, get it filed as soon as possible. I can't guarantee it'll do any good, but I think it might. There are already repercussions from the stories filed by other reporters out in the field who have seen the bloodshed and horror." He reached out a hand to Stone Heart who took it solemnly. "It's a great story. Thank you for sharing it with me. And I wish you the best. Thank you, Miss Connor. Mr. Meeker?"

As the affable young man spoke he shrugged into his coat and gloves, took up his hat. "It's been a real pleasure."

Long after the door closed behind Young, Aiden sat on the bed, feeling as alone as if there was no one else in the room. The very breath of life had been taken from her, leaving only a hollow shell filled with dismay and heartache. What a fool she was to let not only one man, but two, play with her to such an extent, then toss her aside as if she meant nothing. She had not only allowed it, she had practically begged for it. In the morning she would arrange to catch the next stage south to the train station where she could journey back to Saint Louis and her family.

In the far corner, Meeker lowered the chair, stood. "Well, I might as well be on my way. The stuff you asked for is at the mercantile. Paid for by my pelts. I told them you'd pick it up later." He fumbled on his hip, opened his possible bag. "And here's the shears you wanted, ma'am. Hope that's all you need, cause I'm pretty well busted. I kept enough supplies to do me a month or two so I can trap me some more animals, seein' as how them pelts belonged to me. Man's gotta live, you know."

He stood there a moment longer, fidgeting, then when neither of them replied, placed the shears on the edge of the table. Before going to the door he held out his hand to Stone Heart. "I wish you well, sir. It's been good to know you."

"Thank you for what you have done," Stone Heart said and released the hand.

"Reckon I'll be on my way." He eyed Aiden for a moment, and she remembered her promise, the one she had never intended to keep. She stepped forward, stood on tiptoe and kissed him on one whiskered cheek. "Thank you."

Batting his eyes, he touched the spot, nodded, and fled, closing the door hard.

Aiden jerked at the solid thud and fussed with

her hair a moment. A tear ran from one eye and she wiped it angrily, turning away so Stone Heart couldn't see.

He stood stiffly, head high, wishing there was something he could say to her, something he could do to explain his decision. But he knew there wasn't. She would never understand. Never. He wasn't sure he did, himself.

When he was with her the world around him grew brighter, warmer, sweeter. Yet to turn his back on the suffering of his people was not possible. He felt that now, with even more conviction than before. This very moment he felt guilty being in the warm room while they were freezing out there in their dank prison.

He wanted to purge the good food he'd eaten because they were hungry, tear the bedding into shreds because they slept on the frozen ground. He had no right to be with her, to love her, to accept her love in return. It had been foolish to even dream of such a thing.

He tried to explain how he felt, but the words garbled as if spoken through a mouthful of mush, and he could only gaze upon her with despair. If only he could take her in his arms one last time, but in that lay the greatest danger to them both.

"It's my fault, I think," she said.

He shook his head, but still could not speak to be understood.

"Yes. Yes, it is. I pick the wrong men. One is self-centered, prideful, and a pure lout, the other is passionate, blind to his own needs, prideful and...and...Oh, dammit." She threw herself on the bed face down, shoulders shaking.

Her sobs tore at his heart. He reached to touch her, but pulled away. He dare not or all would be lost. He must not give in to what he felt for this woman, could not betray all he held sacred. He would only grow to hate her and the life they might have. But, dear God how he wanted to stay with her. His body ached for the touch of her satiny skin, ached to breathe in her essence, to gaze upon her glorious ivory flesh, to draw life from her warm, moist lips.

He spoke her name softly, knowing she would not hear above the tumult of her sobbing.

"Goodbye. I'm sorry," he whispered. "So sorry. As long as the rivers flow I will never forget you." It wasn't enough and he knew it, but he stopped short of declaring the love that dwelled within him. It was not a thing he could do considering what must soon happen.

Outside, he raised his face to the purple darkness of the sky, opened his closed eyes and felt a single tear flow slowly down one cheek. Stars twinkled above and he drew in several deep breaths. He had to pretend he'd never met her. Wipe away the memories that rushed over him each time he thought of her.

He would never speak nor think her name again. He had to follow the path of Morningstar. And she could not go with him. He would not ask that of her, for he loved her too much. Even in spirit, he could not take her, for to do so would destroy his soul. He must forget her as if she had never lived in his heart.

Through the closed door he could hear the mournful, muffled sound of her crying. A lament that echoed in his heart and mind. In the center of the common, two soldiers walked briskly in the frigid night air, their voices rumbling in low conversation, mist puffing from their mouths to be yanked away by the brutal wind. From the direction of the prison came the weak sound of a baby mewling. On fire with regret, he moved alone through the shadows. He would sleep tonight near his people, and soon they would break out, run to freedom this one last time.

Heartbroken, but determined to go on with life, Aiden rose early after a sleepless night, dressed and hurried to the officer's mess to take breakfast and learn the latest news of the escaped Cheyenne. From there she would go to the stage station and make arrangements for her ticket. Of course, Captain Wessells wasn't there, he was out chasing down the last of the escapees.

Late the previous afternoon the soldiers had brought in seven women and children. With a heavy heart she listened to talk about the eighteen men and boys and fourteen women and children who had crouched in a hole as wide as twelve feet, as long as twenty-four feet. For many days and nights they had managed to fight off soldiers, but had at last been captured.

The excited young lieutenant told the bizarre tale as he shoveled hot food into his mouth. One of the warriors, Little Finger Nail, also known as the sweet singer of the Cheyenne, sang a death song as a mother stabbed her child and then herself to keep from being taken by the white soldiers.

"They shot the captain in the head, and we thought he was a goner, but he was just grazed," he babbled.

As the boy continued to recite the high points of the killings in an excited voice, Aiden choked on a bite of food and it was all she could do to keep from vomiting up what she had eaten. She sat for a long while, napkin squeezed in one fist, thinking of Stone Heart and the fate that awaited him. This was indeed a horrible place to be, and he'd been right. She must go home, quickly. Forget him, forget all this horror.

She left the mess hall and went to the stage station, where she found an elderly gentleman sitting behind a barred window. He raised it when she approached.

"Can you tell me if a stage is scheduled to depart soon?"

"Probably not for civilians, ma'am, not for a few more days."

"But it hasn't snowed in a while. The reporters are coming. Can't the stage get through to pick them up?"

"It's the Indians, ma'am. Running about out there killing everything that moves, the company doesn't want to chance it. We aren't allowed to send any women until they get all them savages corralled or shot. Reporters, well, they're another thing. Some came in with an escort of soldiers. President's orders. You wait a while longer, they'll be a stage. These Injuns won't last much longer."

It was almost impossible for her to keep from shouting at the man like a madwoman. How could those poor people do anyone any harm? They were half dead themselves.

The balding man peered closely at her. Probably noting her swollen, red eyes. "You might as well stay here where you're safe, little lady. Go get yourself a new dress and go to the dance tonight, it'll make you feel heaps better. Come back next week, after all them savages is put down."

As she stepped from the station, she almost ran into the young man who had helped carry food to her quarters the day before. He took her arm while she skidded around on the slick footing, then touched his hat.

"Well, Mrs. Connor? Or is it Meeker? How is your husband feeling today?"

She didn't try to explain her name. "Fine, he's better."

"Oh, good. Perhaps he'll bring you to the dance tonight and allow me to be your partner for one go round. Men out here are accustomed to sharing their wives at our regular Saturday night dances."

Sorrow had burrowed so deeply within her she couldn't imagine attending a dance or any other such function. All she wanted was to nurse her wounds until she could escape this horrid place.

Without replying to the private's request, she excused herself and hurried back to her quarters. Though a weak winter sun shone, it was still bitterly cold, and wind blew across the prairie so hard it whipped her dress tightly around her legs and sucked the very breath from her lungs.

At the doorway, she hesitated and put her ear against the panels. Though Stone Heart had gone, she couldn't help but hope he might have changed his mind and returned. At the same time, if he had, she mustn't see him again. Hearing nothing, she lifted the latch and stepped in cautiously. It was very quiet. The empty dishes remained on the table, the blankets were rumpled in the middle of the bed, and no one was there. In spite of her vow, she began to weep at not finding him waiting for her.

Pushing the door closed at her back, she stood there a moment trying to regain some sort of composure. She couldn't go about the rest of her life like this. It would never do.

The room was cold and so she built a fire from the wood that always seemed to be there. Someone came around replacing it, but she had no idea who or from where they got it. Once the flames crackled through the kindling and licked at the logs, she took off her cloak and folded the blankets on the bed. Finished, she went to the table to stack the dishes so she could return them to the mess hall when she went to dinner. That's when she noticed that the shears were no longer on the table.

A quick look around the room did not reveal them. She found them finally, lying on the floor on the far side of the bed. Beside them lay a long, thick golden braid. Her eyes darted toward the hook in the corner where the uniform had been. It was gone. In a pile in the corner were his buckskins and the heavy elk jacket.

Falling to her knees, she took up the clothing, buried her face in the smooth leather. Stone Heart had returned, made the change from Cheyenne to white. Something must have happened. She had no idea what he might have in mind, but wished he would let her help him. Carefully, she folded each item and put them inside the chest.

Someone tapped on the door and she shoved the braid and shears in on top of them, closed the drawer and went to answer. It was Retha, and she invited her in out of the cold.

Standing next to the stove with her hands held over it, Retha got right to the point. "I came to invite you to the dance. Since my husband is still away tending to these dreadful savages, I thought perhaps we could go together. Private Cash told me you are married, is that true?" She studied Aiden with bright, piercing eyes. "You've been crying."

For a moment Aiden couldn't reply, just nodded her head and tried to hold back fresh tears.

Retha came to her, put an arm around her shoulder. "Did he leave you? Is that what it is?"

"No...yes, but he wasn't...he isn't...my husband. Dammit, why do women cry?" At which point she proceeded to do so quite vigorously.

"There, there," Retha said and patted her shoulder. "We cry because it's the thing to do and it makes us feel better. Especially in our dealings with men. They are such cruel, unfeeling monsters sometimes. They have their own priorities that have nothing to do with what we feel. Only under the sheets with us do they try to please, and sometimes not even then."

Aiden turned away in embarrassment. What the woman said appeared to be so true. Retha patted her some more.

"Oh, do come go to the dance. You'll feel ever so much better."

And surprisingly, Aiden thought she might. How long had it been since she'd been to a dance? She couldn't even remember. She glanced down at the dress she'd worn ever since Retha gave it to her.

As if reading her mind, Retha said, "Oh, don't you worry. I have just the proper frock for you to wear. That one needs a good wash, at any rate. I have some things to take to the Chinese laundry. We'll put it with them. You come with me and we'll take care of this."

Gathering her cloak, Aiden said, "I can't keep taking your clothes. It's not right. If only I had some money, I could buy a frock from the mercantile. But I only have enough to get home. I mustn't spend it on anything so frivolous."

Again Retha patted her arm. "Nonsense, it's been so long since I've had a friend my own age in which to confide, it makes it worthwhile just to keep you around." She glanced at Aiden with a bright curiosity in her gray eyes. "I do hope I helped you by introducing you to that young reporter. How did that go?"

"Well, it went very well, thank you. I'm sorry if I was rude about it."

"Nonsense. It did hurt my feelings, but then I tend to get over slights." Her gaze begged for more consolation.

"I didn't intend to slight you at all." If Retha expected more than that, she wouldn't get it. No matter how kind she had been, Aiden would not reveal information that might very well get passed on to the woman's husband, and thus other army officers.

Stiffly, Retha smiled. "Well, now, come on. We'll eat dinner together, then come back and choose just the proper dress. And we'd better try to do something to that hair. Isn't this wind hard on it? I'll send for bath water and we'll have a gay old time getting ready. It'll be just like we were girls again, with all those handsome young men waiting to ask us to dance. And I promise you, you'll have partners a plenty."

Not without doubts, Aiden followed her. Torn between her need to grieve the loss of Stone Heart and a desire to put it all behind her, she chose this as an escape, for none other had presented itself.

A few hours later the two women hurried along to the recreation hall where the dance was being held. The cold took Aiden's breath away, and she wondered again how anyone ever grew accustomed to living in this country. Most especially those who lived out in the elements. Trappers such as Meeker and the Cheyenne people. She thought of Stone Heart and hoped he was in out of the cold on this very bitter night.

Warmth in the building was provided by two rather large stoves, with a space between reserved for dancing. Even with them burning full tilt, the building was drafty and only comfortably warm near the fires. Coal oil lamps hung in brackets on the four walls, their light golden. Several musicians, all soldiers, had set up near one of the stoves and were tuning up fiddles and guitars. A long table held several glittering crystal punch bowls filled with red and yellow liquid refreshments. Plates offered an array of sweets. There were probably no more than twenty women in the huge room and maybe fifty or sixty men, all in uniform save a few who must be reporters. Laughter and conversation mingled with the wail of the stringed instruments, as if there weren't still men out there in the night murdering helpless Cheyennes. There were chairs around the walls and a few were occupied, though most everyone milled about sipping punch and nibbling cookies, stopping to talk a while, then moving on. The dance had yet to begin, as people continued to spill through the door, letting in drafts of frigid air.

"Oh, look," Retha cried. "There's Captain Wessells. I didn't know he was back. I'd like to ask him about Lieutenant Woods."

Despite her reluctance, Aiden let Retha drag her across the floor to the captain, who at the moment was filling a punch glass. He wore a bandage around his head, so the boy's story of him being grazed must have been true. He looked pale and a bit hollow-eyed.

He turned when Retha hailed him. "Well, ladies, aren't you a sight for these weary eyes. My, you both look beautiful. Does my heart good to behold such treats after so many hours in the saddle."

His nose was indeed quite red, but Aiden thought that might be from something he'd added to the punch, for she caught a familiar whiff. Her older brothers took a glass of ale on occasion and she was well acquainted with the smell.

Retha responded to the captain with a coy thank you and a silly bob of a curtsy. "Could you tell me, sir, when my husband's regiment is expected back? I would certainly enjoy seeing him."

"Woods, isn't it? Lieutenant Woods. They're doing the last of the cleanup. We brought in those survivors from the Last Hole this evening, and we think that pretty much accounts for their sorry asses. Excuse me, ma'am. I beg your pardon." He lifted his hat to them both and tottered just a bit.

The man was indeed, in his cups, as her mama used to say. Before long he'd likely be passed out somewhere, and if some kind soul didn't see him to his quarters, he'd spend an uncomfortable night on the floor in a corner. But what actually occurred to Aiden was something else altogether. He had the keys to the food lockers outside the officer's mess, and if she could somehow manage to lay hands on them, she might be able to get some food to those poor wretches in the prison barracks.

She helped herself to a glass of punch when Retha did, then turned to survey the room once more. On the opposite wall stood a tall soldier with golden hair that shone in the lamplight. Her heart kicked at her ribs and she couldn't breathe, as if the corset Retha had laced for her were much too tight.

But that wasn't it at all. The soldier, who appeared to stare right back at her was Stone Heart. She could not move. Wanted nothing but to run as fast as she could.

Chapter Fifteen

Though he attended the dance to learn more about the intended fate of the Cheyenne, Stone Heart spotted Aiden the moment she entered, her lovely blue dress billowed by the wind. Her red hair, swirled high on her head, was covered by a shawl in the same color as the dress. She removed it with a grace that fisted hot desire into his belly. Long finger curls framed either side of her face, flushed with the cold. Even though the large room overflowing with people separated them, he imagined he could smell the delicate fragrance that was hers alone. He always thought of a spring breeze blowing over a field of wild flowers.

More than once he tried to turn from the sight of her, get back to the business at hand. Yet always, beyond the object of each conversation he joined, she glided through his vision. There she was, head tilted up to speak to a young private, then talking again to the woman she came with. Later the two of them with the pompous Captain Wessells with his head swathed in bandages. Too bad they didn't kill him. The wish came unbidden, and he knew better even as he thought it. One bad white man would just be replaced by yet another, perhaps worse.

Even though he couldn't keep his eyes off A'den, Stone Heart overheard that General Crook would soon reveal what disposition was planned for the Cheyenne. Some of the warriors would most probably be sent back to Kansas to be tried for murder. An impossibly absurd notion. Others might be taken to the Red Cloud Agency to be dealt with more gently. Back east, opinion had swayed as some important people took up the cause of the poor suffering savages. In this he couldn't help but rejoice. Yet even as these conversations floated around him, there was always within his sight the lovely A'den. She had a hold on him that he couldn't break simply by willing it so. If only he could touch her, taste her, breathe her essence one last time.

Fighting the urge, he remained always as far from her as he could. She danced with a young private, her gaze turned upward to catch every word he uttered, while one pale hand rested lightly on his shoulder. He recalled that hand tending his wounds, pressing the poultice gently against his feverish flesh. Round and round the dance floor they whirled, like floating clouds. The soldier laughed at something she said and she tilted her head in a provocative way that made Stone Heart wish he could bust the fellow in his smug face. A lieutenant claimed her for the waltz that followed, and when she gave him her hand, Stone Heart actually bulled his way several feet through the crowd before stopping himself.

Again, he searched out Wessells, leaned in a corner as if his legs would no longer support him. The captain grew less surefooted by the minute while sipping at a glass of punch that must be laced with whisky. With an effort, Stone Heart concentrated on the reason he'd placed himself in such a dangerous situation, and worked his way around the edge of the dance floor toward the captain. With the man so drunk, he might well manage to obtain the keys A'den had said he carried on his person. From the looks of it, he would soon pass out, giving Stone Heart the perfect opportunity. He must be nearby when that happened.

As he moved around a group of young ladies giggling and talking, a dancing couple bumped into him, and he turned to see it was the lieutenant and A'den.

Her eyes met his for a brief instant, recognition sparking hers to a brilliant jade, and then she was gone, borne lithely away in the soldier's arms. Frozen in place, he watched her move out of reach, saw her gaze at him with each turn.

At least now she knew he was here, for all the good that would do either of them. His last leave-taking would not have endeared him to her, and that was the way it must be. Still, he couldn't help putting himself in the place of that lieutenant. Imagined holding her as they whirled round and round, caught up in a world all their own.

Her presence and this ridiculous military garb had him thinking and acting like a white man, which he had vowed never to do again. Somehow he had to shake off the hold she had on him. Think only of the Cheyenne and their fate. Fighting the desire coiled deep in his belly, he moved once again toward Captain Wessells and the prized keys.

From the moment their eyes met, Aiden was lost. After what he'd done she ought to be furious, but he looked so handsome, gazed at her with such open hunger. The uniform fit him superbly. His hair was a bit shaggy where he'd chopped off the braid, but he'd done a credible job of smoothing it down and had even found a hat that fit. Probably stole it, but she couldn't be concerned with such trivial things at that at this late date. Curls caressed his neck and the collar of the jacket. Once a formidable savage, he'd become a majestic soldier, easily the most handsome man in the crowded room.

And he was headed directly for Captain Wessells. She remembered then having told him about the keys to the food lockers, and knew instinctively what he was after.

He'd be caught! What could he be thinking? In

this room filled with army officers and soldiers, he would not stand a chance should Wessells recognize him. The captain had, after all, thrown Stone Heart in prison. Would he remember him? See beneath this veneer of a civilized white officer to that dangerous Cheyenne warrior?

As her partner whirled them closer to Stone Heart, she said, "Oh, dear, Lieutenant. I'm afraid I'm going to have to rest. Would you mind if I...?"

Pouting with disappointment, the lieutenant nevertheless remained a gentleman and deposited her against the wall.

"Would you like a glass of punch?" he asked, holding her hand. "I'm afraid there is no place for you to sit."

With a forced smile, she declined, and gently removed her fingers from his grip. "Oh, that's quite all right, sir. I'll be fine right here. Just let me get my breath. Dancing with all you virile young men has quite worn me out."

Reluctantly, he moved away in search of another partner.

The music stopped for a moment and everyone milled about, conversing and laughing. She took the opportunity to inch her way nearer Wessells, who regarded her with bleary eyes. She didn't think he even knew who she was. Passing the table, she picked up a glass and filled it, quickly glanced over the crowd in an effort to find Stone Heart. So many uniforms, she couldn't locate him right away. Stepped closer to the captain, smiled into his face.

He raised his glass in a wavering salute, took another gulp. The man was so drunk he didn't recognize her, much less know where he was. Good. At least he wouldn't know Stone Heart either. But was he drunk enough to pay no attention to someone reaching in his pocket? No matter. She could not allow Stone Heart to place himself in such a hazardous situation. He'd be caught, and even if she never saw him again, she must remember him wild and free, not locked up in some prison. If she were caught, her punishment would be much less severe than his.

Continuing to smile, she touched the captain's arm and leaned close, as if to say something. No longer able to remain upright, he propped himself against the wall.

"Hlo, my dear. 'Fraid I can't dance."

"Oh, that's quite all right, Captain." Deliberately, she staggered against him, pinning him tightly into the corner, one hand brushing along his pants and into the pocket.

His bloodshot eyes widened. "What's this?" With an extreme effort, he straightened his shoulders, put an arm around her and pinned her tightly. He'd obviously misread her move, and that was fine. The stench of alcohol on his breath made her eyes water, but she let him rub against her while her fingers checked out the contents of the pocket.

No keys. Did she dare try the other one?

The hand holding the drink moved toward her bodice, and she thought for a minute he was going to pour it down the front of her dress in his effort to rub his knuckles over her breast. It was difficult not to fight him off, but she didn't. She had a drink of her own to dispose of if she was to get in his other pocket, so she managed to drink it, sloshing some out, then transferred the empty glass to the other hand and felt along his opposite leg. All the while he pawed ineffectually at her. It appeared he wasn't too drunk to enjoy being touched and actually shifted to give her a better angle.

"Thish is delightshful," he mumbled as her hand slipped into his pocket. Her fingers closed over the keys and slid out.

For an injured man who was also intoxicated, he

had a pretty good hold on her by the time she had the keys in her fist, and it then became a problem to disentangle herself without causing a scene. He actually attempted to guide her other hand to the front of his pants, but the effort failed when she tipped his drink so it spilled down his shirt front.

"Oh, my," Aiden gasped and stepped back. "I'm so sorry, sir. I'll get something to help you clean up."

"Jush bring me nother drinkee, girlee," he said, then slid slowly down the wall to the floor, eyes rolling back in his head.

Nearby, several soldiers laughed, and she took the opportunity to get far enough away from the captain to escape any attention his action might attract.

Clutching the keys so tightly they bit into her flesh, she scanned the room. The last time she'd seen him Stone Heart had been headed this way, but she couldn't spot him in the crowd.

A fiddle tuned up, then another joined in and several couples began to dance. At last she spotted her quarry, standing with his back to her staring at the man passed out in the corner. Quickly, she moved to him, took his arm from behind.

"May I have this dance, lieutenant?"

He stiffened under her touch, and for a moment she thought he was going to bolt. Anything to get away from her. But then he turned, ever so slowly, stared down into her face, silver eyes moist and reflecting the golden lamplight.

"May I have this dance?" she repeated.

The familiar voice sent shivers of dismay down his spine. He couldn't take her in his arms. All would be lost. Frantically he gauged the crowd and the distance to Wessells and the precious keys. Why was she doing this?

He laid a hand on hers. "A'den. Do not interfere. I must get the keys."

She slipped her closed fist between them so only he could see and uncurled her fingers to reveal the cluster of keys that had left red marks crisscrossed on her palm.

While he had been inadvertently caught up in a group of jolly fellows who insisted he join them in a toast, she must have taken them. Put herself in great jeopardy to actually remove them from the man's pants.

A laughing young couple headed for the dance floor bumped them, and he grabbed her in his arms to keep her from falling. All hope of remaining distant from her disappeared, for he couldn't let her go. Stood there holding her, eyes closed, heart thumping. He took one deep breath, then another. Tried with all his might to turn loose. Only succeeded in crushing her against his chest.

He whispered into her silken hair. "Dear God, A'den."

She whispered his name, inched both arms around his waist.

As if there were no one in the room but them, he held her and swayed lightly to the music, tried to deny the pleading of his heart.

A soldier pushed past them. "Y'all gonna dance, ought to get out on the floor."

"Yes, let's dance," Stone Heart said, breath fanning her hair.

Carefully, she lay her hand high on his shoulder, fingers trailing along the warm skin of his neck. He held her closer than was allowed by the decorum of the day. Forgotten was her earlier anger as she gazed up into his eyes, unable to speak.

"You are very beautiful," he whispered.

"And you...you are...how did you . . .? I mean, oh, I'm so glad you're all right." She laid her head against his chest and followed his graceful movements round and round the floor, not sure how she managed to hold herself upright.

Dear God, how would she ever be able to leave him behind? Even his slightest touch made her feel absolutely giddy with passion.

Stone Heart cursed himself for a fool over and over, but he could not bring himself to let her go. Here, in this white man's place, with everyone looking, he held her as he always wished he could, moved her round and round the floor. Learning to dance like the white man had been one of his greatest joys. Cheyenne men danced alone, and if the women did dance, it was not in sight of the men. This was indeed one of the best ideas the white man ever had. It was like making love in public with everyone looking on in approval.

He spread his hand over her back, moved it gently upward, feeling the stiff ribbing of her undergarment, then shifted it below her waist to the hem of the corset. Beneath that rigid contraption, the muscles of her hips undulated sinuously under his touch.

He felt himself grow hard against her, saw her eyes widen as he nestled her closer, waltzed crazily round and round the floor while the lamps swirled golden paths across his vision. Everything but her face blurred. They were alone, flying together, their bodies absorbed in each other, pulsing to the rhythm of the music and their desires, and he knew nothing but her. When the music stopped, they remained in each other's arms, waited for it to begin again.

Others who might have cut in must have realized the futility of such an action and left them be. They remained together as the party continued on into the night. The crowd thinned until only a couple of dozen people remained, not counting the men who had joined their captain to lie in a drunken stupor on the floor.

After assurances from Aiden, Retha left,

accompanied by two young men who promised to see Lieutenant Woods' wife safely to her door.

Stone Heart didn't want to leave, because to do so would break the spell, take her from him, for he could see no other way to do what he must do. But eventually the musicians put down their instruments, the punch bowls emptied, the cookie plates contained only crumbs. The party was over.

"Let's get out of here," she said. "We can't continue to stand here in the middle of the floor like this. Someone will notice."

Though he nodded his head in assent, he couldn't move for yet another moment. Afraid that if he let her go, he would never find her again. She would be lost to him forever. And yet so very aware that such a thing was exactly what must happen.

"Come on," she urged and pulled loose from his embrace, grasped his hand and worked her way toward the door.

She found her cloak on the table put there for that purpose, and he slipped it around her shoulders, draped the blue shawl over her hair just so. In each movement he took his time, delaying the inevitable. At last they moved out into the cold night.

The wind held the odor of horses and the bright taste of winter. Above stars gleamed, appearing so near he might pluck one down for safekeeping. He kept his arm around her as they made their way through the crusted snow. The keys jingled in his pocket, reminding him of what he had yet to do this night. He would first see her safe to her door. The idea of bidding her goodbye weighed heavily on him, but there were no more choices. This had been their final night together. A night he knew he would never forget.

At her door, she slipped the latch and took his hand to pull him inside.

"I cannot," he said. "I must go."

"Let me change. I'm going with you. And this time you can't stop me. If you try I'll only follow you. I've thought of this a lot and it's more important that I be with you no matter where you are than that I be unhappy in a safe place. I know you love me. You can't deny that. Come in and wait while I change."

He followed her inside because he couldn't think of what else to do. She completely confused him as no woman ever had. There was often no way of telling her no.

"Help me undo this dress," she said, turning her back so he could fumble at the row of tiny buttons with cold fingers.

"How did you get this on?" he asked after succeeding in opening only a few.

"Retha. She's been a good friend, the first one I've made out here. Someday, maybe I'll see her again."

He halted, studied the smooth curve of her neck. "Remain here with her while I do this thing. I will come back for you."

Under his hands, she stiffened. "No, you won't."

"Yes, I promise. You'll be safe here, and when it is done, when they are on their way home, I'll come get you. We'll go wherever you want. I'm tired of trying to talk myself into something I no longer want. What I want is to be with you, and I can see that we cannot be together where my people are going." Embracing the truth of what he'd said blazed a bright trail into his heart and mind.

"I'm afraid to stay here and let you go," she finally said, her back to him.

It wasn't the people so much as him she wished to save. Though compassionate for their suffering, she felt no real connection to it. As if they were beings she did not quite understand. But him. This man. He was a part of her, a part she could not lose.

"Why? Because of that other man? The one who left you? I am not him."

She turned then, put her arms around his neck. "I know that, but you are a man. Men like their women to be somewhere in the backs of their minds. Waiting for when you decide you need to be succored. And once you've enough of that, you want to run off somewhere else for more adventure. Well, I don't want to be left behind to be visited at your whim. Since I cannot ask you not to do what you must, then I have to go with you."

"What a lot of nonsense."

"Is it? Look at the women here at Fort Robinson. At how they wait half their lives for their men to spend a little time with them before they're off again on some great adventure that they can't possibly share. My father went to sea and every time he came back he left my mother with child, and then one day he just didn't come back. Left her with my baby brother growing in her belly. And she still weeps for him."

The expression on her face revealed a great sorrow and he kissed her, first on one cheek then the other. She was right. He had wanted to bring her here and leave her. That day when they had left the shelter and started for this fort, it was only because he wanted to put her somewhere so he could continue with his plans. He remembered how he had taught her to walk in the deep snow and how she had curled up in his arms to sleep, keeping them both warm. But now she was wrong. He couldn't leave her again. Ever.

"I want to go with you," she said.

"It is dangerous."

Sensing she had at least partially won him over, she twisted in his arms. "Finish the buttons. I'll put on the buckskins and we can go."

Even after he surrendered to her wishes, it

remained in the back of his mind that he could somehow talk her into remaining here at the fort for a short while. Until he could arrange the escape and see it underway. For her safety, if for no other reason. He did not want to lose her. Found that he couldn't bear the thought now that he'd held her again.

"It's important we get them some food and water. Tonight. Now."

"I know, and I will help you do that." *Then we will be free,* she thought.

With a great sigh, he unlaced her corset and stood by while she transformed herself from a beautiful white woman into a buckskin-clad nomad. Very carefully, she spread the lovely blue dress across the bed, folded the shawl and cloak. She did not plan to return, he could tell by her movements, the way she checked out the room. Watching her slip into the stained leather pants and shirt she'd worn on the trail, he vowed that when this was over, this task finished, he would take her home to her people. Learn her ways and make her happy as no woman had ever been before. In doing so, he was sure he too would finally be content.

Still, he dare not make her such a promise, for fear something terrible would happen. She must have thought so too, for she carefully tied the pouch containing her money around her neck. If something went wrong, she would surely need it.

Wrapped against the brutal cold, they crept out into the deserted common, slipped around the end of the building and made their way to the food storage sheds behind the officer's mess. Before too long, the bugles would sound reveille and hundreds of men would swarm over the grounds.

All but one patrol had returned from the field, bringing in what they deemed to be the last of the captives. Dull Knife was not among them, according to talk at the dance earlier. Stone Heart feared the great leader was dead, but could not bring himself to believe it. It would surely take more than an army of white men to bring down such a spiritual being.

Hunkered beside her between the wooden crates and the storage shed, he tried the keys in the heavy padlock until he found the one that fit. Sliding the long iron bar loose, he inched the door open. It groaned on its hinges and he paused to listen.

"Check for a patrol," he told her and stepped inside. It was even blacker within the shed, and he hesitated a moment or two to allow his eyes to get used to it.

A large vat sat on the floor, and he lifted the lid and sniffed. Perhaps stew meat or beans cooked the evening before and sat out here to keep. Taking hold of a handle, he pulled at the vat. Partially frozen, it was heavy, but not impossible to move.

They could drag it through the snow. Take it first, come back for more. It looked to be enough to feed many but they would have to build a larger fire to thaw the contents. He worried they wouldn't have the wood to do such a thing. Lifting the top of a wooden barrel, he smelled the aroma of bread. Inside, he felt several loaves.

Prying them apart, for they too were frozen, he put as many as would fit into the vat and pressed the lid down. The rest he bundled up in the blanket he took from around his shoulders. A'den could carry that and he would drag the vat across the frozen snow. But they must hurry. Already, the sky to the east held a silver cast. The cooks would soon arrive and they had to be away. He hoped they wouldn't miss the vat while preparing breakfast.

He also hoped there were no guards on the prison overnight, but knew he couldn't count on that, considering the Cheyenne had broken out once before.

"I didn't hear anyone," A'den said when he backed out of the shed dragging the heavy vat.

"On a night such as this, they may not have any guards posted. Only fools would be out and about. Here, can you carry this?" He handed her the bundle of bread, then returned the heavy iron bar to its place and replaced the padlock. "I don't want them to know its gone."

"What happens when they do find out? Won't they guess what happened to it?"

"I'm hoping they'll blame some of the civilians wandering around. Or the Blackfoot camped outside. Maybe even some of the soldiers." He bent to his task, dragging the heavy cooking vessel.

"How will we get this in to them?"

"When they had me in there I checked it out. Good thing they didn't build with logs and chinking, we'd be out of luck. Most of the buildings are planks, and I'm hoping we can pry away some at the back corner where they won't be noticed. I can get help from those inside. They broke out once, they'll know what to do."

"Wessells probably has a key to the prison as well," she said. Gasping in the frigid air, she didn't say anything more for a while, just bent to help him move his burden along over the frozen snow.

He thought they were making too much noise and stopped once in a while to listen to the stillness. Gazing up at the lightening sky, he urged her to hurry.

"It'll be daylight soon, we have to move faster."

"When are we going to get the supplies Meeker bought at the mercantile? He left them there for me to pick up."

"I'd forgotten all about them. I wish he'd figured a way to carry them off himself. They're bound to ask questions when you go in to get them."

"I guess he didn't think of that."

Suddenly Stone Heart held up a hand. "Hush. I hear something." Conversation, footsteps, grumbling. More than one person coming their way.

"Quick, over here," he said and shoved the big pot of frozen soup into an alleyway between two buildings.

She scurried into the shadows with him, so frightened she could scarcely breathe. He pulled her close, sheltering her within his arms. She could feel his heart drumming against her ear. Her breath froze a circle on the woolen uniform jacket.

Four soldiers hurried by. Perhaps cooks headed for the mess tent, for they certainly didn't appear to be on guard duty. Hunched against the cold, they almost ran past the buildings to disappear between two of them further down the row.

Pulse pounding in her temples, she followed Stone Heart back out into the open. "How far is it?"

"Yonder." He pointed to a long, low structure, a black shadow in the snowlit pre-dawn.

It seemed to take them forever to get there. No one watched the doors. If guards had been posted, they'd abandoned their duty and sought warmth somewhere.

"They may be nearby, but we can't wait. It's getting light. Come on." He gave the vat one last shove, sent it careening toward the door. It too would be padlocked. If she was right and Wessells had a key to that lock as well they'd be in luck. Otherwise, they would have to rip off some planks, making too much noise in the silence that would at any moment be broken by the trumpets of reveille and the hue and cry of hundreds of soldiers racing to formation.

Taking out the keys, he began trying them with stiff fingers.

She grabbed his arm. "Someone's coming."

"I can't...how close?"

"I don't know. I hear footsteps."

He continued to work the lock, fearful that perhaps Wessells didn't have a key after all.

"Around the corner, down there," she whispered, pointed.

A lone figure started across the yard. He hadn't seen them yet, but he would any minute.

Muttering, Stone Heart put the last key in the lock and felt it drop open. At that very moment the soldier spotted them.

"Hey, you. You, there. What's up?" The man started to run toward them, and they saw he had a rifle.

Stone Heart swung open the door, shoved the food inside and her after it. "Stay there. You'll be safe." He shut the door, and raced to meet the soldier.

"You stop right there. Halt," the man yelled, head swiveling as if he expected to be attacked by someone as yet unseen. He finally made the decision to point his weapon at the only one he could see.

"Stand down, Private. Is this your post?"

"Sir, I don't think..."

Squaring off at the private, Stone Heart barked, "You don't think what, Private? It's not your place to think. Were you supposed to be guarding the prisoners?"

The confused man saluted, fumbled with the rifle so it was no longer pointed at Stone Heart. "Sir, yes sir, I had to...had to...take a leak, sir?"

"And you left your post?"

The boy settled on remaining mute, waiting out this rapidly growing problem.

"You report to your senior officer, private."

"Now, sir? Pardon me, sir, but he's asleep, sir."

"At his earliest convenience, then."

"What about...?" The soldier gestured toward the prison barracks.

"I'll take care of this." Lowering his voice, Stone Heart leaned toward the private. "Look, son. I know it's colder out here than a well-digger's bones. I can understand you deserting your post. Tell you what, why don't you go to breakfast and I'll explain what happened. I'll cover for you, but just this time. Don't let it happen again." Lord, he sounded just like a white man. How easily it had all come back.

"Huh? I mean, sir, yes, sir."

Practically running, the boy took off in the general direction of the infantrymen's mess.

Inside, Aiden hunkered near the doorway until the private left. Before she could shove open the door and rejoin Stone Heart, a hand grasped her arm tightly.

She turned, and in the smoky, firelit room, gazed into the bottomless eyes of a most ferocious Cheyenne brave, face smeared with what looked like blood. Covering her mouth, she let out a muffled squawk.

At the same moment, the padlock on the outside of the door snapped closed with a solid thunk.

Chapter Sixteen

Minutes after Stone Heart locked Aiden in with the Cheyenne, the fearsome brave continued to stare at her. She wanted to claw at the door, kick it out. The urge was so great she could scarcely contain it, but managed to for the instant it took to think in a rational way. Stone Heart wouldn't put her in danger, of that she was sure, so with teeth gritted she stood her ground.

To convince herself she was safe, she smiled tremulously at her terrifying adversary and dragged her gaze from his black-as-night eyes to take a quick look around. Smoke from a fire in the center of the drafty room burned her eyes and throat. Breathing through her nose didn't help because of the horrid smell of humans too long penned up with no facilities. Cold air sifted in through gaps in the planking, all that saved them from choking to death.

The warrior's intense concentration continued and finally took her mind off her discomfort. In an effort to distract him, she patted the vat. "Food. Cook."

He drew a threadbare blanket tighter around his shoulders, appeared not to so much as blink. Maybe he didn't understand. She reached to slide off the lid, but his arm shot out to block the movement, and she jerked away in fear.

If she laid hands on Stone Heart she'd fix him good for shutting her up in here. But she might not get the chance. He could very well leave her here while he finished whatever it was he had to do. He was quite an adamant man. She should have agreed

to remain in her quarters, not been so stubborn.
What if these people decided they didn't want her
here and killed her? Certainly a possibility, the way
a few of them were staring at her. Death might be
the better of the options left open to her. Still, no
matter what else she might believe, Stone Heart
would not let her come to harm. She clung
desperately to that knowledge.

One consolation was that many of the Cheyenne
paid no attention to her at all. They sat or lay,
wrapped in tattered blankets and soiled animal
skins, more concerned with surviving another night
than dealing with an interloper. Especially a white
woman who could obviously do them no harm.

"I will cook it, shall I?" she finally asked the
silent warrior. His eyes barely flickered.

A young boy, possibly ten or eleven years old,
scrawny body layered in rags, crawled to her. With
eyes dark as a starless night he glanced toward the
warrior, spoke in his native tongue. The man
answered sharply.

"Come, then," the boy said to her, and grabbed
one handle of the cooking vat. "We will put this on
the fire. Help me."

Warily, Aiden studied the stoic Cheyenne who
appeared to ignore her, then glanced at the boy.
"Me?"

He nodded, gestured.

She helped him drag it to the flames where,
with a stick, he raked out a bed of hot coals.
Together they hefted the cooking vessel onto the
glowing embers, and the boy added more wood.
Cautiously, she lifted the lid, removed the bread
and, replacing the cover, lay it on top to warm.

Most of the Cheyenne moved closer and
hunkered in a circle to watch. An old woman with a
stiff leg hobbled over and sat on the floor between
Aiden and the warrior, regarded her with a toothless

grimace.

Aiden nudged the boy. "Tell them it is food. Stone Heart brought it for them."

As the boy spoke, a young woman with a crying baby cradled at her breast, made a grab for one of the loaves of bread. The warrior held her back, spoke a few soft words. The baby continued to mewl like a lost kitten and nuzzle at the girl's tiny breast. It was obvious she had no milk. The child would surely die. How it had ever been born in the first place was a mystery.

While the people discussed what the boy told them, the flames licked higher up the sides of the iron cooking vessel. After a while steam escaped carrying the mouth watering aroma of cooking stew.

The warrior broke off a piece of bread, lifted the lid and dipped it in the bubbling soup. Aiden thought for a moment he would eat the dripping morsel himself, but he gave it to the old woman who handed it to the young mother. She chewed a bite ravenously, swallowed, then bit off another piece. After she had chewed it, she fingered a small amount from her mouth and fed it to the child. She continued to share it that way until it was gone. Though her sunken eyes remained focused on the food, she didn't ask for more as others lined up to claim a portion, doled out by the ferocious warrior as if he were a kindly father. Each time he handed the old woman a share, she passed it on to others.

Watching the starving people ration the offering, tears filled Aiden's eyes and she turned away.

These were Stone Heart's people, once known as the Beautiful People, and her own kind were killing them in the most cruel of ways. It would have been kinder to line them up and shoot them. From what he'd said, they'd done that as well, out there in the icy wilderness where those desperate to return home hid behind rocks and in caves awaiting their fate in the brutal and frigid weather.

She felt their pain cut sharply into her innermost self, where her beliefs in a kind humanity suffered a bad blow. A compassion she had never felt for anyone, no matter the circumstances, enclosed her soul, and she wept for them. Wept as if her heart might shatter.

****

At the very moment Stone Heart turned to fetch A'den from the prison barracks where he had hidden her from the guard, he heard the noisy crunch and squeak of many feet on the frozen snow. At least ten soldiers carrying rifles came around the far corner of the barracks and headed straight toward him, marching in a loose, rather awkward formation. In light of this development he had only one choice. Secure the padlock before they discovered it open, and play his part. So he snapped it shut, locking A'den inside. She would be safe, though she might not know it. When he let her out, he had a feeling he would loose a spitting wildcat.

A sergeant led the group of soldiers, and he threw a quick glance at Stone Heart, took a couple more steps, and halted the group, as if only then realizing what he had seen.

He snapped a sharp salute toward this lieutenant he obviously did not recognize. "Sir, where is Private Holcomb?"

To the east the sky gleamed like polished gun metal, outlining the man's gaunt cheekbones and making dark sockets of his eyes.

Feeling exposed and vulnerable, Stone Heart returned the salute which he'd learned well enough at West Point.

"I relieved him, Sergeant. Sent him to breakfast."

Cocking his head, the sergeant opened his

mouth to speak, closed it, opened it again. "You did what, sir? I'm sorry, sir, I didn't get your name."

"Lieutenant Stone. And you are . . .?"

"Sergeant Holt, sir. Stone. Hmmm. Whose regiment are you in, sir?"

Stone Heart swallowed and stiffened. If he had to fight this man, the others might be confused enough to hesitate before they killed him. Or they might not. Fresh in off patrol, where they imagined savages lurked in every shadow, it wouldn't take much to set them off. He did all he could do under the circumstances. He lied, using information he'd overheard at the dance. The thing about lying well, you attacked your opponent with just enough facts to confuse him. And if you could, you scared the very britches off him in the process.

"I'm here with Colonel Evans of Fort Laramie and General Crook's aide, Lieutenant Schuyler. To investigate the breakout. It's no wonder these people escaped once already. I came out to take my early morning stroll and what do I see?" Without giving the man time to answer, he went on. "I see, Sergeant, the prison barracks completely unguarded. You've sent one young man out here in this cold all night, with no relief and expected him to remain alert. It's an outrage. This entire thing is an outrage, Sergeant." Stone Heart drew himself up, so that his chin was even with the bridge of the astounded sergeant's nose. Drawing on his experiences at West Point, he pointed a glower at the pond-muddy eyes that held only a flicker of rebellion.

"Did you know that every newspaper back east is calling for cessation to this brutal treatment of these poor, starving people? Are you aware that President Hayes himself has ordered an immediate investigation? Heads will roll, Sergeant, and yours may be one of them."

Before the dumbfounded sergeant could call up a response, Stone barked, "Dismissed. I will remain here until you can assign guards who aren't worn out from firing upon helpless Indians."

Snapping another salute, the sergeant marched his men toward the common and the distant call of a bugle. The poor man hadn't even attempted to summon a reply to the verbal attack.

Releasing a huge sigh, Stone Heart quickly inserted the key in the padlock and swung open the door.

Through the smoky gloom, he called her name.

She didn't reply and he stepped inside. From somewhere in the shadows came her lilting, clear voice and the song that had so enraptured him during the blizzard when he'd thought her lost and frozen. The music of her people, he supposed. The burr of her accent was more pronounced with the singing of the moving words that promised a love so strong it defeated sorrow and loss, even death. He located her then, sitting cross-legged near an old woman with a stiffened leg extended in front of her. In A'den's arms lay a baby wrapped in a faded scrap of blanket. With wide eyes it stared up into her face while she sang.

He moved to stand over her as she finished the final strains, and when she looked up he saw tears on her cheeks. He had not found the angry woman he'd expected.

"He will not live," she said in a hoarse voice.

"No."

"Oh, how can this be?" The wail of her question awoke some of those who had eaten and fallen asleep, and they stirred, making startled noises in their native tongue.

Stone Heart spoke to them until they settled, then to her, amazed that he had so quickly grown used to shifting from Cheyenne to English. "Leave him now with his mother. She will see to him. We have to hurry. I don't want you caught here."

"Is there nothing we can do?"

He drew himself up as tall as he could, met the questioning gazes of some of the men. "It is being done," he said, first in Cheyenne then in English.

Nearly sobbing, A'den lay the motionless child in the arms of its mother, grazed the wind-roughened cheek with trembling fingers, then rose and took Stone Heart's offered hand. Released from her earlier fear, she felt an intense grief for these people. And for this man forced to face a reality that might well destroy him.

"Hurry," he urged.

She turned for one last look. "Goodbye," she said. "Goodbye."

Only one answered her, and she saw it was the young boy who had cooked the stew.

Then they were outside, the door closed between her and that dying world. The shock of the frigid air made her dizzy and she gulped great drafts into her smoke clogged lungs. When she lifted her face toward the sky, tiny snowflakes kissed her cheeks and melted into her tears.

He would remain with her, had chosen not to stay behind to die in a hopeless effort to change something that could not be changed. A deep sorrow settled within her, lifted only by knowing that this man loved her and she loved him.

For a long while she couldn't speak, but hurried along beside him, struggling to match his long strides. Finally, she voiced the thoughts that crowded her mind.

"Out here we can surely do more for them. More than we could do if we remained in that dreadful place."

"They are going to be sent to the Red Cloud Agency. Those that don't go back to Kansas to stand charges for murder. It's something, I suppose. It probably means the army has given up on sending them down to Fort Reno and on to Indian Territory."

"At least we can demand they give them food and water, some blankets and more wood for their fire."

He squeezed her hand, stepped onto the wooden planks that ran along the front of the barracks where her quarters were located. He halted at her door. "I want you to get some sleep. You've been up all night."

Lying her palm alongside his icy cheek, she replied, "You too."

He shrugged and the cold look turned his eyes to ice, frightening her. She wanted to soothe him, but wasn't sure how. "What will you do?"

"I'm a lieutenant in the United States Army. I'll act as such. As long as they don't compare notes, I'll get away with it. I intend to play out this charade until I'm sure these people are going to be taken care of, sent home like they want." He gazed down at her, covered her hand with his.

"Will you be leaving...today?"

Swallowing painfully, she gazed beyond his shoulder. "I can't. No, I must stay here."

For a moment his features cleared, then he scowled. "I don't understand. I thought you were going home."

"Yes, yes, I was. But I can't return to St. Louis and leave this...this unfinished business behind. It's hard to explain, but my whole life I've been the only sister, protected by brothers on all sides. If it wasn't one brother it was another, taking the load I should have been sharing. Even my mother allowed it. They spoiled me."

He rubbed his knuckles along the side of her face. "You deserve to be spoiled. I too, would, if only—"

"No. You don't understand. I...while I was inside there, I found a purpose. Learned something about myself I never knew. I've never felt...well, important. Like something I might do would be worthwhile. I was raised to marry some man and make him happy. That was to be my purpose. Can you imagine?"

"Ah, A'den." He leaned down and kissed her forehead. "There's nothing wrong with making a man happy."

"I'm not so sure we can make someone else happy. Maybe we can only make ourselves happy, and when we do that those around us, those we love, will be happy too."

"But you said it yourself. You don't want to live like this, out here in the wilderness. Such hardships. What will you do if you don't return to St. Louis?"

She feared what she was about to learn here, about him and herself, but plunged on, heart in her throat. "I want to help them, however I can. Help you help them. Don't you want me to stay?"

She stared into his face with such yearning that he leaned down and brushed her lips with his, then took her in his arms, holding her as if he might never let her go.

"I want you to stay. But I don't know what will be the outcome of all this. What I can promise you when it's over...settled, we will be together. Are you sure this is what you want?"

"It is, oh, it is."

He held her a moment longer, squeezed her hand. "Then I will return. Perhaps you could go get the supplies Meeker bought, bring them back here and I'll try to arrange to have them given to the prisoners." He paused, dug Wessell's ring of keys from his pocket. "Here. Leave these in the officer's mess, if we are lucky he'll think he dropped them there."

She took the keys and dropped them in the

pocket of the buckskin jacket she wore. Gripped with a growing fear that she would never see him again, she held on tightly. "You will come back?"

"Oh, yes, I will." He kissed her quickly and was gone, striding across the common looking every bit a military man. She shuddered and wondered what it had taken out of him to put on that hated uniform and play the part of a white man once more.

She went inside, stripped off the buckskins and crawled into bed. She slept through breakfast, but woke early enough to wash her hands and face, tidy her hair, and answer dinner call at noon. The dress Retha had taken to the laundry hung on the wall, washed and ironed at the Chinese laundry. She slipped into it, enjoying the feel of clean cotton against her skin.

She continued to take her meals at the officers' mess, as originally invited to do by Captain Wessells. This morning he was nowhere to be seen when she entered the warm building filled with the delicious aromas of food cooking. Probably nursing the effects of too much drink from the night before.

Glancing around she spotted Lieutenant Stone, sitting at a table with a cup of coffee, looking as normal as any of the other officers in the room. She wondered briefly if she should acknowledge him, but he anticipated her, rose and beckoned her to sit beside him.

Smiling, she did so. "Is this wise?" she asked after a private poured her a steaming cup of coffee.

"You are the prettiest woman here. What could be more natural than that a young visiting lieutenant from back east would invite you to sit with him?"

Every day he sounded more and more like the white man he'd once been. How easily he'd fallen back into old habits. She took a sip of the coffee, nodded toward a young man across the way who smiled and bowed his head gallantly toward her. He had danced with her the previous night, as had several others who glanced in her direction.

"They're jealous," Lieutenant Stone said. "They would like to take my place."

"Have you learned any more about plans for the Cheyenne?"

"Yes. They fed them this morning and took in a stack of new blankets."

She squeezed his arm. "Oh, that's wonderful. I will go by the mercantile when I leave here and pick up those supplies."

"For now keep them in your quarters. It seems they will be well fed, for the time at least. Back east they're calling for the court martial of those men involved in shooting down the fleeing Cheyenne. Saying it wasn't a battle at all. Things will change drastically, I think."

The door opened and several captains entered. Stone Heart watched them, eyes slitted. To him, they remained the enemy, men who had murdered his people. He glanced back at her.

"At least, it's a start. I've heard that so many people are coming here to see firsthand what's going on that it's growing difficult for the army to contain them. Reporters from the *Chicago Sun Tribune* arrived a couple days ago. Crook is getting nervous, wants to blame Sheridan for this entire mess, but that brave general has taken off for parts unknown. He's more than happy to let it all fall on Crook's head."

Thoughtfully, he took a sip of coffee, and she did too. Contentment filled her, and she felt, sitting there with him, as if everything would at last be good between them. Both could look forward to beginning their life together.

Their plates arrived, filled with steaming boiled beef and thick homemade noodles. Platters of biscuits and bowls of butter followed. He did his utmost to appear to be the polished officer of his disguise, but having gone so long without enough to eat made that nearly impossible when it came to food.

She didn't bother him about the question of the supplies, what he planned to do with them. To interrupt him while he ate would have been cruel. When he had cleaned his plate and wolfed down four biscuits, she slid the remainder of her meal in front of him. Watched as he made short work of it as well.

When at last he was finished, he lifted his head and glanced around, as if afraid someone had taken note of his appetite. Gracefully, he took up a napkin and wiped his mouth, then leaned back. Surprisingly he didn't feel as guilty about becoming a white man as he'd expected he would. Perhaps it was just a matter of his own survival, after all. Only a fool would want to die for a hopeless cause with a woman like A'den to love. It would take some doing to grow accustomed to a life with her, but he was willing, even anxious to give it a try. More and more, returning to Montana with the Cheyenne was looking less attractive. He could not ask her to live that way, yet he wanted to be with her. Always. If she was willing to give up going home to be with him, then he could do no less.

After they ate he walked her back to her quarters. The sky had cleared to a crystalline blue. Chinook winds off the eastern slopes of the mountains danced across the plains. Encrusted ice melted into puddles of water, and the frozen mud of the passageways grew boggy and bottomless.

The shawl floated from her hair and she turned her face into the warmth of the sun kissed breeze. "What a lovely day. Makes me feel...somehow ordinary...normal. Like everything might be all right after all."

At the end of the boardwalk, he hooked an arm around her waist. "Careful. Don't—"

But he was too late as she stepped blithely off the boards and into the muck, shoes sinking out of sight. If he hadn't been holding her, she would have pitched forward on her face. As it was, he struggled to keep her upright and himself from following her into the quagmire where she now stood, buried halfway to her knees. To add insult to an already sticky situation, several mounted cavalrymen rode by, their horses hooves throwing up great clods that splatted over her skirt. One landed in her hair.

When she turned toward him, laughing, some of the thick stuff oozed down one cheek. And still she laughed. He studied her for a moment, the sparkle in her eyes, the pealing of her voice, and felt growing within himself a great joy such as he'd never known. For those few moments, he forgot the demons that drove him, let go the torturous memories of blood and death on the battlefield and his driving desire for revenge. Through tears of laughter, he eyed the mud and the safety of the boardwalk along the front of the barracks across the way where her room was located. With a lift of his broad shoulders, he waded in and scooped her up. Mud sucking at his boots with each step, he carried her to safety and deposited her high and dry under the porch overhang.

When he put her down, she kept her arms wound around his neck, nose buried against his warm flesh.

Both of them covered in mud, what they'd waded through as well as what had been thrown on them by passing horses, he leaned down and kissed her, deeply and with a great deal of passion. Right there in front of everyone. Caught up in the mood, she prolonged the kiss.

It was not exactly the way to remain unnoticed,

and Stone Heart knew it, even as he held her, lips tasting hers. No officer behaved this way in public and, with a great deal of restraint, he straightened, held her away stiffly. It would not do for an officer to see them like this and begin to ask questions. He was still in danger of being found out. The penalty for impersonating an officer of the United States Army was grave. He'd be lucky if he wasn't shot. Being around A'den had completely addled his brain.

She saw the look of concern alter his features. "I think I should see if I can get this dress laundered and take a bath," she told him, attempting some decorum.

The corner of his mouth twitched, but he managed to control the amusement. "And I have business to attend to. There's a meeting at Wessells' headquarters concerning the movement of the Cheyenne. I'm going to attend."

"Do you think that's wise?" She took his hand, held it concealed in the folds of her skirt.

"Probably not, but I will be careful. As soon as I learn what will happen, and when they will leave here, we can make plans to do so ourselves. I can't wait to get out of this uniform."

"And I can't wait to get back in your arms," she teased.

His fingers tightened around hers for an instant, then he let go and stepped back. Touching the brim of his hat, he tilted his head in farewell, and left her to make her way to her quarters at the far end of the barracks.

She watched him until he went out of sight around the corner, then turned just in time to see a figure in the shadows. Watching her. Though the man slipped out of sight along the end of the building, she thought she recognized Captain Wessells, the bandage on his head flashing white.

Concerned over what his presence might mean,

she stopped at Retha's door and knocked. A tall, bearded man, shirt open at the throat, opened the door, and she recognized him as one of the soldiers who had found her and Meeker and brought them in. This must be the missing Lieutenant Woods.

"Yes?" he asked, a tentative smile on his face.

"I'm sorry to bother you. I wanted to see Retha. I didn't know you had returned. My name is Aiden Connor."

His grin faded. "I know who you are. You're the woman we brought in with that trapper. His wife...you said?"

"Well, not exactly. I'm afraid I wasn't truthful at the time."

"Oh, and why was that?"

She was beginning not to like this Lieutenant Woods, and was sorry, for she did so enjoy his wife's company. "I would think you'd understand. A young woman, alone with a company of soldiers."

"Honorable soldiers. What are you implying?"

"Nothing. Of course, I didn't mean—"

"You were the one sleeping in a shelter with the man. Perhaps it was more to salvage your reputation than anything else, that you lied." With disdain he looked her up and down. "You look as if you've been wallowing in a mud hole."

Weary of the exchange, she smiled coldly. "I'm sorry to have bothered you. I'll call on Retha another time."

"She isn't here or you could speak to her now. Isn't that her dress you're wearing?"

"Yes, she was kind enough to loan it to me when I came in with nothing to wear."

"My wife is a kind woman, sometimes too kind. I'll tell her you called." Without waiting for her reply, he shut the door.

"Well, well," Aiden murmured and backed away.

Inside her own quarters, she took off the muddy

dress. She would have to wear the gown she'd worn
to the dance until she could get this one cleaned.

Dropping it down over her head, she
remembered a day what seemed like a lifetime ago
when she had dressed in her finest to make her
appearance on stage in Benson, only to be attacked
and run out of town. She felt somewhat the same
way after her confrontation with Lieutenant Woods.
The man was insufferable and she wondered how a
sweet woman like Retha could stand to live with
him. Probably all that kept the marriage together
was his being gone so much of the time. Retha never
met a stranger, and she probably contented herself
with many friends during his long absences.

She still held the muddy dress in her hands
when someone rapped on the door. Thinking it was
probably Retha, she ignored the buttons open down
the back of the gown and hurried to open the door. It
wasn't Retha she saw standing there, but a pale
Captain Wessells, hat in hand.

He'd probably figured out where his keys had
gone, and she prepared to defend herself. Instead of
saying anything, he pushed his way inside and shut
the door. The expression on his face frightened her.
This was more serious than lost keys.

"Do you know a Lieutenant Stone?"

He might have hit her. She dragged in a breath,
tried to steady her nerves. Dear God, what had
happened?

"Well?" He took her wrist in a harsh grip.
"Answer me, woman."

"I...well, yes, I guess I do."

"Wise of you not to lie. I saw you with the man
not an hour ago. You were carrying on in a way no
reputable woman would. What is he to you?"

"Why? What's happened?" She twisted, tried to
free herself. "Let me go, you're hurting me."

"I'll do more than that if you don't tell me the

truth. Who is he?"

"Lieutenant Stone. He...he came here from—"

"Enough, woman. No more lies. He's under arrest, and if I have my way, so will you be. For now, you are to remain in your quarters. Confined, unless you'd rather be tossed in the brig, which is where you belong, to my notion. But some of the others don't agree."

Still holding her arm, he shoved her backward toward the bed and one shoulder of the gown slipped off her shoulder. Distraught over what had happened, she simply sat on the edge of the mattress, rubbing her arm and staring up at him.

"What...what will they do to him?" she finally asked.

"Why, they'll put him up before a firing squad and shoot him, of course. That's the penalty for impersonating an officer of the United States Army. And if I have my way, his whore will be right there beside him."

Unable to speak, she watched in horror as the man stormed from the room, leaving the door standing open.

Chapter Seventeen

Aiden wasn't sure how long she sat on the bed staring through the window. The shock of hearing that Stone Heart had been arrested and would be shot left her numb except for the sharp throbbing at her temples. Once that began to wear off, she fought an urge to throw something through the glass. It wasn't fair that this should happen. He loved her, she loved him. They were going to build a life together. Why had this happened now?

Wessells was responsible, she knew it. But how had he known? Stone Heart played the part of a white officer well; no one could possibly have guessed that he wasn't who he said he was. The room grew colder as she sat there, leaving the fire untended, her mind leaping about for answers where there didn't seem to be any. There must be something she could do to stop this. With a guard on the door, she couldn't even leave. But she would not sit here while they prepared a firing squad. When would they do it? Would there be a trial or would they just take him out and shoot him? She dared not wait any longer to find out.

A hundred questions picked at her. Surely there was someone she could ask. Lieutenant Woods was right next door. Perhaps the guard would let her talk to him. Despite his attitude, he might be willing to explain what was happening. Maybe Retha could convince him.

Adjusting her dress, she went to the door and yanked it open. The guard turned, crossed his long rifle over his chest.

"Please, I wish to speak to Lieutenant Woods. He's just right there. Could you...?"

"I'm sorry, ma'am. You're confined to quarters. You can't leave."

"Well, then bring him to me. This is important. I must speak to him. Please, just knock on his door and ask if he'll see me."

The guard's slate-gray eyes darted from her to the nearby door, back again. She could see him wavering, and repeated her plea.

He considered a moment longer, then appeared to make a decision. "Move back into your room, ma'am." When she did he stepped briskly to the adjoining quarters and rapped, never taking his hooded gaze off her.

When the door swung open, she couldn't see who stood in the shadows, but heard Woods' crisp voice. "What is it?"

The guard remained at attention and saluted. "Beg your pardon, sir, but this lady would like a word with you."

Woods leaned out and peered in the direction of the guard's gesture. "What lady?"

Poking her head through the door, she called. "Lieutenant Woods, please. Retha, won't you help me?"

"My wife is not here. I told you "

"Nonsense," Retha said from inside. "What's going on out here?" She pressed past her husband to stand on the boardwalk, hands planted on her hips.

Aiden stepped over the threshold, but the guard barred her way. Furiously, she pushed at him, but he didn't budge.

"You're confined to quarters, ma'am. Sir, she's confined to quarters. If you could possibly come speak to her. She's very distraught, sir."

"Private?"

"Simmons, sir."

"Private Simmons. Have you never dealt with a distraught woman before?"

"Stop that, stop that right now," Retha said.

"Sir? Yes, sir." The guard did everything he could to ignore Retha Woods, who now threatened to join Aiden, and deal with his superior. He appeared reluctant to use force with an officer's wife.

Woods himself grew a bit flustered. "Mrs. Woods, you will conduct yourself like a lady and return to our home, this instant."

"What's going on, Aiden?" Retha asked, ignoring her husband.

"I have to get out. My...a friend of mine has been arrested, and they...they won't let me see him. I have to...they're going to shoot him. Please, help me."

The young guard did everything he could to keep the women separated, stepping this way and that when they tried to touch. Retha finally smacked him on the arm with the flat of her hand.

"Would you please stand still, sir," she demanded, whirled on her husband. "I wish to go inside and talk to her. Tell this...this boy to let me pass, or I'll—"

"Oh, blast and be damned if you'll speak to this whore about her half-breed lover," Woods blurted.

Retha drew herself up, glared at him. "Lieutenan Woods. Foul language is not necessary." Then to the private: "Stand aside, young man, and let me pass."

Though the private towered over her small frame, Retha attempted to shove him aside. Aiden admired her spunk, but wondered if perhaps she would pay later. Her husband had reached the boiling point, and though he didn't seem to be getting anywhere with Retha, he might well be reluctant to use force in front of witnesses. She could imagine him disciplining his wife in private later, and hated to be the cause of such trouble.

"Retha, it's okay. Please, I don't want you to get in trouble."

Fists bunched in front of him, Woods gritted out a command to the private. "Let Mrs. Woods pass and keep an eye on that door. I don't want that...that woman running free. The charges against her...friend are serious. There's no telling what she might do to get him free."

The private saluted, stepped aside for Retha to pass, then planted himself once again in front of the door. As Aiden closed it she heard Woods slam his.

When in Retha's arms, tears filled her eyes and she felt helpless, tangled in a web that held her so tightly there could be no release.

"There, there. You just go ahead and cry. Women shouldn't have to deal with the military. They're bullies trained to kill, and it's frightening. Sometimes I wish I'd never left home and followed Lieutenant Woods to this godforsaken place. Half the time I can't even get sugar for my tea. It's trying to the soul of any woman."

Patting Aiden, she steered her toward the bed where they both sat down. "Now, come on. Tell me what's going on. Perhaps I can help, or get that brute of a husband of mine to do something."

For a moment, Aiden couldn't speak. She fingered globs of mud on the hem of the dress she wore. Retha's dress.

"I'm sorry, it'll have to be laundered again. We...we were walking back from...I stepped in a mud hole. Then these soldiers rode by and...and the horses...threw it...all over me."

She picked at her muddy hair, cried so hard she could no longer speak.

"Well, now, that's nothing to cry about."

"Yes, it is," Aiden cried, put her hands over her face. "Oh, Retha. What am I going to do? I can't let them shoot Stone Heart."

"Oh, my dear. Shoot who? Your husband...I thought."

Struggling to control herself, Aiden shook her head. "No, he's not...not my husband, but I love him. We were going to get married...go away. He's...he's over in the jail."

"Well, for goodness sake. What did he do that they're going to shoot him? My husband called him a half-breed."

"His mother is...was a Cheyenne. He wore your...your husband's uniform...I took it, you see, so he could...could find out about the fate of his people. That's all he wanted to do. It was nothing so terrible, was it? Now they say he can be shot for impersonating an officer."

The thought of him confined behind bars was more than she could bear, but imagining his fury and despair helped her dry her own tears. She blew her nose on a handkerchief Retha dug out of her pocket. "He'll do something foolish. He won't stay there, even if he dies trying to escape. They can't keep him, and when he tries to get out they'll kill him. I have to do something."

"Well, of course you do. Why do they have you confined as well?"

"I think...I think that fool Wessells saw us kissing and thinks I'm guilty of as much as Stone Heart. And I suppose I am, but I have to get out of here. I just have to."

Retha glanced around the small room. "I can't blame you for that. But what will you do, I mean, how do you propose to get him out of jail?"

"I don't know, I'll think of something." She eyed her buckskins. "Help me out of this dress," she said, coming to her feet.

"What on earth?"

"Never mind. I don't want you in trouble too, so it's better if you don't know."

"Oh, don't you worry. I'm glad to help in any way I can. You don't know how tedious it is waiting around for something to happen in this place. You want out, I'll help you get out. It just might add some excitement to an otherwise dull and boring day."

As she undid the buttons of the muddy dress, she hatched her plan, and though Aiden desperately did not want her friend in trouble, she had little choice but to let her help.

As soon as she had slipped into the buckskin pants, shirt, and jacket, Retha set her plan in action. Instructing Aiden to stand to the side of the door, she swung it open.

"Private, would you step in here for just a moment? We need your help."

The boy glanced nervously around, craned his neck and peered inside. "What is it?"

"I...I dropped something behind the chest and we can't seem to move it. Please, it's important."

Giving in to her, he stepped inside, and when he did, Aiden slipped through the door at the moment Retha swung it closed. She would do everything she could to block the private's way as long as possible.

Racing along the boardwalk, Aiden reached the corner of the building. Where the boardwalk ended someone had laid down long slabs of wood across the muddy gap. She leaped over them and into the soft, unmelted snow in the shadowy alleyway. It slowed her down some. Behind her the private shouted for her to halt. He repeated it two, three, four times. On she ran, the muscles in her back taut, expecting at any moment to feel a bullet strike. But he didn't shoot. Instead, he pursued her, his boots pounding along the wooden walk. Burdened by the equipment he carried, he might not catch her. She could outrun him, she was sure. All she had to do was remain out of sight so he'd have no idea which way she went.

She made the back corner of the barracks and skidded around into the long shadows cast by the evening sun.

Behind her she heard more shouts. Others had joined the chase. She reached the grassy rear common, not worn down by the passage of troops and horses. While the ground was wet, the thick grass roots kept it from being muddy. Ahead, the stacked crates near the food storage sheds offered a place to hide if she could make it before the pursuers rounded the corner and spotted her. Legs pumping, she reached the crates and slipped beneath the draped canvas, hunkered down and waited. They hadn't come out from between the buildings in time to see her, she was sure. Panting from the sprint, she tried to hold her breath, but it was no use. Each gasp roared in her own ears.

They'd hear her, find her. And what of poor Retha? Her husband would be absolutely furious. Fighting panic, Aiden curled in upon herself, muffled her breathing and listened until her ears roared in the silence. Only if she remained in hiding would she be safe. If she ran now, they'd catch her, and there'd be no more kindnesses. No more remaining confined to her quarters. They'd toss her in the brig just like they had Stone Heart.

Toss her in the brig.

Maybe she ought to give up. At least then she and Stone Heart would be together.

No, that would be foolish. How would she get him out if she was locked up too?

She hugged her knees up against her chest. Something hard dug into her arm and very carefully she felt the ridged lump with trembling fingers.

Wessells' keys! They were still in the pocket of the britches she'd worn the night before when she and Stone Heart went on their midnight raid. She'd forgotten all about putting them there. And forgotten as well that she was supposed to see they got back to Wessells.

Would a key be there that would open the cell where they were keeping Stone Heart? And if it were, what good would it do her?

Heart kicking in her chest like a wild animal trying to escape a trap, she struggled to remain quiet. Not move or breathe or even think.

She heard footsteps. Running. Getting closer and closer. They stopped. Very close. Nearly on top of her. They'd hear her heart hammering at her skull, hear her breathing, hear the terror fighting to escape her chest. It closed around her like a thick, black fog. Its great fist squeezed her insides. To keep from crying out she pinched her mouth in one hand, squeezed her eyes shut as if that might somehow make her invisible.

"No one around here," a male voice shouted from so close she could reach out and touch him. The fear of being caught filled her belly, sickened her until she almost leaped from the safety of her hiding place to run like a rabbit flushed by the baying of hounds.

From far away, someone called, and he moved off. His boots slushed through the wet grass. There had to be a safer place for her to hide until dark. She fingered the keys. The storage shed, she could go in there, crawl behind the barrels and hanging sides of meat. Even if someone came to get food to prepare for supper, they wouldn't see her. It would be cold, but she could do it. She remembered canvas tarps and gunny sacks she could wrap up in. Somehow she would stay warm, just until dark, when she would find the place where they kept Stone Heart and set him free. Her mind refused to go any further than that. What they would do, where they would go, how they would live, she could not fathom. All that was important was getting him out.

Cautiously, she crept from under the canvas and

looked about. They were hunting for her elsewhere, faint shouts sounded from around and about. Wessells would be furious, maybe temporarily distracted from his vow to have Stone Heart shot. *Oh, don't let him take it out on Retha.* She had to console herself with the fact that Retha had been a willing participant, and she hadn't forced her to do anything against her will. She had lived with the man long enough to know what he was capable of doing to her.

With trembling fingers, Aiden found the proper key to the padlock on the shed, opened it, and slipped inside. Hopefully, when they found it unlocked, they would only think that someone earlier had forgotten to fasten the thing back. Or perhaps they wouldn't. But hiding in there was the only thing she could think of to do. From what they'd learned earlier, there would be too much activity around the Cheyenne prison so she couldn't go there. She would not be safe, not with all the attention they were attracting. There would be reporters, other interested visitors coming and going. Someone would spot her in a minute. No, she was better off here in the storage shed. At least until dark.

Some time later, as she lay curled in the far corner of the shed, beneath gunny sacks that smelled of flour, and a canvas tarp redolent with ham fat and a musty indefinable odor, she heard voices and the creak of the door opening.

A voice raised in denial. "I'm telling you, I didn't leave the lock undone. You must've."

"Not me, but someone did. Probably Elton, he's dim-witted, can't remember his name let alone the rules about locking up when we finish."

"Well, all I know is it wasn't me that didn't lock up."

"Fool, none of us must've locked up. When we finish tonight, you'd better see to it. I ain't catching hell for missing supplies."

The two continued to grumble at each other as they left with whatever they'd come after. Time to prepare the evening meal. Feeling secure, she leaned back in her hidey hole, then sat up with a start. She couldn't remain here. They'd lock her in for the night, and she wouldn't be able to get out till morning when they began preparations for breakfast. How could she have been so stupid? She was purely lucky they hadn't locked the shed up when they'd left. Must be too much trouble what with one or the other running back and forth to fetch supplies for the meal.

Would they lock it as soon as supper call sounded, or wait till after they'd cleaned up and stored whatever was left over? She couldn't take the chance, and so crept over and around the barrels, sacks and crates to the door.

Cautiously, she opened it a crack and peered out. The sun had set. Pink clouds streaked a lavender sky. Long dark shadows lay across the grounds, but it was still dangerous to be out and about with everyone searching for her. Worse, Wessells would certainly expect her to head straight for Stone Heart, wouldn't he? Maybe even put extra guards on. She wished she could convince him somehow that she'd lit out. Disappeared. Left the fort for good and all.

Maybe she could.

She darted from the shed, slipped into the darkness cloaking the back wall of the commissary. No matter how impatient she became, she had to hide out till full dark. Once the buglers sounded the changing of the guard and everyone was inside for the night save the regular grounds patrol, she could move about with more safety.

She watched with interest as several Indian children drifted by. They must belong to the

Blackfeet living in tipis near the outlying corrals where the cavalry mounts were kept. The scampering children reminded her of mud balls, for they had obviously been rolling about. A group of passing soldiers brushed them aside without scarcely sparing a close look. She gazed down at her hands and grinned. Dressed in these buckskins, if she muddied her hands and face, rubbed the stuff in her hair to disguise the color, she'd look much like they did. Such an uncomfortable disguise might be just what she needed to enable her to get close to the brig. Hang around there for a while and see what was what.

Kneeling near a mud hole, she rubbed the black stuff generously over herself, shuddering when she slathered it through her hair. She found a window and checked out her appearance.

"Gah, that's god-awful, but an excellent idea," she said under her breath. Without the red hair and pale skin that stood out like some sort of flag, she could be any one of the urchins running around this place.

Now, to try it out.

Heart racing, she ran from between the buildings and out across the common, brushing past several men who gave her wide passage but scarcely looked twice. It would work. At last, she was free to do what had to be done. And if no one spotted the white woman who'd escaped, maybe Wessells would believe she'd left the camp.

Because she dare not ask directions to the guardhouse, she was forced to wander about in the falling dusk until she found it. The military settlement was so large that the search took a while, and it was full dark before she finally spotted lamps glowing through barred windows of a structure that had to be the guardhouse, what soldiers often referred to as "the brig." Somewhere in there they held Stone Heart.

How she might get to him, she had no idea, but she crept along the back of the building, peering in each small window to see what was inside. For the most part she saw only darkness, but some of the windows shone vague light and she hurried to check them out. The glow appeared to be coming from a main hallway or larger room, falling through the cells and providing just enough light for her to make out figures, most sitting on the floor, a few others standing. Some of the cells were empty, others held several men, a few housed only one lone occupant each.

These she concentrated on, being very careful to take short peeks so she wouldn't be spotted. It took a while to make out more than shadows, but soon her eyes grew more accustomed to the dark and she could see the shape of a nose, the cut of hair, tell if one had a beard or was clean shaven. As well as studying each man in turn without being spotted, she had to be very careful not to be heard or seen by the guards that patrolled the grounds.

It was hair-raising work and her nerves tingled until she jumped at every sound before she finally spotted a man she thought might be Stone Heart. Of course, he would no longer be wearing the uniform, but she had no way of knowing what to expect in the way of clothing. Lamplight gleamed in his hair when he shifted from his seated position to stand with his back to her at the barred door. It was him. With hair like that it could be no one else.

Now what?

She picked up a tiny pebble and scraped it over one of the bars at the window. He paid no attention. Whatever noise she could make to attract him would have to sound normal to the guards and other prisoners, yet cause him to look.

Hoot like an owl? Bay like a coyote? Bark like a

dog? The ideas grew more and more ridiculous. Then she knew what to do. It was so simple, she didn't know why she hadn't thought of it earlier. Often around the barracks crowded with families of the men of the regiment, one would hear someone burst into song. It was a common enough occurrence. Women went about their chores singing, as did some of the older children. Often even the soldiers sang in cadence.

Perhaps no one else would pay attention, but Stone Heart would recognize her voice, of that she was sure. She walked away from his cell, then turned and started back, trying to sound as if she were out for a walk and singing under her breath. It might not work, but she couldn't very well shout, "It's me, Aiden, and I'm right outside your window."

He well knew her favorite, and so she began to sing "Danny Boy," softly so that anyone who listened would not become unduly curious. By the time she approached his window, she had reached the strain, *"From glen to glen, and o'er the mountainside."*

She glanced sideways, kept strolling and singing. Saw him turn, stride toward the opening, check over his shoulder, then peer outside.

"A'den?"

"'Tis I'll be here in sunshine or in sorrow," she sang, turning to walk back to him.

At the window, she moved close.

"Is it you?" He barely whispered the words.

"'Tis I, and it is you must go and I must bide," she sang.

He reached through the bars and she brushed his hand with shaky fingers. "We have to get you out of here. What can I do?"

"Leave this place now. Go far away. There is nothing you can do."

Grief burned her throat. "There must be something."

"No. I have what I wanted. They are letting my people go home. It's over. You must go home as well, A'den, or they'll put you in here with me."

"I can't, it's too late. They're looking for me everywhere."

"Steal a horse, sneak away, do something."

"I love you, I won't leave you here."

"Hey, you, what's going on in there?" Footsteps approached the cell, and Stone Heart slipped to the floor, rested his head on his knees.

Mouth dry and heart racing, Aiden ducked down below the window.

Inside, she heard Stone Heart mumbling and snorting as if making sleep noises.

"Keep it down in there, breed." The footsteps receded.

She remained there for a long while, then raised cautiously. He stood at the window, staring out into the darkness.

"You will be stubborn about this, I think," he finally said.

"Oh, yes, indeed I will. I won't leave until you can go with me, so you'd better come up with an idea fast."

He was silent so long, she thought he wasn't going to do as she asked, then he said, "There's only one way out and that's the front door."

"Then that's the only way in too."

"No, A'den. Don't do that. Don't be foolish."

"When will they...shoot you?"

"Oh, not for a while. First they will hold a trial, then they'll shoot me. I think they'll wait till the Cheyenne are shipped to the agency and all these reporters go home."

"Oh, my God, Stone Heart."

"What?"

"The reporters. I think I can get you out of here. Stay here, be patient."

"Don't worry, I think I'll be here a while."

"I love you."

"And I love you," he replied.

She heard him whisper her name as she scurried away, but she didn't reply. There was no time.

Chapter Eighteen

Running about through the dark, cold night wasn't Aiden's idea of a good time. The moccasins Stone Heart had given her were covered in mud and soaked by melting snow. If she didn't die from exposure, she'd be lucky. But she had to find the reporter Marcus Young. He seemed impressed with Stone Heart's mission, and might be willing to help get him out of trouble. The fort was so huge, with its rows of officers' quarters, separate barracks for both the infantry and the cavalry, she didn't know where to start looking for him. There seemed to be hundreds of men here when they gathered on the parade grounds of a morning.

Still, she would not give up. Night fires cast eerie shadows along the periphery of the parade grounds beyond which loomed countless structures that she hadn't yet searched. Low clouds reflected a pale glow in the sky, making it easy to find her way. Even though everyone had settled in for the night, she hesitated to venture into the light cast by those flickering fires. Actually, resting for a while on the boardwalk in front of the sutler's, she felt quite lost. It was time she stopped wandering about and rethought her options.

A warm wind had blown all day, then laid when the sun went down. Now an unearthly cold crept around her shoulders, biting through the buckskin jacket. She wished for the big ugly buffalo coat Wiley Lawson had given her. It had been lost in the shuffle when the soldiers raided Meeker's camp. She hugged herself and wondered again what she was doing here in this dreadful place so far from the comforts of her home near the docks of the Mississippi River. A home she had foolishly left behind in search of a new and better life. She had expected to find excitement in the world outside St. Louis, but had found only a harsh and extremely unkind environment.

At times like these she so yearned to rest in her mother's arms, enjoy the raucous exuberance of her five brothers, sleep in her own bed. Then she remembered the resignation in Stone Heart's eyes as he peered through the bars of his cell. Thinking of him awaiting execution reinforced her vow not to give up. She must save him, no matter the cost to herself.

Creeping out into the open, she studied her surroundings and saw she had come nearly full circle. Just down the way were the officers' quarters. Retha would know where the reporters were staying. Remembering the mood of Lieutenant Woods, she wasn't sure she dare return to their quarters. He'd be in an even more dreadful mood what with Retha aiding in her escape. She shivered and her teeth rattled. It appeared she had little choice, for if she didn't get in out of this cold, she could well freeze to death.

Having no idea what time it was, for it seemed she'd wandered for hours, she feared they would probably be asleep. Perhaps there would be a guard standing outside the doors of her own empty room in case she returned. Visions of the clean, soft bed and the little stove overpowered any fear she might have. If Retha had retired, she could hide in there until morning. Figure out someway to speak to the woman away from her husband's hearing.

At the officers' mess she cut through and approached from the back, retracing her earlier steps when she'd fled the pursuing guard. Peering from the alley, she saw that no one was about. A patch of light puddled outside the front window of the Woods' home. Someone was awake. Tiptoeing to the window she dared to peek in. Retha sat in a rocker, mending a stocking. Aiden could not see anyone else. Hopefully, that meant the lieutenant was in bed asleep.

She waited for several minutes, not sure what to do, then risked tapping lightly on the glass. Retha kept on rocking and sewing, mouth pursed in concentration. Aiden tapped again.

Retha glanced up, but something distracted her. A muffled voice from the other room. Perhaps asking about the noise. She replied, then looked again at the window. Aiden pressed her face to the glass, wiggled her fingers.

Retha lay down the mending and rose. She glanced toward the bedroom, then fetched a heavy cloak from the hat tree and stepped out onto the boardwalk, closing the door gently behind her. When she got a good look at Aiden, her eyes bugged.

"My goodness gracious. You look as if you've been mud bathing. What're you doing here this time of night?"

"I didn't think you'd still be awake."

"Oh, yes, it's the only time I get any peace when he's home is after he goes to sleep. He's been at me non-stop about your getting away."

"What'd you tell him? Did you get in trouble? Oh, come, let's go around to the side so no one will see us."

"I took my medicine like a good little wife. Let him pace and yell and throw his arms about. He's furious, but I convinced him that women often do foolish things. We must help our friends, no matter what they do." She chuckled. "Men don't understand us, anyway. You can tell them just about anything, and they'll sigh and shake their heads." Retha shivered, and took Aiden's arm. "No one is about.

The guards are on the perimeter. Let's step inside your quarters. It's cold out here. Aren't you freezing?"

Aiden backed through the door Retha unlatched and hugged herself to still the quaking deep in her belly. It wasn't much warmer inside.

"Where's your coat?" Retha asked. "You're chilled to the bone."

"This is all I have."

Retha shook her head and tut-tutted, then bustled through the darkness, returning with a blanket that she wrapped around Aiden.

"I never will be able to say again that nothing much happened while we were at Camp Robinson. Fort Robinson, I guess it is now. Hard to get used to the change. You've added some excitement to my life. But what else can I do for you? I have to hurry back. He might wake up."

Nodding, Aiden rushed to tell her. "I need to know where that reporter Marcus Young is staying. Can you tell me?"

"Oh, dear. Well, do you know where the infantry men's barracks are?"

"Over near the commissary? Yes."

"They've let them bunk in the building furthermost to the rear. I can't imagine how crowded it must be, and how difficult it is for them to concentrate. But you know the army isn't too concerned with the comfort of anyone save the upper echelon. Rank is all, as they say. Lowly lieutenants don't fare as well as the captains and colonels. Privates and corporals take the worst of army life."

Aiden's heart sank. How would she ever get to the reporters without someone seeing her? Maybe she could hide and wait, hope he came out. He would have to eventually, but the circumstances would have to be just right for her to dare approach him. Thinking of Stone Heart sleeping on straw ticking on the cold, hard floor in the guardhouse while he awaited his fate was enough to give her the courage to try.

"Why don't you stay here the night?" Retha said. "No one will think to look for you if you don't build a fire. Anyway, they think you've left the camp. I heard Lieutenant Woods say as much earlier." Again she chuckled with glee. "Imagine. He thinks no one could outwit his soldiers, certainly not a mere slip of a girl. I can't wait until he finds out you've been here all along."

At a tiny exclamation from Aiden, Retha touched her arm. "Oh, dear. Don't worry. I won't tell him till it's all over and done with. But I will have a lovely time in the telling, you can be sure.

"You're so cold. There are blankets here, wrap up in them and get some sleep. I know it's cold, but it's better than being out in the elements all night. Oh, my goodness, I wish there were more I could do for you. You look such a sight, all covered in mud. Even your lovely hair is full of it. Oh, my goodness." She stood there a moment, bundled in her cloak, as if she would say more if she could. "What will you do? Is it true they are going to shoot that young man?"

"Not if I can help it. I'm going to do everything I can to get him out. There's surely something someone can do. Public sentiment freed the remainder of those poor Indians, perhaps it can reach far enough to free him as well. They're going to murder him for doing what he thought was right. What is right, by God."

"It will be a very hard life."

"Pardon?"

"You love him and that will make for you a very hard life."

"How did you know? I mean, yes, I do. He's...oh, I don't know how to explain it so you'll understand."

"Understand? Don't be silly, child. Why, look at me. I love Lieutenant Woods. Isn't that enough said? No one can explain love, not why or from where it comes. Sometimes I think it's a vicious little joke God played on us all, but never mind."

Aiden actually joined Retha in a small laugh.

"I must go." Retha glanced around. "You must be brave. It will all work out. If there's anything else I can do, please let me know. And be very careful. I fear someone will shoot you in the dark, thinking you're some sort of wild animal."

A combination of the cold and the dried mud coating her skin and clothing made for a very uncomfortable night's sleep. Even after she pulled the thin mattress over her shivering body. Lying on the hard floor waiting for sleep to come, she recalled the nights spent in the shelter with Stone Heart. She wished him there beside her, warm body curled around her. Dreamed of the day they would be together once again someplace where the sun was warm.

****

Soldiers loaded the pathetic group of Cheyenne into wagons that morning. With a mixture of relief and sorrow, Stone Heart watched through the tiny window of his cell. Of the over two hundred people who had journeyed here from down south, many fewer than a hundred were left in the prison barracks. There might be more alive elsewhere, he had no way of knowing. He had heard several of the men who would be tried in Kansas for murder were being held elsewhere. He expected no one would ever see them again.

The uprising was finished, over, as were the people of Dull Knife and Little Wolf. These few poor survivors they were loading into the wagons would soon be on their way to the Red Cloud Agency, and from there it was said they could go home to join

Little Wolf and his band. To his sorrow, he'd heard that Dull Knife had died in the fighting. He hoped not, for he liked to imagine the great man home at last where he belonged.

As for Stone Heart, it no longer mattered where he belonged. He would soon die and his spirit would go to join all the others who had been slain here in this awful place. All he wished was that he could see A'den one last time before they filled his body with lead.

Were it not for her he wouldn't be sorry for anything he had done. Now he wished he could return to being white, and she could be with him. He had learned much at West Point that would stand him in good stead in the civilian life. Perhaps in California or Oregon. There they could make a fine life together, and he could forget the hate he felt for his father. Only by putting that behind him could he hope to offer her happiness. But it was too late. It was over. All over. The dreams were but shadows in an everlasting night.

Footsteps approached and he turned from the window and his reverie.

"You have a visitor," a young private announced, and went to stand a few feet away, leaving the young reporter, Marcus Young, outside the bars of the cell.

"How are you?" Young asked.

Stone Heart nodded, unable to bring himself to tell the man his innermost feelings. How much he regretted, how he wished he could do everything all over again.

"They let them go."

"Yes."

"How do you feel about that?" Young held a pad and pencil, ever a reporter.

"I'm sorry I couldn't help them more. I had nothing to do with it, but I'm glad it is over. That no more will die. I grieve for all those who were slaughtered needlessly, though. What a pity it is."

"I filed your story."

Stone Heart glanced at him. "It does not matter now."

"It might."

A strange gleam in the man's eyes piqued Stone Heart's curiosity. "I don't understand. The people are free."

"Do you know of Libbie Custer?"

"The wife of Long Hair? Never met the woman. Nor desired to."

"I hear she's quite vexed, threatened to sue the newspaper. Says her husband was never untrue to their marriage, and certainly never fathered any bastard half-breed children."

Stone Heart snorted with derision. "There's not a Cheyenne nor Sioux woman he hasn't tried to bed, save the elderly and ugly, and sometimes he simply closed his eyes. It is true he was not married when he lay with my mother, though."

"Uh, I don't know if you're aware of it or not, but Mrs. Custer is quite a formidable figure. She has spent every waking hour since her husband's death repairing the cracks in his reputation. She's building a legend and won't sit still for your claim. Is there any way you can prove he's your father?"

Hands gripping the bars as if to throttle them, Stone Heart tried to control his fury. "No, and I don't care to either. I'd as soon forget it."

Young scratched his head and glanced toward the guard, who appeared to have no interest in them at all. "It might be to your advantage to kick up a fuss about this. Could be it would save your skin."

"I'd rather go to my death than claim that bastard as my father. I don't see how that would save me."

Young raised his shoulders, his babyish expression forlorn. "I wish you'd think this over. I'm sure the army will do everything they can to cover up your claim. Could be you could make a deal."

"I think you just want another story to feed your readers."

Young laughed. "Of course, I do. That's my job." Again he shrugged. "But if it could help save a life, I'm all for that too. And think of the story that would make. Besides, I like you and your spunky woman friend. I hear she literally slipped from the clutches of the army and they can't seem to find her anywhere. Bet that put some burrs in Wessells britches."

"Do you know where she is?" Stone Heart asked.

"No, sorry. If I see her should I tell her you're ready to die?"

Stone Heart flexed his arms, and for a moment wished his hands were wrapped around this self-satisfied man's throat.

Young must've seen something in his eyes, for he took a step backward and the guard made a motion to approach. The reporter waved him away. "Look, I'm sorry, but sometimes we have to do distasteful things. All of us. I understand Crook is on his way back here and he wants Wessells' hide for stirring this hornet's nest. You think about it. You tell me all you know about your mother and Custer, dates, places, anyone who might have been there who is still alive, and I'll get you out of here. Think of that pretty little redhead. I'd say whatever you have to do would be worth it, wouldn't you?"

Gritting his teeth, Stone Heart turned away to keep from spatting on the man. "Get out of here, now. Leave me to face my own death in peace."

****

Early that morning Aiden rejoined a group of Blackfoot children cavorting near the guardhouse. They rolled and played in a snow bank piled against the north side of the building. Though she was a bit larger than the biggest boys, the soldiers didn't single her out when they glanced at the raucous bunch. She saw Marcus Young leave the guardhouse and watched with a great deal of interest as he hurried toward the station. Excitement filled her. He had been inside, probably seen Stone Heart, maybe even talked to him. Did she dare approach the man?

Leaving the group of children, she darted across the muddy road and sat down outside the station, back against the planks. It was a long wait, but at last he came out.

After glancing about to make sure they weren't being watched, she hissed his name. Sweeping a quick look over her, he started off the porch, holding his bowler on against a stiff wind. Disregarding the danger, she ran after him, tugging at his coat tails.

"It's me, Aiden. Did you see him? Is he all right? When are they going to do it?"

"My God, woman. They're looking everywhere for you. Don't you look a sight." He appraised the road, then grabbed her arm and dragged her into the barn where extra animals were kept for the stage run. Sweet rose water from his toilet nearly overpowered the smell of hay and horses and leather.

Before he could say anything, she pulled on his arm. "I have to get him out of there. Please, can you help me? Don't let them kill him."

"Easy, settle down." He pried her soiled fingers off his coat sleeve. "What have you been doing, wallowing in a hog trough?" With bright eyes, he studied her for a moment, then began to laugh. "Well, well. Aren't you the smart one? You look just like one of those urchins out there. No one even gives you a second look, do they?"

She shook her head. "Can you help him?"

"I just did. He won't like it one bit, actually ordered me not to, but knowing what I know, I can't just stand by. Wessells is, if you'll pardon my language, a bung hole. Besides, it's going to make one whale of a story back east. People'll eat it up. And if Libbie Custer was fit to be tied before, wait'll she reads the story I just sent. She'll do anything to put a stop to this. The publicity that would follow this execution would keep raking up those nasty rumors about her womanizing husband for years to come. She'd never recover from the stench of it."

"I don't know what you're talking about, and don't really care, as long as it gets him out."

"Oh, I can't guarantee that, but I can guarantee it'll stir up as big a fuss as there's been since the Confederates were given amnesty. All eyes are on this place, and I intend to keep the fires burning. If I could get him to tell me more about his mother and father, I could do more, but he refuses to talk about it. What I'm writing may be enough for the army to put the lid down fast and hard. There're reporters here from Chicago and New York now. Nothing they do will be secret, and I filed the story first."

Anger burned in her throat. "You don't really care if he's shot or not. All you care about is your story."

He patted her arm. "No, that's not true. It's just that I'm not a miracle worker and I won't make promises I can't keep. I could use more information about Custer and your young man's mother, but he's so danged stubborn."

"I want to see him."

Head swiveling in all directions, he said, "I don't see how that's possible."

"Make it possible. I can get him to talk to you. Tell you what you want to know."

He laughed harshly. "I don't think so. He's adamant. Says he'd rather die than claim 'that bastard' as his father. And those were his very words."

Choking back tears, she turned away, stared through the open doors at a rattling freight wagon, wheels deep in mud.

"Okay, if you won't help me, I'll do it myself," she cried, broke from him and ran out into the street. To her surprise, she saw she stood directly in the path of a column of soldiers. At their head rode several officers. One on a magnificent, high-stepping mount out ahead of the others, was a bearded man wearing a great caped coat with a fur collar. He must be very important, for his entrance caused a great stir. She darted toward the guardhouse, saw the boardwalk out front filled with soldiers watching the procession.

They paid little attention to the muddy little Indian who slipped along the wall at their backs and through the door. Gently, she pushed it shut behind her and quickly surveyed the room. A ring of large iron keys lay on the desk nearest a barred door. Without a plan, she grabbed them up and inserted one into the keyhole, then another, until she found the one that worked. Moving now with no conscious plan, just the frantic urge to free Stone Heart, she hurried past the cells, taking only an instant to check each one out.

Then she saw him, back to her, peering through the small window as the soldiers rode past. She wouldn't have known him save for his wavy blond hair, for he wore grubby pants and a loose linsey-woolsey shirt. On his feet, though, were the familiar knee-high moccasins still stained with his own blood.

Almost dancing with urgency, she fumbled a key into the lock. He whirled, crouched, as if ready to fight, then saw her. At first he didn't recognize the grubby creature she'd become, but then she spoke his name, her sweet voice slamming into him with such force he stumbled.

"What are you doing here? They will catch you.

Leave, leave now before they find you. A'den, please do not do this crazy thing."

The lock clicked loudly. "Too late," she said, reached inside and grabbed his hand. "Is there a back door?"

"Through there, but it's locked."

Smiling tremulously, she held up the keys and shook them. "Come on."

Unable to quite believe what was happening, he led her through the maze of cells to the oaken door that opened onto the alleyway between the guardhouse and the corrals. Through it meals were delivered and slop jars were carried out and emptied.

The way was deserted and he sprinted for the corrals, still hanging onto her hand, expecting at any moment to hear a cry of discovery. Maybe someone would simply take aim and fire, saving the army a trial. But no one saw them. Everyone had turned out to watch the arrival of General Crook. The reporter had told him Crook was on his way, and he'd been right. Perhaps he should have paid more attention to the other things the man said. Just maybe the cocky little pigeon knew what he was talking about after all.

At the corral fence, he lifted A'den over and leaped after her. About twenty horses milled into a tight bunch, eying the intruders with ears twitching. He slipped past them and into the stable.

"Look for saddles, blankets, anything we can use, but be quick." Grabbing up a couple of bridles, he eased back outside, picked two long-legged roan geldings. The cavalry liked tall, strong mounts, and she would have to make-do with her shorter stature. With no wasted motion he bridled both and led them into the stable where she waited with blankets. Snubbing both animals he quickly saddled them. She had found saddlebags that looked a little the worse for wear, probably discarded by their owners.

"Roll up any extra blankets you can find, tie 'em behind the saddles. Hurry, we cannot have much time before they discover I'm gone."

She did as he asked, and no more than finished the job when he grabbed her from behind and boosted her high into the saddle.

"I don't...I can't ride," she said.

"Hang on with your knees. Hug him tight. Lean forward to make a smaller target. Stay low and just hang on." He mounted, grabbed the reins of her horse, kicked his in the ribs and they galloped through the wide doors.

The tail end of the cavalry column moved out of sight between rows of buildings as he made for the road that led away from Fort Robinson and into the hills. Wind kissed his face with a promise of freedom, and his heart hammered against his ribs. Yet he dare not hope they would get away clean. Any moment he expected the shock of a lead bullet in his back. He only regretted that she too might be shot down, but he could do nothing about it. It was much too late to turn back or to leave her behind. They were in this together, until the very end.

The first hour or two he pushed the horses hard. Headed north, they climbed up out of the White River Valley. At the hot springs they would turn northwest and make for the Bighorns. They had to avoid the Red Cloud Agency, which would be crowded with soldiers that had accompanied the Cheyenne earlier this morning. On they rode without rest. The sun hung at the peak of its winter apex, a brisk northwest wind blew, and they could not stop moving into it. Amazingly, no one had chased after them, so that meant they hadn't been spotted leaving. Soon though, a search party would fan out to track them and bring them back. Probably dead or alive, since he'd been under a death sentence. They had to put many miles between them and the fort before nightfall, then find a good place to hide, rest the horses and sleep. He knew better than to ride the animals to death. As for themselves, they would need food and water and he wished for a weapon, but they had none of those things. And so he kept riding, leading her mount and not speaking to her of the things that worried him. There would be time for that later.

She didn't complain. Not even when her backsides grew so sore she wanted to cry out with each step. The insides of her thighs throbbed, and her buttocks grew numb. How could anyone ride these miserable creatures all day every day? Her mouth grew dry and her empty belly growled. Still, he didn't stop; and she didn't ask.

The sun dropped behind the distant mountains to the west and darkness crept around them until she could no longer see the ground beneath the hooves of her horse. The air cloaked her in miserable cold, and still they rode. She wanted to beg him to stop, to let her down, but she couldn't. All she could do was wait to die, right there in the saddle. She probably wouldn't even fall off. He'd just ride on and on and when he did finally stop, he'd find her stiff body, clinging to the back of the horse.

And then, blessedly, he led them into a thick grove of trees and the horse stopped moving under her.

She let out a moan and tried to lift her right leg from the stirrup. It wouldn't move.

"Wait, A'den. I'll help you," he said, the first words he'd uttered since they'd ridden from Robinson that morning.

He came to her in the darkness, enclosed her waist in both hands and lifted her off. She fell into his arms, unable to stand, and he carried her to a place where he lay her gently on a bed of pine needles. She could smell water and felt a damp warmth in the air.

"Lay here until I take care of the horses. I will be back."

"I need water," she said, tongue and lips so dry they could scarcely form the words.

It was so dark she couldn't see him, but heard him rustling about. In a moment he lifted her head and gave her a handful of water. It was warm and tasted strange, but she gulped it down and he brought her more. She lay back and knew nothing else until he lay down beside her and took her in his arms.

Now she could die in peace.

Chapter Nineteen

Aiden awoke as she had fallen asleep, cradled in Stone Heart's arms. For a moment she felt only serenity, and thought perhaps they were dead. She could see nothing but an enclosed darkness. No trees, no sky, no moon and stars, no sunlight. But one didn't feel pain after death and her body was one huge aching mass. Snuggling closer to him, she groaned with the slight movement. He spread a hand over her mud clogged hair.

"Hello," he said and kissed her forehead. "Do you hurt?"

"Oh, yes. Ummm. You're warm."

"It's the spring, the steam off the hot water."

She saw he had stretched a blanket over them that captured the escaping heat and held it around them like downy fur.

"I thought I'd never be warm again. Is it morning?"

His arms tightened around her. "Early. I am so sorry, what has happened to you. All I wanted was to help my people and look what it did to you."

"We're together now, that's all that matters." She shifted and dried globs of mud chafed her body. "Ugh. Do you suppose I could take a bath?"

"A bath? Do you think you need one?"

He chuckled and she joined him. He'd actually made a joke. Granted, a small one, but a joke nevertheless. A wonderful contentment spread through her at being there with him. Rather foolish, considering that they had no food or supplies, were in the middle of nowhere and were being pursued by no telling how many soldiers. And when they left she'd have to ride that dratted horse again. She wasn't sure she could.

"Did we really get away?" She was almost afraid to ask the question. "Won't they come after us? Marcus said the army will try to hush it all up because Libbie Custer is making such a stink. Maybe they won't carry out the execution."

He held her so close she could hardly breathe and said nothing for a long while, then whispered, "We dare not count on that."

He was right, of course, but it was a wonderful dream.

Shifting, he began to remove her buckskin clothing, first the jacket, then the shirt. She wore nothing under it but a camisole and he slipped that off as well, his big fingers fumbling with the ribbons that tied it together over her breasts. Though much of the dried mud had been worn away, she remained rather grubby. He licked one nipple clean, took it in his mouth. The moist warmth of his kiss sent ripples of pleasure through her tired, sore body.

He raised his head, nuzzled her throat. "Let's get in the water."

"Kiss me again."

Lifting her, he took the breast in his mouth and slipped from under the makeshift shelter into the hot water of the spring without standing.

Its delicious warmth enclosed her as they went under, his mouth clinging in a long, hungry kiss. When at last they came up for air he alternated between eagerly touching her naked body and removing his own clothing, the awful shirt and pants supplied by the army to its prisoners. Standing waist-deep in steaming water he gazed at her as if seeing her for the first time. In the pink of early dawn, his eyes gleamed, and though she searched their depths she saw no regret. He had left with her and not followed his people. Would he one day blame her for that?

Wrinkling his nose distastefully, he plunged the prison clothing into the water. "I wish I could burn them, but I have nothing else to wear. Do you know where my clothes are?"

She hadn't thought of them at all during the past few days. Not since she'd come home to find the stolen army uniform gone and his buckskins in a pile on the floor.

"I put them away." Threading fingers through his hair, she pulled his mouth down to taste his lips, his tongue, the velvety softness within. Her hands roamed his naked body, slick from the water, and she pressed hers close. Breast to breast, belly to belly, thigh to thigh. Warm and slick and aroused.

He spread both hands under her buttocks and lifted her against his hardness, released a great sigh of pleasure when she took him into her most secret self.

Inside her and cradled in the warm embrace of the spring, he felt more alive, more hopeful, than he had at any other moment in his life. If all he could do was keep her forever, he would never ask for more. Daft as that might sound under the circumstances, he still couldn't think beyond it. For in his heart he knew this time with her would probably be all they ever had. All that was left of a life he'd spent pursuing all the wrong things, seeking vengeance on a man who didn't know or even care that he existed. Ruining his own chances at surviving in a world gone crazy, a world not of his making but one in which he must live or die. Nothing else mattered but her love and it was too late for him to keep that.

He held her so closely, remained so still that she grew worried.

"What is it? Are you all right?" She wanted him

to make love to her, but he simply held her, hands trailing slowly up and down her bare back. He filled her, enclosed her, yet she sensed he had gone away.

When he didn't answer, she leaned back to look into his face. She was surprised to find his eyes closed, tears running down his cheeks. Her ferocious warrior was crying.

"What's wrong? Please, talk to me."

Without opening his eyes, he replied. "I am tired of fighting, tired of watching what is happening. One day someone will come and take all this away from the white men. I vowed, in that cell, if I escaped we would go away somewhere together. Live like you deserve to live. And forget all this. Forget it all. And being here with you now, I know I can do that."

"But your people." She cupped his face, studied the finely sculpted features closely.

His gray eyes shimmered with unshed tears. "You are my people."

Sobs caught in her throat and she kissed him tenderly. "I missed you so much. I love you so much."

"Oh, me too. Me too." The last was muffled against her throat.

Above, streaks of pink and lavender clouds slashed across the blue sky. Too soon the sun would be up and the soldiers would find them, ride them down. It was as if time could not wait to tear them apart.

If only she could hold back the passage of the next minute, make the world stop right then, cradle them forever just as they were. Arms locked around his neck, she arched her back, felt him grow large inside her, reach for the heart of her essence. Touch it and awaken a spirit within she'd only dreamed of possessing. It saw beyond the day, far past the night and on into infinity, where beauty took away ones breath.

Eagerly, she met his rhythmic throbbing with a

demand of her own, soared to an explosion of passion. The water around them roiled in a frenzy. Morning turned to night, stars tumbled and bathed the sky in fire, and she knew nothing but his hands, his mouth, his flesh embracing her soul.

From the root of his desire his heartbeat grew like a storm swallowing the morning, drove him into a land where spirits dwelt. Where drums beat the rhythms of the ancient ones. In his blood, the unholy thunder would always remain, for in this one thing he would forever be a savage. He couldn't let her go, held her tightly, feeling himself rise and fall, rise and fall, within the cavern of her sweetness. Tasting, touching, clinging as if to leave her safe, warm haven would mean death.

Even in rest the water rocked them gently, and still they held to one another. If he turned loose she would not be there. In his arms would be that stinking straw bed, and him sitting cross-legged on the floor in that narrow cell back at Fort Robinson. And he'd never see her again. But the very worst part, this would have been only a dream.

He gasped as if sucking in his last breath, ran his hands over the curve of her shoulders, fingered the tiny bones in the center of her back, cupped the lush ripeness of her buttocks. She was real. He had to believe that.

He could hardly speak, but had to say something. Tie this moment to reality. "I thought I'd never see you again."

She cried against his neck. "All I could think of was them shooting you. I wanted to die with you if that was the only way we could be together."

Even in the water he felt the teardrops against his skin. He thought of what she said and was surprised to find himself smiling. No one had ever loved him this much.

They made love again, this time prolonging each

touch, each kiss. The final coming together stretched into a long, leisurely experience that crested as the sun burst gloriously above the horizon, as if born of their climax.

At long last she stirred, sitting in his lap in the shallows, up to their necks in warmth. "We can't stay in here all day."

"Why not? It is cold and our clothes are wet."

"I know. One of us has to get out and hang them. The sun and wind will dry them and we can move on. I'm afraid they'll catch up with us."

Despite everything, he nourished a small secret belief that the soldiers would not come. He could take her into the Bighorns and there he would build them a shelter from the cold. He could hunt and fish for food and come spring they could move on wherever she wanted to go. The thought of being alone with her in the mountains where no one could find them almost made him sick with longing.

He moved her aside. "I will do it. Stay here."

"Are you sure you know how?" she teased, gazed with pleasure upon his virile, naked form as he climbed from the spring and bent to retrieve their wet clothing.

"It is woman's work, but I will manage." Finding some low shrubbery in the sun, he spread the britches and shirts to dry, then turned to go back to her.

The men came out of the woods on either side of the hot spring, stopped to aim their rifles at her. Shouting orders, one screaming over the other until the words were a blur of brutality.

Choking on his own fury, Stone Heart lunged toward her, not sure what he intended to do. He only knew he must be with her.

"Another step and we shoot her," one of the soldiers shouted. "It's you we want. Doesn't matter what happens to her, but it'd be a damn shame,

301

nevertheless."

The futility of the situation brought him to a halt. It was no more than he'd expected, and he wouldn't get her killed.

"Collier," the same soldier shouted, and one of the men on the opposite side of the spring shouted, "Yo?"

"Take the breed a blanket so he can cover himself. That's disgusting. Cruikshank, drag the woman out of the water."

"Should I get her a blanket, too?"

"Not just yet. She's not so disgusting. How long's it been since you seen yourself a naked white woman?"

"It's been a while, LT."

"Enjoy."

"Bastard," Stone Heart shouted. The man who'd just handed him a blanket hit him in the gut with the butt of his rifle. He grunted from the sharp pain and bent over, dropping the blanket.

"Pick it up," the man ordered and slammed him on the shoulder, sending him to his knees. That the man held back and did not club him to death was enough to tell Stone Heart they had been ordered to bring him in alive. So they could put him up before the firing squad in one piece, he supposed.

"Stop it," Aiden screamed. "Leave him alone. I'm getting out."

Stone Heart watched her crawl from the water, trying to cover herself, one arm over her breasts, the other hand spread between her thighs. Her red hair hung in strands down her back and steam poured from her in the cold air. Anger boiled into his throat and he leaped from his squatting position, hitting the soldier standing over him so hard they both tumbled to the ground.

"Shoot her, Private Cruikshank."

"Noooo," Stone Heart yelled, releasing his grip

on the man's throat.

"Sir? Now, sir?"

"Now, Private."

The man raised his rifle and took aim.

Arms wide in supplication, Stone Heart staggered to his feet, shouting at the lieutenant. "Stop, stop it. I'll go with you. No more trouble. Just don't hurt her."

"Now, LT?"

"No, you can wait, Private."

Aiden hugged herself, fear a live thing that coiled through her system like a giant snake. She shook with it and the cold, could not tell them apart. "Please give me a blanket," she begged, teeth chattering. "I'm freezing."

The lieutenant nodded at Collier, who went to fetch one from his horse, led into the clearing with others by another soldier.

Stone Heart counted maybe half a dozen men and a Crow tracker. They must have sent scouting parties out in all directions and this one cut their trail somewhere. Filthy Crow. If he could get him alone, he'd rip out his heart.

The man called Collier unrolled a blanket and standing in front of Aiden, wrapped it around her shoulders. Closing it over her breasts, he spread his hands on her.

Afraid that if she did anything he would take it out on Stone Heart, she squeezed her eyes shut, shuddered, and waited for him to stop feeling her. When he finally let go, she clutched the wrap tight and staggered backward. Sick at heart, she tried to think of some way to escape. But these men were not about to let that happen. They would drag her and Stone Heart back to Robinson, stand him up against the wall and shoot him, and probably do as they pleased with her for as long as they wished. She no longer trusted any of the white men in that place.

From Wessells right on down to these privates, they were all a bunch of killers. Worse by far than any of the Cheyenne, who had been kind to her even after what the whites had done to them.

Though she knew she ought to watch her mouth, she couldn't resist one last barb. "It seems to me it's the white man who is the savage and not the Indian, Lieutenant."

"Shut her up," the man said, not addressing her directly.

Collier poked her with the barrel of his rifle just hard enough to hurt. "You heard the LT, shut up."

A man appeared leading the two mounts Stone Heart had hobbled nearby. "Add horse theft to the charges. These belong to the U.S. Cavalry." He smacked the flat of his hand on the brand on one of the gelding's shoulder.

"Saddle 'em and let's get moving. I want to be back to Robinson before dark."

They allowed them both to dress, then tied Stone Heart's hands behind his back and lashed his feet together with a rope under the horse's belly. One of the privates tied a blanket around him against the cold. Then Collier tossed Aiden into the saddle and started to do the same to her.

"I can't ride that way," she said. "I'll fall off."

"Put her belly down over the saddle, then," the LT ordered.

Before they had gone a few miles, she regretted that decision but could do nothing about it. After a while, she began to pass in and out of consciousness. She only fully came to when she was dragged out of the saddle at the fort, mouth dry and insides on fire from the long, torturous ride over the saddle. When they gave her water she brought it right back up and began to scream with cramps in her belly. Someone picked her up and carried her away.

Stone Heart watched the proceedings with a

great sorrow in his heart. But he knew that she would recover from her ordeal, and could only hope they would not punish her for her part in his escape. This was no more than he'd expected, and he would prepare himself to die in the Cheyenne way.

A great crowd had gathered when they rode into the fort, even though it was past dark. As he was dragged into the guardhouse, he saw the young reporter who had tried to help him. He looked hopeful and actually grinned. Probably thinking of the story he could write.

****

Aiden awoke in total darkness in a soft bed under clean covers and wearing a soft nightgown. Obviously she wasn't in a jail cell. Still sick to her stomach, she moved gingerly to the edge of the mattress and slid her legs out. When she tried to stand, dizziness overwhelmed her and she fell back. She lay there until her eyes grew accustomed to the darkness. The square of a window looked out into a moonlit night and furniture made formless hulks in the room. A shadow moved across the patch of light. A soldier, a guard. Of course, that only made sense. Finally, she realized she was back in her quarters. Someone had built a fire and made up the bed. None of that comforted her. All she wanted was to be with Stone Heart. Why hadn't they put her in jail? She stole the uniform, she helped him escape, actually made it all possible.

"What is wrong with you people?" she cried out, dragged herself from the bed and across the room where she beat on the door until her hands hurt.

The guard ignored her, and after awhile, sore, sick, and discouraged, she crept back to the bed, crawled in under the covers, and drifted off to sleep. There she could lie in his arms and make believe everything would be all right, even though she knew it never would be.

Someone was shaking her shoulder, speaking to her in an excited voice. "Aiden, wake up. Come on, you have to get dressed. We must go. Now."

Bleary-eyed, she dragged herself to a sitting position. Every muscle and bone in her body throbbed, and she couldn't think straight. "Where are we going? Why? What is it?"

Retha began to unbutton Aiden's nightgown. "Hurry. Come on. I brought you a clean dress. Look at you. Covered in bruises. Someone will pay for this if I have to restrict Lieutenant Woods to the enlisted men's quarters for a year."

Aiden allowed Retha to pull the nightgown off over her head and drop a dress on in its place. "What is happening?"

"No time for a camisole, and as for those corsets, I never wear one except on special occasions. One learns in the west to do away with such folderol. Come on, child. You're like a wet noodle. Stand straight. Let me do something with that hair."

Fists doubled at her sides, Aiden repeated, "What is happening? Is it Stone Heart? Are they going to murder him?"

"No one is going to get murdered. Your hair is a mess. Good thing I thought to bring a brush. I'll do the best I can with it. Okay if we just leave it loose? No time to do it up. It's so beautiful anyway. Where're your shoes?" She rummaged around, found the pair she'd lent Aiden for the dance. "These will have to do, those disgusting Indian things are dreadful. Slip into these. Sorry there're no stockings. I only just found out, and there's no time to lose."

"Just found out what?" Frustration brought tears to Aiden's eyes. She wanted to choke an explanation out of her friend, but knew from experience she would chatter on and tell her what she wanted to tell her, regardless of anything Aiden might say.

"Oh, dear, I forgot to bring you a cloak. We'll stop and get you one. Hurry, now. You look fine, let's go."

She dragged Aiden out the door, went inside her own room briefly and came out with the cloak she'd loaned her earlier, tossed it around her shoulders, took her hand, and off they went at a run.

The entire place was in an uproar. Morning formation had broken on the parade grounds, and great groups of men all hurried in the same direction as she and Retha. The sun had not yet risen, but dawn smeared the glowering sky with a metallic glow. The wind promised snow, as did the low-hanging clouds. Just the kind of day for someone to die.

Thinking that, Aiden sobbed and tears blurred her vision, but she stumbled on behind Retha. "Where are we going?" she finally managed.

"Post Headquarters, and we have to hurry. They're beginning the trial. General Crook insisted, said he doesn't want to be stranded here with the storm coming."

"The trial? Oh, dear God, help him," Aiden cried. "Please don't let him die."

Retha led her toward the double doors of a large building where guards kept the milling crowd at bay. She walked right up to the entrance, but a guard stepped sideways to bar her way.

Someone took Aiden's elbow from behind. She turned to see Marcus Young. He smiled, quite jovially she thought. "Come on, I have a seat for you. These ladies are with me," he said to the guard as he flashed his press pass, then swept them through the doors and into the crowded, noisy building.

Once they were seated, he went up front to join a large contingent of men she supposed were also reporters from various newspapers back east.

Sitting behind a table that faced the audience

were several officers, including the general who had ridden into town the day she'd set Stone Heart free. The bearded man must be General Crook. He was flanked by a couple of other rather important-looking military men. And a rotund gentleman in very natty civilian clothes. He frowned, took a gold watch from his vest pocket, leaned forward, and said something to the man beside him. Captain Wessells was there, as well as some others of the same rank. She knew little of army protocol but did recognize the insignia of a captain from her close encounter with Wessells. She narrowed her eyes, and sent him thick feelings of hatred. He actually raised his eyes and searched her out in the crowd with a vague nod, then glanced quickly away. He didn't look at all happy.

Good. She hoped he rotted out here in this godless place, or froze to the ground. Thinking of her friend Retha and how much she had done for her, she took back the wish, but just barely.

One of the men next to Crook hammered on the table and the crowd settled down. But not for long. A cold wind swept through the place and everyone turned to see Stone Heart, flanked by two armed guards, ushered down the aisle. A rising murmur followed his passage and the hammer pounded once again.

"I will have order," the man boomed, and he got it. He shuffled some papers, then looked up. "Would you read the charges, sir?"

A gangly young man rose, and read from the paper in front of him. "Sir, this man...uh, Stone Heart, Martin Stone as he is known, is charged with...uh, I don't see...oh, yes...he is charged with aiding and abetting in the breakout of the Cheyenne on January ninth, 1879. Sir?" It was clear he was puzzled.

A roar rolled over the crowd, most of whom were

military personnel. The reporters to a man rose and cheered.

What was going on?

While the hammer banged, Aiden stood to try to get a look at Stone Heart, but the celebrating reporters blocked her view. Surely they were going to charge him with impersonating an officer. That's what everyone had said. Even Wessells had said they'd put him up before a firing squad for doing just that. She didn't understand what had happened, and wished everyone would shut up so it could be explained.

Order was finally restored when General Crook rose and bellowed for quiet.

"How do you plead, Mr. Stone?" the man acting as judge asked.

The man she'd known as Stone Heart, with this strange name of Martin Stone, rose. "Guilty, sir."

Again the reporters reacted and order had to be once more restored. She didn't understand why they were celebrating.

"As you've pled guilty before this court, we will now pronounce sentence. Do you understand that there will be no trial under these circumstances?"

"Yes, sir, I do," Martin Stone said.

"You are sentenced to one year in the guardhouse. Sentence is suspended with the understanding that you will go from this place and never return. You may not reenter the United States of America in your lifetime, nor can you reveal such information as has previously been discussed with this court. Is that clear?"

"Yes, sir."

"And you agree?"

"Yes, sir. Sir, may I ask a question?"

"Yes, you may."

"Have my people gone home?"

The man stared at Stone Heart for a long

moment, and the courtroom was so quiet the flight of a butterfly could have been heard.

"If you mean the Cheyenne, yes, they have gone home."

"Thank you."

Nodding, the man smacked the table one last time. "You are free to go. Court is dismissed."

Retha grabbed Aiden and they hugged and laughed, then Aiden broke away and tried to wade through the milling humanity to reach Stone Heart's side.

Breaking through, he reached out, their fingertips touched and she was in his arms. Forever.

Young approached, laughing. "I told you Libbie would get you off, and she doesn't even realize she did it."

"I...I don't understand...what happened." Aiden could scarcely speak for the emotion crowding her throat.

"The army backed off. The better part of valor, etc.," Young said.

Stone Heart hugged her tighter, whispered something in her ear. "*Ne mohotatse.* I love you."

"I love you too." She gazed up at him, saw her own reflection in his clear gray eyes. And saw something else there, too. Something that had never been there before. Serenity. He was content at last.

"But I still don't know what happened," she insisted, gaze locked on his.

"I promised I wouldn't talk," he finally said.

"But you weren't going to anyway," Young said, and they both laughed.

"Talk?"

"You see," Young said, "Libbie Custer doesn't want her husband's memory besmirched. The army doesn't want to add to that by executing the man who claims to be Custer's son and put the story on everyone's lips. We reporters were invited so we could make sure everyone knows that the Cheyenne Stone Heart was set free without another word about Custer being uttered."

She stared from Stone Heart to Young and back again. "But what about your story? The one you wanted to write, about Stone Heart and Custer and...and all?"

"Maybe I'll write a book in my old age," Young said. "Besides, I got the stories I wanted, and they were published. No one can take that away from me. Even if Libbie is going around saying it's all a pack of lies and there's no one who can back me up. It was sensational. I've never had a better time. I may stay out west where all the excitement is."

Stone Heart shook the man's hand heartily. "I'll never forget what you've done for us. I'm sorry I can't tell the truth to your readers."

Aiden listened to the conversation in awe. They'd made a deal with the entire army. Only Marcus Young and Stone Heart knew everything about his relationship to George Armstrong Custer. Libbie Custer would see that anything Young had written would be branded as lies. In return for his silence, Stone Heart would not be shot.

"General Crook had a lot to do with this," Young added, "but I don't think he'll ever admit it. All he wanted was for it to go away. Bad enough what Wessells and these men did to those Cheyenne, and that won't go away so easily. But for the army to turn around and execute a man who was only helping those same poor Cheyenne escape their evil clutches, well, that just wouldn't do at all. Not as far as Crook was concerned. I wouldn't be surprised if Wessells isn't sent to some outpost so remote he'll never see civilization again."

"Oh, no, they mustn't," she said, thinking of her dear friend.

Stone Heart hugged Aiden even closer. "As long

as they don't send him where we're going."

"And where might that be?" Young asked.

"Well, we have to leave the States, so if Aiden agrees, I'm thinking of California. The army gave me an education, and I suppose I ought to use it. Who knows, I might one day be in the legislature out there."

Head spinning, she gazed up at him. "How will we get there? We have only my small purse of money, the clothes on our backs, and those few supplies Meeker traded for."

"Oh, we have a bit more than that," he replied and smiled at Young.

"It seems the army wants us to be comfortable in our exile. At least after I discussed our needs with them. They are supplying us with tickets on the Union Pacific and enough money to see us through a few months until we get settled. They'll take us down to the station tomorrow."

She could hardly believe it. "Why would they do that?"

"Well, let's say it's my share of what they owe the Cheyenne for stealing their homes. Would you like to marry here or wait until we arrive at our new home in California?" he asked, gazing down at her with eyes sparkling.

"Are you sure about all this? I mean, life as a white man may not suit you."

He laughed and hugged her again. "I'm sure we can occasionally go wild out there in California."

"You'll always be my ferocious warrior." She stood on her tiptoes and kissed him, right there in the middle of Post Headquarters, surrounded by cheering reporters and befuddled soldiers.

A word about the author...

Velda Brotherton lives with her husband in the Boston Mountains of Arkansas. She designed and helped build the house in which they live. She continues to write historical books, both fiction and nonfiction. Her previously published western historical romances, written under the pseudonyms of Elizabeth Gregg and Samantha Lee, will soon be available as e-books.

For more information, check her website at
www.veldabrotherton.com
or contact her at
velda at veldabrotherton.com

CPSIA information can be obtained at www.ICGtesting.com
Printed in the USA
BVOW040420310812

299176BV00007B/2/P